Happy Birthday
Pam

love

The Demon Inside

Peter Oxley

Cover Art by Kristina Pavlovic

Edited by Ben Wayw

ISBN: 1543109764
ISBN-13: 978-1543109764

DEDICATION

For Arnie Peters
...and his three blind jellyfish...

OTHER BOOKS BY PETER OXLEY

The Infernal Aether series:
The Infernal Aether
A Christmas Aether: An Infernal Aether Novella

Non-fiction
The Wedding Speech Manual: The Complete Guide to
Preparing, Writing and Performing Your Wedding Speech

PRAISE FOR THE INFERNAL AETHER

"Epic, Epic, Epic, this story was so good I couldn't put it down and was sad that I reached the last page."
—Aviar Savijon, Goodreads

"This no-holds-barred story features golems, bizarre devices, clockwork entities, an airship, soul-suckers, and more (including a cameo by Charles Dickens) and is told with wit and a touch of humor."
—Kathy Burford, Amazon.com

"An awesome read. The author definitely has a handle on his art as a writer. Do yourself a favor and read it and everything he writes."
—Alan McDonald, Amazon.com

"I liked the way the story was told almost as much as the story itself."
—Tommi, Amazon.com

"Steampunk meets sci-fi fantasy horror with a great deal of magic weaving it all together in a real page-turner. With unpredictable twists and characters that I loved and loathed in equal measure it was a thoroughly enjoyable book which I devoured in one sitting. I can't wait to see what happens next."
—Alibel, amazon.co.uk

PETER OXLEY

CONTENTS

ACKNOWLEDGMENTS

As always, there are so many people without whom this book would never have been written, or at least would only be a shadow of what it is.

Thanks to my fantastic beta readers, whose invaluable feedback helped refine and shape the initial drafts - Andreas Rausch, Lynne, Glenn Bordeaux, James Heppe-Smith, Alison Belding and Joe "the Pendantic Paddy" Brennan.

Thanks to Ben Way for an invaluable and insightful edit, as well as unearthing a veritable treasure trove of 19th century slang.

And of course, thanks to Jess, Tom and Sam for your encouragement, support and just being there for me, always.

It goes without saying that, while everyone has played their part in making this as clean and error-free as possible, any errors or alternative facts which remain are entirely my fault and responsibility.

PART I

AUGUSTUS

PETER OXLEY

CHAPTER ONE

Sheffield, 1868

It was the tallest and most imposing-looking door in the street, but it still collapsed as though it were a paper screen as N'yotsu put his fingers through it. With scarcely a grunt he wrenched it from its hinges, throwing it to the ground behind us.

Kate shook her head as she drew her LeMat pistol, a weapon that had been specifically modified by Maxwell to target demons. "Mate," she said, "how many times do we have to tell you? People prefer it when you knock…"

"No time," he said, charging inside. "I am picking up some strong resonances from within. I fear he may be conducting a summoning."

A shadow fell across us and I spun round with my sword held ready to attack, then relaxed as I realised it was just another gas lamp in the street flickering and dying prematurely: yet another sign of the world falling apart around us. Leaves swirled in the half-light, moulded into a dirty vortex by the wind that seemed to follow us wherever we went.

I shuddered and turned back to Kate and the house. "Shall we?" I asked, my sword raised as I stepped ahead of her into the hallway.

She cocked her pistol. "And there was me thinkin' we were just here to collect a kid."

"A young man who could also be a sorcerer," I said. "You know as well as I do that things are rarely straightforward these days."

We dashed down the hallway, senses alert for any threats. By the standards I was used to back in London it was a relatively humble house, its furnishings providing scant clues as to the owner's status as one of the most prominent foundry owners in Sheffield. I cast a critical eye over the decor, comparing it to how I would bedeck my own mansion if I ever fell into my fortune. The artwork displayed on the walls was perfunctory to say the least, as though the inhabitants knew that they should present something but had no idea exactly what would fit. As a result, grimy industrial vistas clashed with gentle watercolours and serene seascapes, with the odd battle scene thrown in for good measure. I frowned, downgrading my opinion of our unwitting hosts with every step I took.

N'yotsu pulled open a door to reveal a set of stone steps leading down into darkness; he nodded to us and then stepped through. Kate had managed to sneak ahead of me while I had been casting my eye over the decor and I cast aside chivalry to push my way back in front of her. I ignored her bemused glare as I focused my attention on the stone steps and the gloom into which N'yotsu was leading us.

As we reached the bottom, it took a second or two for my eyes to adjust to the flickering candlelight that barely illuminated the cellar, although when they did so I found myself yearning for the blissful ignorance of the dark. The centre of the room was filled with a pentagram that had been drawn on the stone floor in red, sticky splashes. There was little doubt that the substance in question was blood, for the air had that peculiar metallic tang to it; not to mention the fact that a pair of butchered goat carcasses lay discarded to one side of the room. The pentagram was in turn contained within a circle drawn neatly in chalk. A stocky young man stood a few feet outside this circle, glaring at us in surprise and irritation, his long dark hair buffeted by a brisk wind that was as strong as it was impossible in that confined space. As we approached, the candles around the room were suddenly extinguished by the wind, and the darkness was lit up by a terrible glow that emanated from a vortex growing in the centre of the pentagram.

It was a whirlwind of colours and shifting shapes, an insane mass of pain and loathing given a semblance of physical form. I was reminded of the portals that Maxwell and N'yotsu had created all those years ago, although this one was different: more primal and raw. Were it not for the pentagram's controlling influence, I feared that this swirling maelstrom would happily consume the whole world.

We shielded our eyes as the vortex grew in volume and resolve, watching as N'yotsu fought against the gale, shouting at the young man to terminate the spell. Whatever the answer, it was rendered academic by a sharp explosion from the centre of the room. The vortex blinked out of existence, plunging the room back into darkness.

My ears rang as I fumbled for a match in my coat pocket, keeping my sword poised for any attack while my eyes and ears strained to pick up signs of anything awry. As my hearing started to return to normal I could make out a low growl, accompanied by the sounds of something large prowling and straining at unseen bonds. It was not the best of signs.

I closed my fingers around a matchbook at the same time as the young man on the other side of the room lit a gas lamp, revealing a huge, muscular demon standing in the centre of the pentagram. The man stared at the creature he had summoned in awe, as though he had expected a kitten to appear instead of a beast from the pits of Hades.

"Oh, good," I muttered, raising my sword.

Kate put a hand on my shoulder. "It's all right," she said. "The demon's still inside the summoning circle. There're protective charms around it. The demon can't get out or hurt us unless the circle's broken."

I blinked at her. "How do you...?"

"The amount of time I've spent around Max and N'yotsu, some of it was bound to rub off at some point." She scowled at me. "What, you think I just spend my days thinkin' about cleaning, cooking and what pretty dress I'm going to wear?"

I muttered an apology and turned my attention back to the scene in the cellar before us. The demon tried to lunge at N'yotsu and the young man, but instead collided with the invisible barrier of the summoning circle, flashes of green energy flying off in all directions as a result of the impact. After a minute or so of frantic but fruitless effort it slumped back into the centre of the chalk circle, a rippling mass of frustration as it glared at us with glowing red eyes. Slick black wings unfurled and flapped behind its back, wafting the smell of sulphur around the room. The creature's face bore a passing resemblance to a human one but was much more angular, with sharp edges in all the wrong places. Its body was wreathed in muscle, but again it were as though it had been designed by someone who had had the concept of the human body explained to them, but without having understood the relative proportions, like a picture painted by a blind man. I was painfully aware of where I had seen something like this creature before: Andras.

N'yotsu had managed to position himself so that he could glare at the young man while also keeping an eye on the demon. "Would you mind telling us exactly what you are doing?" he asked the man.

The man straightened himself up and smoothed down his hair, attempting to portray the air of outraged homeowner. "I might ask the same of you. Exactly who are you to barge in here unannounced and uninvited?"

N'yotsu looked as though he were about to tear the young man's head off, so I took a step forwards and cleared my throat. "Joshua Bradshaw I presume? Allow me to introduce ourselves. This is N'yotsu, over there is Kate Thatcher and my name is Augustus Potts."

"Gus!" N'yotsu and Kate shouted at me in unison. I winced and glanced at the demon, who grinned back at me triumphantly.

"How many times do I have to remind you not to state your name within earshot of a demon?" N'yotsu scolded. I held up my hands apologetically. A person's real name was a gift to certain demons, who could cause a lot of trouble with the power that it gave them. I spent most of my time battling non-magical demons such as Berserkers and so rarely needed to watch out for such considerations.

The young man, Joshua, did not seem to have noticed my slip of the tongue. He stared at us, his mouth fixed in a perfect 'O'. "I cannot believe it: it is really you?"

"It is," I said. "My brother Maxwell has taken an interest in your letters and he sent us to bring you to him."

His affront forgotten, Joshua grabbed N'yotsu's hand and shook it vigorously. "It is such a pleasure to meet you," he exclaimed. "All of you!" He darted round to shake my hand.

"No!" shouted N'yotsu and Kate together, but it was too late: in his haste to reach me, Joshua put his foot through the summoning circle, breaking the demon's containment. With a victorious snarl, the creature grabbed him and held him in front of itself like a shield.

"Make one move and I kill this whelp," snarled the demon.

N'yotsu shrugged. "Do it. I don't care."

The demon frowned at him, but before it could react any further, a gunshot rang out in the confined space. The demon staggered forwards and involuntarily released Joshua, who fell to the floor, covered in the black sticky slime that served as the creature's blood. I grabbed the young man and pushed him behind me, pointing my sword at the demon.

It turned and snarled at Kate, who had the pistol aimed at its head. "Forgot about me, didn't you handsome?" Kate grinned.

The beast took a step towards her but was checked when N'yotsu launched himself at it, throwing it to the floor and aiming a series of blows to its skull and torso.

"Bloody fool," shouted Kate. "I had a clean shot to the head!" She ran to me, glancing at Joshua. "He all right?" she asked.

I shrugged. "Hopefully that gave him enough of a scare to think twice about summoning any more demons in the future." I was watching the fight in front of us intently; I itched to join in but N'yotsu and the demon were struggling at close quarters, which ruled out the effective use of my sword.

After freeing itself from N'yotsu's embrace, the demon aimed a kick at our friend's head, its clawed feet flashing menacingly in the candlelight. N'yotsu dodged aside and punched at the demon's gunshot wound with a hard jab, causing it to scream in pain as it scrambled away to the far wall. As N'yotsu advanced, the demon used its muscular legs to thrust itself like a missile past him and up the stairs. A further series of thuds and crashes signalled its escape from the house.

N'yotsu followed without a word and I moved towards the stairs before turning back to look at Kate and Joshua. "Go," she said. "I'll keep an eye on the village idiot here." I thought to check whether she would be all right alone with him but then stopped myself; her grim expression told me all I needed to know.

I ran up the steps and out of the house, pausing to check the trail of slick dark blood for the direction in which the others had gone. I turned left and ran, my soul exulting with the pull of my sword as it strained to engage in battle. I felt the runic symbols move beneath my skin and suppressed my instinctive resistance to those changes: at that moment I needed all of the strength and speed that my altered state afforded me. In the heat of action it was so much easier to forget my fears and revulsion at what the changes meant, focusing instead on what they did for me, the advantages they gave me.

The wind whistled past my ears as I picked up the pace from a sprint to something altogether more preternatural. I grinned and let out a low growl, leaping into the air and clearing 100 yards in one bound. The unrestrained joy of my condition at times like this were the main reason I managed to stay sane in the midst of the madness that had enveloped the world. It also had the added benefit of making me useful in our unending battles against the creatures from the Aether. This was fast becoming the new drug in my life, for I had no need of the numbness of alcohol or euphoria of laudanum when I could stand toe-to-toe with gods and devils and fight them on my own terms.

The sound of fighting grew ahead of me and I burst into a park to find N'yotsu and the demon once more confronting each other in a clearing. A dim part of me noted the similarity between this and the corner of Hyde Park in which Maxwell and I had first met N'yotsu, all those years ago when he had confronted yet another demon.

The creature squaring up to N'yotsu was clearly suffering from the wound caused by Kate's pistol, but even with that handicap it was still more than equal to its foe, dodging N'yotsu's blows and landing a number of its own. It moved so that its back was to me and I instinctively lashed out, my blade missing by inches but the hilt landing a ringing blow to the side of its head. It staggered and stepped back so that it faced both of us, leering from one to the other with malicious intent. I gritted my teeth against the urge to run away and hide, instead standing firm in front of this creature from the pits of Hell. We stood this way for some moments, feinting forwards and dropping back defensively in turn. I noted that N'yotsu was breathing heavily, clearly exhausted by the pursuit and battle.

"Who are you?" I demanded. "What is your purpose here?"

"I am impressed," the demon said. "I thought humans were all weak and helpless. But then—ah! I had heard that they had recruited demons to their cause; I did not expect to meet you so soon."

"Answer my question," I said, pointing my sword at the creature's neck. "You are already wounded, we can do far worse."

The demon sneered at N'yotsu. "You don't recognise me, old friend? Has it really been that long? Or maybe the rumours of your deteriorating mental state are true after all…"

I gaped at them; while it was entirely possible, nay plausible, that N'yotsu knew most of the demons that we encountered, he spoke so little about his past life that it was easy to forget that he was not of our world.

"I remember you all too well," N'yotsu growled. "Certainly well enough to know that you were never a friend of mine. That is why I plan to remove your head as soon as I have found out what you are doing here."

"Why, I was summoned here by your friend the human sorcerer back in that cellar, ripped unawares from where I was innocently abiding. You know how these things are."

"I do. And I also know that you never willingly stray far from Almadel. To be summoned here you needed to have been in the Aether." My friend's face twisted into a mirthless grin. "Have you been exiled too?"

The demon sneered. "That would make you happy, wouldn't it? To know that I have finally suffered the same fate as you? Maybe I have come here to be your salvation, to save you from the slow decline into oblivion that you are forcing on yourself. Tell me, do you hate your past so much that you would die rather than face it again? Or is it fear that motivates you?"

N'yotsu flinched as though he had been slapped, and the demon continued.

"I wonder how much of that famed pride you still have, whether you would let me help you to live anew? Maybe we could join forces and conquer this world together in the name of the Four Kings?"

N'yotsu grunted. "So the usurpers still rule. But they did not exile you, did they? You are far too canny for that. Even if you had fallen out of favour, they would not let you live. So I would wager that you still act for them. Which could only mean one thing: that you are acting as some form of scouting party, here in advance of an invasion."

The very thought chilled me, even though it was a threat that had hung over us for many years now. N'yotsu had shared precious little of his background, but what he had told us was enough to populate our most desolate nightmares. Creatures forged in the crucibles of hellish worlds stalked the void of the Aether, hungry to devour the riches of our realm like a hideous swarm of demonic locusts. N'yotsu had always painted a picture of an amorphous mass of evil creatures hell-bent on a single goal, but what he had just said hinted at something else: the existence of a demonic society subject to a form of government. Which meant in turn that these creatures were possibly even as sophisticated as us.

"Care to fill me in?" I asked. "Who are you, demon?"

"I am Gaap," the demon replied. "A key member of the Almadite Supreme Council, to be feared and dreaded by the likes of you."

"He is a schemer and a petty functionary," snapped N'yotsu. "A toady for a group of demons that now rule my home realm. Someone who I used to trust until he stabbed me in the back and who is no doubt obeying their wishes even now."

"Why so untrusting?" asked Gaap facetiously. "What makes you think I follow anyone's plans?"

"Solomon said it best when he described you: 'He goes before Four Great and Mighty Kings, as if he were a Guide to conduct them along on their way.' Or do you want to tell me that you have changed your ways so much in only a few short millennia?"

"So bitter, even after all this time," tutted Gaap as demonic figures emerged from the shadows around us. "I just have a knack for picking the winning side, that's all."

"Desist," said a demon from behind us, "and we will let you live."

"No, you won't," said N'yotsu slowly, turning with wary intent.

Taking advantage of the distraction, Gaap batted my sword aside and thrust a clawed fist at N'yotsu, sending him staggering backwards and leaving us exposed inside the circle of demons. I turned slowly with my sword raised and counted eight of the fiends, including Gaap, who extended a fist and shouted: "Hail the Four Kings!" The chant was taken up by the others as they advanced on us.

CHAPTER TWO

I raised my sword and sidestepped a charging demon, swinging to deliver a raking cut down its side. I allowed myself a brief moment of satisfaction at its yelp of pain before spinning around to parry a blow from another demon. They were fast but I was faster, especially as I could feel the changes taking hold of me ever more, the runic symbols flowing beneath my skin like a volcanic river, consuming my weak humanity and leaving pure, demonic intensity in its wake.

The familiar fugue of battle descended upon me, the whole world becoming imbued with a preternatural focus and slowing everything to a half-pace, enabling me to anticipate my opponents' actions and react with what must have appeared to the casual observer as an impossible speed.

A demon approached me warily, keeping just outside the reach of my sword. I lunged forwards and growled in frustration as the creature darted just as quickly backwards. Out of the periphery of my vision I was aware of N'yotsu fending off three of the creatures but I forced myself to concentrate on the job in hand: my friend was more than capable of looking after himself.

I redoubled my efforts, feinting to the right and attacking to the left. The demon spun backwards, throwing me off-balance. I fought to regain a fighting stance but was caught by a sharp blow to the side of my head. I fell to the ground, the world flashing a hot red around me as I realised that I had dropped my sword. The panic of being unarmed overrode my pain and I snapped back into the world with a harsh clarity, scrabbling to my feet just in time to see a clawed foot heading towards my face.

The force of the impact sent me flying, a metallic taste in my mouth as my nose and lips split open in a bloody mess. I landed hard and rolled away, casting around in vain for some form of safety. A clawed hand pulled me up and held me, feet dangling, to stare dully into the murderous face of my attacker. My hand flapped loosely and then connected with the LeMat pistol in my coat pocket. Without wasting time releasing the weapon, I cocked it and fired through the fabric of the coat in the demon's general direction.

The creature grunted in surprise and looked down at its leg. I kicked at the fresh wound and rolled away as the demon instinctively released me with a howl of pain. I batted at my coat to dampen down the flames which had been caused by the gun's discharge and looked around. I could see my sword just a few paces away and ran towards it; however, my sense of balance had been disrupted by the blows I had suffered and I found myself careering from side to side like a drunk in an alley.

Another demon grabbed me by the throat and squeezed. As the world started to grow dim I put my hands over its face, desperately groping with my thumbs for its eye sockets and digging deeply with the reserves of strength that come from the desperate fight to escape death.

My thumbs found their desired target and the creature released me with a scream, putting its hands over its face as I dived for my sword. My fingers wrapped round the hilt and I felt the weapon's supernatural energy flow into me once more, lifting the fog of weary pain from my vision and pouring strength into my limbs. I spun round and drove the blade through the chest of the blinded demon and then twisted to meet the charge of another beast head-on. The creature looked at me with a questioning dismay as it slid to the ground off the point of my sword.

Three demons remained, all of which surrounded N'yotsu. I started towards them but was stopped short by a cold, hard pressure at my back. I turned to see a hooded figure standing on the edge of the tree line. From that distance I could make out very little of its features beyond a huddled form and a distinct sense of dread.

I pointed my sword at the figure but before I could issue a

challenge my whole body froze. I felt as though someone had opened up my skull and poured in ice-cold water, the liquid cascading down to every part of me so that I was little more than a statue.

The hooded figure raised a cadaverous hand and a succession of words seeped into my consciousness, crystal-clear whispers from ten feet away. Each sound was a dent to my willpower, battering into my mind with an implacable intensity.

The words stopped and my body was returned to me, my limbs flexing as though I had awoken from a long sleep. The hooded figure forgotten, I turned to the fight taking place right by me. I knew exactly what I had to do.

I raised my sword and shouted a guttural roar as I ran, swinging my blade at the vile creature's back. At the last moment, N'yotsu dived aside and met my strike with his own sword.

"Gus, what are you—?" he said, his words cut short as I threw another blow at his head.

The demonic whispers from that hooded creature had pulled at the threads of my frustrations with N'yotsu, unravelling and stretching them out before binding me with them so that my every movement was dictated by pure hatred born of those feelings, the irritations of knowing so very little about him in spite of having fought at his side for all those years. The way that he refused to tell us about his prior life as a demon and kept us in the dark about the inner workings of those strange worlds that we collided with on a daily basis. He said he was committed to helping us, but was he really? How could we truly trust someone who had done such terrible things in his life and then refused to talk about them, even if it might help us learn how to win the war against the demons?

N'yotsu stepped away from me, dodging each thrust of my sword and enraging me even more by his refusal to engage in battle.

"I do not want to harm you, Gus," he said, stepping aside from another swing. "But you must know that this is not your doing. You are being manipulated." His words were mere flies battering at the brick wall of my resolve. I charged at him again and he dodged aside with ease, saying: "You need to fight this. I am your friend!"

All I could think of was that I had to kill this pathetic creature: a demon which longed to be human so much that it denied its own nature. My fury narrowed to a point, a red tunnel with N'yotsu at its centre, a murderous hole into which I poured all of my hatred and rage. On top of all of this, he was responsible for what I was becoming: the slow stripping away of my humanity and replacing it with… God knew what.

I grew more and more frustrated as he evaded me, dodging this way and that without having the guts to fight back. I redoubled my efforts, throwing myself at him with yet more violent intent but then blinking in confusion as my sword swung into thin air with my foe nowhere to be seen. I spun around and then everything flashed red before I sank down into nothingness.

My head hurt. My whole body hurt. I groaned as the cold evening swam back to greet me with a sickening lurch, depositing me on the hard ground. I opened an eye to see N'yotsu standing over me, a thick branch held ready in his hands.

"How are you feeling?" he asked.

"Like I've been battered to within an inch of my life," I said. I levered myself up onto my elbows and looked around. We were still in the park, but the demons were nowhere to be seen. "It's all right, you don't need that club. I no longer have the urge to kill you."

He lowered the branch but did not drop it as he offered his free hand to help me to my feet. "Do you remember what happened?" he asked.

"There was a figure," I frowned, trying to make sense of my addled memories. "He—it—did something to me. I couldn't move, I felt like I was made of stone and ice, and then there were these words in my mind. The next thing I knew, I wanted nothing more than to kill you." With a start I looked around. "The demons: where are they?"

"Gone," he said. "They used the distraction of us fighting to make their escape. I have looked around for them, cast some spells to try to locate them, but they are no longer in the vicinity. I did not want to stray too far from you while you were unconscious, so I let them go."

I nodded my thanks, rubbing my forehead as I thought back on the murderous instincts that had consumed me at the bidding of the hooded creature. "What was that thing?" I asked.

"A Mage," said N'yotsu, frowning into the middle distance. "If you are feeling better then we should get back to…"

But I was not listening. I remembered the thoughts I had had when I was under the Mage's influence: my frustrations at N'yotsu for time and again refusing to share information with us, information that could possibly be the difference between us living or dying the next time we confronted the demons. And here he was, doing the exact same thing again. While the urge to kill him had abated, the emotions the creature had manipulated and amplified in me were as real as they had ever been.

"No," I said. "Not until you tell me exactly what a Mage is and why you have not mentioned these creatures before."

"I have not had cause to mention them because we had not encountered them until now. Do you want me to talk you through every single species that exists out there?"

"If there's a chance they will come here and use me as their puppet, then yes I would rather you did tell me!"

N'yotsu sighed. "I did not believe that they would ever be able to come through to this realm. It should not be possible…"

"And yet here it is."

"Indeed. Which either means that more powerful sorcerers exist in this realm than I had believed, or Maxwell's Fulcrum is advancing at a faster rate than we thought."

I clenched my fists. "All very interesting, but please answer my question: what is a Mage?"

For a moment I thought he was going to prevaricate some more, but thankfully he relented and started to talk. "They are a creation of the Warlocks among my people: a demon that can dig into peoples' souls, speak to them, influence them and play with them. In so doing the Mage controls their victims, forcing them to do, think or feel anything they want."

"So on top of the mindless warrior demons we've been fighting so far—"

"The Berserker demons, yes."

"—we also have these things running around as well, forcing people to do their bidding?"

"Technically no, at least not quite. You see, the Mages have no free will of their own: they act only to serve their Almadite masters."

"Is that meant to reassure me?"

"I just wanted to clarify that they are not capable of 'running around', as you put it. They are a weapon, pure and simple, and cannot act of their own volition. They need someone to control them. One of my people—an Almadite, to be specific."

"Like your friend Gaap?"

"Indeed. His presence in this realm is a very troubling development, which is why we should make our way back. Do you agree?"

I nodded slowly; I had at least managed to get him to tell me about the Mages, which was progress of sorts. Getting N'yotsu to talk at all about his people was often akin to pulling teeth. "Could you promise me something though?" I asked. "In future, please could you try to tell us more about the foes we face? I realise you do not relish thinking back on your time as..." I paused, unsure of the wording.

"Andras," he said quietly. "You can say it. The time I was the demon Andras, before I was freed from the evil aspects of his nature."

"Yes," I said warily. "I know that the memories are painful, that you hate what you once were. And believe me, I do not wish to prompt you into another rage-filled rant—"

"Or another one of my depressive spells," he grinned weakly. "Do not worry, I am too tired for any of that. And you are right, again. I shall make sure that you are fully apprised of these latest demon threats. But first we should gather the others and get ourselves back to London. From the spells I cast, it would appear that that is where Gaap is also heading."

He turned to walk away but then stumbled, his breath coming in ragged gasps as he sought to regain his balance. I put a hand out to steady him but he shook it off. "One minute," he gasped.

I nodded and watched him closely, trying not to show my concern as his skin turned translucent and pale.

"It is not getting any better, is it?" I asked.

He took a deep breath as he screwed his eyes tight shut and, with an effort of will, became firmly physical once more. Struggling to his full height, he nodded at me. "I am fine," he said, but the evidence of my eyes screamed otherwise.

"That seemed worse than the last time," I said. "Maybe you should stop using magic for a while?"

"It is not just the casting of spells that drains me; any form of activity takes its toll. I fear that, without the obsidian stone, it is almost as though my body is rejecting this world."

The mention of the obsidian stone made me shudder involuntarily. "I am sure Max will find a suitable antidote soon," I said.

"I think he would be better served finding an antidote for you," he said. "You are still struggling to control your own problems, I see."

My heart sank as I looked down at my hands, which were bright red and prominently scored with the runic symbols. I ran my fingers across my face, my breath fast and shallow as the scale of the transformation became apparent. "How extensive is it?" I asked, not wanting to know the answer but fearing the worst.

"Pretty widespread," said N'yotsu. "Although on the bright side, at least you have not sprouted horns or a tail yet."

"Very funny," I muttered, closing my eyes and clenching my fists. I had to control it. It should have abated: it always did after a few moments of a battle ending. Did this mean that the changes were getting worse or becoming embedded? Were my nightmares coming true and I was doomed to permanently look like this? I cursed my elation when we were chasing the demon and I had felt the changes starting to take hold. I had exchanged the euphoria of one foolhardy addiction—drink and drugs—for another, much more damaging one. What if I was never able to change back? What if my fate was to forever be a freak at a circus show, or worse: an enemy to my own kind? What if—

N'yotsu put a hand on my shoulder. "You should relax," he said. "It is tension and excitement that brings on your changes."

"I cannot look like this," I said, exhaling slowly. "I cannot let her—them—see me like this."

"Kate still does not know?"

"No, and she will not. You know how she would react if she sees me looking... like this."

N'yotsu grunted. "I will help you." He placed his hands on my temples.

"No," I shook him off. "You are weak enough; as you said, I just need to relax." I exhaled deeply and willed my body to calm down, allowing the tide of tension to wash over me in ever decreasing waves.

Slowly, I could sense that my body was returning to normal and

I opened my eyes to see my friend smiling at me. "Good," he said. "Are you fit to move?"

"I am." I looked at my hands, noting with relief the smooth, unbroken skin. All in order, all perfectly natural. It would be different next time, I vowed: I would not allow the changes to take such a hold over me. For a moment, the thought of abandoning the runic sword flitted across my mind only to be shot down. I had to be useful to the cause and, in any case, it was now as much a part of me as my own arms or legs.

N'yotsu turned and started walking. "In which case, let us go back to the others; the mission Maxwell sent us on is now much more urgent. And we have questions for our new friend. That is, if he has not already been beaten into submission by Kate."

CHAPTER THREE

N'yotsu and I grinned at each other as we arrived back at the house. The young man cowered in a corner of the basement while Kate perched on a table, nonchalantly swinging her pistol in her hand. She jumped to her feet when she saw the state of us. "You all right?" she asked. "Looks like you've had quite a punch up."

"We gave a good account of ourselves," winced N'yotsu as he lowered himself into a chair.

"Did you get the demon?" she asked.

I shook my head. "Unfortunately it got away, thanks to some friends it brought along. Everything all right here?"

"Couldn't be better. Although the company leaves a bit to be desired," she said, pulling a face.

I beckoned to Joshua and he reluctantly joined us, keeping a wary distance from Kate. "After all that N'yotsu and I have done and the way we look, and she's the one you're scared of?" I asked.

"No offence," he said, "but in my experience females can be a lot more dangerous than men."

"Well said," grinned Kate. "I can see we're going to get along famously." Her pistol disappeared into the folds of her dress.

Joshua stared at her, clearly trying to ascertain whether or not she was kidding him. Then he looked around at us all and blinked. "My manners," he chastised himself. "I have forgotten myself in the midst of all this madness. We should go upstairs, where things are a bit more civilised. Can I offer you any refreshments?"

I could have murdered for a drink but, before I could say so,

N'yotsu spoke up. "We have little time for pleasantries. We are on an urgent mission and I need you to answer me truthfully. How many demons have you summoned to date?"

"The one you saw earlier was the first," he said.

"Are you sure?" I asked. "Not dabbled with some others, maybe looking a bit strange and cowled?"

"No, I am positive. Today was the first real chance I have had to properly set out the correct ingredients."

I looked to N'yotsu for his thoughts, but he was frowning at Joshua. "Your first summoning," he repeated slowly. "And you happened to successfully call one of the most powerful demons, an act that should take years of practise, decades of experience and training and even then..." He shook his head.

"The Fulcrum?" I asked.

"The Fulcrum," he agreed. "There can be no other explanation."

"The what?" asked Joshua.

"All in good time," said N'yotsu. "We need to get back to London and you need to come with us."

"Me? I'm honoured, but... but why?" Joshua stammered.

"Maxwell believes that you and your powers can help our cause," I said.

"At the very least," added N'yotsu, "we will feel safer if we have you where we can control you."

I cleared my throat; he really was not helping matters.

N'yotsu blinked at me and then nodded. "Sorcerers can study and practise for decades and not get half as far as you have already." He pointed at a shelf on the far wall, which held a dozen or so books. "Those are all of your texts?" The young man nodded and N'yotsu continued: "We have over 100 back in London, plus the combined knowledge of myself and Maxwell. Just think of the great things you could learn and accomplish if you joined us."

Joshua licked his lips and then nodded. "Very well, I will come with you. When shall we leave?"

"Now," said N'yotsu. "Gather up whatever you need and we will help you take it to the train station. We have a carriage waiting for us."

"What about the demons?" asked Kate. "Surely we can't just leave them running around Sheffield?"

"We looked," I said. "Or rather, N'yotsu did. Wherever the

creatures are, they are far away by now."

N'yotsu nodded. "They appear to be heading towards London. In any case, we are highly likely to see the demon again when he tries to kill Joshua. We can take care of him then."

"Me?" said Joshua, turning pale. "Why would it kill me?"

"You summoned it," said N'yotsu. "By virtue of that act it is bound to you, and you could send it back to where it came from if you were able to trap it and then undertake the necessary invocations. The only way it could secure its place here, in this realm, is by killing you."

He sat down. "I didn't…"

"You didn't think that playing with magic spells and demons would be dangerous?" asked Kate, in the voice she usually used to chastise me. "You can't be that clever then, can you, son?"

We were interrupted by a cry from upstairs, a shrill woman's voice: "What in God's name…?"

"Oh, God," muttered Joshua. "Mother. She's back. Is it a dreadful mess up there?"

"A bit," I said. "A demon running through your house tends to do that."

"And I may have slightly ripped your front door off its hinges," admitted N'yotsu. "We didn't really have time to knock and wait."

I thought the young man was about to have a heart attack as he dashed up the stairs. "Ah, Mother, good evening," we heard him say as he reached the top.

"What is going on here?" came the reply. "What has happened to the door? Have we been burgled?"

"Umm… it's a bit of a long story. I have some new friends that I'd like you to meet…"

We sat awkwardly in the living room, shrinking under Mrs Bradshaw's cold glare. At her side sat Joshua's sister, a rather attractive young woman named Lexie who was clearly enjoying her brother's discomfort. I rubbed my hands together, trying to massage some life back into them, having spent the past hour helping N'yotsu to secure the front door in place as best we could. While we had been hard at work, Joshua had tried to explain what had happened, each part of the tale earning him a string of rather inventive rebukes from his Mother.

"So how long have you been encouraging my son in this madness?" she asked us.

"We?" I protested. "We have done nothing: he wrote to us! In any event, we saved him from being mauled to death by the demon he had summoned."

"It is true, Mother," Joshua said. "Anyway, it was you who bought me the magic books and encouraged me to—"

"You be quiet, Joshua Bradshaw," she snapped at him. "I didn't intend for you to start messing around with demons. I thought you'd do something nice and useful with your studies."

He opened his mouth to reply but before he could reply the gas lamps simultaneously flickered and dimmed. Mrs Bradshaw tutted. "I thought it was too good to be true," she muttered. "Joshua, please fetch the candles and get them lit before we are plunged into darkness again." She turned her cold gaze back on us as her son rushed to comply. "So you're those famous demon hunters everyone's been talking about, yes? Although the way I hear it, you were responsible for bringing all the demons to us in the first place."

"It is true that we unwittingly played a part in the creation of the portals to the Aether," said N'yotsu, "but it was the demon Andras who was the active and controlling influence."

"Who is also you, I believe?" said Lexie.

N'yotsu shot her a hurt glance. "Not quite. While it is true that I was once the demon Andras, my kind can split aspects of their personality from their bodies. I have ejected those elements that made me a—" he took a deep breath and I noted that his hands were clenched into fists. Kate cleared her throat and put a hand on his arm as he continued: "—heartless demon. Such as the lack of a conscience and other demonic aspects: the lack of humanity, as it were. I have the memories of Andras but I am not him, far from it."

"A leopard does not change its spots," observed Mrs Bradshaw.

N'yotsu smiled gently. "A leopard cannot divorce itself from its spots. I can."

"Hmm. And what is to say that you will not reacquire those faculties, turn back into the demon and kill us all?"

"They are encapsulated in an obsidian stone, locked away and under constant guard somewhere even I cannot easily reach. There

is no risk of that happening, even if I wanted to. Which I do not."
He fixed her with a hard stare. "I do not ever wish to become that
monster again. I have hurt enough people in my time, and I pay for
it with my every waking breath. Each time I close my eyes I see the
faces of those I wronged when I was Andras. I have wept so many
tears for them, but now I choose to atone through my actions: by
helping to save the world from the demons."

Mrs Bradshaw stared into his eyes for a few long seconds and
then grunted, clearly satisfied by what she saw there. "And now
you wish to take my son with you to London, to drag him into this
battle as well?"

"With all due respect," I said, "he has made himself a part of
the battle. Gaap—the demon your son summoned—is very
powerful." I looked at N'yotsu and he nodded in confirmation.
"The demons are therefore aware of your son's abilities; it is only a
matter of time before they come here to take him."

"Take him?" asked Lexie.

"Either to make him join their cause or to kill him," said
N'yotsu. "For you, the end result would be the same: you would
lose your brother, your son."

"Anyway," said Kate. "Look around you. People are afraid to
go out at night. Strange stuff happens, demons and ghosts and
whatnot roamin' around the country, killin' people or worse. We're
all involved: if you like it or not. The demons don't care whether
you're fighting them: we're just playthings to them. Or food."

"Both, actually," said N'yotsu. "The Prime Minister has given
us the resources of the Empire to fight this threat but we still need
all the help we can get, including the best minds. Your son has the
potential to be invaluable to our cause."

Mrs Bradshaw turned to her son. "And you want to be a part of
this?"

"It's what you always said to us," he said, placing a lit candle
gently down on a sideboard. "To make a difference, to do
something meaningful and worthwhile rather than just churning
out yet more steel for the world. This is my chance."

She took a deep breath and then nodded. "Fine. But on one
condition: you take your sister with you."

"What?" Everyone in the room chorused as one, our objections
silenced with a wave of Mrs Bradshaw's hand.

"It is clearly not safe to stay in this house, given that this demon of yours knows where it is," she said. "I will go to my sister, but it is not fair to inflict that drudgery on Lexie." She turned to N'yotsu. "You said you wanted the brightest minds; my son is not the only one with remarkable talents."

Joshua glared at her while his sister grinned.

"It will not be safe," I said. "We cannot spend our time as nursemaids to your daughter."

"I am more than capable of fending for myself," snapped Lexie. "I am 18 years old, not a helpless babe in arms."

"What sort of talents?" asked N'yotsu, ignoring us.

"A keen mind," said Mrs Bradshaw. "She reminds me a lot of an old friend of mine: a lady by the name of Ada King, Countess of Lovelace. With the right stimuli, I have no doubt Lexie could surpass even her achievements."

"Ada Lovelace, eh?" said N'yotsu. "Maxwell would be intrigued. Very well, we agree to your terms. But we must leave as soon as possible; the Fulcrum fast approaches."

CHAPTER FOUR

"Wow," said Joshua as our carriage clattered to a halt beside the train station. "Is that for us?"

"It is," I said. "One of Maxwell's more useful creations. I am pleased to say I had a significant input into the design. Beautiful, is she not?"

"She really is," said Joshua, drinking in the sight as the full extent of the locomotive hove into view. "Truly magnificent. Does she have a name?"

"The Juggernaut," I said proudly, for truly the name suited the creation. It was a train unlike any other, a beast that was as impregnable as it was fast. The carriages were constructed from a particular mix of metals that Maxwell had proven could withstand a sustained barrage of gunshot and even—if the conditions and angles were favourable—cannon fire. However, it was the engine that really stirred the imagination. It combined the brute efficiency of many of the models already in service with something much more aesthetically pleasing: a snub-nosed and yet sleek frontispiece with the cold, hard metal offset by lanterns and slitted windows, giving the machine the air of a muscular stallion, straining at its reins. This design was a rare victory of mine over Maxwell's ever-present pragmatism, which all too often drained the beauty out of anything and everything he created—function over form, he argued repetitively.

"We believe that it is the most powerful train in existence," I said. "A battalion of soldiers could pepper it with gunshot and artillery for hours and it would just steam right through."

"Impressive," Joshua breathed, the intense look in his eyes mirroring everyone else's who had thus far gazed upon the machine. Well, almost everyone.

"If you boys are quite done with slobberin' over the tin can," said Kate, "shall we board it before it gets too dark?" She pushed open the door and glared at us pointedly.

We muttered our acquiescence, stepping out of the carriage and onto a platform filled with the bustle of last-minute preparations for departure. Soldiers rushed to and fro, gathering munitions and hauling them into the carriages with a rapid precision, like ants around a nest.

I held out my hand to help the ladies down from the carriage. "Thank you, sir," said Lexie, meeting my eyes for a long moment. I blushed in spite of myself: she was attractive in a rather harsh way, but it was the intensity of youth that gave her an added vigour, something I remembered from Kate before the battles against Andras had sharpened her manner and blackened her outlook.

"All ready for the off?" said a voice from behind us. We turned to see a straight-backed, genial officer marching towards us. "I take it you have managed to complete your mission satisfactorily?"

"Good to see you, Albert," said Kate with a grin, giving him a quick hug.

"Captain Pearce," I said, shaking the hand of the steadfast soldier who had helped us out of so many scrapes in the past. "This is the gentleman whom Maxwell asked us to fetch: may I introduce Joshua Bradshaw? And this is his sister, Lexie."

"Nice to meet you sir, ma'am" said Pearce. "The train is stoked and ready to go. Once you are aboard we can be on our way."

I turned to the others and gestured with my hand. "Shall we?" I asked.

We settled into a carriage in the centre of the train, the only one that had not been taken over by boxes of ordnance and noisome soldiers. I sat back in the cushioned seat, looking forward to some rest, but our new acquaintances had other ideas.

"I have read all of your accounts with great interest," said Joshua, leaning in to me. "The thought that such terrible things could have been happening while so many of us were unaware! The battles with demons and golems in the streets of London, the clockwork men your friend created in an attempt to kill you, the Battle of Greenwich… but it is your accounts of the Aether that fascinate me the most. Is it really as terrible as you recounted?"

"Worse," I said, shivering involuntarily as I felt the touch of those cold, dead hands upon me once more, seeing in my mind's eye the hungry void stretching out before us. "We experienced much that I could not bear to relive, even for the sake of posterity. Even if I had been willing to commit them to paper, I had a duty to my readers to tone down what we experienced out there in the Aether, for public safety if nothing else."

"What do you mean?"

"The Aether is a timeless void inhabited by undead creatures that will claw through each other to get hold of anything living," said N'yotsu. "What do you think the reaction of the general public would be if they realised this? Many people still think that it is some sort of magical gateway to the spirit world. If they believed that that was where they would end up when they die, or where their dearly departed loved ones may have gone to fester for all eternity, then there would be riots on the streets and worse."

"Is it?" asked Lexie. "The spirit world, that is?"

"No," said N'yotsu. "At least I don't think so. Although it is home to some particularly malignant spirits."

"But I thought that the Aether was a gateway," frowned Joshua, "a method of getting from one realm to another."

"It is," said N'yotsu. "But in order to get from this realm to another you need to be skilled and powerful enough to first travel through the Aether and avoid being trapped there, or worse. Of course," he grinned mirthlessly, "that is not the hardest part."

"No?"

"No. Getting into the Aether is relatively easy. At least it certainly is these days. The hard part is knowing how to create another portal out of the Aether and point that portal at the realm into which you want to travel. Many of those trapped in the Aether are there because they fell at that hurdle." He went silent for a moment and then added, almost under his breath: "I certainly did."

My ears perked up at this admission, for he could only be speaking of his time long ago when he was Andras, marooned in the Aether before he had been able to escape into our world.

The thought of Andras brought other feelings to mind: the terrible leering grin that mocked the world and found it wanting, the sense of dread which overcame me every time those glowing red eyes turned on me, sucking me into a place devoid of reason, decency or morality. I remembered the cold touch of the demon's claws as my soul was sucked from my body, the gleeful malignancy in the way that he tore us all apart, taunted us and then spat us out.

But then N'yotsu's earnest face reminded me that we had won: the demon's essence was now confined to a cold black stone safely locked away, while what remained fought beside us as our friend and compatriot.

Frowning at the change in our moods, Kate turned to Lexie. "So who's this 'Ada Lovely' your old dear was talking about?"

Lexie smiled. "Love*lace*. Ada King, Countess of Lovelace. She was a great mathematician: some would say a genius. She was a close friend of Mother's. Unfortunately I never had a chance to really meet her as she died when I was an infant."

The name was familiar to me. "Wasn't she Lord Byron's daughter?"

"That's correct," said Lexie. "But her fame lies in mathematics rather than poetry. She corresponded with Babbage extensively on his Difference Engine and Analytical Engine; her Notes is one of my favourite texts."

"I am impressed," said N'yotsu. "That is not an easy text to wade through."

"Certainly not for one with an occult bent," she smiled at him.

"Indeed. But you understand the paper and its principles? The method of calculating Bernoulli numbers through the use of the machine?"

"Intimately," she said. "In fact, I have expanded on them and would welcome the opportunity to discuss my findings with someone of a like mind." She patted the satchel full of papers resting on her lap.

"And that is where my brother comes in," I said with a grin. "I suspect that he will be very happy to meet you." I noticed Joshua scowling at his sister and added: "Both of you."

"So how did you two get to become little geniuses like this then?" asked Kate. "Didn't see much need for that up there in Sheffield when we were wading through foundries and factories and forges."

"Mathematics pervades everything," said Lexie, warming to her subject. "For instance, the smelting of steel requires knowledge of precise temperatures, timings and—"

"You are right, Miss Thatcher," interjected Joshua, cutting off his sister's flow, "in that I was originally intended for the trade. Our Father owned and ran a number of foundries in Sheffield and he groomed me to be his successor."

"So what happened?" asked Kate.

"Our Father died," he said, holding up a hand to stem our muttered condolences. "It was a few years ago now. And I was never really interested in the family business, so…"

"So your Father died and you fell into magic?" I asked.

"In part," he said. "A conjurer came to town and I saw his show over a dozen times, wondering how he did it. Lexie and I figured out that it was all just parlour tricks and sleight of hand—"

"In point of fact, *I* did," Lexie said. "I do not recall you adding much to the calculations."

"Whatever the case," he said, blushing intensely, "I was disappointed and resolved to learn *real* magic, especially with everything that was happening in the world. Our uncle has carried on the management of the foundry business, and in that respect it appears I have had a lucky escape."

"What, because it's so dull?" asked Kate.

"No. Well, yes, it is, but that's not the real reason. The business is struggling: the machinery is becoming less and less reliable. Even the smelting furnaces, which should be good for decades' more work, are failing on a regular basis. Our uncle has tried everything, but to no avail." He exhaled with a short laugh. "I have often wondered whether my studies in magic may be the answer here, by providing us with an alternative means of continuing the family business."

Lexie interrupted his flow with a theatrical snort.

"Don't you believe in magic?" N'yotsu asked her.

"I believe in many things," she said. "But only those that I can prove or empirically observe. So-called 'magic' is not one of them."

"You might be a proper bit of frock, but have you been hiding under a rock these past few years?" Kate asked, her voice dripping with sarcasm.

If Lexie noticed our friend's displeasure, she did a marvellous job of hiding it. I found myself admiring her composure: people

29

often wilted in the face of even a hint of Kate's harder side.

"I have seen many things," Lexie said with a sweet smile on her lips but a hard glint in her eyes, "but as I am sure Maxwell will say: it is not enough to merely see things, the importance is in the understanding of them."

"Be careful about presuming what people might say before you've actually met them," snapped back Kate. I looked down, stifling a smile but also hoping that I would escape being pulled into the argument: after all, Lexie's words were pretty close to what Maxwell would indeed have said.

"All I meant," said Lexie, ploughing on regardless, "is that I am aware of the phenomena that have taken place over the past few years, the so-called demons, the Aether and so on. But I have yet to see or hear of anything that I would describe as 'magic'."

"Whatever the case," said N'yotsu, "you may find that your brother's ideas are not too far from reality—at least if Maxwell's calculations are correct."

Lexie shrugged and looked out of the window, flushing slightly under our combined attentions. With a jolt I realised that we had just witnessed the hard certainty and self-belief that often came with youth, coupled with a good dose of sibling rivalry. Her reaction reminded me of myself when I was an idealistic teenager wilting under the cold logical arguments of my elders. *My God, when did I get so old?*

"You will have the opportunity to see for yourself soon enough, young lady," said N'yotsu. He turned back to Joshua. "You said that you have been studying magic for just a couple of years, and that all you learnt came from those few books you own? No other tuition from any other sources?"

"None yet," he said.

"Fascinating," said N'yotsu, staring at him intently.

Kate nudged Joshua with her elbow. "So you're a bit of a genius, then?"

He blushed as I fought a stirring of resentment over Kate's familiar manner around the young man. "I am excited to learn from you and Maxwell," he said to N'yotsu.

"Be careful what you wish for," said N'yotsu.

Lexie turned back from the window. "I am curious," she said. "You mentioned earlier about something called the 'Fulcrum': that it was approaching, or words to that effect. What did you mean?"

"Maxwell will be best placed to explain it to you," said N'yotsu. "After all, it is his concept. But if he is correct, then it is to be avoided at all costs." The train jerked forwards and he cursed as he looked out of the window.

"Don't tell me the train's failing as well," I said.

"Not quite," said N'yotsu. "Or at least, not yet. We would seem to have trouble of a different complexion." He stood and reached for the door handle. "Gus, come with me. The rest of you, stay here for the moment."

I glanced out of the window as I stood, seeing a number of dark blots on the horizon. I followed N'yotsu as we walked in the direction of the train's travel, walking past the latest of Maxwell's inventions as we did so. To the untutored eye it was merely a collection of crates and ropes, but Maxwell had reassured us that it had the potential to revolutionise travel. It said a lot about the caution with which we treated his untested creations in those troubled times that we were relying on the train rather than risking our lives to that thing.

I glanced out of a window to see the figures still following us. "Gaap?" I asked.

"That would be a logical assumption," he said. "Or the Soulless. Or both. Either way, it is enough of a threat for us to speed up and try to outrun them."

We stepped through to the next carriage and were met with the quiet intensity of a company of soldiers readying themselves for battle, checking and rechecking their weapons under the shouted encouragement of their Sergeant. Their faces were strained in the half-light that was afforded by the narrow slit windows in the armoured walls, which was only marginally assisted by the small gas lamps mounted around the carriage at regular intervals.

We found Captain Pearce at the far end of the carriage, coordinating the action with a cool efficiency.

"Captain," said N'yotsu. "What is it?"

"Not sure," said Pearce. "Something seems to be following us."

"Something?" I asked. "Can the Juggernaut out-pace them?"

"We are about to find out," he said grimly. "Until then, it is prudent for us to prepare for the worst. Sergeant!" A man appeared in front of us and snapped a salute. "Bring all non-military passengers forwards to this carriage. I want men stationed on both sides of the train with their weapons loaded and ready, but no one is to fire until I say so." He turned back to us. "I will get the driver to put everything he has into the engines. Mr Potts, I suggest that you and N'yotsu prepare yourselves for action. Kate, would you like to come with me?"

We turned to see her stood behind us, a grim look on her face.

"I thought I told you to stay with the others," said N'yotsu. "You would be better placed making sure that they are safe."

"Bugger that," she said. "I'll go with Albert, see if I can make myself useful up front. I'll keep this with me in case things get hairy." She held up a Snider-Enfield rifle that she had grabbed from a nearby rack.

I grinned as N'yotsu frowned at her. After what Andras had done to Kate in Greenwich Observatory, N'yotsu had tried desperately to keep her from any further harm, which had just served to infuriate her further. "Tell you what," I said, "I'll get the two youngsters in here; there's not much I can do until we get close enough for me to use this," I said, gesturing to my sword.

"We will need you on a rifle as well," Pearce warned me.

"Yep. Nothing like a bit of wild blind firing to put the fear of God into demons," winked Kate at me as they left the carriage.

"I can shoot," I protested at the closing door. I turned to N'yotsu. "I'm a better marksman than she is."

"I think we both know that's not quite true," he said. "In any case, you'll soon have plenty of opportunities to test that theory. In the meantime, shall we?"

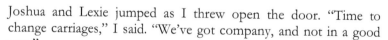

Joshua and Lexie jumped as I threw open the door. "Time to change carriages," I said. "We've got company, and not in a good way."

"Company?" asked Joshua with concern on his face. "What sort of company?"

"Could be demons, could be the Soul-less." I looked out of the window; the figures were definitely drawing nearer, although they were still far enough away for their identities to be uncertain. "They're catching up with us, and we're going at full steam, so those won't be normal horses they're riding. Come with me." I beckoned for them to follow me out of the door.

"The *Soul-less*?" asked Lexie. "I thought they were the stuff of penny dreadfuls, fairy stories to scare children and titillate simpletons?"

I ushered them down the corridor. "You have not been out much, have you?"

"For the past few years, ever since the reports of the strange happenings and the Battle of Greenwich, Mother has been overly keen that we did not leave Sheffield," she said. I detected a hint of resentment in her tone.

I smiled. "As we said earlier, there are plenty of things these days that can't be explained away by science. The 'fairy tales' are very real, as, unfortunately, are the Soul-less."

"But they're just people—"

"They *were* people, but they have been tainted by demons, mainly Andras, tempted by the lure of power or money, such that they lost their souls. When Andras was destroyed, their so-called rewards went with him."

"So they have nothing to live for," said Joshua.

"If you can call their existence living," I agreed. "But they're all the more dangerous for that: they seem to believe that they will still get their rewards if they can just kill enough of the rest of us." I felt a change in the train's motion and frowned. "We're slowing down."

"Why?" asked Lexie.

"I shall go and ask." I ushered them into a corner of the carriage where they could sit without being in the way and left them there with explicit instructions not to move.

I ran as best I could along the swaying carriage, bouncing off chairs and walls in an attempt to stay upright while maintaining forward momentum until I reached Pearce and Kate huddled round the speaking tube in the corner. They were using it to shout questions through to the driver in the engine up front.

"Why are we slowing down?" I asked. Kate pointed to the track ahead of us in reply. I leaned out the left-hand window by where they were standing and then cursed.

Less than half a mile ahead of us the track was blocked by a huge tree, upon which stood a host of howling creatures. Looking to the left, I noticed that our pursuers were taking advantage of our rapidly diminishing speed and were drawing closer. I did a quick tally, squinting into the sunlight: ten ahead of us and another dozen or so bearing down from the west. I ran to the other side of the carriage, muttering a stream of increasingly inventive curses as I spied yet more creatures heading towards us from the east.

Pearce looked at me questioningly, lowering the speaking tube from his ear. Forcing myself to calm down, I told them what I had seen.

"Yes, I saw them," said Pearce. "How many did you count?"

"Ten on the obstruction ahead, then probably a dozen apiece to either side and at the rear. At this rate I would expect them to be upon us in maybe ten minutes, unless we can clear the fallen tree ahead. How many men do we have with us?"

"Only 25, not counting yourselves."

"Not the best odds in the world."

"You play the cards you're dealt. And besides, we have the world's most feared demon hunters on our side!"

"So what's the plan?" asked Kate.

"We can't ram the obstruction: it is big enough to destroy the engine, or at the very least derail us. In any event, we would just be giving the demons on it an ideal opportunity to board us."

"So we stop and fight?" I asked.

"We have little choice. We will abandon the rear carriages and concentrate our defences on the front two: this one and the engine. In the meantime, I believe we should test your brother's latest invention. I will organise my men while you install the device." He put the speaking tube back to his mouth and bellowed down it, ordering the driver and coalmen to make their way back to the safety of our carriage as soon as possible.

I nodded, slightly nervous at the prospect of trusting our lives to Maxwell's untested device, but we had run out of options. "Kate, let's get to work."

We ran through the carriage, our ease of travel now much improved by the slowing motion of the train as it continued to brake. "Do you know how to build Max's thingummy?" asked Kate.

"No," I said. "But he does." I grabbed N'yotsu and quickly explained the situation to him. He nodded and barked out orders and, assisted by two soldiers, we heaved the crates over to the carriage's entrance and began unpacking them. After a few minutes we stepped back and surveyed the contents: a bewildering collection of ropes and harnesses, a large canvas sack and an equally cumbersome black box.

"The good news is that we should be able to install this

relatively quickly," said N'yotsu. "Unfortunately it is going to require us to be on the roof and underneath the floor."

I looked out of the window. We were now almost at a standstill and the demons were approaching at a rapid pace. "Let's get going then," I said. "We probably have no more than a few minutes before we are overwhelmed."

I picked up one end of the heavy canvas sack and, with help from N'yotsu and the soldiers, hauled it to the rear of the carriage. I swung open the doors and pulled myself up the small ladder outside and over the lip of the roof. Lying on my belly, I spun round and reached down to grab the edge of the sack as it was offered up to me. I slid it along to the centre of the roof while N'yotsu and the two soldiers clambered up to join me, awkwardly heaving the black box with them.

The soldiers stood guard while N'yotsu and I placed both objects as centrally as we could, securing them to the roof with the ropes. "Careful with that," called out N'yotsu as I busied myself around the box. "It is extremely volatile. One wrong move and you will find yourself spread over half of this field."

"Thank you for telling me," I muttered, adjusting my stance to ensure that as little of me as possible was above the box's smooth black surface.

We threw the ropes over the side of the carriage and N'yotsu jumped down to help Kate and Joshua secure them round the underside of the train. I maintained my position to ensure that the objects on the roof remained in place, taking the opportunity to check on our pursuers from my vantage point. What I saw made me pleased that I had not looked up earlier, for the creatures were dangerously close, so close that I could make out each slobbering fanged jaw and menacing talon. In their midst charged humans, men driven to a near feral state by their association with the demons: the Soul-less.

I drew my four-barrelled Lancaster pistol and aimed it at the nearest attackers. "I do not wish to alarm you," I shouted down to N'yotsu and the others, "but time is very much of the essence!" A volley of gunshot from below echoed my sentiments as Pearce and his men opened up with their first defensive volleys. I followed suit, nodding with satisfaction as the head of a Soul-less split open in a bloody mess before I moved on to the next target, then the next and the next before reloading.

The runic sword vibrated in its scabbard and I fancied that I could feel it pulling at me to join in the action. I resisted, knowing that I was needed on the roof until we were sure that the equipment was securely fastened. In any case, I did not wish to risk getting in between the soldiers' bullets and their intended targets.

I continued firing until the hammer hit down on an empty chamber. As I fumbled in my pockets for fresh bullets a demon landed on the roof in front of me, eyes glowering like twin flames from Hell mounted atop a snout that housed a motley collection of fangs.

I threw the pistol at the creature's head and drew my sword while it flinched to the side, exulting in the blade's ringing song of release as I threw myself at the beast. I was fast but the demon was faster and it dodged to the side, spinning past me and raking my back with its claws as it did so. The momentum of my swing took the blade down to the carriage roof, thankfully missing the ropes and equipment but burying itself into the vehicle. The demon took advantage of my momentary distraction to kick me aside, leaving the sword buried in the roof. I slid along the smooth metal, struggling for purchase before I plummeted over into the hail of bullets and demons below.

I wrapped an arm around the rail that bordered the roof edge, gritting my teeth against the wrenching pain as my legs continued on and past, threatening to dash me to the ground. I looked up to see the demon advancing with murderous intent and fancied that I could feel claws grabbing at me from below. I kicked down hard with my feet and was rewarded by a satisfying connection with something, providing enough leverage to allow me to launch myself back up onto the roof. I landed awkwardly and scrabbled with my legs, finding a glorious foothold on the handrail that allowed me to arrow myself forwards at the demon, driving my shoulders into its stomach and knocking it off its feet. I managed to get a couple of punches into the creature's chest and head before it shrugged me off with a roar.

I flew through the air and landed hard on my back, the wind pounded from my lungs as the world exploded in a sea of red stars. I shook my head in a desperate attempt to regain my focus before the demon was upon me once more, looking up in helpless horror as the creature bore down on me, fists raised above its head and ready to pound me into oblivion. I tried to will my body to move but it was no use; the blow had temporarily shocked all the strength from me.

Something flashed overhead and then the demon fell backwards with a scream. I gasped and flailed about, trying to pull myself onto my elbows, hoping to make use of this momentary good fortune to escape. N'yotsu appeared at my side and helped me up. "We wondered what you were getting up to," he grinned.

I looked down to see the demon lying prone, my sword sticking from its chest. "Jolly good throw," I gasped. "Thank you."

"You're welcome," he said, reaching down to retrieve the sword from the creature's body with a sickly squelch. "The device is securely installed," he said. "The others are inside; I suggest we do likewise."

"Agreed," I said and allowed him to lead me to the end of the carriage. Looking out, it seemed that the soldiers' constant volleys of bullets were having the desired effect of holding back the demons, at least for the moment.

We slid down the ladder and swung into the carriage, pulling the door shut behind us. The interior was a Hell of smoke and noise thanks to the soldiers' rifles discharging in the confined space. Captain Pearce saw us enter and ran over to us. "Everyone's in!" he shouted. "Activate the device!"

N'yotsu nodded and picked up a small box with a plunger on the top. Two cables led from the sides of the box, leading under the door and presumably to the device on the roof. "On three," he shouted. "One…"

"Everyone," shouted Pearce. "Brace!"

"Two…"

I pushed my back against the wall and wedged myself as best I could between the corner of the car and the doorframe. In common with most people in the carriage, I was not sure exactly what would happen when the device was activated, but I had seen enough of Maxwell's prototypes to be more than a little wary.

"Three!" N'yotsu pushed down the plunger and braced himself against the wall.

For a moment there was silence, aside from the snarling and shouting of the demons outside. I cursed inwardly; had the connection from the plunger to the device been severed? Or was the device simply ineffective?

Then there came an almighty bang from above, as though

something very large and heavy had landed on the roof. We all looked up, hoping against hope that no hole had appeared, and were rewarded with a hissing sound: the noise of a balloon being inflated. After a few more seconds, the carriage lurched to the side, throwing me hard against the wall, then again to the opposing side, as though the whole train were trying to stand up and walk.

The jarring became more pronounced, accompanied by screeches of metal from all around us, the train protesting at the injustices being visited on it by my brother's invention. The lurching continued and we found ourselves thrown from one side to another as though we were on a choppy sea.

"Something's wrong!" shouted N'yotsu.

"Demons?" I asked.

Kate staggered over to us. "I don't suppose anyone remembered to uncouple this carriage from the rest of the train?" she asked.

We looked at each other and then cursed. I grabbed the door and wrenched it open, sword raised ready in case any of the beasts tried to attack through the opening. N'yotsu looked over my shoulder and grunted. "That's not good. The weight of the rest of the train will stop us from taking off, and might just tear the carriage apart."

I looked up. The sack that we had attached to the carriage's roof had been inflated so that it formed the balloon of a dirigible, with the carriage we were situated in effectively becoming the gondola. The balloon was fully inflated and holding fast, but it clearly had not been designed to carry the weight of the whole of the Juggernaut. It was straining to get us airborne, but the ungainly mass of the rest of the train was acting like an anchor, threatening to drag us into the hordes of demons swarming around us, who were in turn only held back by the odd volley of gunfire from our soldiers.

I saw what needed to be done and acted instinctively, swinging my sword down and through the coupling connecting us to the next carriage, the runic sword severing the metal as though it were cotton thread.

Immediately, the carriage jerked upwards with the released end flying into the air while the other end, still coupled to the Juggernaut's engine, remained anchored to the ground. "Well, that's better!" shouted Kate as we slid painfully down the floor to the opposite end of the carriage. Even in that undignified position, she still managed to convey exasperated sarcasm in my direction.

I grunted as I hit the wall and scrabbled for the other door. We were now listing hard as the remainder of the train, primarily the engine, continued to drag us down, this time just from the one end. I could hear the metal protesting, machine and gravity fighting the upward pressure from the balloon above. As I pulled the door open I reflected that it was a wonder that the straps securing us to the balloon had held firm: given the weight of the engine holding us down, it was only a matter of time before they snapped.

I swung my sword desperately and felt the faintest of resistance as the blade passed through the metal of the coupling. The carriage immediately swung upwards, throwing me backwards as I collided painfully with a chair and then some equipment. I flailed around with my free hand in a desperate attempt to find purchase, grabbing hold of someone's arm and clinging on in the vain hope that they would somehow stop me from falling. They didn't, and the back of my head collided with something hard before the world blinked into darkness.

CHAPTER FIVE

I came back to my senses into a world of noise and confusion. People shouted and screamed around me, while above and to the sides was the deafening sound of gunfire. I pulled myself up onto my elbows and looked around. The carriage seemed to have turned through 90 degrees, so that the walls of the vehicle formed the floor and ceiling. A dozen or so soldiers had used the benches fixed to the floor—now wall—to climb up to the windows and were firing out, while others reloaded from below and handed over fresh muskets as needed.

"How are you feeling?" Lexie asked me.

"A bit bruised, I think, but otherwise fine," I said. "What happened?"

"We flew for a bit and then crashed down here. We think the balloon's straps were weakened by us lurching all over the place; eventually they just gave way and snapped. The good news is we think we landed on a few of the demons."

"Bad news is there's more out there though, eh?" I asked.

She nodded. "You should rest for a bit."

"No time," I grunted, pulling myself to my feet. I noticed my sword lying on the floor a little way away and staggered over to it.

"You're really in no fit state…" started Lexie.

I grabbed the sword and felt its power course through me, lending strength to my tired limbs and making the pain a distant memory. I straightened up and grinned at her. "You've got a lot to learn about us," I said. "It takes more than that to lay me low."

I found N'yotsu in huddled conversation with Kate and Pearce. "Ah, you're awake," he said.

"Yes. I'm fine, thank you for asking," I said. "So what's the plan?"

"We're currently penned in," said Pearce. "My men are holding the enemy at bay for the moment, but we're quickly running out of ammunition and are restricted to picking them off on their terms. We need someone to get out there and distract the enemy, push them back so we can get enough bodies on to the roof and inflict some proper volleys on them. That way, we should be able to drive them off before we run out of bullets."

"That's where I thought we could come in," grinned N'yotsu. "Fancy giving that sword a bit of exercise?"

"Delighted to, old chap," I said.

I braced myself on the side of a bench, my back bent to allow full range of movement to the soldier next to me as he leaned up to fire his musket through one of the holes in the roof which had once served as a window. I looked over to N'yotsu, who was similarly perched under the window next to mine and we nodded grimly at each other.

"On three!" shouted the Sergeant from below. "One... two... three!"

I tensed my legs and, as the soldier beside me ducked out of the way, launched myself through the window and into the air, the sword's power lending extra height to my leap. I hung in the air above the carriage for a split second and surveyed the battlefield below. There were probably around 20 or so demons and Soul-less scrambling around the upturned carriage, with at least double that number lying dead or dying on the ground. A long smear of mud and gore indicated where the carriage had slid to a halt, handily taking with it those creatures slow or unfortunate enough to be in its way.

I dropped back down to earth, heading towards a group of Soul-less who were looking up at me hungrily, tattered clothes barely disguising their overinflated muscles. I pulled my lips back in a mirthless grin, spotting my initial targets as I fell towards them. I landed in their midst in a squat with a pleasing amount of grace, having finally perfected the art of doing so without stunning or wounding myself. I snapped my head up, glaring at them before my sword spun into action.

My task was particularly pleasurable for if there was one group of creatures I despised more than demons, it was the Soul-less. Many of them were the soldiers and other unfortunates who had sided with Andras during the conflicts that led to the Battle of Greenwich and the demon's defeat at the hands of N'yotsu and I. Andras had tempted them with promises of whatever their hearts desired, but at the expense of their souls; a deal that I myself had also been briefly tempted by. However, while I had been released from the pact thanks to the actions of my brother, these people had not been so fortunate. Although Andras had been taken from the world, their pacts remained in place. As a result they subsisted, shunned by a human race horrified by what they represented, but lacking the release that only Andras could give them. The demons had quickly recruited them to their cause, recognising kindred spirits with nothing to lose and doubtless showering the gullible fools with yet more promises of riches and power.

At first I had pitied the poor misguided individuals who became the Soul-less: after all, I had been perilously close to joining their ranks myself. However, any sympathy was lost when word started to spread about the atrocities committed by those creatures. While the demons were pitilessly amoral by nature, they came from worlds completely alien to us in every way, and so had no concept of or use for our human morality. The Soul-less, on the other hand, knew full well that what they did was against civil laws and human nature, and as such had turned their backs on their own kind. People grew to fear the Soul-less as much, if not more than, the demons: for while the demons did what they did for their own unfathomable reasons, the Soul-less did it for the joy of undermining everything that they once were. It was this calculating thuggery that particularly riled me, for if there was one thing I could never abide, it was a bully.

My sword swung through their bodies like a hot knife through butter, barely troubling my arm muscles. Although the Soul-less were strong and fast by human standards, they were snail-like compared to me with my enhanced powers. As a result, I was able to dance through them as though they were statues, carving a bloody progress as I picked out my next targets.

A Soul-less landed in front of me, a huge man with long hair as wild as his eyes. With a wordless yell he threw himself forward, thrusting a rusted bayonet blade at my face. I ducked and swung out with my own blade, catching a glancing blow across the man's chest. He did not seem to notice the deep cut, instead lurching forwards once more, clumsily trying to snare me with his makeshift weapon. I batted his arm aside, grabbing his wrist as it passed and using his momentum to pull him down to the ground. He tried to twist round, in the process knocking my sword arm out and to the side, where a passing body knocked it from my grip. Forgetting the weapon for the moment, I focused on my adversary and wrapped one arm round his neck while my other hand grabbed the wrist holding his blade.

He writhed against me, twisting his arm up so that the blade was inches from my face. Without the runic sword's influence I could feel my vitality ebbing away while my foe had the strength of a bear. With a yell I pulled his arm down and then grabbed his head, wrenching it round with a sickening crunch. I threw aside the limp body, swallowing back the bile as I cast around for my weapon.

The runic sword thankfully lay only a couple of feet away, trampled in the dirt but otherwise ignored by the creatures running amok around us. The sound of gunfire was as loud as ever and I marvelled at the fact that I had not been hit by a stray bullet: either someone was looking out for me or the soldiers were incredibly accurate marksmen.

I turned at a motion from behind me to see the Soul-less whose neck I had just broken stumbling to his feet, shaking his head back into position. *Great*, I thought. "N'yotsu!" I shouted. "Be warned: we have Djinn here!"

The man's eyes were as wild as ever but something had changed behind them: a slight red glow, a subtle sign of the Djinn demon that now occupied and animated his body. It was still adjusting to its new host and I took advantage of this pause to decapitate it with one swift swipe of my sword. Head and body parted company in a fountain of blood and I turned without waiting to see them fall. "Can't even trust them to stay still when they're dead," I muttered as I carved into the back of a nearby demon. "It's just not cricket."

I heard a loud bang and looked up to see a rag-tag line of soldiers, two deep, firing on the demons. My heart rejoiced to see this prime example of British soldiery, both ranks firing in turn, raining a constant hail of death down on our attackers.

I returned my attention to my own battles as a demon threw itself at me, its jaws slavering hungrily. I stepped aside and my blade sang as it bit deep into the creature's stomach, barely noticing the spray of blood and exit of wet viscera into the dust as I charged towards my next target, a particularly hirsute demon that was screaming a shrill challenge, the noise sickening enough to curdle blood. I attacked with my blade and the demon parried, thrusting me aside with a long arm. I fell hard and felt the red heat of the runic transformation start to flow through me again.

No, I said to myself, forcing my body to slow in an effort to stem the physical changes. I could not allow myself to transform in broad daylight and only a few feet from the carriage, lest I be mistaken for one of the demons or—worse—my friends and colleagues realise what I was turning into.

This distraction cost me precious seconds and by then a demon was upon me. I swung wildly with the sword, hoping that I would somehow draw blood, but the creature stepped aside and kicked me in the stomach. I rolled with the blow, finding my feet but doubled up with the crippling pain that sucked the breath from my chest.

I staggered and lunged away from blow after blow, fighting to regain my strength while also trying desperately to contain the runic strength so that it did not turn me into that other thing. My attacker grinned through sharp teeth with an overconfident glee. I allowed myself to stumble and fall, sweeping the sword round as I did so. The demon fell onto my blade with one final shriek and I grunted as it landed hard on me.

For a moment I welcomed the demon's dead weight, knowing that it hid me from view and protected me from any further attacks. However, my conscience would not allow me to rest while N'yotsu and the others fought on. I yelled as I rolled the beast off me, glancing at my hands and sighing with relief as I noted that they were relatively unblemished. A small kernel of hope grew in me: maybe I could control the changes after all.

The battle had largely abated by this time. N'yotsu was trading punches with one last demon, their weapons long since lost. On the other side of the battlefield, the soldiers had poured from the carriage and were firing as they advanced on the largely retreating enemy. I allowed myself to relax as I watched N'yotsu finally overcome his demon with a powerful blow to its chin, which lifted it clean off the ground. He swiftly jumped on top of it and wrenched its head round until its neck was broken, before collapsing heavily in a mirror image of my own exhausted state.

I walked over and put a hand on his shoulder. He glanced up at me, his face a study in tortured concentration as he fought to regain his strength.

"Looks like we won," I said.

"This battle," he agreed. "But they'll be back in greater numbers come nightfall." He peered at me. "Are you all right?"

"I had a moment of losing my focus," I said. "The changes were coming on, but I could not let them take hold while I was here, in broad daylight."

"I understand," he said, accepting my hand and allowing himself to be pulled to his feet. "But you are hamstringing yourself if you are fighting not just your opponents but also yourself."

"Those changes are nothing to do with me," I shot back. "They are the sword's doing. I am human." I marched away before he could respond, heading towards the carriage and Captain Pearce, who was busy marshalling his troops.

"Good work," he said as I approached. "We have them beaten for the moment, but we need to move on before they come back."

"Any ideas where to?" I asked.

"We estimate that Nottingham is about a three-hour march that way," he said, pointing to the south-east. "We can get another train to London from there."

"It won't be the Juggernaut though," I said mournfully, surveying the wreckage of that once-great machine. The carriage that had borne us on our abortive flight lay on its side like a fallen tree trunk, the fact that it was still largely intact being a great testimony to the sturdiness of its construction. The sleek engine itself lay at right angles to the rail track around half a mile away, steam still trickling from its funnel. The rest of the train was in similar disarray, carriages strewn in a zigzag across the track, like a child's discarded toy.

"She'll be fixed and back on the rails in no time," said the driver, noting my dismay. "Assuming we can keep the scavengers away from her."

"We will have to trust to luck for that," said Pearce. "I'm not leaving any men here to guard her."

The driver grumbled but had the good sense not to argue; anyone left at the engine would be a sitting duck for the demons when they returned, and we would doubtless need as many men with us as possible as we made our way back to London.

Captain Pearce and Sergeant Jones organised the men and the equipment, parcelling out those items that were to come with us. The driver and his crew set about securing the engine as best they could, disabling it so it could not be easily moved and removing the more portable and precious items, burying those which could not be taken with us.

Thankfully, as civilians, we were spared the need to lug heavy equipment, although after sharing the burdens of Joshua and Lexie's luggage, including a copious amount of books, we were struggling as much as the soldiers.

We set off at a punishing pace, my friends and I firmly encased in the middle of the marching column of battle-weary soldiers. We were all desperately tired and wanted nothing more than to rest, but we also knew that to stay where we were was to invite death; if not soon, then certainly when night fell.

"I've not been outside Sheffield since it all started," said Lexie. "Is night time in open country really as bad as they say?"

"Basically, yeah," said Kate. "If by 'bad' you mean horrendous creatures from our worst nightmares running riot, stealing souls and killing people willy-nilly."

Joshua shuddered. "How long until sunset?"

I took out my pocket watch. "Around five hours," I said. "We should be safely in Nottingham by then, with luck."

After around an hour my feet joined the rest of my body in protesting against the exertions they were being put through. The adrenaline from the battle had long since burnt away and I dared not risk the use of the sword to give me another energy boost, lest I suffer a sudden transformation so close to the others. Instead I focused on putting one foot in front of the other and marking each step as a minor victory, a spur to push me on to the next one and then the next and the next.

Glancing up, I noticed a flash on the horizon and commented on it to Sergeant Jones.

"I know, sir," he said. "They've been with us for a while now, but not getting any closer. I reckon they're just tracking us so they know where we are. They'll soon back away when we reach the town: that's the usual form of it."

His theory proved correct soon enough, as the welcome sight of Nottingham began to loom over the horizon, the hulks of factories and buildings replacing the monotony of trees and bushes. We paused as we reached Radford Station, searching in vain for any sign of trains on the tracks to either side. As we did so, I looked out for our demonic escort and noted with satisfaction that they had faded away.

Pearce shook his head. "We can't wait here. The garrison is at the castle: should be just a few more miles." He pointed east towards the city.

I looked to the sky. "We should get moving then. I would estimate we don't have more than a couple of hours of daylight left.

The Ilkeston Road took us through Radford and then past an engineering works that rattled and clanked through its daily routine, oblivious to our struggles. Rows of terraced houses were huddled in the shadows of the works building, trailing towards the city in a staggered line and containing row after row of curious faces at windows and doors. Children playing in the streets ran after us shouting questions while their mothers watched from doorways, occasionally calling to their son or daughter to keep away from the strangers.

Our route reached a large crossroads, half a dozen streets leading off in different directions like the spokes of a wheel. In the centre of the junction stood a tall man in a dark uniform who was flanked by half a dozen policemen, a cemetery looming behind them. Captain Pearce turned to look at us before walking over to them, N'yotsu and I at his side.

"Who am I addressing?" asked the man. He had a long, drawn face that, combined with his dark clothes and greatcoat, put me in mind of one of those fanatic lay preachers who travelled the country spreading tales of the end of the world.

"I am Captain Pearce of the Royal Welch Fusiliers. We were attacked by a horde of demons on the railroad heading from Sheffield, and we're looking for sanctuary here before we continue our journey to London. And you are?"

"Witchfinder General William Morley," he said. "I am chief of the constabulary here."

"Witchfinder General?" asked Pearce. When there was no further explanation, he continued: "We mean no harm. We merely plan to bivouac with the garrison overnight and will take the next train back to London."

"We will escort you," he said, "to make sure you do not get lost. You will have a bit of a wait, though: the next train is not until the day after tomorrow."

"We will see about that," said Pearce. "We are on urgent government business and are needed in London post-haste."

"One thing that you will find about these parts," said Morley, his eyes boring into us, "is that your government has little sway here."

Pearce stared at him. "*Our* government? Surely you misspeak, sir?"

Morley glared back with a cold calmness. "I never misspeak, *sir.*"

CHAPTER SIX

We endured an awkward trudge through the marketplace and down Castle Gate, crowds of curious onlookers gawping at us in silence, clearly fearful of our sombre bodyguards. The garrison was quartered in Nottingham Castle, a tall and imposing stone edifice that squatted on the top of Castle Mount overlooking the whole of the town. I looked back as we passed through the garrison gates to see three policemen leaning against the wall of a building opposite, watching us with a mournful intensity. "They are going to stay there all night, aren't they?" I said. "Why do I get the feeling we're little more than prisoners here?"

"Probably because we are," said Kate. "Something about this whole place don't feel right. And I definitely don't like him." She nodded in the direction of Morley, who stood near the policemen, watching us closely. "He gives me the willies."

"With good reason," I said. "There have been a few Witchfinder Generals throughout history and they are infamous for having spread fear and misery in their wake."

We were pulled from our dispiriting conversation by Pearce, who beckoned us over to meet the leader of the garrison, a weary-looking old soldier who introduced himself as Captain Gilbert. Satisfied that we were all inside, he ordered the gates shut and secured. "That should keep out prying eyes," he said.

"What exactly is going on here, Captain?" I asked.

"Let us discuss it inside, in the warmth," he said, "and away from any flapping ears."

We followed him in silence to his office, a large room with a fine view over the training ground and the main gates. Orderlies brought in chairs and refreshments and,. as we gratefully fell upon the beer and stew provided, Gilbert began to answer our questions.

"Everyone's been scared stiff of the demons and the Soul-less for the past few years: that's nothing new. However, in the last six months or so, this fellow Morley has started throwing his weight around."

"Who is he?" I asked.

"He was an ordinary policeman, albeit a fairly vigilant one: known for never taking a bribe, always applying the law fairly, that sort of thing. Then his daughter died, his wife went missing and all of a sudden Morley was locked up for leading a lynching of some woman he accused of being a witch. Before we knew it he was back on the streets, had taken over command of the police and imposed his own type of martial law on the city. In a way it's a good thing: it keeps people off the streets, particularly at night when the demons are abroad. But he's taking his 'Witchfinder' duties very seriously. Anyone so much as suspected of conniving with a demon is straight off to gaol. You don't want to hear the stories about what they do to them in there."

"Good God," I said. "It's like we're back in the Middle Ages!"

"Can't you do something about this?" asked Kate. "He can't just start making up laws and enforcing them all over the place, surely?"

"He shouldn't be able to," said Gilbert. "But he is. He claims that he has authority from some higher powers—as in someone high up in government or something—and from what I can see he's probably telling the truth. Every time anyone's tried to stand up to him, they've been sent away with a flea in their ear. Including yours truly."

"And the people stand for this?" asked Joshua.

"The people mind their own business, stay out of trouble and hope that Morley and his men don't come banging on their doors next. Neighbours are wary of each other and no one wants to get accused of any sort of consorting with demons, true or otherwise. That's the way of things here, and I can't see them changing any time soon."

That night I slept the deep, sound sleep of the truly exhausted but I still awoke feeling troubled by our conversation of the night before. I had heard all about the witch trials of centuries past and the misery that they had inflicted, but had truly thought that such terrors were now behind us in our more enlightened times. The fact that a city such as Nottingham could revert so quickly to this mediaeval state filled me with a sick dread. My home, London, had been affected more than most cities by the demon incursions but, as far as I could tell, people continued with their lives as stoically as possible under the circumstances.

When I mentioned this at breakfast, Kate laughed in my face.

"Dear old Gus," she said, "the man of the people! You really don't get out much, do you?"

"I've been a bit busy spending most of my time fighting demons," I retorted, my cheeks reddening.

"And drinking," added N'yotsu, somewhat unhelpfully with a wry grin on his face.

"Fact is," said Kate, "that everywhere is the same, far as I can tell. Folks are scared, and them in charge can do precious little to help. So they fall back on the old ways to fend off the demons. Witches are lynched in London all the time, you just don't hear about them in your circles."

"But Witchfinder Generals? The world has gone mad!" I said.

"At last, he notices," grinned Kate. "Though I'm a bit confused about what's so bad about Witchfinders? I agree that your man out there is creepy, but another person fighting against the demons can't be a bad thing, right?"

"It's not, in itself," I said. "But it's the title itself that worries me: Witchfinder General. It has some very specific connotations."

"How so?"

I rested my chin in my hands. "The last person to hold the title in this country was an individual by the name of Matthew Hopkins, back in the seventeenth century."

"If I recall correctly it was 1645," said N'yotsu. "It was a particularly hot summer."

I stared at him and he waved for me to continue. Frowning, I turned back to Kate. "I think it was a title he had awarded himself, and he claimed to have a particular talent for identifying witches and forcing confessions from them. He settled on a number of villages in and around Essex and accused many men and women there of all manner of fantastical things, which he termed as 'witchcraft.' Before long, neighbour was pitched against neighbour, raising baseless accusations for the sake of settling petty scores that Hopkins jumped on with startling alacrity. Those who were accused would be tortured until they confessed, often implicating others on the prompting of the interrogator. Once they confessed, they were then put to death."

"And if they didn't confess?" asked Kate.

"Often they were tortured to death," I said. "I read somewhere that something like 300 poor souls were murdered in just a couple of years: all due to the actions of Hopkins, the so-called Witchfinder General."

"Of course," said N'yotsu, "this was by no means an English phenomenon. If anything, the English version of the Witchfinders was tame by comparison to their cousins in Europe and the Americas. Heinrich Kramer for example was a particularly unpleasant chap."

"And none of it was true?" asked Kate. "Them people they were accusin' weren't witches or demons?"

"Oh, some of them no doubt were," said N'yotsu. "But the vast majority were blameless, targeted just because they had upset someone or their face didn't fit. Hopkins and his like did not really bother too much with little things like actual proof or evidence."

"Which is why this latest turn of events worries me," I said. "If we have Witchfinder Generals roaming the country once more, then that can only be a bad thing."

"Not surprising though," said Kate through a mouthful of bread. "People are pretty worried about everything that's been going on. If someone in authority comes along and says he can do something about it, they're bound to be listened to."

Nevertheless, I had to understand what was going on and, with another day before our train to London would be ready, I sought out Captain Gilbert and asked for his leave to visit the Witchfinder General.

"Be my guest," he said. "But do me a favour and take a couple of my men with you. If things start to go wrong, they can get you back here before you find yourself in chains with your feet to the fire."

I grinned before realising that this was no jest. "So where can I find this Morley fellow?"

"Just step outside the gates and I'm sure he'll find you. His men have been on watch all night and he's no doubt pacing the street as we speak."

He was right: no sooner had we stepped outside than we were met by two policemen who asked us—politely but in a manner that did not allow for a refusal—to accompany them. I agreed, insisting that the soldiers came with me, and allowed myself to be led into a nondescript house in the shadows of the garrison's gates. The door opened to show a simple room containing a rude table and chairs in its centre. The place smelled strongly of unwashed bodies and burnt food. Witchfinder General Morley was seated at the table, facing the door, and he beckoned for me to sit opposite him.

"Nice place," I said. "Very convenient, and what a coincidence that it has a fine view of the garrison gates."

Morley glared at me with naked hostility. "We will be alone," he said to his policemen. They turned and started out the door, holding it open for the soldiers to follow suit.

"I would feel a lot more comfortable if my associates remained," I said.

"Why? Do you fear me?"

"The welcome you gave us last night was hardly warm. You have kept watch over us all night, and the first time I step outside I get marched here. Yes, you could say I'm a little anxious about what you might be planning to do if the two of us were alone in here."

He held out his hands. "I am unarmed, which is more than can be said for you. What if I allow you to keep your sword and pistol, while your men remain just outside that door, able to come in if you call them? Would that reassure you?"

I looked to the soldiers and could see the doubt on their faces.

"I wish to speak freely with you," Morley said. "I would not feel comfortable doing so if they remained in here."

I nodded slowly. "Very well, as long as you give me your word that all three of us can walk away from here and back to the garrison when we are finished, without any hindrance or interference from you or your men."

"You have my word."

I nodded to the soldiers and took a seat at the table opposite Morley. He was probably a little older than I was, but a lifetime of troubles was etched across his face, worry lines and the ruddy complexion of a hard life lived outdoors giving him the appearance of a much older man. I searched his eyes for some sign of compassion or humour but all I saw was a cold lifelessness, a man who had long ago given up on humanity as a lost cause.

"Augustus Merriwether Potts, I presume," he said. "The famed demon-killer and chronicler of the events that changed the world. Now working for Her Majesty's government."

"I confess you have me at a disadvantage," I said. "I am aware that you style yourself as Witchfinder General, but apart from that...?" I shrugged.

"I am what keeps the wolves from these peoples' doors," he said.

"From what I understand, you *are* the wolves at their doors," I replied.

"Explain." He peered at me intently.

"I understand that the people of this city live in fear of being accused of witchcraft or consorting with demons, with you standing in final judgement over them. We have been here before: a dark chapter in our country's past. I have no desire to see us return to the misery of those days."

"Then it is as well that you have no say in these matters. You and your friends created this new world, where demons and evil spirits lurk behind every corner; it is the least that the ordinary people can ask that someone stand up for them and keep them safe."

I snorted. "How many demons have you killed?"

"It is not always about death and killing, Mr Potts. The demons make vile promises of power and money to lure the innocent and gullible, as well you know. Someone needs to ensure that such transgressions are caught in time and deterred where possible."

"And that someone is you?"

He inclined his head in a curt nod.

"And who appointed you to this role?" I asked.

"I work for the highest powers in the land," he said.

"To clarify, who exactly?" I asked. "Not the army, that much is clear. Not the government: I'd have heard of you and your kind if it were them."

He smiled at me. "I do not need to justify my authority to you. But you are correct, it is neither of those. I work for a higher power than them."

"God?" I felt the familiar hot frustration of colliding head-on with an irritatingly smug obstacle.

"Don't be flippant. In any case, it is irrelevant: better men than you have tested my authority and been satisfied. Or thrust aside."

We glared at each other, two stags locking horns to see who would back down first. After a few moments of staring into the pitiless abyss of his gaze I looked away, focusing on the rough surface of the table to avoid being dragged any further into an argument with this strangely bitter man. "I find myself wondering why you asked me to come and sit with you," I said.

"I was curious to see who would leave the garrison first: whether it would be you or the demon."

I looked back at him. "N'yotsu, you mean? He is no demon."

Morley snorted. "Born of demon, has demonic powers. There is a saying: if it looks like a duck and quacks like a duck…"

"That was almost humour," I said. "There was me thinking that such luxuries were beneath you. Regardless of his heritage, he has done many great things to protect mankind."

"And as a demon it did many things to harm us."

"We have all done things we regret in our past," I said coldly. "Even, I would wager, you."

There was that emotionless gaze again. "A demon is a demon. All of them must be destroyed."

"And I consort with him, so what does that make me?"

"Someone to be watched. And be warned: we certainly are watching you."

"We?" I asked. "You mean you and your flat-footed cronies outside? Or are we talking about your higher power again?"

"Both. You would do well not to mock me."

I rose to my feet, scraping the chair back. "Is there anything of value you wish to discuss? I have the distinct impression that I am wasting my time here."

"Not at all," he said. "I simply wish you to know that you are not welcome here; neither you nor the demon or your other co-conspirators. There is no place here for those who consort with demons or make use of their powers. You will remain inside the garrison until your train is ready and then you will depart, never to return. Is that clear? You should be advised that we know all of the so-called secret passages out of Castle Mount and have them all covered. If you try to venture into any other part of this city, you will be arrested and put on trial. The only reason I have not done so thus far is that I gave my word that you would be unharmed, and I do not yet wish to initiate a conflict with the army."

"Yet?"

"Yet." He met my gaze with a cold intent that made me want to shudder, but I resisted lest I show weakness in front of him.

I forced my face into an unconcerned smile. "Any other messages? Wishes of glad tidings?"

"Yes. Watch your back. My remit extends far beyond Nottingham and the next time our paths cross, you will suffer." He stared at me for a moment, almost as though he were daring me to blink, before shouting: "Constable!"

The door opened and one of the policemen who had brought me to the house stepped inside. "Sir?" he said.

"Escort Mr Potts and his friends back to the garrison and ensure they get inside safely please."

The man nodded and then stepped aside to let me through the door.

I got up from the table and looked back at Morley, who was glaring at me with undisguised hatred. "I do not know what happened to make you as bitter and misguided as you are," I said quietly. "But you should know that we are not the enemy: we are also trying to defeat the demon threat. You should be working with us, not fighting us." I looked at him for some flicker of agreement and then sighed. "I have met people like you before."

"People like me?" the Witchfinder General asked.

"Bigoted, closed-minded. People whose beliefs are so set in a particular way that they will not countenance any difference in others. Dangerous people."

He fixed me with that dead stare again. "That is correct. I am dangerous: to the demons and those who consort with them. A demon does not recognise right or wrong. It is pure evil. They offer no mercy to their victims and so I do not see why I should afford them that courtesy."

"It is not your attitude towards demons that concerns me, but towards other people. The thought of the terror of witch trials returning to our land... frankly, it appals me."

"Why? Because you have something to hide?"

I tried to ignore the sudden heat in my cheeks. "No. Because too many innocent people will suffer unjustly as a result of lynch mobs taking exception to someone for some spurious reason and then being tortured or killed as a result."

"Ah. You are referring to the old witch trials from centuries ago. Do you think we duck witches in ponds or subject them to trial by burning? We are more scientific now than they were back then."

"Do you torture the accused?"

"Those consorting with demons do not tend to offer information voluntarily. An element of... persuasion is necessary to extract a confession."

I folded my arms. "And just as some people will say anything to rid themselves of a pesky but innocent neighbour, so they will say anything to stop themselves being tortured. Tell me, how many poor souls do you have in your torture chamber right now?"

"Right now, none. Although you are sorely tempting me to change that. Would you like to come and examine my facilities? Maybe experience them first-hand? If you have nothing to hide then you have nothing to fear."

"Maybe some other time," I said, stepping outside and noting with relief that the soldiers were standing to attention, ready to escort me back to the garrison. "Good day, Mr Morley."

"Good day," he said.

I could feel his eyes boring into my back as we walked away, an anxious itch that made me want to burst into a panicked run for safety. I resisted that urge and forced myself into a measured march, a walk that seemed to stretch on for miles and miles.

"Everything all right, sir?" asked the soldier to my right.

"Just keep walking. Please," I said through gritted teeth.

Eventually, thankfully, we reached the garrison gates and I endured a long couple of minutes while they were unlocked and swung open. I tried to effect a casual air by chatting to the soldiers but I could not forget the presence of the policemen behind us and my neck bristled as though it could sense Morley's dead-eyed stare upon it, imagining that at any moment I would feel a hand on my shoulder and be pulled towards whatever horrors awaited in his gaol.

I did not relax until we were safely inside the garrison and the gates had slammed shut behind me.

"You all right, cocker?" asked Kate, coming down the stairs to the yard.

    "Nothing a stiff drink won't cure," I said.

CHAPTER SEVEN

We watched from the garrison's high windows as the crowd outside the gates grew in size and ill-temper.

"That one's got a cricket bat, see?" said Kate, pointing at a burly-looking man on the edge of the mob.

"Yes, and I can see at least five others who look like they are concealing weapons of some description or another. On the plus side, they all look human: no demons." N'yotsu turned and grinned at us.

"Was that intended to be a joke?" I asked.

"Of sorts. I thought a bit of gallows humour might lighten the mood."

"Gallows may be very apt," I said. "This gathering has the feel of a lynch mob about them."

"Should we read them the Riot Act?" Pearce asked Captain Gilbert.

"We could," he said, "although I'd prefer it if the police helped us with crowd dispersal. Can't see much chance of that happening, can you?"

We conceded his point; while the police were present in numbers, they were doing little to control the mob. If anything they were encouraging them, chatting to the ringleaders and occasionally pointing towards us as they made a point. I could see Morley standing at the edge of the mob, a dark and looming presence that my eyes were constantly drawn to.

A young soldier approached, saluted and handed Gilbert a piece of paper. He studied it and grunted. "Your train is on its way. Barring incidents, it should be here in a few hours."

"We need to be on that train," said Pearce, "and I suspect that public order here would be much improved by our swift departure."

"Agreed," said Gilbert. "I have some town plans in my office: let us retire there and discuss some thoughts on attack. In the meantime, maybe they will all get bored and wander off home."

I looked down at the growing anger and resentment in the crowd below, peppered with the odd group of opportunistic thugs clearly spoiling for a fight. "Wishful thinking," I muttered.

We stood in the shadow of the huge garrison gates, surrounded by soldiers standing three deep with muskets at the ready.

"Remember!" shouted Gilbert. "No one is to fire unless given an express order. If you are attacked, you are to use non-lethal force only, and keep formation at all times. There are a lot of potentially angry and very upset people out there; do not under any circumstances allow yourselves to be provoked into a reaction. You will take your orders from Captain Pearce." He nodded to Pearce, who was standing at the front of our wedge-shaped company.

The gates swung open and an initial party, led by Gilbert, advanced forwards in line, rifles held ready as they pushed forward to create an opening for us to step into. They shouted at the crowd, barking orders for them to stand back, keep away, stand down. As our party approached, Gilbert's line split in two, allowing us to drive through them without creating any gaps for anyone foolish enough to try to dive into. We stepped through the shouting line of soldiers and into an altogether more oppressive atmosphere. Men jostled and glowered at us, faces twisted in hatred at the mere suggestion of our presence. The tension in the air was palpable, like the closeness that precedes an oncoming storm, and I knew that it would only take the slightest spark to ignite the crowd into violence.

I looked back to see that Gilbert's line had reformed and closed again now that we were through, a solid barrier blocking the entrance to the garrison. They stood, rifles raised, watching carefully as we advanced through the throng.

"That's 'im," shouted a man. "The demon!"

I flinched and looked around before noticing the fingers pointing at N'yotsu. Any relief I felt was short-lived as the mood quickly soured, the jostling and muttering becoming even more pronounced and threatening. I felt the runic sword's presence in its scabbard strapped to my back, an almost tangible hot itch as it longed to be unsheathed and put to work. I clenched my hands into fists and resisted. My turning into a demon before their eyes would almost certainly be the final push they needed to descend into all-out rioting.

The soldiers around us redoubled their efforts, shouting and pushing back with the butts of their weapons. I caught a glimpse of Morley in the background, watching with interest and making no effort to order his men to assist us, but he was soon lost in a mass of scowling, shouting faces. I looked to my friends and companions to make sure that they were all right and shared nods with each of them. N'yotsu was as inscrutable as ever, while Kate was her usual unflappable self, almost seeming to enjoy being the centre of attention. Joshua and Lexie were slightly less sanguine: presumably this was the first time that they had been in such a situation. They clung to each other tightly, Joshua trying to put a brave face on things for the sake of his younger sister, although to her credit Lexie appeared to be making the best of things, glaring defiantly around while her brother stared fixedly ahead.

I put a hand on Joshua's shoulder. "All will be fine," I shouted. "Captain Pearce has got us out of much tougher scrapes than this in the past!" I looked more to Lexie than Joshua as I spoke in an attempt to spare his feelings, but he looked back at me with the desperation of one who wanted to believe every word.

I straightened my back and walked taller, putting on a show of confidence for our younger companions, my physical comportment at complete odds to how I really felt. While I tried to focus on the sturdy backs of our military escort, I could feel my breath shortening as my body tensed in claustrophobic resistance to the masses pressing in on us. I wanted to beat my way through and then run as fast as I could away from this madness, and it took all of my energy just to keep me walking slowly and steadily along with my companions.

Everything blurred into a narrow tunnel as I forced myself to stare ahead and not look round, lest I be panicked by the reality of what I would see there. At the same time I focused on keeping my face fixed in an expression of steely but relaxed determination; I knew that the mob wanted to see us weakened by their antics and I was damned if I would give them the satisfaction.

Wilford Street gave way to a short bridge, which merely served to press the crowd closer around us, in spite of the soldiers' best efforts. We made it to the other side of the River Trent, Wilford Street turning into the wider and longer Wilford Road. In the distance ahead of us I could see the puffs of steam that marked the railway station: maybe we would make it in one piece after all.

Eventually the crowd started to thin in front of us and I looked up to see another line of soldiers ahead, with the redoubtable Captain Gilbert at their centre. Once we had drawn the crowd away from the castle, he had taken a number of soldiers on a swift jog round the back streets, flanking our progress and forming up mid-way along Wilford Road, effectively forming a bottleneck to deny the mob the chance to easily pursue us as we made a last dash towards the railway station.

Gilbert grinned at us as we approached. "Prepare yourselves for some gunshots," he shouted. "As soon as you hear them, start running. The station's 100 yards down the road."

"They're going to shoot at them?" asked Joshua, shocked. "That's not—"

"Don't worry," I cut in. "It will be warning shots over their heads, just to discourage and confuse them and buy us some time." We were through Gilbert's line now. "Get ready," I said.

The words were no sooner out of my mouth than the deafening peal of gunfire erupted around us. We broke into a sprint, urged on by our escorts, as another volley cracked the air.

I counted the steps between each burst as my feet pounded the paving stones, noting how the pauses in between were punctuated by shouting and screaming from the mob behind us. The station drew closer and I saw with relief a strong column of steam reaching into the air from somewhere in the building: a train was ready and stoked. Whether it was in a position to leave just yet was irrelevant as we planned to force the issue.

We raced through the station building and onto the platform, past startled travellers who pinned themselves to the walls to avoid being knocked down like skittles. Pearce sent three soldiers to the engine to ensure that the drivers would comply with our accelerated timetable, while the rest of us bundled into the front-most carriages.

A number of civilians had already settled themselves in their seats and they watched us pass with a mixture of shock and annoyance. I smiled and doffed my hat to a couple of elderly ladies before throwing myself into a seat: a heavy-breathing, perspiring lump.

"You are out of shape," observed N'yotsu as he smiled at me from his seat, a study in calmness in spite of our situation.

"It's all that ale and wine," said Kate. "I said it was no good for you."

"Bugger off," I replied, turning to watch Pearce marshal the rest of the soldiers onto the train while he stood on the platform guarding against any last-minute attackers. As the train started to move, he jumped on board, him and his men keeping their muskets trained on the platform as we pulled away from the station.

I forced myself to my feet and walked over to Pearce. "Will Captain Gilbert and his men be all right?" I asked. "I still think they should have come with us: the city is lost."

"While I agree with you, someone has to hold the rear and protect our backs to certify we are not pursued." He paused as he caught sight of me. "Are you all right? You look a little... red."

"I am fine," I said, wiping sweat from my brow. While the sword gifted me with wonderful powers and stamina while I was using it, when it rested it was incredibly stubborn in refusing to assist me.

"In any case," continued Pearce, "they have horses and will join up with us a little way down the line. As you say, the city is lost. In any case, after them opening fire on the mob, I suspect Morley will stop at nothing to hound them out now."

"Yes... Morley." I said, my mind whirling again at the mention of the man's name. "I am intrigued as to the nature of the authority he claims to be acting under."

"As am I," said Pearce. "Hopefully someone in London will be able to assist us in that regard."

CHAPTER EIGHT

The air was noticeably warmer back in London than it had been up north, and for that I was grateful. I was, however, relieved by the approaching autumn, for that year's summer had been particularly sticky and unpleasant, not helped by the cloying fog created by the various peat and coal fires that still burnt unabated in those areas of the city where humans dared not tread.

We had only been gone just over a week but I still found myself drinking in the sights, the bustle of pedestrians and traffic and the familiar landmarks we passed. There was a certain vibrancy about the city that I had missed on our travels, a liveliness and intensity that none of our other stops had been able to match. And, of course, not being the subject of a lynch mob certainly helped my positive frame of mind.

We swung round the side of Trafalgar Square, staring absent-mindedly at the fountains that were already stained and mottled thanks to the city's smoke and dirt, in spite of being just 20 years' old. The plumes from the fountains played merrily at the front of the columns framing the entrance to the National Gallery. Rounding the corner, we were met with the wide thoroughfare of Whitehall, the ornate and brown brick buildings lining the route down past the Admiralty and Horse Guards towards Westminster Palace and Westminster Abbey.

Our carriage drew to a halt right next to the Admiralty building and opposite Scotland Yard. We stepped down to the pavement outside the relatively unremarkable door to 24 Whitehall, the location of Maxwell's latest residence-cum-laboratory. Its proximity to so many centres of operation for military and policing was supposedly for our protection, although I sometimes wondered whether the true reason was to keep an eye on us. To that end, I had steered clear of The Clarence, a tavern that was conveniently close to Maxwell's laboratory but no doubt also home to any number of prying eyes and flapping ears.

The soldiers guarding the doors watched us closely as we approached, nodding as they recognised us and standing aside only when we confirmed the bona fides of our new companions as well.

We passed through another couple of checkpoints until we finally entered the building proper. Moving beyond the entrance lobby, we made our way through a series of locked and guarded doors until we reached a tall spiral staircase, again guarded by two men at the top and bottom. Joshua turned to me as we descended. "What is in this building that warrants such security?" he asked.

"Max and his inventions, for the most part," I said.

"There's a lot of guards here for just one man," Lexie said.

"He's not just any man," I said. "He's a prime target for the demons: probably the most vulnerable and important man in the Empire."

"The demons still want him? But surely now that they are through from the Aether, and portals are becoming easier to create...?"

"Ah," said N'yotsu. "But we currently—for the time being at least—live in a scientific age. A sustainable portal to the Aether is not yet possible without scientific assistance, and creating a linking portal through to another realm is harder still. Maxwell and his knowledge and experience is a rather unique asset, and one that the demons would do anything to get hold of. Hence our precautions to protect a very valuable person, whose knowledge could be extremely dangerous in the wrong hands."

"And presumably also the obsidian stone containing what is left of Andras?" asked Joshua.

"Safe and secure," snapped N'yotsu. "And not here." He marched off ahead in a way that very firmly informed us that the conversation was over.

Joshua looked at us questioningly and Kate grinned. "Word to the wise, mate: if you ain't figured it out already, don't mention the 'A' word around N'yotsu. He don't like to be reminded of that side of himself. To tell the truth, none of us do."

We walked through a long, low corridor, taking care to bend our necks and walk in single file so as not to brush our hair or clothing against the clammy walls. I had implored Maxwell to find somewhere less damp and dingy to live and work than this upmarket sewer but had been met with firm rebuttals each time; not just from him but also N'yotsu and Kate, who were less swayed by Maxwell's obsession with the array of facilities available than with the simple fact that this was probably one of the most secure living/working quarters in the country. While I shared with them a concern for Maxwell's safety, I also worried about the impact on his welfare and sanity of being cooped up like a common prisoner with no sunlight or fresh air.

N'yotsu reached the door to my brother's laboratory and knocked. Kate elbowed him aside and pushed open the door without waiting for a reply. As we followed her inside our noses were assailed by the usual heady mixture of stale sweat and astringent chemicals that signalled Maxwell was in residence and hard at work.

The room was shrouded in a dim light from a handful of lanterns dotted around the central workstation, which was in turn filled with an alarming number of contraptions all lying around like a toddler's wildest playtime. The outskirts of the room's meagre lighting suggested yet more chaos spreading out towards the edges, lost in the darkness around us. In the centre of this sat Maxwell in his wheelchair, scowling up into the light from behind us.

"Kate, how many times do I have to tell you to wait until I respond before entering?" he said in a rasping voice.

"Well, I tried that once and you kept me waitin' for ages," she said, already bustling around him and lighting more lanterns.

"That's because I was busy: I am in the middle of some very intricate and potentially dangerous experiments. The very slightest disturbance could be fatal."

She stopped and crossed her arms. "So what you workin' on now then?"

He blushed and looked down at the table in front of him and the pot and cup in his hands. "I was making tea. But that is not the point, you did not know that."

"Stop being so grumpy," she said. "You should be pleased to see us; it's been a while."

"Has it?" he asked. "It can be difficult to tell the passage of time down here."

I shot N'yotsu and Kate a look that shouted: 'I told you so,' but they both ignored me.

"We have brought you a couple of guests," said N'yotsu.

"A couple?"

"Yes. Joshua Bradshaw, as requested, and his sister Lexie."

Joshua darted forwards and thrust out his hand in greeting. "Such a pleasure to finally meet you in the flesh, Mr Potts," he said.

Maxwell stared at the young man's hand for a moment before realising that it would be impolite to decline the greeting. "The pleasure is all mine," he said slowly, shaking Joshua's hand before dropping it like a dead fish. He looked back at N'yotsu and me. "But I do not recall requesting that you bring me the entire family."

"It was a condition of my Mother's," said Joshua. "I will make sure that she does not get in the way…"

Lexie elbowed him aside. "I believe our work may be of mutual interest," she said. "I am a keen student of mathematics and in particular the works of Ada King, Countess of Lovelace."

Maxwell looked at her for a long moment. "At what level of advancement are your studies?"

She pulled a thick pile of papers from her satchel. "This is my commentary on Lovelace's Notes."

"The translation of Menabrea's article?" asked Maxwell, taking the papers and thumbing through them.

"Yes," she said. "I found it a most stimulating introduction to the principles behind Babbage's work."

Maxwell looked up at her. "How old are you?"

"I am 18," she said. "Not that that matters in the slightest."

"No, no, not at all." While anyone else would have been flustered by her forthright tone, Maxwell seemed to have hardly noted it. "I am merely fascinated by the fact that you have understood so much in such a relatively short time. When did you commence studying Lovelace's work?"

"Mother has had me learning about her since I was a child. But these notes, well, since I was about 14 years old."

"The Analytical Engine is a concept I have had a great deal of interest in for some time," said Maxwell. "In fact, the mechanisation of calculations could greatly aid my studies by helping me to work through the variables that comprise the boundaries to the Aether."

"I thought as much," said Lexie, just as excitedly. "With a few tweaks to the design it could very easily make the computations that would be required to identify the particular resonances unlocking individual worlds, and by inference which ones could close the barrier to our world once more."

"My thinking exactly! I have mentioned the concept to Charles Babbage on a number of occas—"

"You know Mr Babbage?"

"Of course. I can introduce you to him at some point; he would no doubt be fascinated to find one cut from the same cloth as Ada was."

"Looks like true love," I commented dryly and Joshua turned to glare at me. "Of course," I said softly, then louder: "Max, remember that you do have two guests here, and Joshua has been very keen to collaborate with you on... erm... magical stuff."

"But of course," said Maxwell. "This could be the perfect combination: the prodigies in mathematics and magic, aligned with the knowledge and experience of myself and N'yotsu. I believe, my friends, that not even the sky is the limit!"

Kate sidled over to me. "Where does that leave us then?"

"We, my dear, are the blunt instruments," I grinned, patting the hilt of my sword.

"Speak for yourself," she muttered.

"Failing that," I said, "we will get irresponsibly drunk and invite trouble."

"Now that," she smiled, "is more like it."

N'yotsu put his hand on my shoulder. "There will be time for that later. In the meantime, you and I should pay a visit to Downing Street."

After a short walk up Whitehall we turned right into Downing Street, stepping around the puddles, potholes and piles of horse dung as we made our way to Number 10. A pair of policemen casually watched us as we headed down the surprisingly run-down street, which was the official residence and office of state of the Prime Minister of the United Kingdom of Great Britain and Ireland.

In the entrance hall we encountered a group of bickering functionaries, who glared at us before returning to their business. A flustered official extricated himself, rushing towards us with an outstretched hand. "Mr N'yotsu, Mr Potts. We received your letter. Please follow me and I will see if he can fit you in."

"Hang on a moment," shouted one of the people from the other side of the room. "I have been waiting here for hours, and these two just wander in off the street and are taken straight upstairs? This is an insult, sir!"

I turned my shoulders so that the hilt of my sword became visible. "Important matters of state," I said. "I am sure that you understand."

The man's eyes widened as he finally registered who we were. "Of course. My apologies." He turned away, red-faced.

I grinned back at our official, who had watched the exchange with disguised amusement. "Shall we?" I asked.

"Thank you," he said as he led us up the grand staircase. "Some people do not seem to understand simple English."

I nodded. "It is the least we could do, seeing as how you are being so accommodating to our last minute request."

"Unlike our overbearing friends down there, it is not too hard to get the Prime Minister to agree to a meeting with you. I believe that what you have to say is a lot more… stimulating than his usual fare."

N'yotsu grunted and we shared a glance. I suspected that our enthusiastic patron might consider our latest news to be a case of 'be careful what you wish for.' "I do love this staircase," I said, already regretting the words as they came out of my mouth. N'yotsu grinned at me: small talk in formal settings had never been a strength of mine.

"Indeed," said the official. "It is currently the one part of this building that is in a half-decent state of repair. Would that we could hold all our meetings here."

After a short wait we were ushered into a long and meanly furnished room, at the other end of which, sat behind a huge mahogany desk, was Prime Minister Benjamin Disraeli, a scrawny man with a long face topped off with a shock of curly black hair. He set down his quill and grinned at us. "The conquering heroes return," he said, coming round to offer us an ink-stained hand in greeting. "Please, be seated. Williams, some refreshments if you would be so kind."

"Augustus was just admiring your staircase, Mr Disraeli," said N'yotsu in an amused tone.

"Hmm. Yes, the one section that does at least look the part, and the one section which I sometimes wish *would* collapse, if only to make it harder for tiresome politicians to pester me. So, when did you return?"

"This morning," I said. "We have come straight from my brother's laboratory. Apologies for not coming direct but we had some people with us who we needed to ensure were deposited safely there."

Disraeli waved a hand dismissively. "I am pleased to have something worthwhile to engage with at last. My time seems to be comprised solely with political machinations and that damned Irish question. Honestly, do none of them realise there is a war going on?"

"Speaking of which, sir," said N'yotsu, "we bring disturbing news."

We were interrupted by the Prime Minister's orderly bringing in a tray of tea and waited until he had left before continuing.

"Our train was attacked by a horde of demons and Soul-less just north of Nottingham and we were forced to make an unscheduled stop there, where we encountered some trouble. The local populace were somewhat... restive."

Disraeli frowned and then bellowed: "Williams!" The orderly opened the door after a second's pause. "Yes, sir?" he asked.

"Are Cranbrook and Hampton around? They should hear this."

"I have seen Earl Cranbrook downstairs, sir," the orderly said. "But I believe Baron Hampton is in the House. Shall I send for him?"

"No, no," Disraeli waved a hand. "Send up Cranbrook. He will suffice; we can brief Hampton later if need be."

A few moments later a round-faced balding man with an impressive set of white side-whiskers entered the room. We stood as Disraeli made the introductions. "Gentlemen, I have the pleasure to introduce Gathorne Hardy, the first Earl of Cranbrook and my Home Secretary. Now please, do continue."

"We had cause to make a stop in Nottingham and were met with what can only be described as a lynch mob," I said, "led by a gentleman who now purports to be the supreme authority in that city. An individual who goes by the name of William Morley, supposedly styled Witchfinder General."

I had expected guffaws of laughter or at least outright disbelief, but instead was met with a frantic exchange between the two statesmen.

"I told you that we should have stamped on these characters as soon as they started coming out of the woodwork," said Cranbrook.

Disraeli ran his fingers through his hair. "It is not that simple. You know that, Gathorne." He turned back to us. "How many were in this lynch mob?"

I shrugged. "It felt like half the city. We had to run the gauntlet from the garrison to the train station, and I believe it was only thanks to the bravery of the soldiers that we managed to get away."

"Their ire seemed mainly directed towards me," said N'yotsu. "There was a strong anti-demon sentiment there. Which is understandable, if a little unfair in the circumstances."

"And what did the police do?" asked Disraeli.

"I think you will find that Nottingham's chief constable is the same individual who now calls himself Witchfinder General," said Cranbrook. When Disraeli turned to him he held up his hands in mock surrender. "I have raised this concern a number of times. The rule of law is being supplanted by petty superstitions, and the common constabulary are by no means immune. Especially when idiots like this Morley fellow fan the flames. Every street preacher and half of those behind pulpits are declaring that we are in the midst of the End of Days. Given everything that has happened over the past few years, it is in a sense understandable."

Disraeli glared at his Home Secretary.

"Why not replace Morley and his like with more sensible, loyal types?" I asked. "You are the Home Secretary; you have that power, surely?"

"Ordinarily I would agree. But these are not ordinary times and to do so would be an affront, possibly a treasonous one."

N'yotsu nodded slowly. "Morley said that he answers to a 'higher power.' I take it from what you have said that he means the Crown?"

Disraeli stood and started pacing the room. "I am afraid so. Ever since the events of a few years ago, Her Majesty has been very... proactive."

"Can she do that?" I asked. "Create new posts willy-nilly?"

They all looked at me. "She is the Queen," said Disraeli slowly. "And my predecessor was unfortunately not really in a fit state to challenge her. Not only due to his ill-health, but we have a minority in Parliament and have been somewhat distracted by the Reform Act as well as the whole demon issue. Demon incursions, the Soulless raiding towns and villages the length and breadth of the country; the army has enough on its hands. For a while we were merely happy to have one less thing to worry about, and at least Morley and his kind keep the streets in order."

"I am curious," said N'yotsu, "as to what has motivated Her Majesty to behave in this manner. Does she not trust your abilities to maintain law and order? What is the role of these Witchfinders?"

"Her Majesty sees the current crisis as an existential one, a religious threat as well as a physical one. Demons feature quite prominently in the Bible, after all. As the Head of the Church, she believes it is her duty to ensure that her people are protected from all angles. The Church, for their part, are enjoying their new-found hold over her conscience. Whenever I try to insist that the government and army be allowed to take charge, I am reminded of our failures last time."

"Although," said Cranbrook, "on the plus side, the Witchfinders have been effective at keeping order and the populace in line. Until now, in any case."

"The concept of Witchfinders has always been inextricably linked to religion," I mused. "Especially on the Continent: it was often a handy tool for the local church to rid itself of bothersome heretics."

"Fascinating though all of this is," said N'yotsu, "it is worth pointing out that the Captain of the Nottingham garrison was a powerless prisoner for some time. I would wager that other cities have similar issues."

"If you could persuade Her Majesty to at least make her Witchfinders report to the Home Office, that would go some way to containing matters before it is too late," Cranbrook said.

Disraeli sighed and nodded. "Very well. She is very protective of her Witchfinders, but with this new evidence I may be able to persuade her to rein them in for a time at least. Leave it with me. Was there anything else to report, gentlemen?"

"I am afraid so," said N'yotsu. "We encountered a new demon, a rather unpleasant fiend named Gaap. We engaged him in battle but he unfortunately managed to escape, thanks to the intervention of a creature known as a Mage."

"Is that a type of demon as well?" Disraeli asked.

"Yes. Rather a powerful one too; Gus can testify to that."

"Indeed," I said. "It compelled me to attack N'yotsu. For a while I was hell-bent on killing him, thanks to its influence. It seems that the creature can make people do things against their will. Worse, it can make them *believe* that they want to do the very thing they're being forced to do."

"From what I remember, you have a similar ability?" said Disraeli, watching N'yotsu closely.

"Not quite," replied my friend. "I—as Andras—could only influence people by playing on their desires or fears. So a number of your colleagues were tempted to act in the ways they did because I played on their lust for power, money or other trappings. Such an ability does have its limitations though. The Mage's abilities are much purer: they are able to mould a person's will and bend it as they wish, regardless of the victim's desires or powers of resistance."

"How is it that we have not heard of such creatures before?" asked Cranbrook with a hint of scepticism in his tone.

"I did not think any had come through. It appears I was wrong."

"But you were only planning to tell us after they had come through and corrupted our minds? I am beginning to wonder what other pieces of information you are withholding from us, sir!"

"I can assure you that I have been completely open with you all. But there are myriad creatures out there, many of which will never break through to this world. Would you wish to be jumping at shadows and bogged down in unnecessary details, just so you can say you know everything?"

A thought struck me. "Why did it not affect you?" I asked N'yotsu.

"Pardon?" he asked.

"The Mage. Would it not have been more efficient if it had compelled both of us to fight each other, rather than just me attack you? Or even to just make us stab ourselves and be done with it?"

He frowned. "The ways of demons can sometimes be very inscrutable."

"The demon works in mysterious ways," quipped Disraeli, earning himself a glare from Cranbrook.

"Indeed," said N'yotsu. "It may have acted as it did because it was interpreting the orders it had been given in a very literal sense. The Mages have very little ability to think for themselves, you see. Or perhaps it was operating at the extent of its powers by manipulating you, and could not spare the energy to control me as well."

Disraeli walked round to stand behind his desk. "Mr N'yotsu, Mr Potts, assuming there is nothing more I would speak with my Minister in private."

"Of course," I said, standing up. "We have matters to discuss with my brother."

"Home Secretary," said N'yotsu, "the matter of this demon Gaap. We suspect he was heading down here to London. Captain Pearce of the Royal Welch Fusiliers is conducting searches, and I am also putting out my own feelers. I would appreciate any assistance that the Constabulary could provide."

Cranbrook frowned. "I am not going to order my men to engage this demon if that is what you expect."

"Not at all. If Gaap is spotted, then I just ask that we be informed so we can deal with him. But the more eyes we have looking for the fiend, the better."

Cranbrook grunted. "Very well. My aide is outside. He can take the details from you and make the necessary arrangements."

We arrived back at 24 Whitehall to find Maxwell still in excitable conversation with Joshua and Lexie. We allowed this to continue for a while before deciding to intervene.

"I am sure our new guests are tired from their journey," I said. "Kate, would you be able to take them to the guest quarters?"

"Oh, we're fine," said Lexie.

"Yes, we can manage a while longer," added Maxwell. "They are young and no doubt have plenty of stamina, eh?" His two new protégés grinned at him.

"And you have not yet explained what this 'Fulcrum' is that we keep hearing about," said Lexie.

"Ah, yes," said Maxwell, settling back as though he were about to read a bedtime story to his children. The effect was completed by the enraptured looks on Joshua and Lexie's faces. I sighed and shrugged at N'yotsu; clearly we would be forced to wait a little longer until we could get down to business.

"Many tales from the days before the Enlightenment give the impression of the world as being a place full of magic and sorcery, wizards and demons and such like. For a long time, I had assumed that these were mere folk tales or the fevered imaginings of our uneducated forebears, primitive people who did not possess the scientific methods and wherewithal to explain the apparently miraculous.

"However, our first meeting with N'yotsu made me reappraise my views, having witnessed phenomena such as demons and magical powers with my own eyes. The creation of portals to the Aether seemed to accelerate matters, as did our conversations with the demon Andras. In fact, Andras intimated that science and magic are effectively two mutually exclusive elements that cannot exist easily together. Not only that, but Andras stated that the dawning of our age of science had effectively ended the age of magic, making it difficult—if not impossible—for demons as well as human sorcerers to undertake such actions as passing through the Aether or summoning others from it. Effectively, it was science that trapped Andras and his fellows here in our realm."

"But it was also science—your devices—that released them into this world?" asked Lexie.

"Indeed," said Maxwell. "But my devices also inadvertently punched a hole in the fabric of reality, giving magic a foothold in our world once more. You see, it appears that the Aether is intimately connected to magic. As a result, the continued weakening of the barriers between our realm and the Aether has increased the strength and propensity of magic here also. And because magic and science are mutually exclusive..."

"...science is on the wane while magic is in the ascendancy," concluded Joshua.

"That is correct," said Maxwell. "Which partly explains how you have been so much more successful in your endeavours than many other magicians in the past."

Joshua looked hurt at the insinuation and so I quickly added: "Although of course you are also a highly talented individual, which helped immensely."

Maxwell glared at me, clearly not appreciating the reason for my interjection. He picked up a piece of paper and scrawled a pair of axes upon it. "The x-axis," he said, pointing to the horizontal, "represents time, while the y-axis is, for want of a better term, the relative power or prevalence of elements within our world. I, and most others in my field, have always assumed that 'science'—again, for want of a better term, but by which I mean all of the laws that we have existed by, as in not the supernatural or magical—is effectively stable within this equation, like so." He laid his pencil horizontally, towards the top of the y-axis, illustrating a straight line unchanging over time.

"However," he continued, picking up the pencil once more, "it appears that it is in actuality a declining force, like so." He drew a diagonal line sloping downward from the top of the y-axis to the far right-hand point of the x-axis. "Whether that is a natural phenomenon or something that has been brought into being through our actions is of course open to debate."

"Wait," frowned Lexie. "You are assuming here a linear relationship. But surely, given our observations and what you have said about historical phenomena, it would be more of a polynomial?"

"Yes, yes," said Maxwell. "That is likely to be the case, but I am here just taking a shortened period of time, so we are effectively seeing a very defined segment of the curve."

Kate and I shared a glance. "In English please?" I asked.

Maxwell grunted. "Lexie has very accurately pointed out that it is more likely that the strength of science over time in this graph would look more like this." He drew a wavy line on a separate piece of paper. "That would accord with the fact that historical observations indicated a more magical world, until the dawn of the Renaissance brought about a shift towards a more scientific way of thinking." He moved his finger along the line, moving upwards from the bottom of the curve as he spoke. "I would expect this trend to be accurate over a broad span of time—centuries or even millennia—but if we look at a shorter period then the curve effectively becomes straight: see?" He marked out a very small section of the line and we all nodded slowly.

Maxwell returned to his original graph. "Newton's Third Law states: 'To every action there is always opposed an equal reaction,' from which we can deduce that there must be a force acting in opposition to that which I am terming for these purposes 'science'."

"Magic," nodded Lexie, as Maxwell drew another line on the graph, this time running at a 45 degree angle from the bottom left-hand corner all the way up, forming an 'X' with the other line he had drawn.

"Indeed," said Maxwell, pointing to the new line. "Represented by this line and acting in direct opposition to 'science'."

"This is extraordinary," said Lexie, "and perfectly logical. If we have readings along various points then we could extrapolate the exact points of convergence, not to mention estimate when the balance will swing back again."

"Which is what I have been attempting to do," said Maxwell. "I have taken measurements and done extensive calculations, and I believe that the balance is continuing to tip over time, meaning that we are fast approaching a point at which the dominant element in our world will move from science and into magic. This point I have named the Fulcrum." He tapped the centre of the 'X' and smiled at us all, still proud of the name he had given the phenomenon.

"But what would that mean?" asked Lexie.

"Until we reach that point, we can only hypothesise," said Maxwell. "But I believe that science will become redundant in favour of magical methods that were once merely the stuff of fairy tales. Of course, if there is a relationship then there must be a way to influence it, and effectively reverse what has been happening."

Lexie leaned forwards, a note of urgency in her tone. "This relationship between the two forces would also account for the increasing failure of machinery, and the corollary being the increasing faculties available for successful magical experiments."

"That is correct," grinned Maxwell, looking younger and more animated than I had seen in a long time. Maybe bringing him these protégés was not such a bad idea after all.

Lexie turned to Joshua. "It would seem that I owe you an apology, big brother."

"In what way?" he asked warily.

"It would appear that your assertions as to your magical studies being the key to reigniting the family business were not as hopelessly juvenile as I first thought. If Mr Potts' Fulcrum theory is correct, then the foundry and all the other machinery were always bound to fail, while your magical methods truly will be more important and useful going forwards."

"Which is not necessarily a cause for celebration," interjected Maxwell. "Do not forget that the demons are significantly more gifted in magical methods than we are. And the approaching Fulcrum makes portals to the Aether and beyond that much more feasible, giving them a doorway to our world. Unless we can find a way to stop it."

"May I see your calculations?" asked Lexie. "I may be able to help come up with a solution."

"Of course," said Maxwell slowly. "Although this is something that has taxed me for some time."

"Even so," she said, "a fresh pair of eyes may be of some help."

"Maybe," he said, "although time is fleeting and so I do not wish to waste it on dead-ends."

"And that is why we need everyone at full strength and rested so that they can work as effectively as possible," said N'yotsu, staring pointedly at Maxwell.

"But of course, you are right," said Maxwell, finally getting the message. "Kate, please escort them to their sleeping quarters and then you may retire yourself for the evening."

Joshua and Lexie left reluctantly, while Kate paused in the doorway to glare at us. "What are you lot up to?" she asked.

"Absolutely nothing at all," I said, doing my best to effect an air of innocence as I pushed the door shut behind her. I waited a few moments before locking it.

"That will not do much good," said Maxwell. "She always manages to unlock it."

"Have you tried changing the locks?"

"Constantly. At first I thought she was taking copies off the locksmith before I realised that she is just incredibly good with a pick."

I smiled. "Ah yes, the benefits of a lifetime of education on the streets."

"All I can say is that I am glad she is on our side," said Maxwell. "Now, what news?"

"Gus's affliction appears to be worsening," said N'yotsu. "Have you come any closer to a treatment?"

"As a matter of fact, I believe I have," he said. "I have managed to isolate the particular resonances that the Aether emits when it is attached to living tissue. I have constructed a device," he gestured behind him, "which will attack only the Aethereal elements, leaving human tissue undamaged."

N'yotsu and I examined the machine he had indicated. The main portion was a large glass dome, not unlike an over-sized fishbowl, into which ran an alarming number of pipes, tubes and wires. A metal rod was rammed through the centre of it, flowing into the floor and ceiling at right angles. The pipes and tubes trailed into a number of bowls and vats containing differing substances, some of which looked like water, while others seemed considerably more viscous as they bubbled and smoked away. At the end of it all, the wires terminated into what was at first sight a writing desk, but on closer examination contained a frankly unnecessarily large number of dials, knobs and levers.

N'yotsu clearly did not share my disdain for Maxwell's device. "Ingenious," he said. "Do you believe this will work?"

"But of course," Maxwell bristled. "I have tested it extensively on a variety of organisms and the results have been emphatic: anything Aetheric is destroyed while those elements originating from the Earth remain undamaged."

N'yotsu looked up. "You tested it on organisms? What kind of organisms?"

"Plants at first, then mice and rats."

"What *Aetheric* organisms did you experiment on?"

Maxwell met N'yotsu's gaze for a few seconds. "To be sure it works, I needed to test it on suitable creatures. Namely those that we are seeking to eliminate."

"You have killed demons in this thing?"

"Yes."

"Including the ones we captured the other week, maybe?"

"Yes."

N'yotsu threw his hands in the air. "You cannot do that! Sitting here in your laboratory, subjecting innocent creatures to this... torture chamber!"

Maxwell fixed him with a stare that matched the coldness of his voice. "There is no such thing as an innocent demon."

"I beg to differ," N'yotsu said. "The creatures we brought back the other week were harmless."

"I fail to see how anything straying from the Aether to our world can be considered harmless. In any case, you brought them to me for examination."

"Examination, yes—not extermination!"

"If I am to perfect my methods, I must test them," Maxwell said in a measured voice as though he were addressing a five-year-old child. "Although my theoretical calculations are usually impeccable, it is not uncommon for errors to creep in to the overall models, or for there to be aspects in reality that were not anticipated or accounted for in my calculations."

"I appreciate that, but even so—"

"I sense this is becoming a bit of a circular argument," I interrupted. "Max, can we ask that you consult us before you next experiment on any other creatures, demonic or otherwise?"

"It seems highly unnecessary, not to mention a delay—"

"Max!"

He scowled at me. "Very well. Any further creatures, I will consult you first. Can we get back to the matter in hand? Would you like to see my calculations and results?"

N'yotsu nodded with a scowl.

A couple of hours later I was seated in the centre of the device, looking out at my friends through the curve of the glass surface. The curvature lent them a strange, bulbous aspect that shifted as they moved, making me feel more and more like I was in a goldfish bowl. For their part, they busied themselves with the machinery and the various calculations, largely ignoring me. I was not surprised by this, but it served to increase the sensation that I was merely a creature to be studied or dissected rather than a brother and friend.

"So you are sure that this will work?" I asked again.

"Yes, positive," said Maxwell. "None of the non-Aetheric test subjects have shown any indications of distress or physical degradation."

"Did it hurt?"

"They declined to tell me. Of course, I don't actually speak rodent so I wouldn't know. But they did not shriek in agony if that is what you mean."

"Thanks for the reassurance," I muttered.

I kept my agitation under control as much as I could while I watched them prepare the equipment. I was acutely aware of the lightness on my back where my sword should have been: given its occult nature, we did not wish to risk subjecting it to whatever procedure I was about to endure. I focused on the desired outcome—if it worked then very soon I would be free from the ever-present burden of turning into a demon. I had mixed feelings at this prospect. While I was keen to unburden myself from the constant threat of turning into an inhuman beast without warning, I was also fearful of what I would become without my powers.

Would I still be of use to the others if I could not fight on equal terms with the demons? How could I really contribute to the cause without my powers? I remembered how things were before I was given the runic sword, how I was a hindrance at best and a drunken liability at worst.

But then I remembered the visions and nightmares I had had over the past few months: of turning into a mindless beast, a stranger and even an enemy to my friends and allies. I had to go through with this.

Finally, satisfied that all was in order, Maxwell turned to me, his hand on a lever. "Are you ready?" he asked.

"Not really," I said. "But let's get this over with."

He nodded and I noted a slight hesitation in his bearing; with a flash of understanding I realised that, in spite of his confidence in his equipment and calculations, it was quite something else to experiment on one's own brother rather than rodents. "Max," I said, "I want you to do this. I cannot keep turning into that... whatever it is. I would rather die than become your enemy."

Our eyes met, a mutual understanding passing between us as I saw the fear and uncertainty on his face. Above all else, though, I knew that he wanted to help me and he nodded, taking a deep breath and then pushing down on the lever.

There was a slight hum and then... nothing. I held my breath: had the device malfunctioned?

Maxwell and N'yotsu scrutinised the dials; whatever they saw there did not give them any cause for alarm.

"Dial 'A' is rising," said N'yotsu.

"Dial 'B' is holding steady," replied Maxwell. "Both 'C' and 'D' are starting to increase."

I forced a chuckle. "Could you not have thought of more original names for the dials than the alphabet?"

Maxwell sighed without looking up. "If you would rather I

wasted my time thinking up pretty names or acronyms rather than making my devices safe and accurate, then I will bear that in mind for next time," he snapped. "Now please be quiet and let us concentrate."

I nodded, holding up my hands as they continued their conversation. After a while they stopped and I peered at them, again trying to see if there was any change in anything connected to the device, as there seemed to be precious little taking place within my fishbowl. "Is it working?"

"As far as we can tell so far. But again, please be quiet!"

I folded my arms, biting back a comment about his lack of bedside manner as I noticed a faint mist seeping into the chamber by way of one of the pipes. It curled around the inlet and snaked towards me, a slow-moving tendril of faint white intent, lazily creeping across the floor and up the sides. My heart started to beat hard in my chest as I realised what this reminded me of.

"Erm, Max?" I said.

"Not now," he replied, not looking up.

I pulled my feet up off the floor, squatting on the chair and looking around to make sure that none of the mist could touch me as it blanketed the lower part of the sphere. Memories came back of a similar substance in a house occupied by a poor, possessed girl named Milly and a mist that brought with it the leering spirits of malicious children, taunting me with ghastly rhymes. Then there was the same mist emerging from the portal that Maxwell had created to the black abyss of the Aether, a place where hungry hands reached out from withered bodies desperate to devour anything living and suck away all of our vitality to feed their insatiable appetites. And then I was back in the Aether itself, holding the door firm against the pressure from the ghouls without, seeing the mist everywhere and knowing that that was the only tangible feature of the void in which we were trapped.

The mist curled up the chair legs, reaching up to me, coiling and writhing in a hungry dance as it made its determined way ever upwards. "Max!" I shouted.

They both looked up. "What are you...?" asked Maxwell. "The steam is perfectly harmless. It is simply a medium for the transfer of the serum that will then latch on to the Aetheric elements within you. I need you to relax. Let it cover you and breathe deeply."

"It is just... it reminded me of the Aether..."

"Ha, yes I suppose it does resemble the Aetheric mists somewhat," he said, treating my comment more as a matter of vague interest than a genuine concern. He peered at it for a moment and then finally noted my panic. "I assure you that it is in no way connected to the Aether. Quite the opposite in fact. Now, please do your best to relax and sit still. I promise I will not allow anything to harm you."

I stared into his eyes and then nodded. He had trusted me plenty of times in the past and I now needed to do likewise. I gingerly lowered myself back into a sitting position and placed my feet back on the ground, flinching for a moment as the mist enveloped my lower legs. When nothing untoward happened, I relaxed a bit more and allowed my hands to drop down into my lap. Slowly, the mist swirled and rose around me, reaching up to my torso and shoulders. As it stretched its gossamer tendrils towards my mouth I found myself reflexively holding my breath and straining my chin upwards. Clenching my fists, I forced my chin down and took a deep breath in.

A part of me was pleasantly surprised to note that I did not fall into an abyss or start to corrode from the effects of the mist on my lungs. If anything, it smelt faintly of fog, but a clean fog rather than the pervasive and cloying wall of misery that often obscured London's streets. It had a fairly moist quality that was rather soothing to my skin and throat, putting me in mind of the bowls of boiling water that Mother would make me lean over when I had a cold as a child, draping a towel over my head to fully encase me in a small world of soothing, decongesting steam.

Warming to the idea, I closed my eyes and took another deep breath. When I opened them again, the mist had covered my head completely and the world had taken on an other-worldly view from within my mist-filled bubble. I could still discern the figures of Maxwell and N'yotsu outside but they were indistinct and fuzzy, as though they belonged to a place far away, somewhere I could never comprehend.

Maxwell's voice came to me as though over a long distance, enhancing my light-headedness. "We are about to commence the next phase and introduce the compound containing the serum. Are you comfortable?"

"I am fine," I called back, looking at my hands in the strange light. "Are you sure it will not hurt?"

"I believe not, but as I said I could not be totally certain. Please keep us appraised, and if it becomes too much then we shall discontinue. Are you ready?"

No, I thought. "Yes," I called back.

I could vaguely make out a flurry of activity from outside the bubble as they pulled levers and turned knobs, N'yotsu darting from one side of the bench to the other to call out readings and accept instructions from my brother. I was aware of a slight increase in the humidity within the chamber, a thickness in the air that tasted faintly of copper. For a moment I wanted to rebel against this serum as my mind dwelt on all of the things that my special qualities had enabled me to accomplish—the heightened awareness, the increased speed, incredible strength and stamina. What use would I be to the world without such things?

But then I again remembered the physical changes that came with those abilities, not to mention what they represented: the panic when I first saw the runic symbols run like water from the hilt of the sword to my hand and wrist, spreading red liquid tattoos up my arm and across my body. I remembered a vision I had had of what I would become if I were to allow those changes to continue until they permanently took hold: the sight of me as a snarling demonic creature with hunger in my eyes, lacking in all mercy, morals or humanity. I could not allow myself to become that thing. I would not force my brother to kill me to protect others.

I took another deep shuddering breath, followed by another and another. The enhanced mist felt hot as it seeped into my lungs, a warmness that went from pleasant to uncomfortable in very quick order. I looked down at my hands to see the runic symbols visible once more, swirling slowly beneath my skin. As I watched they grew agitated and started to whirl with an increased intensity, almost as though they were fighting to escape from my body. My breath caught in my throat: it was actually working!

The sensation was unpleasant, but I was ready for that and gritted my teeth as the intensity increased, feeling it spreading from my hands, through my arms and shoulders and into the rest of my body. Every part of me vibrated as though I were comprised of millions of tiny bees all held together by little more than common purpose, ready to break free into countless different directions at the slightest whim. I gasped as the vibrations continued to increase exponentially: the hive was getting angry.

My skin was a river raging fast over the shifting sands of my veins, sinews and bones, no part of me now fixed or solid. While I still sat on the chair, I was also within it and under it, the normal rules no longer applying to me, if indeed they ever had. With a jolt I realised that sight no longer had any meaning for me, nor did any of my senses: I was nothing more than mist.

But then the mist repelled and attacked me, a swirling red angry mass that wanted nothing more than my annihilation. *Who are you?* a distant part of me shouted out into this hideous hatred.

Your doom came the reply in a cavernous voice that would have taken my breath away had I any to steal.

Why?

You are abhorrent, an abomination. You do not belong here; none of you do.

A million crows attacked me, gnawing into my very soul. From somewhere far off, someone screamed, a terrible cry that felt like the loss of everything. Then there was a light in the distance, and dimly I wondered if this was the gateway to heaven. Was I going home at last?

A figure stepped into the light, batting away the swirling mist and carrying me out, his face etched in painful determination. N'yotsu bore me from within the shattered globe and out into the room, laying me on the ground as carefully as he could before collapsing beside me in agony.

CHAPTER NINE

"What exactly were you doing?" Dr Smith asked again. When Maxwell remained silent, the doctor sighed. "If you cannot tell me what has afflicted your brother and your friend then I cannot readily treat them. Really, Maxwell; I understand the secretive nature of your work but I have been your physician for a number of weeks now and have betrayed no confidences. You really *must* trust me."

I peered at the doctor through cloudy and unfocused eyes. What I could see of the man through my distorted view was distinctly underwhelming: my vision was filled with a beak-like nose protruding from a shiny, patrician-like face. He was a new addition to Maxwell's carers, having replaced the previous doctor at some point during our trip to Sheffield, and he was apparently among the finest physicians in the country.

After N'yotsu had dragged me, insensate and near death, from Maxwell's device we had both been brought to a room further down the corridor that now served as a makeshift hospital ward. It seemed that I was not the only one who had had a negative reaction to Maxwell's concoction. N'yotsu was similarly afflicted and Maxwell himself had complained of blistering to his skin. As for the soldiers who came to our rescue, they had burst into fits of coughing as soon as they entered the room. Thankfully, however, their exposure was considerably diluted compared to my extreme dosage.

After the doctor was satisfied that they had suffered no lasting ill effects, the soldiers had left with little more than quizzical glances back at us: they were clearly used to Maxwell's experiments. Thankfully, Kate seemed to have actually taken Maxwell's dismissal earlier as an order to be followed. I could not bear to face her at that time; with my swollen and blistered skin I looked like a burnt cadaver pulled from a house fire.

I shifted in my bed and a sharp burst of pain ran through my body. "Max, please," I croaked.

"Very well," Maxwell sighed. He passed the doctor a sheet of paper. "These are the compounds with which I dosed him."

Dr Smith frowned at the list. "What an odd combination. I cannot imagine these being anything other than benign. What were you trying to accomplish?"

"We were attempting to separate Aetheric matter from his human tissue. Unfortunately something did not quite work according to plan, or maybe it worked a little too well. I have not had time to consider this, as my brother's welfare is my primary concern. Can you treat?"

"Of course I can treat him," the doctor snapped back and for once I saw Maxwell affronted by someone else's lack of courtesy. "I will need to run some tests, but it appears that your compound has uniformly attacked every part of your brother's body."

"Which would suggest that the Aetheric elements are too closely bound to the human ones," Maxwell muttered.

"The same goes for Mr N'yotsu here, although his symptoms are not quite as acute."

"That is correct," said N'yotsu from the bed next to mine. "I was only in there for a few seconds to rescue Gus. And I held my breath throughout."

"It is for the best that you did," said the doctor. "For it appears that your sensitivity to the compound is significantly greater than that of Mr Potts."

"That would make sense," said N'yotsu. "I have spent a lot longer in the Aether than Gus."

"Not to mention the fact that you are not of this world," said the doctor. "Are you?"

N'yotsu glared at him. "I thought that we were discussing treating Gus's ailments, not my family tree."

The doctor raised his eyebrows as he turned back to Maxwell. "You also appear to have been affected by the compound, as were the soldiers who entered the room before your concoction fully dissipated."

"Yes," he said. "That was an eventuality I had not planned for."

"Indeed. I am confused: you said that Aetheric elements had been bound to your brother's body?"

Maxwell looked to me, not willing to share my secret without my consent.

I nodded slowly. Thus far, I had been incredibly careful to only share the truth of my condition with Maxwell and N'yotsu. This was for very good reasons, as I feared what would happen if anyone knew what I was turning into. The best scenario that came to mind in my less fevered moments was being a prime exhibit in a travelling freak show.

I looked at Dr Smith. He was a professional, but still very much an unknown quantity. As a doctor, he would surely view my transformation as an ideal subject for examination and experimentation, thereby playing to my worst fears. But then again, maybe a medical professional would have insights into my condition that Maxwell and N'yotsu lacked. And surely he had a duty of care to me, as his patient?

"Doctor, you have sworn an oath, am I correct? The Hippocratic Oath, in part meaning that you cannot discuss what I, as your patient, tell you in confidence?"

"That is correct."

I took a deep breath. "I have a sword that is imbued with certain... occult properties."

"Your runic sword; yes, I am aware of it. It is sharper and stronger than anything else known to man, is it not?"

"Indeed. But there is another property of the sword that we do not advertise, and which I am keen to keep between those of us in this room."

"Do tell."

I looked at him closely, trying to satisfy myself once and for all that I could trust him with this, my deadliest secret. With a deep breath, I dove in. "The spells that give the sword its powers, the runic symbols etched onto it, also infect the person who wields the sword. At first it was in the form of heat given off through overuse, which we assumed was just an unfortunate side effect. However, it soon became apparent... that it also makes me stronger, faster and gives me more heightened senses and awareness than any man, and indeed many demons."

"Fascinating. So the spells that power it actually make you a part of the weapon as well?"

"In a manner of speaking, yes. However, a further side effect is that the results have been more and more potent over time and also more and more, ah..."

"Are you saying that you are turning into a demon?"

I studied his face, unable to decide whether his excitement was a result of scientific curiosity or something more sinister. "Effectively, yes. And that is what Max was attempting to cure me of. But it appears that he was unsuccessful."

Dr Smith stared at me for a long moment. "Maybe I can be of assistance. It may be useful for an *actual* medical doctor to help you." Maxwell bristled at this but stayed remarkably quiet as the doctor removed more instruments from his bag and started to examine me.

"I am sorry, Gus," said Maxwell. "I genuinely thought that it would work. It would appear that I can rely on precious little these days without suffering from the malign influence of the Fulcrum..." His brow furrowed in impotent frustration.

I shrugged. "Do not blame yourself; I agreed that you should do it. The important thing is that we try to find a cure for my... condition."

"But not at the risk of it killing you."

"Agreed," I managed a half-grin. "I would prefer that as well. So what do you think this means for my cure?"

Maxwell ran his fingers through his hair. "It means that I must go back to first principles. Clearly an invasive and violent treatment like this will not work, not without also killing you."

"But if, as you said, the Aetheric elements are too closely bonded to my humanity, then doesn't that mean I'm already well on my way to becoming a fully-fledged demon?"

"Maybe. Although the fact that the rest of us were also affected does suggest that the compound is not targeted enough. If it attacks all living matter then that is obviously little use as a cure."

"So it's worthless," I said.

"Not quite," Maxwell said slowly. "You see, while I am of course focused on finding a cure for your... ah, condition, I am also charged with finding a way to end the demon threat. The side-effects of the compound I used on you may provide us with an answer."

"But if it also kills everyone else?" asked N'yotsu.

"That may be a price we have to pay," said Maxwell. "We would just need to put measures in place to mitigate the damage."

"*Mitigate* the damage!" I exclaimed, immediately regretting it as the exertion brought with it a stabbing pain in my chest. I forced myself to continue. "You are talking about people dying. If you unleash that substance then it could be a disaster: are you willing to have that on your conscience?"

Max glared at me. "I have been charged with ending the demon threat to our world, *through any means necessary*. In case you have forgotten, we are at war. Sometimes in wars people die."

"For the greater good, eh?" I asked.

"Spare me the moralising. The Fulcrum is fast approaching and all of my efforts to stop it are proving for naught. I believe it is now inevitable that we will soon find ourselves in a world where science becomes redundant, leaving us at the mercy of the demons and their like. We need some way of defending ourselves, and this could well be it." I shook my head as he continued. "Think about it: we could create a portal to the Aether and then send the compound through, directing it at the demons."

"And what if they threw it straight back at us?"

"He's right," coughed N'yotsu. "Remember that every portal thus far has been accompanied by vicious winds blowing towards us. Therefore any attempt to send a gas through would just blow it back our way, killing everyone on this side."

"Can you not modify the compound so that it is more targeted?" asked the doctor. "So that it only attacks demons, for example?"

"I thought I had done exactly that," said Maxwell. "I wonder whether my energies would be better spent finding a method to deliver the compound more effectively."

"You've made a portal before," said the doctor. "I have never understood why you don't have another one already set up."

Maxwell shook his head. "My previous devices worked in a time when magic and science were in relative calm, with science very much in prominence. But with everything now in flux, there needs to be a precise balancing of magic and science within the device, taking into account our status vis-à-vis the Fulcrum, to enable me to get anything close to a sustainable portal. Which is why I summoned young Joshua to assist me. Speaking of which, I must get back to my work." He gestured to his orderly, who wheeled him out of the room.

I slumped back in my bed, staring up at a ceiling that seemed to swirl and shimmer like water above me. My heart sank as I considered the implications: I was surely doomed, as the voice had said to me when I was being torn apart by Maxwell's serum. There really was nothing left for me; the question was whether I could hold on long enough to be of use to humanity's cause, and then… the images from a nightmarish vision I had experienced last Christmas forced themselves back into my mind: of me being reduced to a slavering, mindless creature, just another enemy for Maxwell to vanquish.

"I am sure that your brother will come up with a cure," said Dr Smith. "After all, he is quite the genius—I can tell. But surely it cannot be so bad? Many people would kill for powers like you describe, not to mention your ability to recover from physical wounds. Most would not have survived the ordeal you have just been through."

"Let's call it a mixed blessing in that case," I muttered.

"Hmm. Then again, if you are turning into a demon, even superficially, then I could understand your reticence. But surely your friends and colleagues would understand?" He finished examining me and grunted. "I will look at you again tomorrow, but from what I can tell you should be fine. The blistered tissue is already healing, and your internal organs seem to be operating normally. There is a little bubbling on your lungs, which I would like to check again later, but the best thing you can do for that is to inhale plenty of steam to clear any obstructions."

I noted the irony of this prescription, but was more distracted by his words as he moved off to examine N'yotsu. I thought about Kate and how she had looked at Andras all those years ago back in Greenwich: the hatred and revulsion that would surely also be directed at me if she knew what I was turning into. Not to mention the army, who by now had developed a keen reflex for shooting demons on sight.

I was brought back to the room by an argument at N'yotsu's bedside.

"I do not need your attention, physician," N'yotsu was saying. "I shall be fine and can recover perfectly well without your intervention."

"I really must insist," said the doctor. "It is plain to see that you are not well, and I do not just mean the injuries you sustained in that machine."

"I am fine," said N'yotsu through gritted teeth.

Dr Smith stared at him for a long moment before packing up his equipment, leaving the room without another word.

We lay there in silence, listening as the doctor's footsteps receded until they were cut off by the slamming of Maxwell's door. "I think you hurt his feelings," I said. I tried to lever myself upright but subsided when I was pinned back down by an implacable wall of agony.

N'yotsu chuckled, then lapsed into a coughing fit. "You should rest; even the great Augustus Potts has his limits it would seem."

"Just like you, eh? Thank you, again, for rescuing me."

"It was nothing, really."

"You could have died. In fact, by the sound of your breathing you nearly did."

He coughed again. "I suspect that my death is in any case not far off, as my condition worsens by the day. It cannot be long before my body finally betrays me. So I am afraid that my death is inevitable and to suffer it by saving a friend would be a fine way to go."

I turned my head to look at him. In spite of his brave words, I could see the fear in his eyes. "Surely Maxwell will find a cure for your condition?"

"I have seen what his cures do to people," he said. "I think I'll take my chances, thank you very much." Our laughs tailed off into coughs and groans.

"Seriously, though," I said once recovered. "There must be some way round all of this."

"Maxwell and I have considered it at great length. My body cannot survive indefinitely while being separated from the demonic aspects that are trapped within the obsidian stone. Short of our new friends sparking some fresh lines of inquiry, I am stuck with a choice between a slow, drawn-out death, or the highly unpalatable alternative of turning back into Andras."

"But let us hypothesise: if you were to get back the obsidian stone, surely you would be a different person when recombined with all of the elements trapped there? Surely all of your feelings and emotions must overpower what evil remains within Andras?"

He shook his head. "Maybe in the short term. But, over time, the core of Andras' nature—*my* nature—would win out. The issue is the very nature of demons: they—we—are beyond anything that you might consider morality, in much the same way as a tree does not share the morality of the birds that nest in its branches. Demons have a whole view of the universe that is at odds with your ideas of good or evil, although the outcomes are in many cases very much in line with what you may consider to be evil. No matter how much I have absorbed in terms of emotions and empathy while living in this state among you all, I would be helpless in the face of such amorality."

"But I do not understand why you cannot continue as you are. You have survived this long…"

He smiled. "We have gone over this before, old friend. My kind are not meant to separate their personalities for as long as I have; sooner or later I have to fade away. Think of me like a chicken whose head has been chopped off, running round the farmyard. This body does not yet realise it is lacking a head, but the day is fast approaching when it finally will. Then I will die, and with me Andras, and the world will be a better place for it."

"I refuse to believe that," I said. "You have done so much. Surely you cannot be so resigned to this fate?"

"I am not," he said quietly. "Every waking moment I dread death, while my sleep is disturbed by visions of those I have killed and tortured over the millennia, seeing them beckoning me to them, welcoming my eventual torment." He took a deep, shuddering breath. "I really, really do not want to die, and would give almost anything to prevent it. If there was a way… I am sorry, I have said too much. You do not want to hear me wallowing in self-pity."

"I do not mind," I said. "After all, you have listened to plenty of mine."

He managed a half-smile at this before closing his eyes and I watched him for a few minutes, trying to imagine the terrible torment that he was suffering. Next to that, my own trials and tribulations were insignificant.

I limped through endless corridors, my ears filled with the drip-drip-squelch of falling slime. I stumbled forwards, propelled by a sense of something breathing down my neck. A part of me wanted to turn and see my pursuer, but that was overridden by my body's primal urge to escape it as quickly as possible.

The blank, featureless walls around me were shrouded in semi-darkness, the edges of the black void reaching out to me so that I was forced to keep to the centre for fear of being pulled in by its dark touch.

Doors loomed out of the darkness to either side and I knew without testing them that they would all be locked. I shambled onward, the breath of my pursuer tickling the back of my neck and forcing me into as much of a run as my damaged legs would allow.

My breath came in short, sharp snatches, each more painful than the last. I looked down and saw something moving beneath the skin on my hands and wrists: the runic symbols were awake and fighting for prominence. I tried to calm them but found myself getting more and more panicked. I had to escape that place.

I started pulling at the doors in desperation, in the hope of finding some form of solace or escape from this Hell. My panic rose as each one did indeed prove to be locked fast and I darted along the corridor, fearing at any moment that I would be seized by a cold, dead claw from behind.

The fifth door I tried gave way as I tugged on it, grinding open with a slow deliberation, stones and dust and rust protesting against the disturbance. I yelled out with the effort and found myself face-to-face with another person who stared back at me in a mixture of shock and revulsion.

"Rachel?" I asked.

The apparition stared at me for a long moment before letting out a long, shrill shriek, her clothes dripping with deep red blood that pulsed from the wounds on her neck and body. She collapsed inwardly to be replaced by Kate, who glared at me and then spat. "Demon," she hissed. "Just like all the rest. Scum."

The door slammed shut in my face and I hammered on it impotently before a rasping breeze from behind reminded me of my pursuer. I ran to the next door, which opened easily, and slammed it shut behind me.

As I emerged back into consciousness I realised I was lying down on my bed, the room bathed in faint light from the one remaining candle. I could hear whispering from nearby and turned my head slowly to see a figure that my addled mind interpreted as the doctor kneeling by the side of N'yotsu's bed. I held my breath as I listened to what he was saying.

"...such a shame for you to waste away like this, a grand creature that has lived for so many, many years. Think of all that you could still do if you did not restrict yourself to such fleeting mortality." His voice seemed different, distorted and scratchy, as though he were speaking from within a tin can.

"But it would come at too great a cost." N'yotsu's voice was slurred, sounding as though he were drugged.

"You are strong enough to control your urges. And anyway, the world is a different place to what it was, no longer as hidebound by the old ways."

"I cannot be that... thing again." Despite his weakened condition, I could still hear resoluteness in N'yotsu's voice.

"You always have been and always will be Andras. It is a part of your nature just as much as the rest of you is. The act of merely trimming your hair does not automatically make you a new person. Only the surface changes, what is beneath remains."

"I... am... not..."

"In denying yourself—your true self—you are merely tearing yourself to pieces, which is in turn harming your friends and distracting them from their cause. Soon you will become a liability, and one of them may be forced to sacrifice themselves to aid you. What good will your precious stubborn morality be to you then?"

There was a faint gurgling sound from N'yotsu. I listened incredulously: was he sobbing?

The doctor continued. "If you persist on this path you will die; it is inevitable. Is that what you want?"

"It is no less than I deserve, given what I have done."

"But it was not you who did those things. You have changed, and still can. Do you really want to die?"

"You know the answer to that."

"Do you know what fate awaits you? An eternity of Hell and damnation, all because you were too stubborn to take a risk."

There was a pause and then N'yotsu muttered something quietly in response. I shifted to get closer to what was now being said, and the doctor's head snapped round at the sound.

His face was distorted, as though I were watching it through a waterfall, and the light shone red and hot on his features. But the candle was behind him so how could it be…? Everything started to swim before his glare and I found myself falling back into the corridor, the door once again slamming shut on me.

Back in my dream state, I ran on as best I could, seeking somewhere to hide but met only by the end of the corridor. With nowhere else to go, I turned slowly to face my pursuer.

Red-hot eyes glared at me from a face pocked and scarred with runic symbols. The symbols twisted and turned beneath the skin like cogs in a clock mechanism, giving the features an oddly angular and yet fluid appearance. I recognised the creature from my nightmares: it was what I was likely to become if the runic sword's influence on me were to run its course.

While I had always been petrified and revolted by the thing's appearance, at that moment in time I found myself oddly calmed. We regarded each other and I found myself observing a bizarre type of elegance and grace about the creature, the way it moved. There was an intensity to the eyes that—while still as murderous as ever—was also quite beautiful. *This is not so bad,* I found myself thinking. *What was I afraid of?*

Something intensely cold reached into my head, pulling me back into the world with a jolt.

I was lying on my bed once more, blinking into the well-lit room. Kate sat between me and N'yotsu. "Mornin' sleepy-bones," she grinned at me.

"Um, morning," I said. "Was I…?"

"You were having some sort of dream, that's for sure. How ya feeling?"

"Sore," I groaned as I pushed myself up on my elbows. The doctor's earlier comments about my powers of recovery were proving true, in that I certainly felt a lot stronger than I had the previous day. The thought of the doctor brought to mind what I had experienced that night and I turned to look at N'yotsu, who was propped up on his pillows.

"Did the doctor come in here last night to talk to you?" I asked him.

"No," he said. "At least not when I was awake. Hopefully he got the message from yesterday. I do not need help from physicians."

"Are you sure?" I asked, watching him closely.

"Yes." His face was a picture of bemused innocence. "Why do you ask?"

"I thought I saw him in here last night, speaking with you about your... condition." I rubbed my head. "It must have been a dream; I was having some rather bizarre and terrifying ones."

"What like?" asked Kate.

"Oh, just..." My mind flashed through the various images I had seen, already starting to blur in the light of day. "Actually, I do not remember any details," I lied. "I just remember how bizarre they were."

"So what exactly did Maxwell do to you two, anyway?" she asked. "He's being really cagey with me, won't tell me nothin'."

"Oh, well, you know what he's like when his experiments go awry," I said, as nonchalantly as I could.

"So...?" she asked.

"So what?" I asked.

"What did his experiment do?" She glared at us. "The truth: don't sell me a dog. Honestly, I'm beginning to think you lot are actually hiding something from me."

"Nothing of the sort, Kate," said N'yotsu. "He thought that he had a new way of healing wounds quicker, of harnessing the power of the Aether to aid our recovery. Unfortunately it had the opposite effect, as you can see."

"Hmm," she said. "Even for Max, that's a pretty glocky idea."

"I agree it sounds idiotic," I said, gratefully picking up N'yotsu's lead. "But the implications would be fantastic. And he had tested it on mice, which indicated it would work fine."

"So why didn't it?" she asked.

"Oh, you'll have to ask Max," I said. "You know what I'm like with all this science stuff. Probably something to do with the Fulcrum: it usually is."

"I think I will ask him," she said, looking from me to N'yotsu and back again.

"Why, Kate," N'yotsu said, "it sounds almost like you don't trust us."

"The day I start trusting everything you lot say is the day you should get worried."

She left the room and I shared a relieved grin with N'yotsu. "But what about Max?" I asked. "What if he gives her a different excuse?"

"He won't," said N'yotsu. "I agreed the story with him in advance. Don't worry: your secret is safe."

The atmosphere in the room soured a few minutes later when Dr Smith entered once more, making a beeline for my bed while N'yotsu pretended to be asleep. "How are we feeling this morning, Mr Potts?"

"I am well," I said, watching him closely as my mind replayed the nightmare, the way the figure that seemed to be him but somehow was not had appeared sinister and otherworldly as he spoke with N'yotsu. I was almost disappointed to note how perfectly ordinary he seemed in the cold light of day.

My suspicions must have been clear from my bearing and manner, for he looked at me and asked: "Are you sure? You seem a little... distracted."

I shook my head to clear it of the poisonous thoughts; after all, it had only been a dream. "No, really, I am fine. I'm feeling much better."

He grunted and turned to examining me, occasionally glancing up as though looking for some other indication of my suspicions. After a few minutes he sat down next to me, packing away his instruments. "Well, you appear to be healing well. Your heart rate is now normal and the skin is much recovered. I think that in another couple of days you should be strong enough to try moving around, but for the moment you should continue to rest and take plenty of fluids." He leant in to me. "I was thinking about your condition last night. Your... other condition, that is. Tell me, how does it manifest?"

I looked at him for a few seconds, unsure as to what extent I should let him into my confidence again. I took a deep breath and mentally shook myself; after all, he was a doctor and might be able to help Maxwell find a cure for me.

"At first," I said, "the sword displayed remarkable powers; it could cut through any material—steel, wood, bone, stone—as though it were wet mud. But more than that it seemed to speak to me, to guide me as to how to react to any threat. But there was a downside to its use in that it became overly hot when used too much, so I could at first only wield it for around five minutes or so before it scorched my hand.

"However, over time I noticed that my tolerance to this heat increased, and I was able to use it for longer and longer periods. At the same time—it was when we were in Windsor at night, fighting a pack of Hell hounds a few days before Andras opened the portal at Greenwich—I found that my perceptions were greatly increased when I used the sword; I could see much more than I should be able to. My senses were effectively taking on a preternatural edge.

"Then I noticed more… profound effects. When in battle the runic symbols seemed to flow from the sword onto my skin. At first I thought it was just a delusion borne of the rage that descends on one in battle, that peculiar focus when you are in the midst of a fight. When your world is consumed by the anger, strength and joy of the kill."

I caught myself and looked up. "I am sorry," I said. "That was too graphic; I do not want you to think that I am some form of unhinged monster."

He waved a hand. "Of course not. So these changes were not, I take it, an illusion?"

"No," I said. "Unfortunately they were very real, and they have increased in intensity over time, on every occasion that I use the weapon in fact."

"So why do you not simply stop using it? That seems to me the most obvious solution."

I felt my breath quicken at the suggestion. "It is my sword," I said. "It is a part of me. I cannot give it up: I *will* not…"

He looked at me, a quizzical expression on his face. "I see why you and N'yotsu get along so well," he said. "You are both as stubborn and fixed as each other."

"I am not—" I stopped myself and took a deep breath. "You do not know what it feels like to wield the sword in battle. And, worse, how it feels to be divorced from it for any period of time."

"I can tell," he said, looking pointedly at my bedside, where the sword lay. "If we were talking about a narcotic, I would say that you were displaying all the symptoms of full-blown addiction. And the best prescription I can give to the addict is to separate him from the source of his addiction. That would be my advice to you, but I can see that you will ignore it."

I looked over at the sword and said nothing. I knew that he was right but the thought of losing the sword… that was a price I was not yet willing to pay.

"I can understand your concerns," he continued. "Any sane man would feel the same; you do not wish to be seen as a monster.

And that is what the sword makes you: a monster that has no place amongst humanity." He leaned in closer. "How much longer can you continue this charade do you think?"

I blinked at him, shocked by the intensity of his words. "I thought you were meant to make me feel better, not worse?"

He stood. "Sometimes a cure is only possible by making the patient feel worse. Reflect on my words." He turned to N'yotsu. "I am assuming by the way you are feigning sleep that you still do not require my attentions," he said.

"I am not feigning sleep," said N'yotsu. "I am affecting indifference to your presence."

"Very well," said Dr Smith. "I will attend to the older Mr Potts, who is by far the most sensible and least intractable of the three of you."

N'yotsu chuckled as the door closed behind the doctor. "I never thought I would hear anyone say that: Max as the most flexible of the three of us!"

I grunted and managed a smile, but Dr Smith's words rang sourly through my head.

CHAPTER TEN

A few days later, feeling strong enough to venture from our beds unaided, N'yotsu and I made our way down the corridor to Maxwell's quarters. We found him in conversation with the ever-present Dr Smith, with Kate at his side and the Bradshaw siblings sat at a table surrounded by papers.

"Ah, the patients have arisen," grinned Maxwell. "How are you both?"

"Good," I panted, "although in need of a rest. I never realised how long a walk that is."

"Your strength will return," said Dr Smith. "You just need to take time with your recovery."

"Time is always a precious commodity for us," said N'yotsu. "There are demons abroad, and I dread to think how the army have managed in our absence."

"I'm sure Albert'll be overjoyed to hear you say that," said Kate. "They're big boys, and they're more than able to handle themselves."

"I'm sure you are right," said N'yotsu. "But I for one itch to rejoin the fight." He looked to me for confirmation, but I found myself only able to mutely nod under the doctor's gaze.

"There is a way you can aid the fight, Mr N'yotsu," said Joshua. "I would be grateful for your insights in relation to some lines of inquiry I am pursuing."

"Show me," said N'yotsu, hobbling over.

"I really must insist," said Dr Smith to Maxwell, clearly

continuing a conversation they had been having before we entered the room. "The lack of fresh air is harming you considerably. A day or two in the open air would do you the world of good."

"The answer, as ever, is 'no'," said Maxwell. "I will take the air when I wish and I do not need you to accompany me."

"Very well," sighed the doctor, pulling out his stethoscope in what seemed an overly ostentatious manner. "Then I shall conduct my tests. It would aid me if you would remove that bracelet."

Maxwell shook his head. "Again, we have discussed this before, and again I shall not. The bracelet stays on."

"As I understand it, the bracelet protects you against any demon interference," said Dr Smith. "There are no demons in here, and removing it would make my examinations a lot easier and quicker."

"Doctor," said Maxwell, "you have known me for some weeks now; have you ever observed any indications that I might be open to taking undue risks with my wellbeing or those of my friends?"

The doctor looked pointedly in my direction. "Well…"

"Aside from that," said Maxwell, clearly irritated. "And as far as I was aware, the risks with that procedure were minimal; the prior tests had uncovered no suggestions that it would affect my brother in the way that it did. Regardless, the bracelet stays on my wrist and I will not be accompanying you on any expeditions to take the air. Now, please, undertake your examination post-haste."

Dr Smith complied perfunctorily, and I grinned remembering how he had described Maxwell as the least stubborn of us all. I looked at the table beside me, picking up the papers that were laid out there. It was a pile of drawings showing an elaborate and intricate series of buildings, varying in detail and all picked out very carefully by hand. At the bottom of the pile was a set of parchment with rough sketches in a scrawled cursive.

"Be careful with those," said Maxwell. "The bottom ones are originals sketched by Henry VIII himself."

"Henry…? These are of Nonsuch Palace in Surrey, are they not?" I asked, my weariness forgotten as I peered at the drawings. While they displayed different views and perspectives—not to mention varying degrees of skill—they all showed a set of buildings that were awe-inspiring in their ambition and grandeur. A multitude of turrets reached to the sky atop long ranges of walls in which were carved the most intricate reliefs and images, rivalling the best that even Italy had to offer. Certainly the drawings supported the boast that gave rise to the name, that there was no such place in all the world to rival the palace's magnificence.

"They are indeed," Maxwell said. "Fascinating, aren't they?"

"Beautiful," I breathed, drinking in the details of some of the more intricate documents. Remembering who I was talking to, I looked at him quizzically. "But why do you have these? Nonsuch has been no more than ruins for centuries now. Why the sudden interest in archaeology?"

"It's not sudden," said Kate. "He's been obsessing about that place for bloody ages."

"Kate is right," said Maxwell. "As you would know if you showed any interest in my studies."

"I might have if I realised you were looking at stuff like this," I said. "Rather than all those dull formulae and the like."

"But they are interlinked," Maxwell said, destroying the meagre romanticism in the room in one fell swoop. "For I believe that Nonsuch was deliberately designed along lines that were not merely architectural, but also a mixture of the scientific and occult."

"Oh really? Pray tell," I said.

Maxwell failed to pick up on my sarcastic tone. "At first it was merely a hunch, a theory if you like. However, my investigations have uncovered mention of a number of sorcerers in the reign of King Henry VIII. One in particular, most commonly referred to as 'Mr Wood', claimed before the Privy Council that he was learned in the arts of Solomon."

"As in your book about Solomon? The one listing all the demons and spirits he supposedly conjured?"

"The Lesser Key of Solomon, yes. Which also, remember, speaks of Andras; not to mention Gaap, whom our young friend over there somehow managed to summon." He nodded at Joshua before continuing. "This 'Mr Wood', in a number of different guises, also appears in the King's court itself to engage in various discussions, including the acquisition of the lands at Cuddington, near Ewell, which became the site for Nonsuch Palace."

"What does this have to do with us?" I asked. Kate rolled her eyes at me; clearly I was retreading old ground here.

"I believe that the very situation and design of Nonsuch was deliberate so as to facilitate the movement of bodies into the spirit world. Essentially I believe that it was intended to be an experiment into the potential for applying Solomoniac principles vis-à-vis the transfer of entities across and between realms, but on a massive scale."

I frowned as my ears and brain fought to keep pace with my brother's thought processes. "Are you saying that the whole palace was designed as some form of rudimentary portal?"

"I believe so, yes. Although not overtly, and I doubt whether King Henry was aware of the hidden intent behind the plans. But in order for it to work, it would need to tap into huge quantities of arcane forces and powers. I believe that this may be the epicentre of the Fulcrum." He sat back and grinned at me.

"The epicentre of the Fulcrum? So if that were true then... what?"

"It gives us a physical location to focus our efforts," he said. "Once we have come up with a method of halting the Fulcrum, we can focus it there. In any event, by knowing the location of the epicentre, we get closer to understanding the phenomenon."

"Clever people them Tudors, eh?" said Kate sarcastically.

"Wait a minute," I said. "History is one of my strong points. Henry VIII was incredibly controlling and he was personally involved in the design and commissioning of Nonsuch. How could something as big as this have slipped past him?"

"Yes, but those with the biggest egos are also the easiest to flatter and deceive," said Maxwell. "In any case, it is possible, following your logic, that he *was* aware. After all, King Henry was always looking to increase his prestige, and how better than to discover and conquer new worlds? Or at the very least to give him a new hunting ground?"

I thumbed through the papers, unconvinced. "Aside from chancing upon a name of a sorcerer who may or may not have been involved in planning the palace, do you have any other evidence to back up your claim?"

"Of course I do. It is not a matter of public record, but Nonsuch has been the site of a number of unusual disturbances since its construction began in 1538. And why else was such a magnificent palace torn down less than 150 years after it was so painstakingly built?"

"I thought that was to pay off the gambling debts of some Countess or other?"

"But surely the building as a whole would have been worth

more than breaking it up and selling it piece by piece," said Maxwell.

"I would have thought that that would depend on what those pieces were, and what people were willing to pay for them. As I said, do you have anything concrete aside from rumour and speculation?"

Maxwell pointed to a stack of papers by my right elbow. "Those are a series of reports into alleged hauntings and disappearances centred around Nonsuch since 1540, when the construction of the buildings were well advanced."

I frowned as I flicked through the documents. "I do not recall hearing about any of this."

"Some of them are not public record. Given the unrest at the time, with the dissolution of the monasteries, the suppression of Catholicism and so on, any rumours that one of the King's own palaces was cursed would have been a boon to his opponents. And in any event, they were no doubt keen to ensure that any stories that might hint at the building's true purpose were suppressed. In relation to those that *were* published… well, it is not unusual for a large manor house to be rumoured as haunted. Indeed, at several times in history such a thing has been considered rather fashionable."

"That is not all," said Joshua appearing at my side. "If you take the sketch of the grounds from this picture," he pulled a piece of parchment from the pile of drawings, "and overlay it with a pentagram you can see…" He held it up for my analysis and I grunted. Certain buildings, rooms and outhouses seemed to broadly align with the points of the pentagram.

"Do you not think it is a bit spurious?" I asked. "Surely you can see a pentagram anywhere if you really look hard enough."

"Normally I would be the first to agree with you," said Maxwell. "But the evidence keeps mounting up. I have had a number of readings taken there, and there is a definite Aetheric residue across the site where the building once stood."

"One of Andras' portals?" I asked.

"I did wonder whether the demon had tested its portals there, but the nearest two sites were Windsor and Greenwich."

"Which were also the strongest and most damaging portals," added N'yotsu.

"Indeed," said Maxwell. "And while Nonsuch is not quite

equidistant between the two, it is as near as dammit: 18 miles from Windsor and around 15 miles from Greenwich as the crow flies. Three miles, which when we're considering the distances between realms is but a rounding error!"

"My, my Max," I grinned, "you are using swearwords. I must say I have not seen you this animated in quite a while."

"Indeed," said Dr Smith. "Maybe you should use this enthusiasm to venture outside and visit this Nonsuch place."

Maxwell glared at him and then continued. "There is still much investigation to be done, but if some form of connection is proven then the implications could be profound."

I flicked through the papers, my mind running through the possibilities and mulling over what could have motivated people from so long ago to undertake such an experiment—if that was indeed what they had done. My mind's eye imagined fat King Henry atop a horse galloping at the head of a hunting expedition, charging down demons to satisfy his bloodlust and desire for conquest. Or even an army of Tudor soldiers marching through a portal to conquer lands unknown. These were scenes that would be worthy of Jules Verne himself and I smiled, wondering whether I should write to him and suggest that we collaborate. It would be a fine thing to finally write fiction, rather than chronicling the terrible reality we lived every day.

N'yotsu and Maxwell were discussing in more detail his theories about Nonsuch, which involved some rather intense conversations about obscure occult principles. I perked up when I heard mention of a field trip to retrieve more data. "I would be happy to attend also," I said.

"Assuming you are well enough," said Dr Smith.

"I will be," I replied, a little harsher than I had intended.

"In any case," said N'yotsu, "there is also the matter of Gaap. It is a worrying development on its own that a demon of his standing has come through, but the mention he made of the 'Four Kings' is particularly concerning."

I remembered Gaap and the other demons chanting about those Kings before engaging us in battle, although it had meant as little to me then as it did now. "You know of them?" I asked.

"I am afraid so," he said. "Rather intimately in fact, although I wish I did not. They are four of the most powerful demons from my realm. Asmoday, Abaddon, Bileth and Belial." He spat out the names as though they left a sour taste on his tongue. "Gaap is but their lackey."

The doctor dropped his bag, spilling implements all over the floor. He held up his hand in apology and scrabbled around to collect them.

"And they're bad?" asked Kate.

"They are vain, power-hungry and utterly ruthless," he said. "It was they who were responsible for casting me—or rather Andras—from Almadel: my home." Noting our interested expressions, he added: "But that is a tale for another time as it is not really relevant to the matter at hand."

"Indeed," said Maxwell. "So tell us more about these Four Kings. Presumably this is a threat we should be guarding against?"

N'yotsu bent over to hand the doctor a phial that had rolled under his chair, then took a deep breath and began. "Asmoday you will remember from the Lesser Key of Solomon, where he is listed as the 32nd spirit: a great King, strong and powerful. He has appeared throughout human history as a leader among demons and his name is often connected to jealousy, anger and revenge.

"Abaddon likes to be known as the angel of death, destruction and the Netherworld. He leads the armies of Furies, his footsoldiers who are invincible on the battlefield.

"Bileth is headstrong and emotional, known as a mighty and terrible King. He is also listed in the Lesser Key of Solomon: number 13 if memory serves me correct. In some ways he is the group's weakest link, but is quick to anger and when he is in a rage there is little that can stand in his way.

"Finally there is Belial, who in my opinion is the most dangerous. His appearance belies a terrible nature; while he seems beautiful and mild, he is in fact full of treachery, recklessness and deceit. Many poor souls have fallen victim to his charms, and in human folklore his name has often been interchangeable with one that you will be very familiar: Satan, or the Antichrist."

"And then there's Gaap?" asked Joshua.

"Ah, yes. My dear old friend Gaap. He is a lower level demon but when I left he was acting as adviser to the Four Kings, and was particularly to blame for my fall from grace and banishment to the Aether." He glared at the floor in a way that did not invite any further questions.

Silence descended on the room as we considered these words.

"So, a bit worse than Andras then?" said Kate.

"Andras would never admit it, as they are sworn enemies; and it is worth pointing out that it took all four of them working together to defeat Andras. But yes: if they are here on Earth then we have much to be concerned about."

I smiled tightly at this understatement. "But it's still an 'if' though, is it not? Gaap and his fellow demons only said: 'All hail the Four Kings', not 'The Four Kings are here and about to kill you all'."

"Agreed," said N'yotsu. "They are not the types to sit around quietly, so the fact that we have not heard of any widespread mayhem so far is an encouraging sign. But the mere fact that their followers are here is worrying enough. If Belial and the rest have not arrived yet, then you can guarantee that they will be trying their damnedest to get here."

"And the Fulcrum will no doubt aid them in that," said Lexie.

"Indeed it will," said Maxwell. "This merely reinforces the urgency of our task."

Kate turned to N'yotsu. "So is that all of the really bad demons we need to worry about? Or are there others?"

"There are always others," he said with a tight smile.

CHAPTER ELEVEN

I sat as patiently as I could while Dr Smith examined me with a slowness that bordered on the glacial.

"Is this going to take much longer?" I asked again.

"When a person has been subjected to a large amount of stress such as yourself," he said, "it is usual for his doctor to conduct a thorough examination. I would not wish to release you only to find that you collapsed a few metres from the doorway."

"There is little chance of that happening. I am fully recovered."

"I shall be the judge of that, Mr Potts."

I relented and sat back, breathing and coughing and raising various appendages on command. Kate put her head round the door. "You about ready?" she asked. "Only we'd quite like to leave this year."

"A few more minutes, Miss Thatcher," the doctor said. He handed me a small phial filled with a purple liquid. "Drink this, please."

I held it up to the light. "What is it?"

"A mixture of natural herbs to aid your recovery and give you strength." He raised his eyebrows at my sceptical look. "If you do not trust me then do not drink it," he sighed, reaching for it.

I held up my hand. "No, no," I said, putting it to my lips and swallowing. "Is there laudanum in there?" I asked, smacking my lips together as I handed him back the empty phial.

"A few drops, to aid its ingestion. Not enough to influence your mood; especially not a person who is as accustomed to it as you."

"Good," said Kate. "We need sensible Gus, not drunken Gus. You've got five minutes, you hear?"

When she had left the room, Dr Smith looked at me. "Are you worried about what will happen if you should find yourself, ah, succumbing to your sword's influence?"

"In what way?"

"As in the physical changes. Given their profundity it would be quite a shock for anyone not expecting them. Such as Miss Thatcher, for instance."

"If you are advising me to tell her what is happening to me, then you are wasting your breath," I said. "She has suffered enough horrendous demonic interventions in her life and I am not going to add to them."

"You may have no choice. You said yourself that the changes occur unbidden whenever you are in the heat of battle."

"Then I shall avoid battles," I said. "This is a reconnaissance mission, nothing more. Max just wants us to run some tests. We shall be back before anything demonic happens."

He straightened up, putting his stethoscope aside. "Well, I wish you luck. You appear in good health, although I would recommend that you ease yourself into action slowly and do not exert yourself too much."

I pulled on my jacket and grinned. "The thought had not even crossed my mind, doctor." My chirpiness though belied an inner turmoil, for his words had once again struck a raw nerve. What if I did transform into a demon in front of my friends? I took a deep breath as I walked out of the door, resolving to do anything to stop that from happening.

"So this is Nonsuch?" I asked, staring out at a large mound of grass on the edge of the road running between North Cheam and Lower Cheam.

"Somewhere round here," said Joshua, holding up a map. "At least this is where Maxwell's calculations have pointed us to."

"I thought there'd be ruins," said Kate. "Like old castles and whatnot. There's nothing here."

"When they tore the house down," I said, "they pretty much took away every part of it, right down to the bricks and mortar. I would wager that we would find bits of the old palace in the building blocks of every house for miles around."

"Isn't that a bit disrespectful? Given this was the King's palace?"

"By the time it was torn down it hadn't been in Royal hands for quite some time: Charles II gave it to his mistress, who pulled it down years later when she needed money to pay off her gambling debts. In any case, there is a delicious circularity about it being recycled. Nonsuch itself was built out of stone and other materials plundered from old monasteries and churches."

N'yotsu had started walking across the field. "Illuminating though this conversation is," he said over his shoulder, "we should get started with our experiments so we can be heading back before nightfall."

"Couldn't agree more, sir," said Captain Pearce.

"Maxwell always loved conducting his experiments in the open air," I said, rubbing my hands together to keep them warm. "Especially when the weather was as crisply inclement as this. It is a shame he could not join us; a bit of fresh air would have done him the power of good."

"You are sounding like that infernal doctor," said N'yotsu. "As you know, the risks would have been too great, especially if Maxwell is correct and this is a centre of demonic activity. If Max were to fall into the demons' hands, the end of everything would lurch that little bit closer. He is safer where he is, protected by the army and my spells."

"You don't like that doctor much, do you?" asked Kate.

"There is something about him that intensely irritates me," said N'yotsu. "While I do not doubt his abilities, he has a manner that is annoyingly familiar."

"In what way?"

"That is part of the problem: I do not know." He stopped and hammered his heel into the ground. "Shall we take our first readings here?"

The day crept by with the monotony of the scientific experiment, with dials adjusted and nonsensical numbers and letters scrawled on pieces of paper. The soldiers and I occupied ourselves with lugging about the equipment as ordered and keeping an eye out for anything untoward.

The afternoon was rapidly waning as we finished the last of the readings and packed up, getting ready to head back to our transport. As our carriage came into view over the hill I had a profound feeling of something not being quite right, a tension in my temples and a quickening of my heart rate akin to that which usually indicated a nearby demonic presence. I looked to N'yotsu, who was glancing around intently, clearly having sensed the same as me.

"Captain," I said. "We need to leave very quickly. Something is not right."

Pearce nodded, having learnt some time ago to trust in our intuitions, and sent a handful of soldiers ahead to the carriages to ensure that they were fully secured.

I drew my sword and turned slowly as I walked, scanning the horizon for any sign of activity. I grew more and more tense as we continued to be faced with nothing other than fields, sheep and the occasional tree.

They attacked when we were mid-way through securing the equipment onto the wagon, 20 demons seeming to materialise out of thin air with Gaap at their head. Captain Pearce barked orders at his soldiers as N'yotsu and I ran grimly towards the demons.

Gaap pointed a scimitar at us. "Hail the Four Kings!" he shouted, a cry that was echoed by the others.

N'yotsu met Gaap head on, while I ran into the midst of the demons to his side, swinging my sword and screaming wordlessly as I advanced. Dimly in the distance, through a deepening red haze, I could hear the crack of rifles as Pearce's men sent a hail of lead into our attackers' other flank.

My sword swirled, an angry red and silver wall of enchanted steel that cut through those around me as though they were stalks of wheat before a scythe. The red mist had descended on my world, a swirling concoction of rage that had only one focus: the destruction of all those around me.

Time ceased to have any meaning, my progress marked only by the swing of my blade and the thud of bodies and body parts as they hit the ground at my feet. There was no counting the numbers I had slain, my instincts were now too base to allow anything as complex as thought processes. Instead I shouted with each swing, hoping that that would suffice.

I revelled in the destruction, marvelling at my powers and the ease with which I cut through the creatures. At the back of my head, a dim part of me questioned: *This is too easy, surely?* but the main part of me ignored it, lost in the glory and adrenaline of battle.

As soon as it had begun, it was over. My sword swung round into open air and I looked around to see piles of dismembered demons at my feet. N'yotsu stood a little way away, watching me. He advanced slowly, hands out and saying something in a language that I could not comprehend, words that offended my ears. I roared at this sorcery, the trickery from this fiend, and darted forwards with raised sword.

"Gus?"

Kate's voice cut through my madness and I jolted to a halt, my vision snapping round to see her staring at me in horror. Beside her, Joshua and Lexie gaped in revulsion. Captain Pearce was holding out his hands and I realised that he was ordering his men not to fire at me.

"...need to calm down, Gus," N'yotsu was saying. "It is over. You need to calm down."

I looked down at my hands to see the runic symbols swirling violently across my skin. A hand to my face confirmed my fears: angular bumps sat in stark relief to my otherwise smooth features.

N'yotsu put a hand on my shoulder and I turned, snarling, feeling my teeth jutting forwards in my mouth. *What had I become?* Without thinking, I thrust him aside and charged off, dimly aware of the shouts as N'yotsu and the others gave chase.

PART II

KATE

PETER OXLEY

CHAPTER TWELVE

I hitched up my skirts as I ran after N'yotsu, my lungs burning as I fought to match even half his speed, with Gus—or whatever that thing had been—already a small speck in the distance. After running half the country, or at least that's the way it bloody well felt, I caught up with N'yotsu who had stopped and was staring into space, hands on hips.

For a moment we stood and panted together, trying to get our breath back.

"No use Kate," N'yotsu said to me eventually. "Better to follow by horse."

"He's quick," I managed. "How'd he get so damn quick?"

Pearce caught up with us. "Are you all right, Kate?" he asked, reaching out to touch me and then stopping himself at the last moment.

I nodded. "Not me I'm worried about," I said. "What's happened to Gus? That *was* Gus, right?"

N'yotsu pulled a face. "Yes, that's Gus. I think we have a few things to explain to you."

I felt my cheeks redden as the pieces started to slot into place: the whisperings behind closed doors, the sudden injuries the other week. "I'd say you do. This ain't no surprise to you, is it?" Guilt was written all over his face, like a dipper caught with his hand in a gent's pocket, and that made me even madder. "This has happened before, hasn't it? And you didn't think to tell me?"

"Let's get in the carriage and then we can talk," said Pearce, ever the diplomat. "He was heading towards London, would you agree?"

"Absolutely," said N'yotsu, clearly glad of the distraction. "If I am not mistaken, assuming he carries on heading towards the city, then the nearest crossing of the Thames is Fulham Bridge." As they talked I fixed N'yotsu with my hardest stare, just to let him know that he was nowhere near off the hook.

He tried to get on horseback, using some flimsy excuse of having better eyesight than the soldiers, but I steered him into the carriage. Lexie and Joshua followed and I thought about turning them away as I wanted to beat the truth out of N'yotsu on my own, without witnesses. But there was nowhere else for the kids to go, so I allowed them to sit back and watch.

"Speak," I said.

"Really, Kate," he said, "the priority is to find Gus, and I would be much better placed to—"

"Speak," I said again. "When I'm happy you've told me everything—and I mean *every*thing—then you can go back to your friends out there."

He sighed and gave in, as I knew he would. "Very well. That was indeed Gus, and those changes have happened to him before." He looked at me as though that was enough, and I raised my eyebrows threateningly at him. "I don't know when the first time was," he continued, "but I know that the cause of the changes is the runic sword."

"What do you mean?" I asked.

"Of course!" blurted Joshua. "I noticed that the runic symbols were really powerful—those symbols that Mr Potts allowed me to examine in any case—and it makes sense that they would not only influence the weapon but also the bearer..."

He tailed off as he realised that I was glaring at him for getting in the middle of my interrogation. "I'm glad you find this so damn fascinating," I said. "But I'm more interested in what's happened and how I get my friend back." I turned back to N'yotsu. "Carry on. What do you mean about the sword?"

He cleared his throat, looking a bit confused. "Just what Joshua said, actually: the runic symbols are immensely powerful, turning an ordinary steel sword into something a lot stronger and more powerful than it should be. However, the spells that give the sword its power have also... infected Gus."

"Infected?" I asked. "What, like a disease?"

"In a way, yes. At first it seemed beneficial, making him more powerful and faster than the demons. You must have noticed that?"

"Well, yes, but I thought that was just the magic sword doing its magical stuff. I never thought it was really Gus..." I frowned, thinking back to all the times I'd seen Gus fight. Had it been right there under my nose all that time and I'd just not noticed? How could I not have realised?

"And you were right," said N'yotsu. "But over time it became apparent that the changes weren't just limited to the sword. The runic spells are powerful, but they are also demonic. And when you cast such a spell over a human, the results are—"

"Geezer turns into demon," I said. "So why didn't he just stop using the sword?"

"We asked him to, ordered him, begged him," said N'yotsu. "But you know how stubborn Gus is. And he seems almost addicted to it. After a while, the changes were so embedded in his body that there was no real point in him stopping using the sword, however much he wanted to."

In a flash I remembered last Christmas, when Gus and I had both been trapped in the cellar of a run-down house in the slums of St Giles, waiting for the demons holding us prisoner to do their worst. He'd been under the influence of booze and God knows what else, and been ranting and raving when I found him, talking about dreams and stuff that was happening to him. When it was time to escape, he'd really not wanted to get his sword back, even though we needed him at full strength. At the time I'd assumed it was just him coming down from the effects of the laudanum and cheap gin, but what if...

"Hang on a minute," I said. "*You* made that sword for him. I remember: it was you that made the demonic spells which make it all powerful and stuff."

He looked down at his feet and the vision of a naughty schoolboy was complete. "I know. And not a moment goes by that I don't regret it. But it was done when I was firmly under the influence of Andras, before I managed to free myself, and the whole world, from his malig—"

"All right," I interrupted before he could lapse into another self-pitying speech. He looked up and as our eyes met I searched for something that would tell me the real truth. I believed everything he'd said so far but there was something else, something that didn't quite make sense—I wasn't being told the whole story. "I'm not going to ask what Andras would want out of turning one of us into a demon," I said, thinking aloud, "as that's the kind of nasty trick he'd get a thrill out of. But why didn't Gus tell me?"

"He didn't want anyone to know," he said. "He was worried about what people would think, or what they would do. So we worked on finding a cure, a way of purging the demonic changes from his body. And Maxwell really thought he—"

"Wait," I said. "Maxwell knew as well?"

"Well, yes: they are brothers."

"Yes, but Max tells me everything." I felt as though the world was spinning around me, that I had been the butt of a secret joke that everyone knew the punchline to except me. "Who else knew? Did you two?" I glared at Lexie and Joshua, who shook their heads quickly.

"I promise you," said Lexie, "we had no idea."

"What about Pearce?" I asked. "Or the other soldiers?"

"As far as I am aware," said N'yotsu, "they did not know. Gus did not trust the army's reaction. For all he knew, they would have had him imprisoned or experimented on or executed."

"So he didn't trust the army to not go all demon-hunter on him, I get that. But did he really think I would have...?" I had an overwhelming urge to punch someone. Did he really think I was so thick-headed, so... disloyal, that I wouldn't have sided with him in a flash?

"Now Kate," N'yotsu said quietly, "you must know that we never thought for a second that you—"

"Just shut yer sauce-box," I said. "I don't need you treating me like a sulky kid. So just you and Max knew about this?"

"And Dr Smith," he said. When I glared at him he added: "After the accident the other day, we had to tell the doctor what had happened so that he could treat Gus effectively."

"I knew there was something fishy about what you lot were up to," I said. "So Max was trying to cure Gus then? And it failed?"

"Quite disastrously, as you saw."

"Hmm," I said, biting back the temptation to point out that this was what happened when they cut me out of things. I had plenty more anger to go round, but I wanted to save some for when I saw

Max. The important thing was that we found Gus, and for that we needed everyone looking. I banged on the roof with my fist and shouted for the driver to stop.

"What are you doing?" asked N'yotsu.

"We all need to be searching for Gus," I said. "There's room up front with the driver." I pointed to Lexie and Joshua. "It'll be a squeeze but the three of us should sit up there. Better view from there than sitting back here."

"What about me?" asked N'yotsu.

"What do you mean?" I glared at him: did he really need me to talk him through everything? "Grab a horse and start looking. Don't just sit there!" I climbed out before he could ask me any more stupid questions.

Maxwell looked up at me sheepishly as I stormed into the laboratory. In spite of my best efforts, N'yotsu had got there before me and that just made me even more cross.

"Now, Kate, I know what you are going to say," he said, "but Gus made me—"

"If you know what I'm going to say then you'll know that I thought we had a deal, I thought we were a team. Turns out there's two teams here: you lot, and me."

"That's not true," he said. "I really value your—"

"What? Cleaning? Cooking?" I snarled. "Ability to wait on you hand and foot at all hours of the day and night? Have you forgotten about how I've always been there for you, even after what that demon did to you, after what he did to me…?" I felt the tight line of the scar on my cheek throbbing angrily in sympathy.

I almost felt sorry for them as they looked at me, but not quite. Even Max—dear, sweet, socially inept Max—seemed to realise just how much they'd upset me, although that didn't make the pain of being stabbed in the back by my closest friends any easier. I really thought I'd put all that sort of stuff behind me, that I'd finally found some friends who really did care about me and wanted me to belong, count me as one of them. *Not like all the other times…*

I pushed the thoughts back down. It was always the best thing to do: push away the unpleasant stuff and focus on the everyday, otherwise you'd find yourself drowning in a river of shit. What was important at that moment was that we found Gus. I'd show them how grown-ups behave, and let them suffer through guilt.

"Kate," said Max. "I am so, so sorry. We never meant to hurt you, we were just doing what we thought was right. I realise we should never have kept this from you, but Gus was adamant that he wanted no one else to know. He cared about what you thought of him, didn't want you to see him as another one of those—"

"I'll deal with Gus when we find him," I said. "And that's the main thing now, right? Finding him."

"Or whatever is left of him," muttered Max.

N'yotsu and I glared at him. "What do you mean?" asked N'yotsu.

"Well, for the changes to have manifested so spontaneously and prominently, and to have not ebbed away, suggests that the demonic part of him may be well advanced. I believe he is fighting a particularly nasty internal civil war and is currently on the losing side. The fact that he has not come back to us tells me that he is still in a demonic form." He caught the expressions on our faces and held up his hands. "But I am sure that my brother is still in there, somewhere."

"He is still your brother," I snapped, clenching my fists to stop me from slapping him across the cheek. "He could have killed N'yotsu out there, could have killed all of us, but he didn't. And the look on his face…" I remembered the terror and confusion in his eyes: past all the red scales and horns and stuff, he looked like a little boy lost, struck dumb and helpless. My first reaction had been shock and disgust; surely this couldn't be my friend, the guy I'd fought alongside and laughed with for years? But then I'd seen those eyes and realised there was still a real person stuck in there, and he desperately needed our help.

I put my hand on N'yotsu's arm as we approached Gus's apartment and pointed at the soldiers gathering in the street ahead of us. "There's quite a lot of them for one man, don't you think?" I said.

"Hmm," he said. "I don't suppose this means that they're intending to have a nice chat with him?"

I spotted Captain Pearce. "Let's find out," I said, marching towards our friend and ignoring the soldiers who tried to block our passage.

"Albert," I shouted as we approached. "What in God's name is going on? Have you found Gus?"

He gestured frantically with his arm, looking like some strange sort of street entertainer.

"What the Hell does that mean?" I asked.

"I think he wants us to be quiet and go over to him," said N'yotsu, grabbing my arm.

I allowed him to lead me over and then looked questioningly up at Pearce.

"We are just about to break in," he said. "I wanted to make sure we had enough back-up in case things got... difficult."

We looked around. "Looks to me that you may have overdone the welcome party," said N'yotsu.

"Have you tried knocking?" I asked.

Pearce looked at me as though I were mad. "You saw what he did over at Nonsuch, what he's capable of."

"What he did," I said, "was fight off a load of demons who were trying to kill us. Or did you forget that part?"

"I did not forget. But we need to protect the public against any demonic threats, whatever shape or form they may take."

"So all those years Gus fought alongside you count for nothing? All it takes is—"

"For him to transform into a slavering, homicidal demon?" he finished. "What has happened in the past does not matter: if he is now a threat then he needs to be dealt with."

"And what do you mean by 'dealt with'?" I asked, planting my hands on my hips.

N'yotsu stepped in between us. "Captain Pearce, for the sake of all the times that we have fought together, please let us try to speak with our friend before you wade in with your guns and swords. At least grant us that courtesy. He will not hurt us and, and even if he proves to be uncontrollable you are all here to back us up."

Pearce looked from N'yotsu to me and back again, and then sighed. "Very well. But at the first sign of trouble we will not hesitate to take decisive action."

I grinned triumphantly at Pearce and his soldiers as we walked past them and towards the building. N'yotsu knocked on the door and we held our breaths as we strained our ears for sounds from inside. After a few moments of nothing much, I turned to N'yotsu. "Still got a key?" I asked.

He blinked. "Actually, yes I do." He rummaged in his pockets, frowning. "Do you?"

"Yeah," I said, "just not with me." When he looked questioningly at me I held out my skirts and said: "Nowhere to keep it safe."

After testing a ridiculously large number of keys, he eventually found the right one and pushed the door open, grinning at me.

"If he *was* in there," I muttered, "he'd have heard us by now, with all the knocking and rattling and whatnot."

We searched the apartment even so, but it was clear that Gus had not been there for quite a while; in fact it looked like the last person who'd been there was me when I came to get his belongings while he was recovering from the effects of Max's experiment. The drawers were neatly closed, something that Gus would never do, especially if he was on the run.

"So what next?" I asked as we left the house and stood outside.

Before they could answer, a soldier on horseback charged through the streets, stopping just in front of us. "Sir," he said to Pearce, "a demon has been spotted in Fulham. It matches the description of the one you are looking for."

"Are you sure? Where is it?" asked Pearce.

"It's apparently drunk and was last seen running away from a whorehouse," said the soldier, "on the High Street."

"Well, that certainly sounds like Gus," said N'yotsu with a grin.

I shot him a glare and then shrugged, realising the truth of what he'd said.

By the time we got to Fulham's High Street Gus was long gone, leaving a slightly excited mob in his wake. We managed to work out what had happened: he had thrown himself out of a brothel window and then run through the streets, half-naked and chased by soldiers. The girl he'd slept with told us how he'd looked normal at first but when she woke up later there was a demon lying next to her in bed. She'd screamed and he'd fled, thankfully without trying to hurt anyone. I allowed myself a little smile at this. Whatever he looked like, he was still our Gus deep down.

We followed his trail over the Thames and down past Putney Heath and Wimbledon Common, although the trail had gone cold by the time we reached Morden . As the night fell, we carried on to Merton and lodged in a run-down tavern on the side of the Carshalton Road, thinking through our options over warm ale and cold stew.

"We need to spread the search," said Pearce, leaning over a map. "I will send men in these directions," he ran his hands down, left and right, "in twos or threes to see if any of them can pick up signs of where he's gone. Door-to-door searches, outbuildings, cemeteries, woodlands, that sort of thing."

"And if he is sensible enough to not go poking around peoples' houses?" asked N'yotsu.

Pearce gave him a hard stare. "We have to start somewhere. It is very difficult for anybody to travel for any length of time without leaving some sort of a trail, especially looking the way he does. He'll need to eat, if nothing else."

I thought he was doing Gus down but bit my tongue; I didn't want to give them any more reasons to fear our friend. "So which way will *we* go?" I asked. "I fancy this direction." I pointed down, towards the coast.

Pearce sighed. "I really think that you would both best serve our cause by going back to London, just in case he heads back that way or sends a message."

"Come on!" I protested. "He was run out of town: there's no way he's heading back to London. Last time he did something stupid and had to do a runner he went straight for the Continent. That's where he'll be going I'll wager: France."

"That's as maybe," said Pearce, "and you might well be right. But what if he gets held up on the way or forced to change his plans? There are a dozen ways at least that he could get over the Channel and in any case he'll know we're after him and may look for the least obvious route to get there. If you just blunder south then there's every chance you'll miss him, and then we won't know where you are to contact you, if and when we do pick up some sign of him. London is the best place for you, and it's the best place for you to be contactable: for Augustus and for us."

I could see the sense in what he was saying, but I still didn't like it. "So we go back to London and you find Gus. What's to say you and your men won't just kill him without a by-your-leave?"

"You have my word of honour," Pearce said. "We will do everything in our power to apprehend him without causing undue harm, and if we are able we will get you before we approach him."

"Your word of honour, sure," I said. "But what about your trigger-happy privates out there? How are they going to know that it's Gus they're up against and not some other demon?" I turned to N'yotsu for support, then gasped as I saw the state of him.

He was slumped against the table, thin as a skeleton and just as pale. Jumping to my feet, I grabbed his shoulders to pull him upright and his eyes rolled up at me like two loose eggs in a jar. Finally he focused on my face. "Kate," he rasped through thin, dry lips.

"N'yotsu, what on earth...?" I said.

"It's getting worse," he whispered. "I... don't know how much... longer..."

"You idiot," I muttered. "You should have said." Of course, I knew all about the way he'd been getting weaker the longer he was separated from the obsidian stone: they'd not been able to hide that from me. But N'yotsu had always put a brave face on it, reassuring us that he could hold himself together. I hadn't believed a word of it, seeing him wear the same stupid brave face that all men put on when they don't want to be fussed over, but he had recently seemed stronger thanks to all that time spent resting after Max's failed experiment.

However, this was a bigger and more sudden bout than I'd seen before, and the difference between his usual brute force and the empty shell before me was like a blow to my stomach.

I looked up at Pearce. "I need a fast carriage to take us back to London, right now," I said.

Ten minutes later we were ready to depart, having got N'yotsu safely in the carriage and as comfortable as possible thanks to the efforts of half a dozen soldiers. "He's heavier than he looks," one of them had remarked to me as they stepped away.

I grabbed Pearce's arm. "You gave me your word, right?" I said. "You won't harm Gus if you find him, and you'll let us know as soon as you do?"

"I promise, Kate," he said. "You look after N'yotsu. With Augustus gone, we need him now more than ever."

CHAPTER THIRTEEN

The journey back to London was the longest of my life, every bump on the road making N'yotsu cry out in pain so that by the time we were only a few miles into the journey my nerves were shredded. I wanted to shout to the driver to slow down, but I didn't know how much longer N'yotsu had left: any delay could have been the death of him.

I contented myself with stroking his hand and trying to keep him as comfortable as possible, all the while murmuring stuff I hoped was soothing. It was funny how easily the old habits came back: playing nursemaid had once been second nature thanks to being the big sister to a never-ending stream of kids. There had been times when Ma and I had joked about how we felt more like we were running a hospital for sick kids than a family of grafters. Of course, that was before Pa killed Ma and it all went sour...

My mind wandered back to those days, happy days for the most part with me and the other kids bustling round Ma while she did her chores, always singing as she went. The sun always seemed to shine in those days, the only shadows coming when Pa came home.

I loved him, like any daughter loves her Pa, but I feared him too. And sometimes hated him, when I saw what he did to Ma, the way he'd shout at her for no reason, beat her for the smallest thing. The rest of us, too – he was free with his fists after he'd been in his cups and was quick to anger. It was then that I really hated him: when he'd beat us kids and force Ma to watch. At first I wondered why she let him do that to us, but then I saw the look in her eyes as we took our beatings, the helpless terror swimming behind her tears. She knew not to get in the way or beg him to stop – that just made the beatings harder and longer.

It was me that killed her, really. I should have just said yes when Pa told me to start working the streets to sell my body instead of the junk we kept on our barrow. I was of age, he said, and it was about time I started making a proper contribution to the family. After all, he knew I'd had plenty of practice.

I'd flinched from him as he said that and leered at me, and something in Ma snapped as she finally realised what he'd been doing to me all them years. She went at him, all fists and feet, a screaming fury. In that moment she was a different beast to the caring, singing soul I knew: she was a cornered bitch protecting her litter.

Pa's shock at this sudden change of events didn't last long. He floored her with a mighty fist and laid into her with his boots. I tried to pull him off but he just threw me aside, a ragdolly landing awkwardly against the far wall. Little Tommy had come to me and started whimpering in my arms and it was then that I realised the thing Pa was beating was no longer our Ma: she'd gone. He'd turned her into a lump of meat leaking blood and still he kept pounding on her with his feet.

We'd run, and I'd not stopped running since. The bitter memories brought tears to my eyes and I blinked them back as I took a deep breath and forced myself back to the here-and-now.

I looked down at N'yotsu's restlessly sleeping face, smiling in spite of the situation. It was not too long ago that I would have happily let him die, given all that he represented and had done. The sensible part of me knew that Andras was a completely different beast to N'yotsu, but there was too much pain there for me to just forgive and forget. It didn't help that our friend looked so much like his evil cousin, or whatever he was. Every time I saw him I was reminded of the things he'd said and done, the way he burned a scar in my cheek with just a stroke of his finger.

The scar throbbed as I thought about it, reminding me once again that I was damaged goods. I had never been vain like those painted and perfumed dollymops that strutted round town, but I was always aware of the ragged line across my cheek. A man could wear that sort of thing with pride, a mark of his strength and a sign that he had been in tough situations—a fight, a war, whatever—

and lived. For a woman, though, it was something to be ashamed of: everyone just assuming it was from a jealous lover or a telling off by a pimp. Most people had been amazed that I was happy to be seen out in public with such a disfigurement, thinking that I should hide my hideous face away so they didn't have to feel sorry for me. Of course that just made me want to parade it in front of them even more.

N'yotsu moaned again and I shushed him, putting a hand on his forehead and trying not to pull back: his skin was clammy and cold like wet clay. He was wasting away before my eyes and there was nothing I could do but try to soothe him like he was a sick infant. I bit my lip as the helplessness of it all washed over me, flushing away any thoughts of Andras, tears welling in my eyes as my throat closed up. The sight of him lying there, moaning and panting and fading away, brought to mind so many other people I'd seen when growing up in the East End. Every time I closed my eyes I saw men, women, boys and girls huddled on the streets, unable to find food or even a roof over their head, begging for help before death grabbed them and dragged them to the potter's field. Or even worse, the ones who just gave up. A face flashed in front of me: little Jonny—or was it Mikey? There had been too many over the years, and so much had happened. I remembered him looking up at me with eyes too big for his face, the dullness in his gaze telling me that I'd lost him already, even though his body was still working: for the time being at least.

Things had been so right for a while: me, Max, Gus and N'yotsu against the world. We'd been a team, a family, maybe not perfect and perhaps not quite unstoppable but we had lived well and worked hard together. I remembered days of Max and N'yotsu peering over some invention or curiosity, pretending to ignore Gus and me drinking and joking in the corner. Finally I'd had a place where I belonged, where I was useful and wanted for more than just... but now those days were gone: Max had gone into his shell and become more bitter than ever since he lost the use of his legs thanks to Andras breaking his back in two when he'd refused to join the demon's side in that final battle in Greenwich. What's more, Gus had disappeared to God-knows-where, and now N'yotsu was just fading away before my eyes.

I sniffed and wiped my nose on the back of my hand as N'yotsu's face blurred before me.

133

No. I wouldn't cry. Never show weakness, never show fear, always be strong: those were the lessons I'd learnt the hard way. I took a deep breath and pushed the tears back inside, deep down into my stomach where no one would know they even existed. I had to be strong for N'yotsu, I had to get him to London and to Maxwell and whoever else could help him.

"You're not going to die, N'yotsu," I said through gritted teeth, my voice getting stronger with each word. "I will not let you. You hear? *I will not let you!*"

After another hour we finally made it back to London, with N'yotsu thankfully still in the land of the living. The carriage came to a stop outside the door to 24 Whitehall and I shouted out the window at the two soldiers who were on guard outside. "Don't just stand there, come and help us!" They stared at me blankly and I opened the carriage door. "This here's N'yotsu and he needs to get in there now. Do you want me to report you to your superiors as the ones who dithered and let him die?"

That decided them and within no time they had summoned a dozen soldiers to help get us inside, down the stairs, and over to the beds by Max's room. As we passed his laboratory I threw open the door and looked around. "You," I said, pointing to Dr Smith and ignoring Max's protests. "You're needed next door, now. Move yourself."

"What?" asked Max as the doctor did as he was told.

"It's N'yotsu," I said, running over to grab the handles of his wheelchair and pushing him out the door. "He's taken a turn for the worse. You're coming too: I think we're going to need all the geniuses we can get."

Time passed, but no matter what they said to me I wouldn't leave N'yotsu's bedside.

"Please," said Dr Smith for at least the twentieth time, "you would be better off getting some rest. I need space to examine him and he needs quiet."

"I'm small," I said. "And I'll keep my mouth shut."

"But really…"

I looked at him. "I'm beginning to wonder why you're so keen to get rid of me," I said. "What are you planning to do to him?"

He met my glare in impressive style. "My *job*, Miss Thatcher. I am trying to help him, an action that is hindered by you repeatedly distracting me." He turned to N'yotsu, leaving me to glare at his back.

"...wasn't distracting you until you started talking to me," I muttered under my breath, then straight away felt petty for speaking like that. I looked at the door and wondered whether I actually should go and maybe see what Max was up to; he had jotted down a few things while the doctor had been going through his tests and then asked Lexie and Joshua to take him back to his lab.

Then again, I knew I would just be in the way there, and bored into the bargain. At least staying at N'yotsu's side I felt like I was doing some good, letting him know I was there and cared about him. Anyway, I felt guilty about what had happened: I'd been there when he'd collapsed and hadn't seen it until it was too late. I had to stay with him; I owed him that much.

I shifted back on my seat and then realised that I was sitting on the edge of a bed. I swung my legs round and lay back, propping my head up on an elbow so I could still see my friend. The doctor turned to glance at me and I glared back defiantly before everything started to swim around me and I fell helplessly into a deep sleep as the efforts of the past few days finally caught up with me.

I swam through a thick muck that clung to my arms and legs but left no trace or smear. Everything was slow and heavy, a swamp of nothingness crushing down on me. There was nothing to see and yet I had the feeling that I had been there before.

All around were holes, gaps that reminded me of the rags we'd drape over doors and windows back home when I was a kid, flimsy little walls we'd construct across the middle of the room using string to give us some privacy when we wanted to wash or dress so the others living there couldn't see us. As soon as I thought this, I found myself in a tunnel made out of a long row of these rags, with gaps—windows, doors, whatever—open at regular intervals.

I walked along, dreading what was through each gap and fighting the desperate urge to stop and look through.

"Kate? Kate is that you?" A frail voice called out to me from a nearby gap and I raced over to see my little brother Tommy, huddled under a blanket of snow, just like he was that night we ran away from home, the night Ma... "Kate, I'm scared," he said.

"It's all right Tommy," I said. "Don't worry, it's all right." I wanted to reach out or step through to comfort him but something held me back.

"Is he gone?" Tommy asked. "Will he hurt us?"

"Don't worry," I said. "He—"

"Girl!" came a shout from another gap right by me, making me jump. I turned to see Pa's thick face and broken, bulging nose peering through, his pig-like bloodshot eyes glaring at me. "You come back here, girl. You don't run from me you little bitch!"

I turned back to the other hole but Tommy was gone, no doubt cowering in terror. The sound of Pa's voice made me feel ten years old again, small and helpless and terrified as I tried to run away from the man who had killed my Ma, who killed all our childhoods with his drinking and endless beatings.

"You work for me," he continued from behind me, the voice following me as I ran. "You're mine to do with as I please, and you'll make more money working the streets than you will standing behind a barrow. Now come 'ere!"

A hand touched my arm and I turned to see N'yotsu standing strong and firm before me. But as he reached for me again his face twisted and cracked until there was Andras leering at me with those blistering red eyes. "Once a whore, always a whore," the demon chanted at me, reaching a clawed finger at my cheek, burning me inside and out again and again and again.

I ran away and found myself lost in a thick fog, one of the really deep and cloying ones that come in the winter when all the fires are lit across London. Voices wafted through the grey wall and I reached for them, clawing forward, until I could see something, a small square like a stage seen from the very back of the stalls. Snatches of words and sentences came to me, nonsense at first but then slowly meshing together into something I could recognise, even if I couldn't understand.

"...only hope... no other... won't be as bad... you must consider... do you want to die?"

I could see N'yotsu there and someone else bending over him, a hunched figure who was kind of familiar.

"Do you know what awaits you in the afterlife?" the someone else was saying. "Do you think the afterlife cares that you split off some tiny part of yourself? You'll suffer all the same, but not just for what you did: for much more than that. That's not really fair now, is it?"

N'yotsu stared back at him, not saying anything, his eyes giving nothing away.

"Only one chance," continued the other person. "I can help you. You can still do so much to help, so much to further the cause…" He turned and looked at me, and I found myself reeling in terror at what I saw. Everything was muddled about his face, as though he was standing on the other side of a waterfall and glaring at me with pure evil, but the waterfall was red, the red of running blood, so much blood.

The world swam and I fell backwards into the thick mud again, which grabbed at me and pulled me, sucking me in and never letting me escape…

I woke up with a shout, gratefully sucking in air in the cold room and earning myself a glare from Dr Smith. "Is everything all right?" he asked curtly.

I looked around. Everything was the same as it was before: the beds, the lamps, the polished floor and whitewashed walls. The doctor and N'yotsu didn't seem to have moved either, and I wondered how long I'd been out for. "Nothing," I mumbled, "just a dream." The memory of what I had imagined swam back into my mind, in particular the bits involving N'yotsu and the other person, the strange-looking one who'd been talking to him. "Has anyone else been in here while I was asleep?" I asked.

"No," said the doctor. "Just us. Why?"

"I just… nothing." I suddenly needed to get out of that room. I got off the bed and walked to the door. "I'm just going for a quick walk," I said. "I won't be long."

"We're not going anywhere," said Dr Smith wearily.

CHAPTER FOURTEEN

I marched into Max's lab, slamming the door behind me when they didn't look up.

"Kate," said Max. "How is N'yotsu?"

"No change, I think. I don't like that man."

"What man?"

"The doctor. Dr Smith. I don't trust him. He's always busying around people."

Max put down a piece of paper and picked up another one. "Kate," he said slowly, "he's a doctor. That is what they do."

"I'm not a child," I said, "so don't talk to me like one. I know what doctors do. I'm just saying that there's something about him I don't like. He's been sticking his nose into everyone's business too much. And why's he so keen to get you out of here, eh?"

"He believes that some fresh air will be good for my on-going recovery, which is hardly a novel idea. I am pretty sure that any doctor in the country would say the same; it is just that my particular circumstances and our needs are not conducive to travel at this moment in time."

I stared at him. "So you're saying you're on his side?" I couldn't believe what I was hearing.

"There are no 'sides' in this, Kate," Max said. "Or rather, we're all on the same side."

I opened my mouth to tell him about my dream but then thought better of it. I didn't think Max would take too kindly to it, probably dismissing it as some childish flight of fancy. "What are you lot up to?" I asked. "Found a way of curing N'yotsu yet?"

"I am afraid not," Max said. "As you know, I have been working on this for a long time now. I was hoping that our friends here would be able to provide some fresh insights, but so far..." He shrugged.

There was a knock on the door and I opened it to see a soldier standing there. "A letter, Miss," he said, holding out a piece of paper.

"Thank you," I said, handing the letter to Max. "What does it say?"

He read it. "It's from Gus. He says he's all right and we're not to follow him." He looked up at the soldier. "Where did this come from?"

"It was delivered on the early morning post, come in by train to Clapham Junction first thing."

Max turned to Lexie. "What do you think? Given what we know, can you extrapolate where Gus was when he sent the letter?"

She peered at the letter over his shoulder. "Do you have a railway map and timetable?"

He nodded and pointed to a pile in the corner of the room. "You will find the latest Bradshaws over there."

Lexie grabbed a thick book and pored over it for a few moments, her lips moving as she worked through something or other. "Based on when we know he left and when the letter arrived, plus the route that the mail train would have taken, I believe he posted it in Basingstoke yesterday morning," she said.

I went over to see what she'd been looking at but could see nothing aside from a few maps and a load of numbers and words.

"That was my inference also," Max said, nodding as if it was the most obvious thing in the world.

"How did you work that out?" I asked.

"Mathematics," she grinned.

I stared at her, not sure if she was making fun of me. "Really?"

"Yes," she said. "You see, the letter came into Clapham Junction, meaning it must have been brought in on the London & South Western line. We know when he left London—two days ago—and that he was on foot, and likely to have remained as such, which gives me an outline area of the distances he could have travelled. In his enhanced, demonic form I understand that he can run roughly three times as fast as a normal person, but the lack of

140

sightings would suggest he is only travelling at night. As a result, we can estimate that he would have travelled approximately these distances over the period of one, two, three or four days." She drew circles with her finger as she spoke, each one bigger than the last and covering a greater area of the map. "The mail would travel at this speed," she gestured again, "meaning that I just needed to see where all of these inputs overlap. Here." Her finger ended up on a word I didn't know starting with 'B'.

"Basingstoke?" I said slowly and then smiled when she nodded. Max and Gus had given up on teaching me my letters some time ago, but the odd lesson had stuck. Of course, the rest of the word had been a hopeful guess.

"If he was there," said Max, "then it is very likely that he was heading towards either Portsmouth or Southampton, assuming that he intends to travel to France."

"Which is probably the case, going on past behaviour," I said, on safer ground at last.

"Indeed," said Max. "Which is why you need to go there, ideally before the army."

"Who, me?" I asked.

He nodded and then cocked his head as Dr Smith muttered something from behind him. I blinked: I hadn't seen the man enter the room.

"All of you," said Maxwell, nodding. "You, Lexie and Joshua. I cannot go, and I do not want you travelling on your own, regardless of how formidable you are."

I wrinkled my nose. "Yes, Joshua should come but Lexie should stay with you."

"Why him and not Lexie?"

"He'd be handy if I get in trouble," I said.

"Have you met him?" snorted Lexie.

I ignored her as I continued: "It don't make sense for both of them to come with me. What about all that stuff you lot were doing?"

"Our studies have hit the proverbial dead-end here, and if new variables come up when you are on the road then there would be considerable benefits to you having Lexie and Joshua with you to help solve them. Both of them have different strengths; Lexie in particular could be very useful."

Lexie put her hands on her hips. "But Maxwell, what about my thoughts on utilising the frequencies to erect a barrier—"

"As I said, we have hit a dead-end," said Maxwell, cutting her off with a raised hand.

"But…" she started and then frowned as he turned away from her.

"I really think…" I said, then tried to deal my last card. "I won't leave N'yotsu. Not when he's like this."

"I will stay here and keep an eye on N'yotsu," Max said. "There's nothing you can do apart from comfort him, and I am more than capable of performing that function." I bit back a laugh as I tried to figure out whether or not he was joking. Amazingly, he wasn't. "The more important task for you is to bring Gus back to us safe and sound, before the army have a chance to riddle him with their beloved .577 bullets."

We sat in silence as our carriage rocked slowly over Battersea Bridge, weaving our way through the endless stream of people, carts and animals, most of them passing in the other direction. Joshua and Lexie stared out of opposite windows like a pair of quarrelling lovers. I would have found it funny if I wasn't going to be spending the next few days cooped up with them.

I could tell Joshua hated the fact that his sister had once again come along for the ride, getting in the way of him and his chance to do his own thing. Lexie, on the other hand, clearly resented me for my clumsy efforts to stop her joining us.

"Don't worry about keeping me company," I said to them. "I know you'd be happier with your books than sitting staring into space with me."

"I don't need books to distract me," said Lexie. "I prefer to observe the mathematics at work all round me, and play with the concepts in my head." She frowned. "Why did he not listen to me?"

"Who?"

"Maxwell. He knows that I am getting somewhere with my work looking into the frequencies that the Fulcrum phenomenon is giving off. And yet he described it as a dead-end."

"Maybe it is," said Joshua. "He has been looking into this for a lot longer than you have."

"No," she said. "There is nothing wrong with my calculations and he knows it, so why did he dismiss them so readily?"

"How can you be so sure you're right?" I asked. "Max is pretty good at these things."

"So am I," she huffed, turning her back on us to sulk silently out of the window.

I grinned at Joshua. "How have you been getting on with Max? He been helping you with your magical learning?"

He turned that shy smile on me. "It has been fascinating, finally being at the heart of things, and he has so many books. But the opportunities for practising magic have been limited I'm afraid."

"Why?" I asked. "Max boring you with his inventions?"

"Not at all," he said. "We have simply been focusing more on the mathematical and scientific side of things and so I've not had much chance to explore magical possibilities. I have mainly been studying the literature that he has amassed over the years."

"Your turn will come," muttered Lexie. When she felt me staring at her, she added: "Soon Joshua's knowledge will be the more important. Who knows how much of what the rest of us know will still be relevant?"

She turned back to the window and I shrugged at Joshua.

"So your Ma seemed happy enough for you to be doing magic and stuff rather than having a proper job running your foundry," I said to him. "Why's that?"

"What do you mean?"

"I don't know much about your family, but surely she'd see being a factory manager as more worthwhile than mucking around with books and whatnot?"

"With most parents in our social circle, you would be correct," he said, "but Mother has always been quite different. Once Father died and took with him all his expectations that I would carry on the family business, she was happy for me to follow my own interests. And we still own the foundries so will keep receiving the income. Although that is of course diminishing all the time, thanks to the effects of the Fulcrum."

Lexie smiled as she turned back to us. "That's not the whole story, though, is it? Tell her the real reason you didn't take over the family business."

"It wasn't really for me," he said in a small voice, looking down.

"Joshie doesn't have the right temperament for managing

people. Especially not those who are stronger willed than him," said Lexie. "By which I mean most people." She smiled slyly at her brother.

"I am simply not cut out for that line of work," he said quietly.

"They walked all over him," she said. "Father said it was all due to first impressions and putting your foot down, and Joshie didn't really excel at either, did you?"

My heart went out to him as he blushed and stared at the floor. "Well, we all have different things we're good at," I said. "There's plenty you can do that I can't."

He blushed even more and I wondered whether I'd somehow managed to hurt his pride. After a few moments of silence he looked up. "You have experienced plenty that I would love to hear about," he said. "The confrontations with Andras and the other demons, for instance."

"Ah, well," I said. "You're better off speaking to the others: they were more involved in the ins-and-outs of what happened. I was just there to pick up the pieces."

"But you were there in the Aether as well," he said. "What was that like?"

"Very black," I said, remembering that huge dark place, filled only with the horrible mist that clung to everything. And then there were those creatures: I shuddered as I remembered them slowly pushing against the doors to our small room, hungrily trying to claw their way inside. I never saw them but Andras' words had been enough for me, what the demon had said when we were all trapped together in the Aether, listening to the sounds outside our hiding place.

"Concepts such as time and death do not hold here in the same way that you have always known them," Andras had said. "Many of the creatures outside this room have been stranded here for millennia, never ageing, never dying. Never knowing the blessed release that you will eventually crave. They would rip you apart and you would know nothing but an eternity of pain. It will consume you and you will become one of them."

I drifted back to the here-and-now to see them both staring, waiting for me to go on. "Not much else to tell you," I said. "It's not a place I'd go back to in a hurry, though."

"Was it really that terrifying?" asked Lexie. "I mean, I asked Augustus about it once and just the thought of it... well, he looked like he'd seen a ghost."

"Yeah, well, Gus was hit hardest of all by it. He says he saw and heard stuff from that place..." I got hold of myself, remembering who I was talking to. Max might have taken them totally into his confidence, but that wasn't to say the rest of us should. "Look, it's not my place to speak. If Gus wants to talk about it, fine, but I'm not going to do it for him."

"Fair enough," said Joshua. "But then there was the time that you fought against the army of golems?"

"Oh yeah," I grinned, happy to be on safer ground. "Big ugly things made of clay. Apart from Derek, that is. Derek's lovely."

"Derek?" asked Lexie.

"Kate managed to replace the *Shem* in one of the golems, the words that animate and control them, turning it from an enemy into an ally," said Joshua.

"I swapped around some bits of paper in his head, yeah," I said. "That was kind of fun. I still see Derek around; he's working down the docks."

Lexie laughed and clapped her hands. "Derek? What a wonderful name!"

"I thought so," I said. "The others thought I was touched in the head."

"And he's still in London?"

"Yeah, at the new Royal Victoria Docks," I said, waving my hand towards the east. "We can go and visit him when we get back if you want."

"And what about N'yotsu's spells?" continued Joshua. "For example when he pushed that demon through solid concrete?"

"Yeah, that was weird," I said, not quite sure there was anything I could add to all he'd clearly read.

"And Andras? When you all confronted an actual demon, a Marquis of Hell, that must have been terrifying?"

A door slammed shut in my head before that leering face could fill my mind with poison again. I looked out the window so they couldn't see the fear in my eyes. "Enough talking," I said.

After a while I managed to doze off, waking up to see Lexie draping a blanket over her sleeping brother. I watched them for a moment, the way she looked at him as she gently folded the cover over his chest and legs, and felt a stab in my heart as I remembered all the times that I had done the same for my own brothers. Before they…

I shuddered as I fought against the bad memories. *Lock them away, Kate*, I told myself.

Lexie looked up. "You're awake," she whispered.

I nodded, stretching and rubbing the sleep from my eyes. "You know," I said, "I thought you were a stuck-up, selfish spoilt rich kid. But you're not, are you? You really love him?"

"He's my brother," she said, then frowned as the rest of what I'd said registered. "And I'd like to think I'm not stuck-up, selfish or spoilt. Do you really think I am?"

"No," I said. "I don't think you are. I'm starting to think there are some ways we're actually pretty alike."

"You're rather a tough character," she said. "I'm not sure the others could survive long without you."

"Glad someone noticed," I smiled. "You seem to have a harder edge to you than he does."

"Comes from growing up in a man's world, with a Mother who was determined I was not going to be another useless breeder." She blushed when I looked at her with a question on my lips. "It's what Mother calls the girls who are brought up to have no opinions or use beyond being a wife and mother, a breeder of the next generation for their ignorant husbands."

I smiled, liking the sound of the word. "Your Ma sounds like she don't have a very high opinion of men."

"She doesn't. Father always used to turn a blind eye to it: he needed the family money, you see, and then he was too afraid to do anything but agree with her. When he passed, Joshua bore the brunt of her ire."

"Doesn't sound very fair," I said, looking at her brother. "He seems a decent enough sort."

"He is," she nodded. "Although he could do with being a bit tougher at times. I think Mother hoped that she could bring him out of himself."

"And did she?"

She glanced at him, checking that he was still sleeping. "You should ask him," she said quietly.

I nodded. "You two always been close?"

"I suppose. After a fashion. Spending these past weeks away from Mother has helped." She smiled. "I used to be so jealous of him, you know. Hated him for the fact that he was lined up to inherit everything while I'd just be a thing to be cared for, assuming I wasn't married off."

"Most people I know would kill for that kind of future," I said. "Forgive me if I don't burst into tears of sympathy."

She laughed. "I love how honest you are. But I knew loads of girls who were quite happy with that fate. I have always wanted something more. I suppose it's Mother's fault really. I want to achieve something, to be someone noteworthy."

"What like?"

"I quite like the idea of building on Ada Lovelace's legacy. There is so much potential in the idea of the Analytical Engine. Imagine if there was a machine that was capable of answering any question you asked."

"Such as?"

"Anything you like. Mathematical problems, train timetables, weather forecasts, industrial applications…"

"Don't you have books for that?"

"Well, yes, but what if you had the knowledge of every library in the world all contained within one machine, ready for any question you could possibly ask?"

"Sounds pretty fanciful to me," I said. I looked out of the window. "Anyway, time to wake up sleeping beauty: we're about to arrive."

It was a misty early morning as we reached Portsmouth's dockside, our carriage pulling up at a scene straight from a battlefield. Crates, boxes and equipment were strewn everywhere, puddles of blood and gore showing where people or demons had fallen. Probably a dozen or so demon corpses were piled up against a wall, although I couldn't see any human bodies.

A number of men and women stood around, held back by Peelers and a handful of soldiers. "What happened here?" asked Joshua in horror.

I opened the carriage door. "Let's find out," I said, stepping down to the slick cobbles.

I walked over to the soldier who seemed to be doing most of the organising. "Oi, you," I said. "What the Hell happened here?"

"You need to move on, Miss," he said. "We are still clearing up the site and this is no place for civilians."

"We ain't civilians, mate," I said. "I'm Kate Thatcher."

"Of course you are Miss," he said. "And I'm Prince-bloody-Albert. I still need you to move on, though."

He ushered us away and I looked around, feeling the eyes of Lexie and Joshua on me. I fixed on the bodies of the demons and my heart started to beat fast. "First things first," I said. "We need to see if there's anyone here who we recognise."

Joshua and Lexie ran to keep up with me. "Do you think Mr Potts could be…?" asked Joshua.

"Hopefully not, but only one way to find out," I said.

No one tried to stop us as we peered at the creatures, trying to match what was left of their faces to what we could remember of Gus and how he'd looked that other evening. After a few moments I let out a sigh of relief. "He's not here," I said.

Lexie nodded. "So what now?"

I glanced at the soldiers, hoping to see Albert or another friendly face. A passing Private paused and did a double-take as he saw me, and that was all the invitation I needed.

"Hello, darlin'," I said, treating him to a big, friendly smile, "I know you, don't I?"

He saluted me, which made me like him even more, and then nodded, a slight redness to his cheeks. "Yes, ma'am. Battle of Greenwich: I helped escort you and Mr Potts from the battlefield."

"Yeah, that's right," I smiled, "so how's it been going?"

"Busy, ma'am," he said, looking around to check that his officers hadn't noticed him chatting.

"So what's been going on here then?" I asked. "Found my mate Gus yet?"

He opened and shut his mouth and looked around again.

"Come on," I said, taking a step towards him and dropping my voice a little. "We're all on the same side here. You never know, I might be able to help."

"Well," he said, and then took a deep breath, dropping his voice to match mine, "there was some big set-to here, with a huge crowd of demons attacking a load of folks, all claws and teeth and the like. Luckily the Witchfinder General turned up to help fight them off."

He nodded over to the far side of the docks where a group of people were gathered. I squinted and could make out the dark figure of Morley, the strange man who'd as good as hounded us out of Nottingham the other week.

"Lucky he was around, eh?" I said, more to myself than anyone.

"Yeah," said the Private slowly.

"Don't suppose any of the demons were caught, or maybe gave themselves up?" I asked.

He gestured around us. "Some were killed but, as far as we can tell, more managed to escape. There's word of them heading north: I think that's probably where we're headed next."

"Makes sense," I said. "I think I might have a quick word with that Witchfinder General and thank him for his hard work, or something like that."

"Are you sure, ma'am?" he asked. "Only he don't seem like the friendliest gigglemug in the world, you know?"

"Don't worry about me," I smiled. "Me and him are old friends."

I strode over to Morley, with Joshua and Lexie again running after me. When we were halfway there the Witchfinder rose to his feet and stared at me intently.

"Two can play that game, mate," I muttered and set my face into a hard stare.

"Miss Thatcher, I presume," he said as we got near. "We did not really have the pleasure back in Nottingham, but I would recognise your face anywhere. I am not acquainted with your young friends though…?"

"Never mind them," I said, before they did anything stupid like introduce themselves. "Just thought I'd come over and find out what happened 'ere last night."

"We stopped some demon scum attacking a group of innocents," he said proudly. "Made sure that they could not hurt anyone again."

I looked around us. "How many demons were there?"

"At least 100, maybe more. They're now either dead or scattered to the four winds."

The group around him was no more than 20 people at best. "What, just 20 of you beat back a 100-odd demons? I'm very impressed."

"There were more of us last night," he said. "I managed to

muster up a group that out-matched them in numbers, spirit and determination."

"A lynch mob, you mean?" I asked.

He shrugged. "Call it what you will. We are on the side of light and justice."

Something felt odd. "So you managed to get together a big mob at just the right time to stop a load of demons attacking a group of folks? That would have taken ages, surely? So you must have known the demons were going to be here?"

He smiled at me in a way that made me want to punch him on the nose.

"How did you know?" I asked when it was clear he wasn't going to say anything else.

"I have sources and I have my methods," he said.

"Yeah, Gus told me about your methods. How many people did you torture to find out?"

"Does it matter? The information was correct. By the by, how is Mr Potts?"

I tried to maintain my best poker face. "He's fine."

"Is he with you, perchance?"

"Not right now, no."

He stared into my eyes as though he was trying to look into my brain. "You see, I picked up from our meeting in Nottingham that he was somewhat well disposed to the demons, at least through his association with your friend N'yotsu. I had hoped that that was as far as it went, though; he seemed to be a decent man at heart."

"What do you mean?" I asked slowly.

He stepped towards me and I resisted the urge to move away. "The strangest thing happened last night. One of the demons, a particularly fierce-looking beast and apparently the ringleader, confronted me. It knew my name and who I was." He smiled, but his eyes were still as cold as ever. "Now, I have quite the reputation for being effective, but this area is new to me and I did not expect my fame to spread this far so quickly. Of course, the demon could have been to Nottingham or somewhere else I have worked, but…" His eyes seemed to be digging right to the back of my skull and it was all I could do to keep calm. It was a battle to keep my breathing under control, although I fancied he knew that my heart was beating like it was going to burst out of my chest.

"The demon knew me, and I felt like I knew it too. There was something very familiar about its voice and the way it talked. When I looked hard enough, when we were face to face in the field of battle... well, it was the strangest thing. It seemed to wear Mr Potts' face, under that demonic facade, and it wielded a sword that bore a striking resemblance to the one your friend uses. A sword that I had thought was unique..."

"Very interesting," I said, trying to sound almost bored, although I doubted I fooled him for a second. "And what happened to this demon?"

"It got away. I believe they are headed north: we plan to accompany the army now that we are satisfied that the demons have left this town."

"Good idea," I said, turning to look back at the soldiers.

He grabbed my arm and said: "Miss Thatcher," in a low voice.

I glared down. "If you value the use of that hand," I said, "you'll let go right now."

He did as he was told and stepped back, holding up his hands. "I meant no offence, so please forgive me for my presumptuousness. I have to say, though: if you know anything that can help us in our battle against the demons, you would do well to share it. We are on the same side, after all."

I looked at him, studying his long, stern face for any signs that I could trust him. I failed. "Are we really?" I said slowly. "Maybe. Maybe we are on the same side, but I can't forget the way you tried to set a whole city against us. If that's how you treat your friends, well..."

"You were harbouring a demon," he said. "Do not forget: your so-called friend N'yotsu is the cause of all the madness infecting our world."

"He did not—"

"Once a demon, always a demon. A leopard cannot change its spots, eh? Or should that be a demon cannot change its horns?"

We followed the soldiers northeast but were met at Guildford by a grim-looking Albert. "Captain Pearce," I smiled. "Whatever is the matter?"

"Trouble," he said. "You're needed back in London. Now."

"Why? What's happened?"

"I'm not at liberty to tell you at the moment. There are others in London who will explain. But I need you to come with us right now."

I raised an eyebrow. "Albert, what's this all about?"

"Please, Kate," he said. "I have my orders. Don't make this any harder than it already is."

CHAPTER FIFTEEN

I spent the journey feeling like a criminal being escorted to prison, but with no idea what I was supposed to have done. Captain Pearce and the other soldiers completely ignored me and I was in no mood for small talk with Joshua and Lexie, so the road back to London was a long and miserable one.

I stared out the window and wracked my brains for anything I had done wrong that could make them treat me this way. At one point, as we slowed to let a drove of sheep pass by, I thought about opening the door and making a run for it but stopped myself; it would be worse to be dragged back in chains, and might make me look guilty of whatever it was they thought I'd done. At least this way I could go into London with my head held high.

We pulled up outside 24 Whitehall to be met by yet another group of soldiers. As the carriage stopped, Captain Pearce appeared at the door and helped me down. "If you'll come with me Miss Thatcher," he said.

"Do I have a choice?" I asked. "What's going on, Albert?"

"They agreed I could escort you," he said. "As a favour. Please, just come with me."

I opened my mouth to snap back at him but then stopped myself. I could feel the eyes of Joshua and Lexie on me and wanted to show them I could be strong and sensible in spite of everything.

Inside the building was chaos, with orderlies, soldiers and Peelers running in all directions while officers and important looking people in suits shouted instructions. As I entered the front room, everyone went quiet for a moment as they stopped to look at me.

"What they all staring at?" I asked. "Why do I feel like I've killed the Queen or something?"

Pearce took my arm. "This way," he said, leading me down towards Max's lab.

"I know where I'm going," I said, and then paused. "Has something happened to Max? Or N'yotsu?" I looked up at him but he stared straight ahead, not letting any emotion show on his face. Tears threatened to rise up in my eyes and I fought them back with a wave of anger; the amount of times I had fought at his side, and this was the way I was treated. But I wouldn't show any weakness—not even to Albert.

Rather than being taken to Max's lab or the room where N'yotsu was being treated, I was instead led to a small windowless chamber that had always been used as a mess room for the soldiers guarding us. The usual clutter had been pushed away into the corners, leaving just a table and a couple of chairs in the middle. Pearce turned to leave. "Someone will be with you shortly," he said, keeping his eyes firmly fixed on the floor.

"Where are the others?" I asked.

"Lexie and Joshua have been taken to another room for questioning," he said.

"Questioning? About what?"

"Someone will be with you as soon as possible," he said, maddening me by still refusing to make eye contact. Before I could say anything else he left the room, shutting the door behind him.

I paced the floor for a few moments, trying to calm down enough to think of my next move. I found myself facing the door and opened it, a bit surprised to find it unlocked but not surprised to see a soldier standing outside.

"Back inside please, Miss," said the Private, who I didn't recognise, firmly pulling the door shut.

"What if I need a drink?" I shouted. "Or the privy?"

"Just wait a few minutes please Miss," came the reply from the other side of the door.

I paced the room for ages, occasionally amusing myself by shouting at the guard outside. When I finally heard someone coming down the corridor I quickly sat down in the chair facing the door, folding my arms in an attempt to look unconcerned and innocent, yet impatient and annoyed at how I'd been treated.

A tall man walked into the room and sat opposite me, placing a pile of papers on the desk in between us. I stared at him with raised eyebrows as he arranged them into neat piles and then shuffled through them, occasionally glancing at one or other. He was built like a stick, with the sort of body that came from too much worry rather than not enough food. He was probably in his fifties and had a long, drooping moustache that hid his mouth, the fringes of which flapped slightly as he breathed.

"And you are?" I asked when I couldn't stand the silence any longer.

He looked up at me as if he hadn't even realised I was there. "My apologies, I have not had sufficient time to prepare but I did not want you to be forced to sit here and wait on your own for much longer." He took off his glasses. "I am sorry, my manners... I am Detective Inspector Simmonds of Scotland Yard. And you are Miss Kate Thatcher, correct?"

"That's right," I said slowly.

"Good," he said. "I wanted to ask you some questions about a few matters, and also about your friends."

"Which ones?"

He looked at a piece of paper. "Mr Augustus Potts, Mr Maxwell Potts and Mr... ah... N'yotsu."

"What about them?"

He looked at me for a few long seconds. "All in good time. Now, if you would not mind—"

"Where's Captain Pearce?" I interrupted.

"Elsewhere," he said. "You will see him soon enough. Now, if we could—"

"I want to see him now."

He sighed and put down a sheet of paper. "I am afraid that is not possible. He should not have escorted you here, given that you two have associations going back a few years, but we had little choice."

"Associations?" I snorted. "What are you saying?"

"That the two of you are friends and comrades. Is that not the case?" I shrugged and he continued. "Having him escort you here put him in a difficult position, given that he was under orders not to divulge to you the reason for your summons. That would put a strain on any friendship, so please do not hold it against him. The reasons will become clear soon enough, but for the moment I would like to ask you a few questions, if I may?"

I shrugged. "I suppose so."

"Very good." He balanced his pince-nez on his nose and picked up the sheet of paper. "When was the last time you saw Mr Augustus Potts?"

"About a week or so ago," I said. "Over at Nonsuch. When I was with Captain Pearce and a load of other soldiers. Haven't seen him since. That was why I was on the road, to try to find him."

"And you have had no contact with him since?"

"Nope."

"And when was the last time you saw Mr N'yotsu?"

"It's just N'yotsu. No 'mister'. It was a couple of days ago, before I set off for Portsmouth with Joshua and Lexie, the other two who were with me before your men split us up."

"And how did he seem when you left him?"

"Weak, poorly, sick. At death's door. He was with the doctor."

"Ah yes: Dr… Smith? Tell me about him. How long have you known him?"

"Dunno. A few weeks. When we got back from Sheffield."

"Who exactly assigned him to the role of Mr Maxwell Potts' physician?"

"I don't know," I said. "Dr Jenkins was his physic when we left to go up north. Something must have happened when we were away, as we came back and Dr Jenkins was gone, Dr Smith was there instead. Max seemed fine with it and I never had the chance to check the hows and whys of everything, given what else was going on."

"Would it surprise you to know that there is no record of a 'Dr Smith' in any of the official papers, and nor is there any record of him being assigned to the role of Mr Potts' physician?"

"Well, yeah, that would surprise me," I said. "He'd been let through all the checkpoints to come down here, so we didn't think to question it. Max needs constant check-ups: we weren't going to start asking to look at his papers or references." I shook my head. "Look, what's this got to do with me? It's not my fault if you've lost some records or them upstairs let in someone they shouldn't have."

"But you did have contact with this doctor, correct? And none of the guards upstairs have any memory of admitting a doctor called Smith or otherwise over the past few weeks."

I laughed. "Then they're fibbing! He's been here pretty much every day!"

"And yet the only people I have spoken to so far who claim to have seen him are you and Captain Pearce..." He stared at me.

I kept my mouth shut, determined not to give him the satisfaction of a response. "You calling us liars?" I asked eventually when the silence dragged on for too long.

"Not at all," he said. "Captain Pearce has satisfied me that he is telling the truth, and I have no doubt you are doing likewise. But the mystery remains."

I shrugged. "Maybe you need to ask more of the soldiers, find someone who did see him." My mind was racing through the soldiers' faces, those I'd seen every day over the past few weeks. I tried to think of anyone who would have spoken to the doctor or seen him, but I kept coming up with blanks: Dr Smith always just seemed to... appear. I felt the colour drain from my cheeks. "You think he's a demon?"

"I do not know. You are better versed in these things than me."

I frowned and stared at the wall. "There was something about him... he seemed fine, did all the things you'd expect a doctor to do. But... he had a way about him that wasn't quite right. Can't describe it, just not right."

"Could you give me an example?"

"Yeah, like when N'yotsu was ill, just before I headed down south on Max's... orders, Dr Smith was really keen for me to leave him alone with N'yotsu, even though I wasn't in the way." I shuddered as I remembered the dream I'd had when I drifted off in that room. "And then there was the way he was always so keen to get Max out of this place, and he was really interested in the bracelet Max wore..." The world felt like it was spinning around me. "Shit. The bracelet: the one N'yotsu gave Max to make sure no demon could harm or take him. The doctor was really keen to look at it. Max never let him, but..." I looked back up at the Inspector as my thinking caught up with something.

"Just me and Albert?" I asked.

"Pardon me?"

"You said that the only people you'd spoken to who'd seen the doctor were me and Captain Pearce." I leant over the table. "What about Max?"

157

"In good time," he said. "Tell me when you last saw Mr Potts."

"No!" I shouted. "Not until you tell me what's happened!"

He stared at me and then put his eye glasses down on the table. For a moment I thought he was going to walk out the room but instead he nodded. "Mr Potts—Maxwell—has disappeared. As has N'yotsu and Dr Smith. We have people out looking for them. When we examined the laboratory, though, we found this." He pulled something out of his pocket and put it on the table. It was Max's bracelet.

I stared at it, not wanting to touch it in case it made this whole strange nightmare real. Every word he'd said had blown another hole in the bottom of my world so that it seemed like there was nothing left. First Gus, then N'yotsu's illness and now this. It was the same old story: just when I thought I'd got everything worked out, life came along and messed it all up.

I wanted to shout, I wanted to kick something, I wanted to weep. But no: that wouldn't help anything or anyone. I was hit with the image of Max being taken away against his will, helpless in his wheelchair, to God knows where. Probably a big den of demons or something. We needed to do something. Now.

I stood up. "Then I need to help," I said. "Let me see the lab. I might find something you've missed: I've pretty much lived there these past few years. I can help walk the streets, I might know some places they've gone."

"That is what we're hoping," he said. "But first I need to be satisfied that I know everything about this case." He picked up another piece of paper and put his glasses back on, motioning for me to sit down. I stared at him, clenching and unclenching my fists. I wanted to scream at him: my friends were out there—weak, alone, with God knows who or what—and he wanted to read me questions from his bit of paper. Instead I controlled myself and sat down slowly, clenching the corners of the table until my knuckles turned white.

"So you last saw Mr Maxwell Potts…?"

"Just before I left for Portsmouth, a couple of days ago," I said slowly. "Max wanted me to take Joshua and Lexie with me. I told him one of them should stay with him, but he wouldn't have it. He can be pretty pig-headed when he wants to be. So I left, and that was the last I saw of him."

He nodded slowly. "What do you know of the obsidian stone?"

"What, N'yotsu's special rock? It's where he put all the bad bits that made him into Andras. But that's locked away—we've not seen it in years." I frowned as something twitched in my mind, a nagging memory.

"What is it?" he asked. "Is there something else?"

"No, well, I suppose... that day when I was at N'yotsu's bedside and the doctor wanted me out. I wouldn't leave him so I had a lie down instead and, well, I had a bit of a nightmare." I blushed. "It sounds silly, but I remember dreaming that the doctor was talking to N'yotsu, asking him if he wanted to die, saying he could help him..." I shook my head. "Didn't say anything at the time as it was just a dream and anyway next thing I knew I was being sent to Portsmouth. But in the dream the doctor turned to look at me and he did seem pretty frightening, almost demonic..." My heart pounded as I realised what I'd done; I could have stopped all this from happening if I'd just said something to someone. I gripped the table even harder, the wood digging into my fingers as I fought the urge to shout or punch or throw something.

The Inspector opened his mouth but it was me that spoke first.

"The stone," I said.

"What about it?" he asked.

"N'yotsu was weak, right? And getting weaker all the time. We didn't really understand it, but it had something to do with what he'd done to get rid of the evil bits that made him Andras. By taking them out of himself and putting them in the stone, it made him weaker. It was like he was fading away over time. But there was one thing that would stop it: if he undid all that and went back to being Andras. But N'yotsu would never..." I paused and looked at him, a cold chill running down my back. "You're not just here because some people have gone missing, are you?" I said slowly.

He put down the sheet of paper again. "I am afraid not. Just as pressing is the obsidian stone. You see, it has also disappeared."

CHAPTER SIXTEEN

Our carriage swung down Tower Hill, but rather than carrying on along the Thames it turned off towards the Tower itself.

"What's going on?" I asked. "Why are we going in here?"

"As I said, the obsidian stone has been taken," said Detective Inspector Simmonds. "We are going to inspect the place that it was taken from."

"But it was being held in the Mint," I said.

"It was," said Pearce, "but then it was moved here."

"When?"

"The day before it was stolen."

I laughed. It was always down to me to put two and two together. "Well, there's your first suspect, ain't it? What idiot made that decision and why weren't they stopped?"

Pearce cleared his throat. "It was moved here on the orders of Her Majesty, Queen Victoria. People don't tend to question authority like that."

"Why would she do that?"

"Maybe you should go to the Palace and ask her."

I pulled a face at him. "No need to be snippy. But you have to admit this don't make sense."

Simmonds leaned forwards, clearly trying to break up our little spat. "My people are making enquiries of Her Majesty's staff."

The Tower of London loomed over us as we passed under the Middle Tower archway and then over the mud-and-grass ditch that was all that was left of the Tower's moat. The next archway was thick, dark and oppressing and I held my breath as we passed through, half-expecting the portcullis to crash down and trap us in there.

Safely through, we clattered along the cobblestones running through the inner and outer battlements, high walls on either side of a carriageway that had more the feel of a long alleyway than a Royal castle. After a couple of hundred yards we swung left, turning sharply through a low archway.

"The Bloody Tower," said Pearce, nodding at the left-hand side of the arch as we passed through the other side.

"No prizes for guessing what they do in there," I muttered as I felt the familiar dread that came from being surrounded by thick stone walls and huge towers, as though all the centuries of pain and torture were bearing down on me. As a kid I'd heard about the beheadings and torturing that happened in the Tower in years gone by—some said they still carried on even to this day—and my folks would threaten to haul us off to the Tower if we were naughty. It said a lot that that threat usually worked a lot better than the beatings Pa would regularly hand out.

"It is where Richard III had the Little Princes murdered, so they say," said Pearce. "Pretty apt name, all things considered."

I grunted, pleased that he had forgotten to mention Traitors' Gate as we'd passed it. I still remembered a boatman pointing it out to us as we'd drifted by when I was a little girl, telling us how all those who went through that water-bound gate were never seen again. I'd had nightmares for weeks after about being dragged along the Thames and through the arch, the muddy water washing over me as the gate dropped down behind, cutting off the world and all hope with it.

The carriage bounced to a halt at the foot of a wide flight of stone steps leading up into the main open square in the centre of the castle walls. As we climbed out I looked round: it seemed so much bigger than usual.

"I'm not used to seeing this place without tourists," I said.

"We shut the place down as soon as we realised the stone was missing," said Pearce.

I looked around as we climbed the steps, taking in the sights of the main part of the castle, a mishmash of towers, crenellated battlements and rows of domestic houses clustered in a rough square around the sides of the inner walls. Neat lawns and rows of trees made me think more of a country park than a centuries-old castle, although the effect was spoilt by the soldiers searching the grounds. To our right, not quite in the centre of the walled space but still looming over the rest of the buildings like a mother hen surrounded by her chicks, was the White Tower. It was more light browns and creams than white, a huge square thing with tall towers at each corner and long thin arched windows dotted all the way up the sides until they reached the battlements at the top.

We entered through a tall, thin door at ground level that was being guarded by a flustered-looking soldier. Steps led down from the door into a series of caverns with walls that were white at the bottom but grew darker with soot stains as they reached up to the vaulted ceilings. At the bottom of the stairs we passed a long lead trough that had intricate patterns picked out on its sides. I looked inside to see that it was filled with dirty water.

"Cisterns," said Pearce. "For putting out fires."

"You expect many down here?" I asked, looking around at the stone walls.

"This is where we keep the ordnance," he said. "Guns and gunpowder don't tend to mix well with flames."

We walked through the first room and then under a rough stone archway into another long chamber. Racks of rifles and muskets filled every wall, while the floor was crammed with boxes that I guessed contained gunpowder and ammunition.

A man had joined us, an officer who looked like he hadn't slept in days. "This is where it was kept," he said, pointing to an empty table in the corner.

I had made a point of counting all the doors and checkpoints we'd passed on our way in. "So let me get this straight," I said. "The country's finest guarding six gates, doors and checkpoints, and someone still managed to waltz in here and blag the stone?"

"I'm sure it wasn't as simple as that," said Pearce.

"As I explained before," said Simmonds. "There did appear to be extenuating circumstances."

I shot them both disbelieving looks. "Yeah. So Max disappears, there's a big hue-and-cry and in all the confusion the next thing you know, N'yotsu goes and then so does the stone. That about right?"

"The disappearance of Maxwell caused a large amount of concern, coming so soon after Gus disappearing too," nodded Pearce.

"So the whole of London got distracted?" I asked.

"Not quite the whole," he snapped. "But everyone was on alert to look for him. Resources are stretched very thin, and so some of the guards from the Tower were sent out to join in the search. It would appear that our thieves were aware that this would happen and were ready to take advantage when it did."

"So we can be pretty sure that the two disappearances are linked," said Simmonds.

"And Dr Smith is the main suspect," I said.

"Well, not quite," said Simmonds. "After all, N'yotsu had the most to gain from the stone being liberated."

"Impossible," I said. "Albert, you saw N'yotsu. He wasn't able to walk, let alone rob a place like this."

"She's right," said Pearce. "If it was N'yotsu, he would have needed help."

"But N'yotsu was dead-set against going back to being Andras," I said. "There's no way he would have agreed to take the obsidian stone."

"Unless someone persuaded him when he was at his weakest?" asked Simmonds. "Such as when he was at death's door?"

I shook my head. "He said loads of times that he'd rather die than go back to being that... thing."

"Let us hope you are right, Kate," said Pearce.

Just as with Max's lab, there was nothing we could spot in the Tower that hadn't already been identified by the soldiers and policemen who'd combed through the place over the past day or so. Max's lab had looked like it had been burgled, with stuff thrown all over the place, and there was a worrying amount of blood splattered around the room. The Tower, on the other hand, looked like a targeted raid with nothing untoward apart from the missing stone.

After an hour or so, I sat down on a stone step, drained to the point of wanting to keel over but knowing I couldn't do that until I'd found my friends.

I looked around the room and spotted Lexie picking her way through the bustling soldiers like a lost child looking for her parents. "You, genius girl," I called to her. "You got any bright ideas on how or where we'll find them?"

She picked her way over to me. "I'd probably consider places of importance to them, somewhere they would be most likely to want to visit."

"We've already tried Max's old house at Bedford Square," said Pearce. "Nothing there. Same for Gus' apartment."

"But what if, for argument's sake, N'yotsu had got the obsidian stone," said Simmonds. "Where would he go then?"

"As far away as possible," I muttered. Then, louder: "Greenwich. That's where it all happened, where he spat out the stone and got rid of Andras. He'd go to Greenwich."

I'd not been back to Greenwich since that final battle just over two years ago, being more than happy to just get reports from Albert about how they'd cleaned up the place and started turning it from a battlefield back into a town and a collection of grand old buildings. As our coach wound its way through the clustered streets and the hills that stood over them, I kept thinking back to that day when we fought against Andras and his army, the boys travelling up by boat while I hitched a lift on the back of my friend Derek the golem. I wished I had him with me at that moment; I felt like I was fast running out of friends.

The image of Max alone and helpless in a den of demons slammed into my mind again and I bit back the urge to shout in frustration. We were doing everything we could to find him, but that still felt like bugger-all to me.

As we walked up the hill and squinted through the wind and rain towards the Royal Observatory I felt like I was stepping back in time. The Queen's House had been spared the worst of the fighting and so had suffered little damage, standing proud behind us in its gardens. Groups of people gathered round the doors and on the lawns, as the palaces were now mainly used as houses for all those still homeless thanks to the demon invasion.

I held my breath as the onion dome of the Observatory came into view over the trees: the squat, round building still partly demolished thanks to Andras' portal and our own little fight with him. I looked round, remembering walking back down the hill with Gus, both of us still smarting from the fight with Andras, while Derek held Max's broken body in his hands. That was when it had all been over, or so we'd thought.

Once again a lump rose in my throat. Where was Max now?

What were they doing to him?

Pearce pointed at the roof of the building. "There's someone up there," he said.

I squinted to see a figure dressed in a top hat and long coat, holding a cane in his right hand. "N'yotsu," I breathed, my heart skipping a beat as I realised that maybe things weren't as bad as we'd thought. If he was well enough to climb up on that roof then he was well enough to join the search for Max and Gus. We'd get the old gang back together and then we'd save the world all over again.

Once inside the Observatory we made our way to the roof and I pushed in front of the others, ignoring Pearce's protests. If my friend was going to speak to anyone, it would be me—if only to answer for leading us on this ridiculous chase when we could have been out searching for Max.

I stepped out into a now howling gale, the wind whipping my skirts up around me. I held them down and approached my friend, who still had his back to me. I couldn't tell whether that was because he didn't know I was there, or just didn't care.

As I got nearer I saw that his coat was hardly moving, as though the wind was refusing to have anything to do with him. A few steps further and I realised this was because he'd managed to find one of the few places up there that was sheltered from the atrocious weather by the remains of a high wall. As I stepped into that shelter the noise of the gale fell away like a door had been shut and I was able to speak normally rather than shout.

"N'yotsu?" I asked.

His shoulders straightened a little at the sound of my voice. "It's strange how little this place has changed, given how long has passed," he said. "I never dared come back here until now. Funny, eh?"

"Yeah, great," I said, hearing Pearce and the others catch up with me. "Same here. Look, are you all right?"

"Never better," he said, still keeping his back to me as he stared out across the grounds to the palace and the river beyond.

"N'yotsu," I said, "where's the obsidian stone? You know where it is don't you?"

"Oh yes, it's perfectly safe," he said, holding his right arm out to his side, his fist closed tight. He turned his hand so the palm faced up and then opened his fingers to reveal... nothing.

166

"Oops," he said and then turned to face us, his face shifting from my old friend to a picture from every nightmare I'd had for as long as I could remember. An impossibly wide grin split those hideously sharp features. "Missed me?" asked Andras.

CHAPTER SEVENTEEN

Pearce raised his pistol and his men followed suit. "What have you done?" he asked.

"Me?" asked Andras. "Why, I've done the one thing that all living creatures strive to do: survive."

"Where's N'yotsu?" he asked.

Andras raised a clawed finger and tapped his forehead. "Where he's always been. He's here. And so am I."

"He's insane," muttered Pearce.

"No!" Andras snapped. "For the first time in a long while I am thinking clearly. You do not understand just how much trouble you are all in: *we* are all in. You children have had long enough to mess this all up; now it's the turn of the grown-ups to sort it out."

"I remember the last time you stepped in to sort things out," I said. "Didn't go so well then, did it?"

"Ah Kate, always a pleasure. I know you're still smarting over the things I said back then, but now is really not the time."

I clenched my fists and took a step towards the creature, ignoring Pearce's hissed warning. "Not the time?" I said slowly. "You crippled my friend, scarred me, said…" I bit back the wave of shame, disgust and terror that threatened to flood over me as those memories rushed back. My fists were balled tight, making my arms so tense I thought they would snap. "And that's not saying anything about the whole nearly-destroying-the-world thing. So we're not going to do this. We're not going to talk with a monster. You've got a choice: either give us back N'yotsu or we'll fill you so full of lead…"

Andras laughed, holding up his right hand as he wiped his eyes with his left. "I'm sorry, but do you really think that that sort of threat works on the likes of me? You and I both know that it takes more than those little toy guns to hurt me."

I pulled my LeMat pistol from the band at my waist. "Recognise this?" I asked. "Seem to remember this smarted a bit the last time I shot you with it."

Pearce grunted. "I've got one of those too. Been itching to use it."

The slightest flicker of a flinch passed across the demon's face. "You won't use those. Want to know how I know? Because you don't want to harm your dear old friend N'yotsu."

"That's right," I said. "So give him back to us."

He shook his head. "We are one and the same; always have been, always will be. I am N'yotsu, and I am Andras. One cannot be without the other, just like you cannot be without your anger or hate or joy."

"Any of this making sense to you?" Pearce asked me.

"Not really. How about we shoot first and ask questions later? Not to kill him, just make him squeal a bit." I cocked my pistol and pointed it at his knee. "It'd make me feel better, if nothing else."

"N'yotsu—I—was dying," Andras said. "And now I am very much in rude health. And I have more important matters to attend to than standing here bickering with you two, so if you don't mind…" He flew towards us, that hideous face filling the whole world, blotting out the light as I lurched backwards and fired blindly. I heard yells from around me as I landed hard on the roof slates then looked up to see the soldiers crouching and casting around wildly with their rifles.

Andras was gone.

Pearce helped me to my feet. "Did we get him?" I asked. "Where'd he go?"

"Your guess is as good as mine," he said, turning to his men. "Sergeant! I want everyone out searching: a tight radius, search parties of no less than three men apiece. If anyone sees the demon they are to engage immediately with lethal force."

"Sir!"

As we looked around from the rooftop we knew it was a pointless effort. Andras was long gone. "Just when you thought things couldn't get any worse…" I muttered.

I followed Captain Pearce and General Gordon into Downing Street, trying to look like I went there all the time. The first thing that struck me was how ordinary it all looked: this was supposed to be where the geezer who ran our country worked and I'd expected it to be bigger and more organised. Instead it was a fairly dingy house just like Max's or any other wealthy person's.

Pearce grinned at me. "I know that face, Kate," he said. "You're itching to order them all to get this place sorted."

"What, just because I'm a woman you expect me to be obsessed with tidying up?" I bristled. "But if you're saying it's messy, I have to say I hadn't noticed."

"Personally I think it's a bit of a shithole, if you'll pardon my French ma'am," said General Gordon with a wink. There were few men in their kind of society who'd comfortably swear in front of a woman, but Chinese Gordon, the Hero of Taiping, had been around us long enough to know I didn't care for airs and graces. "You'd expect our seat of government to at least look vaguely presentable. But then again, we are at war." He led us through a door and into a large room filled with a long table and lots of very pale old men.

A tall man with a face like an unhappy horse topped off with a shock of curly hair looked up from the other side of the table. "Ah, General, so good of you to join us," he said.

"I came as soon as I was able, sir," he said. "Although I apologise for the slight delay; I had to receive an update from one of my men. I brought him with me as I believe you should all hear what he has to say for yourselves. This is Captain Pearce."

As they greeted him I could feel the eyes of the men on me and tried my best to ignore them, forcing myself to stand tall and straight.

"Pleased to meet you, Captain Pearce," said a short, balding man nearest to us. "Shall we receive your report in, ah, private?"

I glared at him, my cheeks flushing; he wasn't saying it direct but I knew exactly what he meant.

The horse-faced man had been watching and came round the table to stand in front of me. "Am I right to assume that we have the pleasure of meeting Miss Kate Thatcher?" he asked.

"That's me," I said slowly.

He took my hand and kissed it. "I am Benjamin Disraeli and have the honour of being Her Majesty's Prime Minister. Madame, I believe we all owe you a huge debt. I have heard of the great work you have done supporting Messrs Potts and N'yotsu."

General Gordon chuckled from behind me. "I think you will find, sir, that she has been the driving force behind a lot of what they have done. She is a rather formidable young lady, wouldn't you say Captain?"

"I would, sir," said Pearce. I could hear the grin in his voice and felt the heat in my cheeks grow stronger.

"In which case," said Disraeli, leading me to the table, "I do not believe anyone here would begrudge you a place at this council. After all, you have more experience in these matters than all of us combined."

"Hear, hear," muttered a few voices. I looked around as I sat down in the chair Disraeli held out for me, forcing myself to look them in the eyes and show them I wasn't just some weak woman. Those that met my gaze nodded with smiles that were almost patronising, but most just looked down or chatted among themselves, ignoring me.

Disraeli sat opposite me and then gestured to Gordon and Pearce. "If you please, gentlemen, let us hear your report."

I sat and fidgeted as Pearce set out what had happened over the past day or so: Max's disappearance, the fake Dr Smith, the return of Andras. "We have men scouring the city for the demon," he finished, "although from past experience he will not be easy to find, let alone capture."

Disraeli drummed his fingertips on the table. "So we are now without all three of our champions, and have yet another enemy to contend with."

"Sir, now is the time to invoke Martial Law," said one man. "Use it to get the Queen's men under our control as well, and then we can properly funnel our resources where they are really needed."

"Funnel them? Into what?" asked another. "We still do not know whether we're fighting one unified threat or lots of autonomous individuals. The country needs to see a presence on the streets and the current arrangements achieve that just fine. We should avoid unnecessarily centralising the army until we know whether the benefits of such a step really do outweigh the risks."

They all started shouting and talking at once and I gave up trying to follow what was being said.

Disraeli held up a hand and quiet slowly fell on the room. "Miss Thatcher, I am interested in hearing your views." He gestured to me with an open palm.

I gaped at him for a moment, wondering if he was being serious. I was suddenly aware of all their eyes upon me. Pearce and Gordon nodded and smiled, while the rest of the men tried their best to look like they were interested in what I had to say.

I took a deep breath. "Well, Andras is the big threat here." My voice cracked but I cleared my throat and forced myself to continue. "Him coming back has to be linked to Max going missing. But I don't think N'yotsu knew this or planned it."

"Surely though N'yotsu had to be involved somehow?" asked a man next to me. "Could he have been turned back into that demonic creature against his will?"

"Maybe. I don't know." I frowned as I remembered the dream from just a few nights ago; it seemed like a lot longer since it happened. In the dream it was almost like Dr Smith was forcing N'yotsu to do something he didn't want to do. "We know that Max's doctor wasn't who he said he was, and I'm pretty sure he was really a demon."

"Sent to bring back Andras?" someone asked.

I shook my head. "No. I think Max was the real prize he was after. Andras didn't have anything to do with Max disappearing."

"How could you possibly know that?" asked Pearce.

I turned to him. "He wasn't trying to hide when we found him on that rooftop earlier. Behind all that bluster I think he was as confused and lost as the rest of us. Maybe him coming back was a great distraction for the doctor—or whatever he is—to snatch Max from under our noses."

"So where is Andras now?"

I shrugged. "Last time, Andras wanted to create a portal to bring his demon chums through and create Hell on Earth. I'd bet on him having another bash at that. There's only one person who can make that portal though: Max."

"So if we find Mr Potts then the chances are that we'll find the demon as well," said Disraeli slowly. "The question is, where?"

They all started talking at once, just as some thoughts hit me. "Shush!" I yelled. To my surprise, they fell silent and stared at me. "Max was working on a few things. He kept bangin' on about the Fulcrum: he reckoned there was a place where it would all start to happen, magic taking over, demons coming through, that sort of thing. Him, Lexie and Joshua were working on figuring out where it was."

"Sounds sensible," said someone. "Did they find it?"

"He thought it was somewhere called Nonsuch. That was where we were when Gus turned…"

"Indeed," said Pearce quickly. "And the fact that we were attacked there by demons might point to it being the place we were looking for."

"Yeah," I said. "Except Max seemed to think the readings said something different. 'Hit a dead-end' were his exact words."

"That's not like Mr Potts," said another man. "I always found him stubborn to a fault."

"Maybe it was the Fulcrum," I suggested. "He'd been getting more and more worried about it coming and making all his beloved science redundant. That's why we brought Josh down to work with him."

"The young man from Sheffield?" asked Disraeli. "Did he disappear as well?"

"No. He and his sister are safely under guard back at Maxwell's laboratory," said Pearce.

I clapped my hands together. "They've been working really closely with Max: chances are they can figure out where the Fulcrum is. If we find that, surely we'll find Max."

"Could it have a connection to Nonsuch even in spite of Maxwell's comments?" asked Pearce.

"Maybe," I said. "It's worth sending some men there. Josh and Lexie'll know better than me whether it could be an option. If you'll let me and the genius twins have a go at Max's lab we might be able to figure something out."

"Very well," said Disraeli. "For the time being we have to assume that there is a real risk of demonic invasion through a portal created by Mr Potts, Andras or both."

"Again," muttered someone.

"Max wouldn't do anything to harm us," I protested.

"I am sure he would not. Voluntarily, in any case. But we

cannot rule out the risk of him being coerced into acting against his will," said Disraeli.

"Never," I said. "Last time, Andras couldn't get him to work with him even after breaking his legs."

"But there are these new demons that Mr N'yotsu said he encountered in Sheffield. Mages, I believe they are called?"

I nodded slowly. Gus and N'yotsu had seemed pretty shaken up after meeting the Mage up north. "The creature could make people do things. Might explain why no one saw Max leave his lab and how Andras managed to break into the Tower and steal the obsidian stone from under the noses of London's finest."

"If there are demons here that can make people act against their will," said a man next to Disraeli, "then how can we trust anyone any more?"

"We cannot," said Disraeli simply. "Which is why it is imperative that we act quickly. General, investigate this Nonsuch connection and keep in contact with Miss Thatcher. I am charging you to act in the interests of the country; if I or any of your other superiors order you to act against those interests, then you have my express authority to disregard those orders. Do you understand?"

General Gordon nodded as the suits in the room started to protest. Disraeli silenced them with a barked word. "Enough! Unless you forget, General Gordon was one of the few people who stood firm against Andras' influence a few years ago. Indeed, there are many in this room who were not as steadfast." He glared round before fixing his gaze on me. "Miss Thatcher, gather the two youths and do what you need to do. Please keep us appraised, but be in no doubt: your priority is to find Mr Potts before Andras does. I shall go and update Her Majesty."

CHAPTER EIGHTEEN

We stood in the doorway to Max's lab, staring at what was left of his experiments and notes. "What a mess," muttered Joshua. "Where do we start?"

"He will have taken everything he needed," said Lexie. "So we start by figuring out what isn't here."

"They'd have been in a rush," I added. "Hopefully they left something that'll give us a clue where they've gone."

"Agreed," said Lexie. "Maxwell will kill us for this, but we need to organise everything properly." She started clearing a space in the middle of the room and Joshua and I rushed to help her. "So we shall start by categorising what is here." She picked up a bundle of papers and worked through them, placing them on the floor one at a time. "Anything to do with Nonsuch goes here, general portals here, the compound here..." She looked at Joshua and me. "Well, if you'd like to help?"

Joshua grabbed a nearby pile and started to follow suit, but I stood there and glared at her. She knew I couldn't help; was she really going to make me say it? After a moment of staring at me, the penny dropped. "Of course," she said. "I am so sorry. You don't... you can't..."

"No, I can't read," I said. "So maybe I'll just gather and move stuff, and leave you two to the sifting through and whatever else it is you're doing."

Half an hour later I realised I wasn't being much help so I decided to take a breather, offering to get them both a drink. The kitchen was upstairs, the pot piled high with dregs, and so I stepped outside to empty it. As I emptied the tea leaves out into a flowerbed I had a feeling I wasn't alone. I turned slowly to see a grinning demon perched on the far wall.

"Kate," grinned Andras. "What a pleasure to see you again."

"Can't say I feel the same," I said. "You've got a right nerve coming 'ere."

He jumped down and straightened his waistcoat and jacket. "Security seems somewhat light. I get the impression your soldier friends are all off gallivanting around looking for some devilishly handsome chap."

"Very funny. You know I could just yell and you'd be clapped in irons faster than you can spit."

"Of course. And then I'd break free and we can start this mummer's farce all over."

I sighed, keeping a firm grip on the teapot in case I needed to defend myself. "What are you doing here?"

"I thought it would be nice if we had a bit of a chat, without your soldier friends lowering the tone."

"I'll chat when you give us back Max."

"Now, you see, that's the thing." He leaned back against the wall. "I believe we have common cause in that regard."

"You don't know where he is either, do you?"

Andras shook his head. "So... seeing as we both want the same thing, how about a friendly chat about how we can come to an arrangement?"

"Wait," I said. "What do *you* want him for?"

He tapped a clawed finger on his nose. "All in good time."

I snorted. Some people never change. "I'll speak," I said. "But I won't help you; I'll only speak to N'yotsu."

"That's what you're doing."

"No. I want to speak to just N'yotsu, not you."

He laughed, a piercing, high-pitched sound that made me want to tear my ears off. "You don't get it, do you? We are the same person: one and the same, indivisible, inseparable."

"Not quite," I said. "He managed it before, spat you out into a stone."

He waggled a finger at me. "Ah. But I won't be tricked into doing that again. Quite a prolonged way to commit suicide, and it very nearly worked. Nearly, but not quite." He grinned proudly at me.

"Why are you back?" I asked, trying a different tack.

"It was that or die, and I'm not sure I'm quite ready to meet my maker just yet. As far as my people are concerned I'm an exile and an apostate, and we have some pretty vengeful gods. Meeting them is a nightmare I'd like to delay for as long as possible."

"That's not what I asked," I said. "I meant, how did you come back?"

He held out his hands to either side. "Stone, plus me, equals…" He clapped his hands together. "Me!"

"This is hopeless," I muttered.

"Aw, poor little Kate," he said. "Language and thinking never were your strong points, were they?"

I felt the anger rising in me and started for the door. "If you came here just to insult me, then I'm off."

"Now now, let's not be too hasty," he said, holding his hands up. "I'm sorry, I did not mean to hurt your feelings. I was trying to sympathise with you. To be honest, this whole thing with human feelings and emotions is something I've never really got the hang of. I'll try harder to be nice."

I stopped and stared at him. "So," I said. "How did you get the stone? It was under lock and key, and the last time I saw N'yo—you, you weren't able to stand, let alone trek across town and break into the Tower."

"I had help," he said.

"Go on. What kind of help?"

"Helpful help."

"You're wasting my time," I said, turning towards the door again.

"It was the doctor," he said. "Dr Smith. He said he could cure me. I agreed and… well, here I am."

"But N'yotsu was always dead-set against being turned back into you," I said.

"So he said. But deep down he was as terrified of death as I am, and behind all those brave words lay someone who would happily sacrifice his principles if it meant delaying an eternity of pain."

"No," I shook my head. "Not N'yotsu."

"Then how do you account for my presence here?" He grinned. "Aha! You cannot!" He leaned back, satisfied.

"All right," I said. "Let's just say that you're right and N'yotsu wanted to get the stone back. Why did the doctor want to help you?"

"He's a doctor," shrugged Andras. "That's what they do: help people, cure them, make things better."

"Yes, with medicine and tinctures and tonics. Not turning them into evil monsters."

"I am a demon, not a monster."

"Same difference."

"To you maybe," he sniffed. "I have feelings too, you know."

I frowned at him. "You jokin' with me?"

He grinned. "Do you not think I am a lot more fun like this? No more of that boring moping around, feeling guilty about everything." He screwed up his face into a serious frown. "It is all my fault," he said in a deep voice. "I must suffer my punishment, I deserve it. Boo hoo."

"So you're saying you feel no guilt for what you did?"

"Why should I? Things happened, most of the people affected are long gone."

"Mainly because you killed them."

He shrugged. "Mere semantics."

I bit back my frustration. "Let's go back to the doctor," I said. "Who is he?"

"Dr Smith? Funny you should ask." He hopped back up onto the wall and reached down the other side. "I suspected something towards the end. I knew he wasn't just any ordinary doctor. He has some interesting criminal connections, that's for sure. How else do you think he got me the stone? Other than that, he didn't tell and I wasn't really in any condition to ask. You ever heard the expression: 'Never look a gift horse in the mouth'?"

"So you don't know anything?" I asked, ignoring his question.

"Oh, I know plenty. I know about worlds beyond your wildest imaginings, where fantastic creatures swim across skies of liquid fire. I know the secret of life and the meaning of death and what comes after. I also know how short and pathetic your lives are compared to mine."

"Is that a threat?"

"No, not a threat, just an observation, a simple statement of fact." He examined his fingers. "At the time I suspected that Dr Smith was not just a physician, although he didn't confide in me who he really was or who he was working for. But I'm pretty sure that his main purpose was to get his hands on Maxwell rather than to liberate me. I was a side effect, a diversionary tactic, as it were. As much as it pains me to say so, although I am quite pleased with the end result."

"Kind of figured that out for myself," I said. "Tell me something useful: do you know where he took Max?" I asked.

"Not yet. But I now know who Dr Smith really is." As casually as though he was picking up a couple of small sacks, he lifted two bodies from the other side of the wall and dumped them in the yard in front of me. They landed heavily and moaned slightly. "I believe you already know these individuals?"

"Spencer and Bart," I said. "Funny how you two keep popping up." They were two of the lowest of the low, small-time crooks I was unlucky enough to know back when I was working the streets. Those were the dark days after I ran away from home and before Max and Gus rescued me and gave me something to do which didn't involve lying on my back and hating everyone, including myself. Spencer and Bart used to work as enforcers for Jason—my pimp—until he was taken out of business by N'yotsu. After that, they'd gone back to petty crime but with half an eye on making money from the demon invasion. Last time our paths had crossed, they'd kidnapped me and Gus and sold us out to a pack of demons in St Giles'. "I thought you two were banged up."

"Got let out, didn't we? Got ourselves pardoned," grinned Spencer. He was a short, thin rat-like man with retreating hair and clothes that tried to be fashionable but failed thanks to their age and the fact that they were nearly rags. His partner was a huge bear of a man with a rug on his chest peeking out through a stained vest, shovel-like hands being more fur than skin and a thick but patchy beard covering his face. Strangely, it was at his ears where the hair ended, making him look like he'd been born with his head on upside down.

"Pardoned? Who would do that?" I asked.

"Dunno. Some bloke in a suit. Everyone listened to him so we guessed he was a high-up toff or somethin'. Didn't bother to check his credentials; just pleased to not be on a boat to the Colonies, that's all."

I spat on the floor. "Me, I'd have hung you." I looked at Andras. "What've they got to do with all this?"

"Why, they were the ones who liberated the obsidian stone for me."

"These two?" I laughed. "They could barely rob a chicken coop without mucking it up. There's no chance they could break into the Tower!"

"We did," said Bart. "It were all us. Ouch!" He glared at Spencer, who had elbowed him in his ribs.

Andras cleared his throat and Spencer paled. "Y-y-yes," he stammered. "We did."

Andras smiled triumphantly at me.

I narrowed my eyes at him. "What have you done to them?" I asked.

"Just a little bit of persuasion. I simply encouraged them to be truthful."

I folded my arms across my chest. "I know all about your tools of persuasion."

"Oh, don't get all moral with me. We don't have time to be gentle with them." He nudged Spencer with his boot. "Tell her what you told me."

Spencer swallowed and then looked up at me. "It was us what did it, stole the stone thingy. But we went nowhere near the Crown Jewels or any of that stuff: we were told that would keep us out of real trouble."

"Who told you?" I asked.

"The bloke what hired us. He helped get us in and did some sort of mumbo-jumbo to make sure no one knew we was there. We just walked in and out without no one seeing us. Weird like, but it was the easiest job we've ever done so there was no complaining. He promised he'd look after us."

"Who is 'he' exactly?" I asked.

"Well, I say 'he', but it was a demon. He seemed normal at first, but I'm used to dealing with them types so I can tell."

"What'd he look like?"

"Bit short, blondish hair, big nose, glasses, kind of weasel-like."

I nodded. "Sounds like our doctor."

"Yes!" said Spencer. "He said he was a doctor. Smith: he said his name was Smith. But the other demons called him something else. Carp, I think it was."

"Carp? Like the fish?"

"Yeah, which I thought was odd as he didn't look like no fish. At one point—and this is when I knew he was definitely a demon—he had these really big wings."

"Big wings," I said, as deadpan as I could while I wondered whether this was something he had seen or if he'd been on some of Gus's drugs.

"Yeah, just for a moment." He leaned forwards, speaking as though he was the biggest expert in the world. "The demons do that sometimes, when they're tricking us to think they look like normals. It's like they stop concentratin' for a moment and you see a bit of what they really look like."

"So did this… Carp… tell you what he wanted the stone for, or what his plan was?"

"I dunno," he said.

I turned to Andras. "This make any sense to you?"

"I'm afraid so."

"So you know this Carp he's talking about?" I asked.

"It's Gaap, not Carp, and yes I do know him. What is particularly annoying is that I did not recognise the low-born backstabber at the time. If I had, I would never have allowed him to help me." He kicked the wall, knocking a ragged hole in the stone.

"I know that name," I said. "He was the demon Josh summoned in Sheffield. That demon had wings when we first saw him."

"That is correct. Gaap and I have associations going back many millennia. Back in my realm, it was he who was responsible for me being exiled to the Aether. But he's a politician, an adviser. He only follows real power. As Solomon said, he always goes before four great and mighty Kings."

"Wait," I said. "Four Kings? Like what N'yotsu heard that demon say in Sheffield?"

"The very same. Asmoday, Abaddon, Bileth and Belial." His face was now bright red with bottled-up fury.

"Still," I said, "the fact that they've got you this upset just makes me want to like them more."

He stared at me, those red eyes making me want to be anywhere but there. "Then you're a damn fool. They are the driving force behind Almadel—my realm—and its efforts to conquer every other realm. If they succeed then your world will be destroyed forever, with what dregs remain of the human race reduced to slavery."

I rubbed my head. "But you wanted them *here* before," I said. "You said that you made the portals so you could bring your people through and make Hell on Earth. Those were your very words, I remember it clearly. What's different now?"

"*I* am," he said. "As I said to you earlier, I'm no longer wholly Andras nor N'yotsu: at least, not the creatures you knew. I am a hybrid of both, incorporating the experiences of both. You might not believe me but it's true. And I have grown somewhat fond of this realm and its people over recent years, in spite of how you have treated me. Call it an infection, but one that I am reluctantly learning to embrace. In any case, I used to believe that by handing my kind the keys to this realm they would welcome me back with open arms. Having spoken to some of the demons who came through my portals, I now realise that I was sadly deluded."

"They've cut you off!" I said. "They want you dead as much as they want us dead. But then why bring you back? Why not just let you fade away as N'yotsu, or cut you down when you were so weakened?"

"As much as it pains me to admit it, I was a useful distraction: a way of diverting you all while they got their hands on their prize. Namely Maxwell Potts, the genius who can accelerate the coming of the Fulcrum, show them exactly where it will emanate from and thus give them the portal they need to invade and overrun this realm. And there would be no honour in killing me when I was incapacitated; they would much prefer to strike me down in my prime, in full view of all, to act as an example."

"So you're going to help us?" I asked.

"I'm going to help *me*," he said. "It just so happens that our interests coincide for the time being."

"And when our interests stop coinciding?"

He smiled. "Now why would you spoil a perfectly lovely conversation with such thoughts?"

"So why are you telling me all this? Why bring these two filthy blackguards here?"

"I don't have any more use for them but I thought you might enjoy putting them back behind bars or something. It's possible that I'm getting soft in my old age: time was, I'd have stolen their souls and banished them to the pits of Hell, but…" he shrugged. "As for the information, I know that you and the two children in there are trying to piece together where Maxwell has gone. When you find out, you'll need all the help you can get." He leapt back onto the wall and then bowed. "I will be ready, willing and able to assist when the time comes, although you will need to be quick."

"I'm still struggling with what's in all this for you. Why not just let them invade us?"

"Augustus turned into a demon when he wasn't supposed to. Maxwell was snatched away, and I have been restored to my former glory as an afterthought. Back in Sheffield, that sniffling scrote Gaap started shouting about the Four Kings. They are playing with my toys without asking for my permission, and that makes me very cross. I am also highly vindictive and jealous: the Four Kings and Gaap denied me my rightful place amongst my people a long time ago and I would take a great deal of pleasure in doing likewise to them here." He dropped down the other side of the wall and out of sight.

I turned to Spencer and Bart. "You're going to stay here while I get some soldiers," I said. "No trying to escape."

"No fear," said Spencer. "Just keep us away from that thing, all right?"

After making sure that Spencer and Bart were firmly under guard, I made my way back downstairs to Max's lab. I opened the door to find Lexie and Joshua in excited conversation, standing in the middle of piles and piles of notes like giants in the middle of a paper town.

"Kate," grinned Lexie. "I think we have something."

"What?" I asked.

She grabbed my arm and led me into the middle of their mad organisation. "These are Max's notes on Nonsuch." She pointed at three thigh-high stacks leaning into each other.

"Yeah, so?" I asked. I'd lived through his obsession with that place.

"It's all there," she said.

"Good," I said slowly. "Well done." I looked round for some sort of useful clue.

"No, you don't understand what I'm saying. *It's all here*: he didn't take any of this stuff. However there are other papers that at the time we thought were obscure and meaningless, but which are now missing."

"Then that means…"

"Nonsuch was a dead-end," she said, picking up a paper and waving it in front of me. "The initial readings we took from our visit there showed very little, but Maxwell persuaded us to carry on our workings as though there was something that would turn up."

"But if he knew there was nothing there, why would he make you do that?"

"So that he could get us doing something useful but without giving us all the information on what the true target was," said Joshua. "We think he was trying to distract us from his real intentions."

"Which were?" I asked.

"Did he ever mention St Albans to you?" asked Lexie.

I rubbed my head. "Ages ago. Must be at least a few months. I got a load of maps and stuff for him, but that was the last I heard of it."

"We still need to check," she said, "but I think that might be a place worth checking." She pointed to a couple of stray pieces of paper. "That's all that's left of his St Albans research; he must have taken the rest with him."

"Of course," said Joshua, "the big question is why he felt he had to keep this from us. I thought we were a team."

"So did I," I said. "But it turns out he's been doing loads of stuff without telling me—I mean us." They both stared at me and I sighed. "All that stuff about Gus turning into a demon, the experiments… he didn't tell me anything, even after all we'd been through. I thought I knew him, but…"

"I'm sure he only meant to protect you," said Joshua. "They really value you, you know."

I laughed. "Yeah." It was the way it always had been, the only way I knew: me against the rest of the world. It was better that way so I didn't get hurt by so-called friends. At that moment though, I needed to set things right so there would still be a world left to work against me.

I went over to the door. "Where are you going?" asked Joshua.

"To sort out some transport," I said. "We need to go to St

Albans."

"I want a little longer to look through a few things," Lexie said. "There are some other items of interest here."

"We need to move fast," I said. "The longer Max is gone, the greater the risk of—"

"I know," she replied. "But I don't want us running off down another dead-end."

"You've got three hours," I said. "I'll see if I can get us some reinforcements."

CHAPTER NINETEEN

I ran up the stairs to find Pearce bossing his men around. "I see you've been busy," he said, nodding at Spencer and Bart, who were in the process of being walked out to a waiting carriage.

"Yeah," I said. "They say every backyard in London's full of rats; turns out even Whitehall's infested." I raised my voice to shout at them: "Take care, boys. Don't rush back, eh?"

Pearce was glaring at me. "Care to tell me how they came to be here?"

"I had a visitor," I said.

"Andras?"

"That's right."

"And you were planning on telling us... when?"

"I'm telling you right now, aren't I?" I folded my arms. We were pretty close to a breakthrough in finding Max and there he was, telling me off like a naughty little girl.

"Kate," he said, "we're supposed to be a team. But that's not going to work if we keep stuff from each other."

"Funny," I muttered. "That's just what I was saying down there." I sighed. "Look, let's start again. It happened not that long ago and as soon as he'd gone I sent for your boys, which is clearly why you're here, right? I would have asked Andras to sit around and wait until my friends and their guns arrived, but I'm not sure he'd have been too keen."

I told him what had happened and then watched as he sent guards out to scout around, just in case Andras was still lurking.

"There's more," I said. "Lexie reckons she knows where Max has been taken: St Albans."

"Is she sure?"

"She wants to do some more checking, but she seems pretty certain. I was heading up to sort out transport but now you're here, maybe you and your boys would fancy joining us on a trip?"

"Of course," he said. "When do we leave?"

"I told her I'd give them a couple of hours to double-check."

Pearce checked his pocket watch. "Very well. I'll see you back here at four o'clock."

I busied myself by gathering together some weapons and supplies for our journey and checking up on Lexie and Joshua. Thankfully, they seemed to grow more and more certain as time went on. "We're close to pinpointing it exactly," explained Joshua. "There seems to be a certain set-up in the road design that accords pretty closely to a magical theorem I came across in one of Max's texts a few days ago. A text that is now missing."

"Great," I said. "So we can go now?"

"Just a little longer," begged Joshua. "I could save us a lot of wasted time searching randomly once we get up there."

I wandered upstairs as the clock struck four, surprised to see that Pearce was late. Humming softly to myself, I wandered into the backyard to check on the weather.

"We have to stop meeting like this," said a voice from behind me.

I spun round. "Andras. You're back," I said.

"I understand you've had a breakthrough," he said.

"How did you…?" I asked.

He tapped his ear. "I'm a demon. Enhanced hearing is one of my particular talents. I hope you weren't planning to keep this information from me." He wagged a clawed finger at me in a mock telling-off and I flinched without thinking.

"It's interesting that you had an instinctive reaction to my finger," he said. "Tell me, does it still hurt?"

I touched the scar on my cheek. "No," I said, not wanting to give him the satisfaction. "Hardly think about it these days. It's a part of me now."

He frowned and I thought for a brief moment that I could see a glimpse of the old N'yotsu. "You never were a very good liar, you know," he said. "For what it's worth, I feel... I believe the correct term is remorse."

I laughed. "I didn't think that was something your kind was able to recognise, let alone experience."

He looked down at the ground. "I shouldn't be able to but then I always have been somewhat unique. My talents just tended to be a mite more useful in the past. I do not know how you cope with all these emotions."

I looked at him, suddenly seeing him as a lost creature struggling with something he didn't quite understand. "If I didn't know better, I'd say you've changed. Got a bit more... human."

He whipped his head round to glare at me. "I'm still as dangerous as ever, never fear. I could snap your neck in two, hollow you out, devour your soul and then use your desiccated husk as my marionette."

I put my hands on my hips. "Then why don't you?"

"Because you're still useful to me alive."

"No, that don't wash. You could use me even better if I was your puppet. Letting me run free, not being controlled by you, that's not your style. You like to make people dance to your tune."

He paced over to the wall and kicked it. "I am not weak," he snarled. "I act as I choose to."

I smiled, enjoying the show. "No," I said. "No, you don't. You miss being around me and the men. You're more N'yotsu than you'll admit."

He darted over to me, making me start as I suddenly found myself nose-to-nose with him. I was struck by his smell, like sweetbreads softly roasting over a fire. I forced my body to stand firm; I would not show him weakness. For a moment we stood there, locked in a dance that neither of us really knew how to end.

"If you're getting bothered by all those emotions," I said, trying to keep my voice as level as I could, "why don't you just do your magic and chuck them out into a stone or something, like you did before?"

"I can't. No, that's not right. I could, but if I did so I would just end up as I was before, teetering on the brink of death. My kind are not meant to—"

"That's a lie," I cut him off. "Me and N'yotsu had loads of talks about this sort of thing: it was the demon bit which you lot ain't supposed to be separated from. Emotions are completely different: they're not naturally a part of you, so you could happily run around without them."

He grinned. "Good old Kate, not quite as dim as they all assume, are you?" I bit back an angry response as he continued. "I guess you're right. As insufferable as these emotions are, I cannot quite bring myself to undertake the change that would happen if I lost them." He stood up. "Now, when do we leave?"

"We? What do you mean? What makes you think we want you with us?"

"Because I'm the only supernatural being on your side right now. If you're planning to go into battle against Gaap and his cronies with your toy weapons, then you're a bigger fool than everyone thinks. We don't have time to mess around here."

"Why?" I asked. "What's the urgency? Aside from needing to find Max, that is."

"I have been asking around, speaking to a few demons who have lately come over to this realm. It turns out that the recent manifestations of high-level demons are not as random as we first thought. My people have been busy, pulling together a rather intricate plan to invade this world. And more to the point: to destroy me."

"What do you mean?" I asked. When he sighed I folded my arms. "If I'm going to let you come along, I need to know you're not hiding anything from us."

"When the Fulcrum takes place, it will create a rift in reality, but one that is naturally occurring, as opposed to Maxwell's rather shoddy and violent effort from a few years ago."

"The one you used to try to destroy us all, you mean."

He tutted. "You have to keep bringing that up. But, yes, that is the one. While that particular portal was inherently unstable, this one would be a natural outcome of what is happening to the world and the Aether. Kicked off, ironically enough, by Maxwell's original portal."

I stared at him. Did he really think all this waffle was an explanation?

"It will be large enough and stable enough to allow an army to come through," he said slowly, as if speaking to a child. "It will act as a permanent bridge between your world and the Aether."

"So basically it'll do what you tried to do last time," I said. "Only this time you want to stop it?"

"No. There is no stopping the Fulcrum: something Maxwell would have realised if he had not allowed his emotions to override his common sense. We cannot stop the Fulcrum and the portal to the Aether it will create, but we can delay it for long enough to find a way to stop *them* from coming through. You see, the Fulcrum can either be a slow, natural event or a big bang; it's the latter that Gaap and his people want to create, a sudden rupture through which they can storm and overwhelm us before we have a chance to hit back. The key to all of this is knowing where the focus of the Fulcrum will be: the physical epicentre from where it will all flow. As far as I can tell, the demons have half of the equation, namely the point in the Aether on their side where it will occur."

"And Max will be able to tell them where in this world it will be," I finished for him.

"If he hasn't already. So you see why there is a need for urgency. Especially as I suspect that there is more to Gaap's plan than just this."

"What do you mean?"

"He is a politician," he spat the word, "and will always have a back-up plan, just in case."

"Which is what?"

"No idea. That is why we need to foil the plan we know about as soon as possible, so that we can flush out the next one." He turned to look at me. "The Witchfinder man: Morley. Ever wondered how he fits into all of this?"

I blinked. "I just thought he was another madman kicked out from under a rock by everything that's been going on."

"No. Everything happens for a reason, especially when the likes of Gaap and I are involved. Morley knew exactly where to be when we got to Nottingham. And again, when you were in Portsmouth. I would put good money on him not being too far away when Pearce arrests me. What do you say, Captain?"

I turned to see Pearce and his men in the doorway behind me. "Wait," I said to him.

Pearce ignored me. "You might recognise these," he said, hefting his rifle. "You helped design them when you were N'yotsu as a way of stopping some terrible demon called... Andras. You. We have half a dozen pointed at your head. You can resist us if you want but if you do I promise it's really going to hurt."

Andras snarled and for a moment I thought he was going to pounce on my friend, but then his shoulders slumped and he raised his hands in supplication. "Very well. I surrender, Captain."

"You are not going to fight us? No threats?" Pearce asked.

"No. I suspect that running will be futile. And besides," Andras glanced at me, "it may not be a bad thing for all of the attention to be focused on me for a while."

I followed Pearce and his men as they led Andras through the house. "Albert," I said. "Where are you taking him?"

"Somewhere he can't do any more harm," he replied. "I am under strict orders to—"

"Yeah, yeah, I know," I said. "He says he wants to help us stop Gaap."

"I think we can manage without help from the likes of this duplicitous creature."

"Such confidence from the humans," mocked Andras. "Do you realise how powerful Gaap is? And if he has a Mage at his command as well, then yo—"

"Be quiet," snapped Pearce. "What did he say to you?" he asked me.

"He says there's something big brewing, something connected to what Lexie reckons she's found in St Albans. Gaap's going to create some big, everlasting portal to bring a demon army through and Maxwell's the key to him being able to do that."

"Tempus fugit," said Andras. "Time is fleeting... you know, your chances of success would be much improved if you had me fighting beside you."

"And then we just watch as you double-cross us once again?" Pearce sneered. "I think not."

"I would not do that," said Andras.

"You did it before,"

"Granted, it would very much be true to form for me, but—"

"Your words mean nothing here," Pearce interrupted.

"On the contrary, you would do well to listen. I am not the threat here. I have had no hand in what Gaap is planning, and I have always been opposed to him on a matter of principle. We are mortal enemies, and Gaap works for creatures who en masse are infinitely more dangerous than I could ever hope to be."

"Again, we have only your word for all of this."

"Agreed, but you can use the evidence of your own eyes. What about the increasingly bizarre decisions of your leaders?"

"What do you mean?"

"For instance, your Queen creating the Witchfinder General posts, which have had the sole effect of confusing and scaring half the population, setting them against each other and actually getting in the way of your efforts to combat the demonic threat. And then there's your very recent conversation with your Prime Minister."

Pearce blinked. "How did you...?"

I looked from one to the other: Pearce was suddenly thrown off-guard, while Andras grinned back at him. "Albert, what's he talking about?" I asked.

He frowned at Andras and then turned back to me. "I went to the General to request troops for the expedition to St Albans, as we'd discussed. He was with the Prime Minister. I was ordered to stand down and tell you to gather more evidence before we proceeded. When we have enough information, the Prime Minister wants it to be discussed by a full committee before any action is taken."

"But that'll take ages, surely? Doesn't he know how urgent this is?"

"Both the General and I tried to explain but we were given very firm orders." He turned to Andras. "Do I detect your hand in this?"

"Alas, no. I can influence people to do my bidding, but it needs to be in line with what they would otherwise do if they were given some firm and enticing incentive. I think even I would struggle to tempt Disraeli to put his country in mortal peril."

Pearce frowned at him, clearly still not convinced. "And yet you knew about our conversation. How?"

"I am a demon," he shrugged. "It surely is not beyond the realms of the believable to imagine that I can hear things you cannot."

"Let's just say we do believe you," said Pearce. "What could have made the Prime Minister behave in the way that he has?"

"Do you remember when Augustus and I told you of our encounter with the Mage back in Sheffield?"

I felt a cold chill run down my spine. "You think that thing is controlling Disraeli?"

Andras nodded. "As well as your Queen."

Pearce frowned but before he could say any more there was a banging on the door. One of the soldiers went to answer and was roughly thrust aside as the door swung open to reveal a man in a dark cloak and tall hat.

"Morley," I hissed.

"Ah, Miss Thatcher," he said. "Strange how we keep bumping into each other in such circumstances. People would start to think there was something unusual going on that we needed to discuss."

"What do you want?" asked Pearce.

"Your prisoner. I believe you are holding a certain demon here; I have a warrant that enables me to take possession of the creature." He handed over a piece of paper.

"Signed by the Queen herself," said Pearce slowly. "But how did you know we had Andras here?"

"I have my sources," he said, starting to make his way past us.

"No, but really," persisted Pearce, moving to block him from passing. "I did not know until I arrived here that the demon was in this house, and it has been less than ten minutes since we apprehended him. No word has gone out from my men as to what is going on here, so how could you possibly know? Let alone arrange a warrant from the Queen?"

Morley glared at him. "There exist protocols and intelligence that are beyond the wit of a mere army Captain," he spat. "Just be satisfied that we are all working for the common good. Or do you wish to set yourself against us?"

I looked from one to the other, suddenly feeling very lost. I did not trust Morley and I certainly was not stupid enough to even think about trusting Andras. The demon had tricked us before, turned plenty of people into his puppets and there was every chance he would try to do the same to me. But that being the case, what he had said did make a kind of sense.

What if the Queen and Prime Minister were being controlled by a Mage? That would mean that they would try to make sure we didn't get in the way of Gaap's plans, which would mean that the last thing we should do is let Morley have his way. There was something about the thought of handing Andras over to Morley that just didn't feel right.

Morley stepped forwards. "I should advise you that I have nigh-on 50 well-armed men outside. And if I were to let it be known that you were harbouring not only a demon but the hated Andras in here then, well, you will find that pretty much the whole of the local populace would join us in beating down your door and tossing you on a bonfire. Ask yourself, Captain: do you wish to sacrifice not only your job and your reputation but also your mens' lives? All for the sake of this... *fiend?*"

Pearce glared at him for a few more seconds and then stepped aside. "Hand him over," he said to his men.

It felt wrong. We were giving Morley exactly what he wanted, and didn't understand anything about his plans or who he was working for. I opened my mouth to speak but felt something in my head, almost like a comforting hand telling me to stand down. I turned and looked at Andras and he gave me a small nod. *Let it go,* the feeling in my head said. *Use this distraction.* I blinked; maybe there really was more of N'yotsu in there than he was letting on.

Morley gestured to two of his men, who stepped round carrying what looked like blunderbusses with some form of blunted grappling hooks wedged in the muzzles. Andras held out his hands. "Don't worry lads, I'll come quietly."

Morley nodded and the two men fired their weapons. I flinched, expecting the loud bang of gunfire to echo round the room, but instead there was a slight fizzle as the grappling hooks flew out, embedding themselves in Andras' sides. The demon immediately fell to his knees, his face screwed up in soundless agony. "I know you will come quietly," said Morley. "And this will make sure that you do." He turned to his men. "Get the creature up and into the wagon."

"What is that?" I asked, watching as Andras was bundled to his feet, no more than a helpless shaking invalid.

"A new weapon we've been saving for just this type of occasion," said Morley smugly.

"How'd you get it?"

"It was developed by our finest scientists."

I frowned at him. "I've spent the past three years with the only person in the world who could've made something like that, and I've never seen its kind before. There are no other geniuses out there who make weapons like this: I'd know. At least, none that are human..."

I thought I saw a flicker of doubt in Morley's eyes, but it was gone as quickly as it appeared. "Really, Miss Thatcher, do you truly believe that you are the conduit for all knowledge in the Empire?"

He held out his hand to me. "We would like you to accompany us as well, please."

"Me? Where?"

"Back with me for questioning. I trust I will not have to use force?"

I saw Pearce bristle at this, but I put a hand out to tell him to hold back; I didn't need him wading in and making things worse just yet. "Questioning? About what?"

"Your associations with the demon Andras, for one thing. I need to be sure that I have all of the facts."

"Under whose authority are you planning to try to take her?" asked Pearce.

"My own, conferred upon me by Her Majesty the Queen. I am Witchfinder General after all, and this type of matter falls directly within my jurisdiction."

"I cannot allow you to take her," said Pearce hesitantly.

Morley cocked an eyebrow at him. "You do realise that if you interfere with my duties then you are effectively committing a criminal offence? Not to mention mutiny against your sovereign, which I believe is classified as high treason? And did not the Prime Minister directly order you to assist me?"

Pearce seemed to collapse inside. "I will come with you as well."

"You will stay here at 24 Whitehall and keep the Bradshaw children under guard in Mr Potts' laboratory. After all, they are still important to the cause, and there are dangerous demons about."

Pearce took a deep breath, fists clenched, and I could see he was about to do something he'd regret. "It's all right Albert," I said. "I can handle myself. I'll be back in no time. You're more use out here than being locked up with me. Remember the Prime Minister's orders," I said this last bit as pointedly as I could, hoping the sense of my words got through to him in spite of his agitation.

Pearce glared at Morley. "If you harm so much as one hair on her head…"

Morley nodded without waiting for him to finish. "Very good. Now, Miss Thatcher, if you don't mind?"

I shared a nod with Pearce and then started to walk out with Morley. "You do realise that you're playing into the demons' hands here?" I asked him. "While we're busy talking, they could be ending the world."

"Then all the more reason for us to get back so that you can tell me everything you know."

CHAPTER TWENTY

I sat in the carriage as far away from Morley as I could, refusing to give him even a glance as we rattled our way through the traffic round Trafalgar Square and then on up the Strand. I looked out at the buildings as we passed, the grand hotels and taverns, wondering if this was the last time I'd see them. People on the streets went about their business, some stopping to curse and glare at our horses and coaches as we forced them to squeeze to the sides of the road, blissfully unaware of who was inside and the threats they posed to their ordinary little lives.

A sudden shaft of sunlight glanced off a window and made me shield my eyes. By the side of the road, a man with a pail of water stepped back from a window to admire his handiwork. A pair of Peelers wandered past and I wondered whether I should try shouting out for help, pull open the door and throw myself on them. But then I remembered that Morley was one of them, and they'd like as not just hand me back to him. At least if I was going with Morley without kicking up a fuss then hopefully he'd treat me right in return.

Going along for the ride also meant that I could find out where he was taking Andras. The demon had been a helpless shell in those strange hook restraints, offering no resistance at all as they'd bundled him into the carriage behind ours. Again I wondered about the technology they'd used in controlling him: where did they get it from? The more I thought about it, the more it made sense—the Queen and who knew how many others must be being controlled by some sort of demon, and right now Morley was helping them by making sure we couldn't get in the way of their plans.

I forced myself to turn and look at him. "You never said where them restraints came from," I said.

"No, I didn't," he replied, staring at a wad of papers on his lap.

"You've got to admit, it's a bit odd that you've suddenly found a way to control demons, ain't it?"

"It is a useful tool that will greatly aid us in our struggle to regain control of our world. I tend to make it a habit not to look a gift horse in the mouth."

"Getting on four years now we've been fighting demons," I said. "Me, Max, Gus and N'yotsu. Four years, two of them with full access to everything the British Empire has to offer, and all we came up with was the pistols and swords Max and N'yotsu made. Then you bowl in with these strange manacles that suddenly turn a big scary demon like Andras into a gibbering wreck."

"Clearly you and your friends were not as talented or as diligent as you were made out to be. Or maybe you were not privy to all of the devices that Mr Potts has created."

"I was with Max day and night. I knew everything," I said fiercely. How dare he suggest I was kept out of things?

Morley looked up at me. "Everything? Really? So tell me: where is Mr Augustus Potts right now?"

I blushed and looked away, angry with myself for letting my guard down so quickly. I remembered what Gus had said about the Witchfinders back in the day, what they'd do with a few careless words here or there. I had to be careful with what I said, as people like Morley would look for any chance to twist my words and use them to incriminate my friends.

Morley sighed. "Miss Thatcher, you really should learn to trust me; we are both on the same side here."

I snorted and folded my arms. "You keep saying that, and the more you do the less I believe it."

"How can I prove to you that my intentions really do align with yours?" he asked. "That we both want the same thing?"

"Let me go so I can get to St Albans and help fight the demons. Come with me and bring all your men and lynch mobs and strange tools; I reckon we'll need all the bodies we can get. But do it now, before it's too late." The carriage jolted and there was a shout from outside, which reminded me about the other carriage in our little convoy. "And free Andras so he can help us as well." This last bit came out of nowhere and for a moment I bit my lip. It made perfect sense though: if Morley wanted Andras locked away, and Morley was acting on the orders of the demons who wanted to take over the world, then the best thing to do was to set Andras loose. After all, we were running short of allies powerful enough to fight the demons.

Morley raised an eyebrow. "Let us say for one moment that I take leave of all my senses and do as you suggest. What is at St Albans?"

I thought for a moment; while I didn't want to do anything to help this foul man, there was surely little damage in him knowing a bit of what we knew. "The end of the world. Max talked about a thing called the Fulcrum, where—"

"Yes, yes, I know all about that theory. I have read the papers."

"How did you...?"

"I have authority in many things," he said. "My employer allows me access to anything that might assist me in my work. But do continue."

"Well... we reckon that the Fulcrum has an actual location where it's going to emerge, and that's in St Albans."

"I thought it was supposed to be Nonsuch?"

"So did we. But when we went to Nonsuch there was nothing there."

"Apart from the demons that attacked you."

"Yes." I frowned at him. "Why do I get the feeling you know everything already?"

He inclined his head. "Pray continue."

"When Max disappeared, it was the papers about St Albans that went missing, and we've seen nothing convincing about Nonsuch. Lexie and Joshua have been doing their sums and they reckon it's a definite that St Albans is where the Fulcrum's going to be. Which is why we need to get there right now."

"Why the urgency?"

I wanted to throttle him. "The demons are going to create another portal, right where the Fulcrum is, and they're going to bring an army through to invade."

"And you know this... how?"

"Andras—" I stopped myself but it was already too late.

"Because the demon said so," said Morley with a smug grin on his face. "What else did he tell you? That I'm the enemy? That all your superiors are working against you to try to make this demon threat happen?"

I pursed my lips and kept my teeth clenched tight.

He put his papers onto the bench beside him. "Miss Thatcher, you of all people must realise that demons are not to be trusted. Particularly not the one we have in captivity back there. There is a very specific plan to save the world, and we all need to work together to achieve it."

"What is it then?" I asked.

"Pardon?"

"What is this grand plan to save the world? You said we all need to work together, we're all on the same side and I've been a part of a team at the centre of what the army and government have been trying to do all these years. So I'm wondering what this plan is and why I've not heard of it."

Morley let out a short laugh. "It is I who is supposed to be questioning you, not the other way round. But... very well. The demons are a stain, a blot on our world. They corrupt and pervert all that they come into contact with. They spread fear and confusion, infiltrating families and tearing them apart." I could see a real hatred in his eyes, which got bigger and bigger the more he spoke, lit up with righteousness. "Innocents are turned into hateful monsters at the behest of the demons, playthings of these creatures that think themselves gods. There is only one true God and He is the opposite of everything these creatures represent." He glared at me and I reckoned I could see tears just behind those hard, cold eyes.

I hated the demons but what I saw in his eyes was something more than that. "What did they do to you?" I asked as softly as I could.

"What do you mean?"

"To make you hate them so much. This isn't just a job for you, is it? They did something horrible to you. Or was it your family?"

For a moment I thought he was going to say something but then the shutters came down. "No more talking," he said. "When we reach the Tower you will tell me exactly what you and Andras have been discussing."

"The...?" I asked, and then looked out the window. While we'd been talking we'd made our way beyond St Paul's and wound down past the brand new Cannon Street Station and onto East Cheap. The road curved round to the right and there, down at the bottom of Great Tower Street, I could see the dark walls of the Tower of London. My heart beat hard as I heard my Pa's barking voice: *"You behave, girl, or I'll take you off to the Tower. You know what they do to people in there?"*

I looked back at Morley. "Why are we going there?"

"Why, did you not know?" he asked. "It is my base of operations when I am working out of London. A very useful location, and full of everything I need."

I looked away so he couldn't see the fear I felt as I remembered Gus' talk of the confessions that the old Witchfinders forced out of people through torture. Of all places, it just had to be the Tower, didn't it?

CHAPTER TWENTY-ONE

Our carriage was waved through the big dark wooden gates by a pair of soldiers who didn't give me a second glance. Time was, they'd have saluted me; had things really gone downhill so quickly?

We clattered over the drawbridge, through the next set of gates and over the cobblestones running along the inner wall. We stopped and the carriage doors were wrenched open by two men dressed in dark clothes just like Morley, who grabbed me and pulled me out. I struggled against them but they held me firm. "Hey," I said, "I've come here by my own choice!"

"Indeed you have," said Morley. "That is why you are not in chains. But even so, you will forgive us if we take some precautions, given the severity of the situation."

As my feet hit the ground I looked up to see a stone archway in front of me, dipping into the river on either side, a thick gate shut firm below it. Traitors' Gate. The nightmares came flooding back once more as I stared at it, wondering if this was an omen. Thankfully, I was pulled away before I could dwell on it any further.

I watched as the door to the other carriage was pulled open and the helpless lump of Andras was half-dragged, half-carried out. He was thrown to the ground and then picked up by the shoulders and hauled through an archway ahead of me, heels digging shallow furrows in the mire.

We went through the arch and up the stairs beyond and as we passed I noticed how the soldiers standing guard did anything to avoid eye contact with me. Rather than turning right towards the White Tower, we were dragged round to the left and towards a grey stone building that looked like the White Tower's little brother, dumped in the middle of a load of brown stone and timbered houses. We passed a small green in front of a chapel and Morley leered at me. "Do you know what that is?" he asked. I refused to give him the satisfaction of replying but he continued anyway. "That is where they used to execute the traitors held prisoner here. And this is where you're going to stay." He pointed at the building in front of us.

I was practically thrown down a flight of stairs and into the grey stone building while Andras was pushed and pulled through a small doorway to the left. I could see a narrow spiral staircase beyond before the door was slammed shut and bolted behind his escort.

"Wait here please," said Morley behind me as the door to the outside was slammed shut, leaving me alone in the room.

"Like I have a choice," I muttered as I heard the ominous clank-scrape of a key turning in the lock.

I turned and looked around the room, which was lit by flickering torches. It was roughly curved on the sides directly opposite the main door, with archways picked out at regular intervals containing narrow slit windows. A large fireplace stood to the left of the arches, filled with wood but unlit. To the left of the door I had entered through was a stained-glass window, like you'd see in a cathedral or stately home. I looked out to see two of Morley's men standing guard, their backs to me.

I turned back to continue examining the room. The remaining wall to the left of the window was straight and covered in hooks, bolts and nails. I saw something dark lying against it and went over to get a closer look, flinching when I saw it was a pair of leather manacles hanging about seven feet off the ground.

The flickering torches and the faint light from the windows showed that the walls were covered in rough etchings, words and simple inscriptions that looked to have been done by many different people over a long period of time. With a sinking heart I realised that they must have been left by the poor souls who had been locked away in this room over the centuries, with nothing else to do but try to leave their mark on a world that had turned its back on them.

In the middle of the room was a long table, a solid wooden

bench with straps set in it. Next to it was another table covered by a cloth. I walked over and slowly pulled back a corner of the stained material to see a few pairs of pincers, and then a dozen wicked-looking knives and various other implements that made me shudder just to look at them. I picked up a small but razor-sharp knife that looked big enough to do some damage but small enough to hide in a fold of my dress. I arranged the other knives on the table so it wasn't obvious there was a gap and then pulled the cloth back over them. *That'll teach them to leave me in a room with weapons in it*, I thought with a mirthless grin.

I wanted someone to come in at that moment so I could keep myself occupied with action, but there was no sound from outside the room so I busied myself with learning the feel of the weapon, swiping it to and fro in the air a few times and then secreting it in the waistband of my dress, the space where Morley had taken my pistol from. I practised whipping it out a few times and then, happy I'd got the action down pat as well as I could, wandered round the room, straining my ears for any sort of sound from beyond the locked door.

There was nothing but the crackle of the torches, and that silence was worse than if I'd heard screaming or pleading; at least those sounds would have kept me company of sorts.

I hummed a few tunes, desperate to fill that silence with something, anything. I put a hand on one of the walls, peering at the words and symbols scratched there. How many others had paced around that cell before me, I wondered? How many people had been tortured and killed inside these walls over the centuries, or just left to rot and die? Was I going to be abandoned there too, slowly turning into a gibbering wreck while my friends were slaughtered and the whole world turned to ashes?

My toes curled at how helpless I felt and I suddenly realised how cold I was. Goosebumps broke out on my arms and I paced harder, stamping my feet and swinging my hands as I went. My mind kept going back to all the stories I'd heard of the people who'd been held in the Tower over the years.

A hunched shadow in the corner of the room could almost have been the headless body of Anne Boleyn, still raging at how she'd been cast aside by fat King Henry. I fancied I could see her reaching out to me, begging me to join her in Purgatory.

I remembered the story Pa used to scare my brothers, of the

two princes that had been entombed in the Tower by the hunchback King Richard so he could take their throne. Two scared little boys, not even given the chance to grow into young men, locked away forever. Maybe they'd been trapped in this room as well? Was that shadow...?

I felt so helpless and alone, so very aware that I had only the clothes I was wearing and the small knife at my waist between me and whatever terrors Morley had planned.

I jumped as a key clanked in the lock and the door creaked open. I reached down and felt the weight of the knife. *Wait until the right moment,* I told myself. *Let him get close enough.*

I glared at Morley as he entered the room, noting that the door wasn't locked behind him. The guards were probably still outside, but I'd deal with them in good time.

"I am sorry to keep you waiting," he said.

"No you're not," I snapped back. "Look, what's this all about? You trying to scare me by putting me in here or what?"

He shook his head and walked over to the covered table. I held my breath and tried to look as casually innocent as I could while he glanced beneath the cloth. I let out a relieved shudder when he looked back up without showing any sign of suspicion. "Not at all. We have only been given a few rooms in this building and I am afraid they all lack home comforts. But they serve a purpose. As I said, I just need you to answer a few questions and then we can move on."

"To what?"

"Well, to whatever it is that we need to do to ensure that we defeat the demon threat."

I walked casually round towards him, trying to keep the side where I'd hidden the knife away from him. "So you'll let me go?"

"All in good time. But first, tell me when you first encountered Andras. After the initial confrontation in Greenwich, that is."

I folded my arms. "Aren't you going to offer me a seat? Not very gentlemanly of you, is it?"

"Really, Miss Thatcher, you are the one who keeps saying how urgent everything is. Would it not be in both our interests if you just told me all that you know without engaging in silly pantomimes? But if you want to sit..." He gestured to the table with the straps on it.

"No, thanks," I said, trying hard not to look at it. "They're using you, you know: the demons. You think you're fighting them but everything you've been doing has just been playing straight into their hands."

"In what way?"

"Stopping us, holding us back, getting in our way." I gestured with my free hand. "Locking us up here. If there's a demon attack on its way, how does it help our cause if I'm stuck here?"

He laughed. "I think that you overestimate your capabilities, Miss Thatcher. N'yotsu and Augustus were formidable fighters. Maxwell is a genius. But what did you do, exactly?" He was now close enough that I could make out the stains on his teeth in the flickering light and smell his foul breath.

"Thing is," I said, "People have always underestimated me. Usually it's the last thing they do." Just as I'd practised, I whipped the knife out and brought it round to slash up at his face and neck.

He batted my fist aside and the knife flew out of my hand, clanging against the far wall. My right hand was numb with the force of the blow so I launched at him with my left, snarling as I threw my head at him as well.

He picked me up and slammed me down on the bench. I struggled against him as I fought desperately to get a limb free. Then there were others in the room, pinning my ankles and wrists, strapping me down. After a few minutes I was stuck fast to the solid wood.

Breathing hard, Morley stepped back. He waved away the others who'd come into the room and then glared down at me. "I had hoped that we could do this the civilised way, but if not..." He pulled the cloth from the other table. "I have much quicker and more effective ways of getting what I want."

PART III

AUGUSTUS

PETER OXLEY

CHAPTER TWENTY-TWO

The world became a swirl of wind and green and dark as I ran into the twilight away from Nonsuch, desperate to escape but knowing that I could never flee from the one thing that terrified me the most: myself. The memory of their faces was still raw in my mind: N'yotsu trying to coax me back to my senses, Captain Pearce ordering his men to hold fire, the look of disgust from Kate...

Night had fallen by the time I staggered to a halt, collapsing into a hedge and welcoming the darkness that came from being enveloped in its spiky embrace.

I awoke when the moon was high in the sky, its huge full face casting judgement down on me. "I am not one of them," I said through gritted teeth. "I am not!"

I ran my tongue around my mouth and noted that all seemed back to normal. I looked down at my hands and then touched my face: I was human once again. I crawled out of the hedge and collapsed to the ground, sobbing, the memory of my friends' faces still fresh in my mind.

It was late afternoon the next day by the time that I reached the Thames and staggered over Fulham Bridge with the rest of the traffic, looking and smelling for all the world like just another vagabond come to try my luck in the big city. I rummaged in my jacket for my purse, feeling the weight of the coins there as I eyed the hansom cabs running by. In spite of all the time I had spent travelling alone, I still had no plan of action. I needed inspiration and so headed for the nearest tavern.

Firmly ensconced in a darkened corner, I considered my options. My friends and the army would clearly be looking for me, the latter most likely intending to capture me. I imagined N'yotsu's protestations of my innocence being overridden by Kate and Pearce arguing that I was now just another mindless, homicidal demon. In a way they had a point: I had nearly attacked N'yotsu and in the heat of that bloodlust I would have probably tried to kill him.

Regardless of my friends' reactions, it seemed that I was approaching the stage that I had been dreading for some time—I was becoming a danger to all of those around me. That was a risk I was not willing to take; while the sword's powers had at first been a boon, now they were a hindrance. Not for the first time I considered getting rid of it, removing the source of all those terrible changes. However, the sword's pull on me was too great: even the thought of being without it made me shiver in panic. I would need help to undertake such a painful divorce.

I thought back to what my friends would do when they saw me next. Would they be supportive or would they try to imprison or kill me? Time and again my mind's eye flashed back to Nonsuch and the looks on the faces of Kate, Joshua, Lexie, Pearce and the soldiers. I had been out of control; it was a wonder that I had not been gunned down where I stood.

Nor could I just roam free, for if I was a risk to my friends then I was also a risk to the general public. I was caught in a dilemma— a fugitive who did not wish to be imprisoned but who also knew that imprisonment was probably the best thing for me and everyone else.

Two ales later, I made my decision. I would go back to my friends and surrender myself in the hope that they would welcome me and help to find a cure for my condition, whether that was by removing the sword from me or even something more invasive. Neither thought appealed to me but I had brought this upon myself by ignoring what had been happening for far too long. I needed to do something before it was too late, before I turned permanently and irreversibly into a demon.

Thus resigned to my fate I had another drink to seal in my courage, then another to work up the courage to leave the pub, and then…

The girl who sat at my table was clearly a whore but by that point I no longer cared; if this was to be my last night of freedom then I was determined to enjoy it. To my addled senses her grimy face and gap-toothed grin were a vision of loveliness, and in any case I was too soiled and travel-stained to complain about another's personal hygiene.

More drinks were followed by a drunken stagger to a nearby establishment where I parted with yet more coins in return for a room key. I threw open the door to the bedroom and allowed her to push me onto the bed, clothes ripping away in urgency before...

I awoke to the sound of screaming. Groaning, I grabbed a pillow and held it over my ears. The screaming did not stop and I opened one eye, realising that the sound came from nearby. I rolled over to see the girl having backed away into the corner of the room, a sheet pulled around her as she stared at me with wide, terrified eyes and continued to scream.

I held out my hands to placate her and then stopped, staring down in cold shock. Those were not my arms, they could not be my arms. These were red and veined and angular and covered in runic characters that flexed and coiled under my skin.

I darted over to the mirror. "No," I said. Then louder: "No-no-no-no-no!"

A demon shouted back at me, mimicking my words, a demon that seemed to have borrowed some approximate outline of my form, but a demon nonetheless. Three horns sprouted from atop an angular head that was patterned around and around with the swirling runic symbols, sickeningly dancing before me. My eyes in turn were large, triangular and bright red, while sharp teeth protruded from an over-wide mouth. The runic symbols continued down my body and...

"What's going on in there?" shouted a man's voice from outside, followed by hammering on the door.

"It's a, it's a—" stammered the girl, before screaming again.

"Please," I said, lisping through the unfamiliar teeth. "Please, calm down. It's all right, I won't hurt—."

She continued to scream as whoever was outside the room started kicking at the door. I looked around; I did not have much time and if I was caught in this state I would surely be lynched. I grabbed the sword and my clothes and threw myself out of the window.

I hit the ground hard, but an impact that would have wounded or killed a human barely made me pause. People scattered around me, screaming, and I heard a shout from the right. Turning, I saw two policemen running towards me, truncheons raised. I snarled; I could easily take them on.

"No." The word from my lips shocked sense back to me in spite of my rising panic and I turned and ran.

I lay on my back in a derelict building, sucking in sobbed breaths as my ears strained to pick out any sounds from my pursuers. All seemed clear and so I returned my focus to my body, willing it to change back. I closed my eyes and concentrated on my breathing, on slowing my heartbeat and calming my mind.

Minutes or maybe hours passed and I felt myself drifting into a serenity that should surely have been impossible given the day I had just had. Since fleeing from the brothel, I had found myself pursued at every turn, with no shortage of witnesses to point out my whereabouts to the police and the army that was in pursuit. I had a sudden affinity with the fox chased by horse and hounds, knowing that there was nowhere I could hide that would not eventually be sniffed out.

The main problem was that I was in London, or at least its outskirts, which was far too densely populated to allow me to sneak away without being noticed. That left me with a limited number of options. I could seek out my friends and fall on their mercy; however, Whitehall was by that point many miles away and my route was blocked by my pursuers. Alternatively, I could head for one of the areas of the city that were still under demon control; the police and soldiers would definitely not follow me there. However, there were drawbacks to this option as well. Even if I managed to get there without being killed or captured, there was every chance that I would not be welcomed as I had killed enough demons in my time to make me a very well-known enemy to them. Worse still, going there would simply reinforce any views my erstwhile friends and colleagues may have had that I was now just another evil demon that needed to be put to the sword, or worse.

That only left one option: to flee London and take refuge somewhere secluded, reassess my options and then decide what to do next. This I did, and my enhanced demonic speed enabled me to quickly outrun my pursuers once I was away from the streets and out into the open fields of Surrey.

I had stopped once to try to find some food, to eat something while I rested my tired limbs. The smell of fresh bread wafted out of the window of a nearby cottage and I sneaked up, taking care to keep low and in the shadow of the trees and bushes. There was no one around and I chanced a sprint towards the house, reaching into the window to grab the loaf cooling on the side. I spun round at a gasp from behind me to see a little girl standing on the path, a ragged doll hanging limply at her side as she stared open-mouthed at me.

I held out a hand, wordlessly begging her to stay calm and be quiet.

Her face had twisted into one of pure terror and revulsion and in that moment I had a flash of empathy with Mary Shelley's monster, misunderstood and despised by everyone just because of the way I looked. I had run, the girl's screams ringing in my ears, not stopping until I ended up in an abandoned barn.

I sat up and opened my eyes, looking hopefully at my hands but then letting out a stream of curses when I saw them still unchanged. I slammed down a fist, breaking through the rough floorboards and wedging my hand into the ground beneath. With a roar, I pulled it loose and looked around for something else to vent my frustration on.

"You know, for someone who's supposed to be in hiding you're not doing a very good job of keeping quiet."

I whirled round to see a figure leaning against the wall, shrouded in shadow.

"Who are you?" I asked.

The figure stepped forwards and revealed himself to be a short, squat man with dark hair and a round face covered in a vast beard. He removed his hat and I was shocked to see a pair of furry pointed ears sat atop his head. "The name's Byron," he said, "and I am a demon, like you."

"I'm not..."

"I know, I know," he said, holding up a hand to ward off my offence. "I'm a Pooka, not exactly like you. But we're still kind of kin, distant brethren. I saw you being chased around and thought I'd see if I could lend a hand."

"Lend a hand?" I asked. "When exactly? I don't remember any

help being offered when I was being chased through London by a blood-thirsty mob."

"Well, no. But I'm here now, aren't I?" He glared at me. "What do you expect? I'm a Pooka: we know better than to throw our weight around in public. Not like you lot."

"Us lot?"

"You warrior demons; although I have to confess I don't recognise your race. You're not Almadite, are you?"

"No," I said. "I'm human."

"Yeah," he laughed. "And I'm really Lord Byron, back from the dead—I just had a few too many drinks!" His laughter tailed off as I glared back at him. "You weren't joking, were you?"

I clenched my fists. "Thank you for your offer, but I need no assistance. Especially not from the likes of you. Good day, sir."

Byron looked at me and then folded his arms. "Now, I may be many things, just ask my Ma, but I've never turned my back on a soul in need. And you, my friend, are very much in need if you ask me."

"I am not your friend," I said through gritted teeth. "And I need no help."

"Really? Let us appraise the situation." He paced the room, ignoring the fact that I had drawn my sword and was pointing it at him. "You have spent the day with most of London chasing you. There's a question of why you found yourself in the middle of the human area of London with no back-up: even the most dull-witted of warriors know better than to do that. Even worse, no demons came to your aid in spite of the rumpus you created, meaning none were inclined to help you. And you say you think you're human." He perched himself on an old cart. "I would say you really do need help and, given all I've said, I don't think you're in a position to turn down any help that is offered to you."

I glared back at him, but I could not help but acknowledge the sense in what he said. "And why should I trust you?" I asked.

"There's a human saying I quite like: beggars can't be choosers. Quite apt, no?"

"That doesn't answer my question."

He sighed. "I'm beginning to think you really are human; no demon would ever be this pig-headed and suspicious. Look, if what you say is true and you are a human stuck in a demonic body, then you're in real trouble—the humans will kill you and the Almadites will do far worse."

"And you?"

"Like I said, I'm a Pooka, which is great news for you."

"And why is that?" I asked.

"Because the Almadites hate me even more than they will you, so we've got something to base our blossoming friendship on. Now, could you please put the sword down? It's making me nervous."

I glared at the creature for a long while, trying to decide whether or not I should trust him. Then again, if he had planned to attack me or had a horde outside waiting to overwhelm me, then I would in all probability already be dead. In any case, I had nothing left to lose. I lowered the sword, returning it to the scabbard on my back.

"That's quite a fine weapon you have there," said Byron. "Where did you get it?"

"A friend forged it for me."

"From what I can tell, there are some pretty powerful symbols etched into it. And etched into you too, for that matter. I'm guessing they're the source of your power?"

"Maybe."

He sighed. "Look, if we're going to be friends then I'm going to need a bit more out of you, as I get bored very easily."

"I told you, we are not friends."

"All right." He walked towards me. "Let me be clear. I'm proposing an arrangement that will work for both of us. You clearly need help, if only guidance on how to get around without making half a city eager to kill you. Also, if you really are—or were—human, then I can help you come to terms with your powers. In return, you can do something for me."

"Which is?"

He grinned. "It's a tough world, with lots of people wanting to kill the likes of me on sight. More and more of them each day, it seems. Over the past few weeks many of my people have disappeared, and I don't intend to be one of them. I need someone who can fight with me if things ever get rough. Four fists are better than two, as they say. Swords also."

"You need a bodyguard," I said, then remembering something I had once said to Kate, I added: "A blunt instrument."

"Exactly," he grinned. "Like I said, the perfect team!"

I grudgingly agreed that Byron could stay in the barn with me overnight, although this meant that I spent most of the time jumping at every sound and movement, fearful that the demon would attack me when my back was turned. As the sunlight broke through the cracks in the wooden boards that made up the walls I gingerly touched my head and face, heart sinking as I realised that I still had not changed back. Was this the way I was doomed to remain? Had the sword finally caused irreversible damage to me? I slumped to the floor and stared up at the rafters, trying to force myself to work through my options calmly.

It was no use. Every time I tried to concentrate my mind swam back to the faces of my friends, those faces that would never look at me in the same way again. My life as I had once known it was over; I was destined to be hunted and reviled for the rest of my days.

"You know," said Byron, "if you wanted to make a run for it somewhere, you really should have done so before the sun came up. It's a bit busy out there now."

I levered myself upright and looked through a crack in the wall. The road passing by the building seemed to have a constant stream of traffic, while the fields beyond were being tended by a gang of labourers. "No matter," I said, slumping back down to continue my examination of the barn's vaulted ceiling.

"You never gave me an answer last night," continued Byron, "as to whether or not you'd be agreeable to working with me."

"No. You're right, I didn't."

"So...?"

I sighed. "I am having trouble deciding whether or not to trust you."

"Aha! So you're not as stupid as you look!" He held up his hands when I turned to give him a baleful stare. "All I'm saying is that you're right to do so. Those who trust strangers blindly these days tend to find themselves minus a major organ. Especially when it comes to demonkind."

The silence stretched out between us until I felt compelled to fill it. "Every demon that I have ever met has tried to kill me. Why should you be any different?"

"Why indeed? Well, I told you the main reason last night: I'm a Pooka." He sat back as though that answered everything.

I shrugged. "That means nothing to me."

"Nothing? You're a demon. Where have you been hiding not to have heard of the Pooka?"

"I told you last night. I am not a demon. I am—"

"—human, yes, you said. And I'm beginning to half-believe you, apart from the big horns on your head, the pointy teeth and the severe sunburn. Care to explain them?"

I frowned. There was every chance that this creature would sell me to the highest bidder if he knew who I really was. I had managed to avoid giving my name to him and it would serve me better to preserve my anonymity until I understood his motivations a little better. If it were possible to understand a demon's motivations, that is.

"Very well," Byron continued. "Let's leave that for the moment and assume that you in fact have absolutely no knowledge about demons apart from the fact that we've got bumpy heads and come from far, far away. That a fair starting point?"

I nodded my head slowly.

"I come from a realm that your people sometimes call Tir nAill, sometimes Tir na nÓg. It was a peaceful place, where rivers ran gold and green under mountains that touched the stars. The sky was always crowded, with five suns and three moons and herds of Beithsc'athanach carving through the clouds."

"What?" I asked.

"Big things with wings: taste delicious. Anyway, we were and always have been a peaceful people, never a threat to anyone."

"Apart from the Beith-things."

"Well, yes. And other food besides. Look, do you want to hear this or not?" I held up a hand in apology and he continued: "As I said, we have always been a peaceful race. But then one day the portal opened to Almadel." He looked at me.

I shrugged. "You say that like it should mean something to me."

He stared at me for a moment. "Almadel is home to most of the creatures you now see invading this realm. It is a terrible place, home to beasts whose only desire is to conquer and destroy. They have some utterly ruthless leaders—"

"Like the Four Kings?" I asked.

"Aha, so you're not as ill-informed as you appear. Yes, like the Four Kings. Although they were minor leaders when my realm was invaded. The leader at that time was a creature named Andras." He noted the sudden intent look in my eyes and nodded. "I see you have heard of him. The God of Lies, the Soulstealer." He shuddered. "They swept into my world without mercy, killing anyone who might be a threat and enslaving the rest. Within a generation we were reduced to slaves, along with all the others whom the Almadites have invaded over the millennia."

"And so you managed to escape slavery?" I asked.

He shook his head. "Oh no, not me. I've never been a slave. I was one of the lucky ones. When the Almadites invaded I was posted in the Eternal Mines, deep down, protecting the miners there. You see, I was a soldier and we had received intelligence that it was the mines that were the Almadites' target. We never thought they would risk an all-out assault on our home, or that they even knew how to reach it. How very wrong we were. When we heard about the invasion it was already too late: we were outnumbered and our home was overrun." He shuddered for a moment, then looked up and grinned. "The great thing about the Eternal Mines is that they lead everywhere and nowhere, which means that those who know their way around them can lead those who don't on a merry dance. The Almadites sent warriors down after us… for all I know, they're still down there, wandering round."

"How long did you remain in the mines?" I asked.

"Time ceased to have any meaning. There's light down there, from plants and creatures and rocks, but it doesn't correspond to any particular time of day or night. Luckily there's plenty of food and water too, but it was still hard. Occasionally we would launch attacks on the surface to try to rescue our people…" He shuddered again.

"What?" I asked.

"To know how truly terrible the Almadites are, you need to see what they do to your home. I remember going to the surface what must have been a few years after the invasion. All that I had known was gone; the once beautiful sky was a bitter miasma—a cloying, pungent mist. The rivers were black and steaming with foul effluent. The mountains were being broken down by slaves, the once perfect peaks now little more than jagged shards, as though they had been beaten insensible by a million hammers wielded by a million spiteful children. And as for the slave camps…" His eyes welled up with tears and he took a deep breath before continuing.

"Everyone they had not killed had been forced into camps,

where they were stripped of everything: not just their freedom but their free will and even the knowledge that they had once been free. They were little more than shells, empty vessels for their new Almadite masters to do with as they willed."

There was a long pause while he tried to recover his composure, staring at the floor as he relived those horrors, the torment flickering across his face like storm clouds on a sunny day.

"I had a family. A wife, children, parents, friends. I saw them there. I wanted to help them but they just looked straight through me. They did not recognise me: the Almadites had taken even that away from them.

"I wished... I wanted so desperately to help them, to rescue them, but there was nothing I could do. One of the slaves realised I was not one of them and before I knew it everyone was shouting, including my wife and children. I ran and escaped back into the mines, but only just. It was then that I realised I no longer had a home. I ran and ran and eventually found myself here." He looked up at me and managed a weak smile. "As I said: the Eternal Mines lead everywhere and nowhere."

"I am sorry," I said softly.

"Why? It was not you who did it."

"It's just, that's the sort of thing we say..."

Shock dawned slowly on his face. "You really are human, aren't you? Underneath all of... that."

"Yes, but how...?"

"In my experience, only humans would display such pointless empathy." He wiped his eyes. "So, you've heard my life story. What about yours?"

"I have not heard your whole life story. When did you come to our realm? What happened then? How were you received?"

He grinned. "Nice try, but that's a tale for another time, not that I'd have any qualms about telling it. But it's your turn now."

I stared at him. While my instincts were still to not trust him, and there was every chance that the story he had just told had been engineered to gain my confidence, there was something about what he had said and the way he had said it that elicited genuine sympathy in me. Besides, if what he said was true, he could be a very useful ally.

"Very well," I said. "I was—I am—a human. But a friend and my brother created this sword for me, which has some fantastic properties. Unfortunately it also seems to have somehow infected me, turning me into the creature you see before you."

Byron was watching me closely. "May I see the weapon?"

After a moment's hesitation, I drew the sword and laid it on the floor. "Do not touch it," I said to him.

"Believe me, I do not wish to." He bent over it to read the inscriptions and then looked back up at me. "What is your name?"

I hesitated and then said it, the words feeling like a blessed release: "Augustus Potts."

"Andras gave you this sword," Byron said slowly, backing away from me and the blade.

"No. N'yotsu did."

He laughed hysterically. "You know what the word 'N'yotsu' means in the old tongue, yes? Destroyer of Worlds! I was going to trust you and all along you've been working for that monster. Well, you will get what you deserve!"

"No, that's not true," I protested. "N'yotsu has expelled everything that made him Andras; all of those elements are safely locked away. He is a good man, he has done so much to help us."

"Like give you the sword that turned you into this?"

"That was different. Back then he was being manipulated by Andras. But no longer; he is his own man now."

"He is a demon, and don't you forget it," Byron spat. "Once an Almadite, always an Almadite."

"No. You do not know him, he's different now. All the time he has spent on Earth has changed him, made him realise how terrible the things he did were. Trust me, he suffers each day for everything he has done."

"And you know this?"

"Actually, I do. The torment is literally tearing him apart, but he will not accept the one thing that would save him, as that would mean him reverting to Andras: something he cannot countenance."

Byron shook his head. "He's still manipulating you even now. There's a reason they call him the God of Lies, you know. There will be some grand scheme behind all of this, and his supposed sacrifice will be at the heart of it. He cannot change his nature. He cannot."

My mind ran through all of my interactions with N'yotsu and Andras, the many times that my friend had saved our lives. But I could not help but also remember the long, drawn out plan that

Andras had once concocted just so that he could achieve his goal of getting a portal to the Aether: manipulating our lives, killing our parents to push Maxwell into his secluded studies, sending N'yotsu to nudge my brother's experiments in the right direction, manipulating so many people across the country so that they followed him without question, tricking me into selling my soul so that Maxwell had one final incentive to do the demon's bidding…

Could we still be dancing to Andras' tune? The demon had proven himself more than capable of planning and scheming into the very long term. It was not inconceivable that he could have foreseen a defeat by N'yotsu, and may have even have intended it.

I shook my head. "Andras may have a grander plan, but N'yotsu is definitely not a party to it. Of that I am certain."

"Whatever the path you take, the outcome will be the same," said Byron. "And I cannot be a part of whatever Andras intends. Come nightfall, you are on your own. I wish you well, but I fear you will need more than that."

"What do you mean?" I asked.

Byron looked around, clearly torn as to what he should do or say next. However, there was still plenty of daylight left and we were effectively trapped together in that barn. "The inscriptions on your sword are incredibly powerful. There is no way that a human should be able to wield it in anger beyond a very short period of time."

"That is correct," I said. "When I first used it, I could only swing it for a few minutes before it became too hot for me to hold. But over time my tolerance to the heat built up."

"The sword's inscriptions started working on you as soon as you first grasped it. Think of it as a parasite; it needs a host to survive, and if one is not quite right then it will either alter the host so it suits its purpose, or kill it and move on. Clearly you—and it—were lucky."

I looked down at my red hands, the inscriptions marked out on them like deep angry scars. "I am not quite sure I would call this lucky."

"You would rather be dead? Actually, you are partly right, as you are approaching a tipping point between the demonic influence of the inscriptions and your latent humanity. What you do over these next few weeks will be crucial to how you end up, and if the inscriptions should prove to be in ascendance, well…"

"Well what?"

"You may not wish you were dead, but the rest of us surely will: you will be an Almadite, just like the rest of them. Cold and heartless, without a care for your friends, family or indeed anyone. But on the bright side," he sneered, "you'll be all-powerful, if that's what you want."

"But if I could control the inscriptions? Could I be human once more?"

Byron shook his head. "You are too far gone to ever be able to call yourself truly human. Nor will you be a pure-born demon either, even if the inscriptions do their work and take your body and soul completely. You will always be a half-breed, neither one nor the other."

"But could I stop myself becoming an evil demon? Could I stay... good? Or at least of good intention?"

He laughed. "Ah, you humans with your 'good' and 'evil'! Everything has to be one or the other with you, doesn't it? You could retain your human sense of morality, and even choose to be governed by it if that's what you mean. You could even control your physical form so that you appear to be human, so as not to scare your friends."

"How?" I asked.

"There are techniques and methods," he said. "Ways that we learn how to control our powers, to keep them in check."

"And this works for all demons? Even...?"

"Almadites are different in that they do not see the need to control their powers. But if they did..."

"Like N'yotsu?" I asked, remembering how he had helped me a few times in the past to try to control the changes, to help me revert back to appearing human.

"Maybe in theory, although I refuse to believe that any part of Andras is capable of self-restraint," Byron said dismissively.

I sat back and considered this. Could N'yotsu help me to learn how to bring the changes back under control? If so, then why had he not done it already? Did he not remember how?

Then I remembered N'yotsu's own struggles and in particular his ailing health. Could it be that the way his body was fading away was in some way connected to his own innate inability to exercise self-restraint? Even if not, there was no guarantee that N'yotsu would be fit and strong for long enough to be able to help me, but at that moment I had a creature with me who could.

"Help me," I said.

Byron looked at me through slitted eyes. "Why should I?"

"Because I can also help you. Like you said: I am strong, I can protect you. And in any case, if you are successful then there would be one less Almadite in the world. If you don't help me..." I spread my hands wide and shrugged.

"That sounds suspiciously like blackmail," he said slowly.

"Call it a mutually satisfactory arrangement," I grinned.

CHAPTER TWENTY-THREE

We knelt in a ditch on the outskirts of a large wood, staring intently at a tree.

"What exactly am I expecting it to do?" I asked after a few minutes.

"Shush," said Byron. "Just look, and then tell me what you see."

I looked. "I see... a tree."

"I thought you were supposed to be a writer," he said. "Look properly and *describe* what you see."

I sighed and then focused my gaze on the stick of wood, digging down into my mental reservoirs to reawaken my artistic instincts, a part of me that had been woefully underused while I had been preoccupied with the tasks of being a warrior and protector. Not to mention a slavering, homicidal half-demon.

I regarded it curiously, conjuring up words to describe the view before me. It was dark, the air having that particular scent of late evening in the midst of autumn, a heady mix of freshly fallen leaves and the sharp tang of distant bonfires. The tree stood apart from a copse, as though it were an advance guard sent unwillingly forward to scout for threats. At first, the waning moonlight was not yet strong enough to pick out all of the details, reducing the tree to a stubborn silhouette standing on a dark muddy carpet.

As I stared, though, the light seemed to improve so that I could make out more details. It had shed most of its foliage, although a few leaves stubbornly clung on to the uppermost branches. The bark was gnarled and twisted, such that I fancied I could see 100 shapes and faces carved there…

I gasped. "I can see the leaves, each one of them, their colours, the creases and veins on them." I turned to him. "Has the light lifted?"

"No, just your perceptions; you're seeing like a demon now. Carry on."

I looked back at the tree. "At first I thought it reached straight up to the sky, but now I can see each of the different ways it climbs upwards, every limb carving a different path, all of them doing their best to capture the sun. I can see it waving in the breeze. No, that's not quite right: something is pulsing inside it. My God, I can see the tree breathing and sending life up and down its body, its limbs…" The sensation reminded me of another time, the thick of night in Windsor Park when, in anticipation of battle, the veil of darkness had lifted to show me a multitude of things that I should not have been able to pick out, as well as a fair few things I wished I could not see. The shock of remembering those sights snapped my attention back to something Byron had just said.

"I thought you were teaching me to control my demon side, not enhancing it?" I asked.

"First you need to accept what you are: you can't control something if you keep fighting it. Now stop whining and keep looking."

I tried my hardest to throw myself into the studies that Byron had set for me, although I found myself at times frustrated by the seeming irrelevance of them. Such as examining trees, when I could be learning more important things like how to control my appearance. However, I could not doubt that his methods were having results and I was learning a great deal about my new powers and abilities.

The first thing he was keen for me to master was my self-control, particularly how to manage the rage that often took over during battle. Byron was very open about the fact that this was partly through self-preservation, as he did not want me to rip his head off the first time we found ourselves under attack. This in turn seemed to involve me becoming more intimately engaged with the various powers that I had unwittingly inherited. And so I found myself sitting in fields staring at trees.

To minimise the risk of me being provoked into battle before I had had a chance to master my abilities, we had decided to head south, away from all of the problems that London presented. This also had the benefit of taking us towards France; both of us were in agreement that it would be wise for me to put some distance between myself and my friends until I had learnt to master the runic sword and its influence. I felt pangs of guilt at removing myself from the fight at the time when—if Maxwell's theories were correct—the Fulcrum was fast approaching, an event that could herald all manner of chaos. This was outweighed, however, by the sure knowledge that my friends were better off being able to focus on the battle at hand rather than worrying about controlling me or trying to cure me.

Against Byron's advice, I had sent a short note to Maxwell, sneaking it into a postbag at Basingstoke Station while the stationmaster was temporarily distracted. In the note I told him that I was safe and well and seeking help, and would return to them when I could. I also implored them not to try to find me. Although I was not so naïve as to assume that this would stop them, I had to at least try to deter them somehow.

Byron himself was an interesting creature, full of contradictions. For all of his otherworldly nature, in his manner and bearing he was more akin to a cockney barrow boy. When I pointed this out to him, I was met with a sniffy rejoinder: he considered himself to belong to a much loftier social circle than that, it seemed. Indeed, he was more conscious of class than even the most aspirational upper-middle class careerist.

"Maybe," he mused, when I mentioned this a few days later, "but there is much to admire about your own social structures: the way that, although birth is a highly important factor, it is not the be-all-and-end-all and it is possible to haul oneself up to a higher social standing through luck or marriage or hard work."

"Is that not possible among your own people?" I asked.

"Oh no. Not impossible, but very uncommon. We are born into specific castes, each with a particular role or talent, and remain that way until we die. I was a soldier. You, by the looks of you and the inscriptions that made you, are also a warrior."

"What other castes are there?"

"My people, the Pooka, have Workers, Warriors, Sorcerers and the Ruling Council. The Almadites are slightly more varied: to our four you can add Warlocks, Mages and, of course, Slaves."

I ran through the terms in my head. "What is the difference

between Sorcerers and Warlocks? In my experience the two terms are interchangeable."

"You may think so, but there is a very wide difference in practice, believe me. Sorcerers tend to direct their energies towards largely benign activities, like healing or teaching, creating transportation spells or other methods of helping their society to progress and work properly. The Warlocks, well…" He shuddered. "Let us hope that you never have to meet them. They are single-minded in their pursuit of power for the good of their race, if you can call it that. Through their pet Mages they can make you do anything just by looking at you." He stared into the distance, his face pale.

"I encountered a Mage once," I said. "It compelled me to fight N'yotsu, to kill him."

"And yet you both survived? Such things usually involve a battle to the death."

"Oh, I wanted to kill him, believe me. But he managed to free me from the creature's influence."

Byron stared at me. "Did N'yotsu manage to break its hold on him? I did not know such things were possible."

"As far as I know, it only cast a spell over me. I assumed it could only influence one person at a time. At least, that was what N'yotsu implied."

"No. N'yotsu would have known better than that. One Mage can control an entire army of people if it so wishes. If it only controlled one of you, then there must have been a reason."

"It just wanted to distract us?"

"But why? Surely it would have suited the demons' purposes better if one or both of you were dead."

I frowned. The same thought had niggled at me at first, but events in the meantime had pushed those doubts to one side. They now came back in force: why indeed had the demons let us live? The machinations of those ghastly creatures was nothing new to me, but there was clearly a longer game at play here than I had anticipated. "Gaap," I said slowly.

Byron's head snapped round to look at me. "What did you say?"

"The Mage came to the assistance of Gaap, a demon who had been summoned by a young man in Sheffield—"

He interrupted me. "Gaap is here? In this realm?"

"Yes. We have been trying to find and kill him, although he's proven difficult to hunt down so far. N'yotsu seemed to think he was pretty dangerous."

"To say the least." Byron started fidgeting, his fingers drumming a rapid beat on his thigh. "If Gaap is here then we have a duty to do something about it." He stood up. "Enough wasting time. We need to get to Portsmouth as soon as possible."

"Why Portsmouth?" I asked. "We thought that Gaap was heading to London. In fact, my friends were working on pinpointing his location and may have done so already. If anywhere, shouldn't we go back there?"

"If that is the case, then great. But I have friends in Portsmouth who will know where he is and how to stop him." He started marching away and, after a moment, I shrugged and followed him.

As we travelled I started to learn from Byron how to disengage my consciousness from my body, drifting away from all of the mundane concerns that consumed my waking hours to a place that was free of tension, worry and frustration. I found this more refreshing than sleep itself and looked forward to our regular dose of meditation, a chance for me to forget all about my troubles and the constant creeping tension that came from knowing that I had turned away from a battle that was nowhere near won.

"It's all about your mind," Byron said one evening as we squared up to each other. "Demon brains and human brains are different, and you're fortunate to have a bit of both. The trick is to make sure that you use the best of each. That's what we need to focus on." He was holding a long, thick plank of wood and as he finished speaking he swung it at me, catching me hard across my head.

I fell to the ground. "What was that for?" I asked, stunned.

"We're training," he reminded me. "And you're supposed to be a fearsome fighting machine. Are you afraid of a bit of wood?"

"No." I struggled to my feet. "But I'd welcome at least a bit of warning that you were going to do that." I ducked out of the way of another swing of his plank, but was caught across the back of my head by the return. I staggered forwards.

"I don't want to hurt you," I said, feeling the red mist start to descend. "But I'm not sure how long I can fight this off if you keep doing that."

"Why do you think you need to fight it?" he asked, catching me in the stomach and winding me. "What if you embraced it rather than resisting it all the time?"

I gasped for breath, expecting him to hold off on his attacks but I was sorely mistaken. While I trusted Byron's logic, the very thought of letting go and embracing my demonic side filled me with terror. It was as though I were standing at the top of a sheer drop, staring down into a black abyss. The thought of throwing myself over was enticing but also terrifying in equal measure. What if I kept falling forever, my humanity lost for all time as I plummeted into a hellish reality where I could never again be the person I was, a stranger to everyone I had ever known and loved?

The risk was too great, even though a part of me knew that I should heed Byron's advice. I teetered on the edge of the abyss but could not force myself to take another step.

The idiot hammered at my back and then my head, plunging me face-first into the dirt. The creature that rose from the floor was angry. I watched through the red mist as my body stalked towards the Pooka, catching the plank one-handed and throwing it aside. Byron turned to run but I leapt over him and landed in his path, snarling. The little creature would pay for this.

I came to my senses just before snapping his neck, blinking as I stared at him, unsure as to what had pulled me out of the fugue state but deeply ashamed of what I had nearly done. I released him and staggered away. "I'm sorry," I muttered.

"No," he said. "My fault. I thought you were more…"

The words hung between us. I had failed and would carry on failing until I was lost forever.

CHAPTER TWENTY-FOUR

The remainder of the journey to Portsmouth was largely without incident, with us encountering very few people on the route. We passed the time by talking, and Byron told me about how his people had struggled to find a home since theirs had been destroyed. The vast majority, it seemed, had settled on Earth, either mingling seamlessly with humans or giving birth to many myths around such creatures as leprechauns, pixies and goblins, to name but three.

"I have to ask," I said, late one evening, "why have you chosen the name 'Byron'? I'm guessing that it is not the name you were born with. Are you a lover of his prose?"

He laughed. "Well, yes, but not only that. You see, he and I were drinking partners for quite a while. I tell you, for a human that man could really consume a lot of intoxicating substances."

"You knew Lord Byron?" I asked, unsure whether or not to believe him.

"Of course. It was a few years after I came through into this realm, and he took me under his wing, so to speak."

"Was he not put off by the way you... you know..."

"Look? Oh no, not at all. You see, I am very adept at blending in in all sorts of situations. A master of disguise, Byron always used to call me. Just as you'll learn how to control your appearance, so can I. At least after a fashion."

"So you managed to make yourself appear human? Then why do you not do that now, so that you could blend in rather than having to sneak around at night?"

"Oh, I do sometimes. Where do you think I get food from? But it's very tiring, so I can't keep it up for too long. Luckily, Byron liked to frequent very dark places, where a demon can happily obscure himself. And in any case, he was usually at least three sheets to the wind, so whenever he saw me sprouting horns or the like, he just assumed it was the drugs or the brandy."

"So tell me, what was he like?" I had been an avid reader of Byron's works since I first stumbled upon them on a very high bookshelf in the school library. At first I enjoyed them for the scandal that always attached itself to his name, but after a while it was the sheer pleasure of the way he could wield a phrase.

"Everything he is reputed to be and more," the Pooka said with a smile. "He was often out of control, almost as though he were daring humanity to stop him. That was one of the many things I loved about him. When he passed, I adopted his name in tribute. I like to think that he would have seen something deliciously subversive in there being a shape-shifting demon walking the lands wearing his name.

"Wait a moment," I said. "Lord Byron died around 45 years ago. How old are you, exactly?"

"Difficult to say, especially if you were to try to measure my age by the passage of time in this realm; and the way we measure time in my realm would mean nothing to you. I came through to Earth when the French Revolution was in its infancy—those were interesting times to acclimatise myself to I can tell you, talk about out of the frying pan and into the fire!—and I was well into my adulthood by then. If your question is more along the lines of how long do I have left to live, well, by your realm's terms if I were allowed to live to a ripe old age, I would outlive you by at least a few centuries. Although now you're a demon maybe you will outlive me."

I shuddered. While the idea of being almost immortal at first seemed attractive, the thought of seeing my friends and family wither and die while I stayed constant as a hideous—but forever young—demon did not appeal to me in the slightest.

We finally found ourselves in an abandoned storehouse on the outskirts of the port, breathing in the salty air and staring out at the grey-black horizon. It had been too long since I had last stood near the sea and I relished the thought of once again immersing myself in its wild freedom. However, the thought of Gaap still weighed heavily on our minds; any thoughts of flight were on hold until we knew that whatever threat he posed had been dealt with.

Byron headed into town to gather food and intelligence, asking me to remain in the safety of our hideaway while he did so, as I was still painfully conspicuous with my horns, markings and distinctly inhuman features. He returned an hour or so later with a tall hat and high-collared greatcoat to replace my stained and battered clothing. Thus disguised and under cover of darkness, we headed into town to find a community of demons that Byron knew of old.

I was surprised to find a ghetto of demons living openly not far from Portsmouth's main thoroughfares, teeming around a street that was not unlike those full of inebriated sailors just a stone's throw away. Indeed, if one did not pay too much attention to the people walking to and fro, it could have been much like any other street. I looked around in wonder as we passed, at demons chatting as they walked, buying items from costermonger demons or singing raucous songs from the gutter using familiar tunes coupled with words that were both alien and beautiful at the same time.

I was not the only human (or part-human) in the street, for we passed the odd group of men and women transacting with demons, both races seeming to co-exist peacefully. A couple of sailors pushed past us, leering at a barely dressed female demon who beckoned to them in a way that could be seen in any busy town the length and breadth of the land.

Byron laughed as he saw my expression. "What, you didn't think we had brothels too? Pooka prostitutes are some of the best you will ever experience: they can do things you never thought physically possible, and can last all night..."

"It's not that," I said. "I am just surprised to see humans, well... is it even anatomically possible for them to...?"

"We all have bits and pieces in similar places," he said. "They just vary in size and shape and what we do with them. There have been stories of humans and demons copulating since time immemorial: you ever heard of the succubi and incubi?"

"Of course," I said. "I just never expected to see them in such familiar surroundings."

He grinned. "I would have thought you'd feel right at home here." He pointed at a door, above which swung a sign showing two demons fighting with horns of ale in their hands. "Here we are, the Fighting Heads."

"A tavern?" I asked. "You are right, I am indeed starting to feel at home. It has been far too long since I last had a sup."

He put a hand on my shoulder as we entered. "You need to make sure you remain inconspicuous. We don't know who to trust in here yet, and you're quite a striking-looking chap. So keep your head down and don't talk to anyone."

I nodded. "That is my favoured modus operandi in these establishments. Put an ale in my hand, and I shall be the model of an antisocial gent."

We stepped inside and were greeted by a wall of smoke and noise, a blanket that I embraced like an old friend. Groups of demons gathered in various places around the room, enjoying themselves in time-honoured fashion. Byron led me to the bar where we grabbed two jars of beer before walking over to a corner where a group of demons conspired around a long table. Byron gestured for me to remain in the background while he approached the largest one, a fat demon with features strikingly similar to my friend's. I allowed myself a wry smile. I was becoming so familiar with the demons that I was beginning to be able to tell them apart as individuals, rather than them being just a generic bunch of undesirables.

Byron barked something in a tongue that I did not recognise, a guttural mix of consonants merging together in a way that reminded me of the Welsh language at its most obscure. The big demon responded in an almost offhand manner, prompting laughter from the others. Byron joined in, an uneasy smile on his face.

The conversation continued for a few minutes until Byron gestured in my direction. Unsure what to do, I kept myself in the shadows and took a long drink, the tip of my hat hiding my features.

With a resigned sigh, Byron beckoned for me to step forwards. "He wants to see what you look like," he said.

"Who does?" I asked, staying where I was.

"The one person who can help us. His name's Kingdom. Step forwards so he can see you."

I reluctantly complied, removing my hat as I did so. The impact on the group was immediate; they muttered what were clearly curses and made gestures with their hands. The big demon, Kingdom, barked something and Byron translated: "Put the hat back on now."

I did as I was told and Kingdom made a series of noises. When I failed to respond, he said in faltering English: "Byron here says you're a human."

"That is correct," I said. "Or at least I used to be. I am not quite sure what I am now."

"Almadite scum," snarled a demon next to me, who then shirked away when I turned to look at him.

Kingdom held up his hands to quell any further comments. "Byron vouches for you and that's good enough for me. Your name?"

I cleared my throat and looked around nervously. I had been pretty prolific in my demon-slaying activities and the thought of revealing my identity to this mob worried me, particularly as there were a large number of bodies between me and the exit.

Byron nodded to me. "Don't worry, it's safe."

I took a deep breath. "My name is Augustus Potts."

They collectively shrugged in indifference. I was incensed: did they not realise who they had in front of them? The threats I posed to their wellbeing? "Augustus Merriwether Potts," I said a little louder and firmer, reasoning that maybe they just had not heard me clearly enough. There was still a complete absence of any recognition from around the room and I waved my beer to make my point as I continued. "With my brother, Maxwell, and our friend N'yotsu, we fought back the invasion of Greenwich a couple of years ago."

"Wait," said Kingdom. "Maxwell Potts? And N'yotsu? I know of them. So you're the other one, eh?"

I bit back the affront at only being known through association. After all, they were not reacting by trying to tear my head off, and for that I was grateful.

The demon gestured for me to sit at his table. "So you know N'yotsu?" He held up a hand as I tried to explain that my friend was not evil. "Do not worry, I am aware of his status since he created the obsidian stone. I am also aware of his rapidly declining state of health. There is very little that I am not aware of among demon-kind."

"Then why didn't you know about me?" I was painfully aware that I was almost whining as I said this.

"I did. I just wanted to be sure you were who you purported to be. So, tell us about your encounter with Gaap." The crowd around the table grew silent as I described our trip to Sheffield, the battle with Gaap and the Mage and then our escape back to London.

When I had finished, Kingdom nodded. "Your instincts were correct; Gaap is in London. And there is a wider plan involving your friends and you as well."

I felt a chill run down my spine. "What do you mean?"

"I believe that your brother calls it the Fulcrum, the approaching confluence that will bring science and magic back into balance in this realm. It is coming very soon and Gaap intends to use it for his own ends."

"His own ends?"

Kingdom nodded. "An army approaches from the Aether. That is why we depart in the morning."

I gaped at the sea of nodding faces around me. "Depart... for where?"

"Over the Channel. There is an access to the Eternal Mines in the mountains known to you as the Alps. We plan to escape to another world: this one is lost."

CHAPTER TWENTY-FIVE

I stared at them for a long moment, trying to comprehend what I had just heard. "So the world is falling to pieces, the Almadites are going to invade and you're planning to just run away? That's your plan in its entirety?"

Kingdom met my gaze with eyes that were bottomless pits of indifference. "It is not our fight. Our priority is to save our people."

"And what about *my* people?"

He sighed. "Some humans have been good to us, true, but the vast majority have been anything but. Especially recently. Since the events of a few years ago, your people have been increasingly hostile towards us and our kind. There's not a person in this tavern that hasn't been driven away from places they called home by vicious lynch mobs led by your precious Witchfinder Generals. And then there are those who just disappear, probably killed and dumped at the bottom of the sea for all we know."

"But they do not represent my people…"

"Really?" he said. "What was your instinct when you first met a demon?"

I looked around the room for support, to Byron who was supposed to be on my side. It was clear, though, that I was on my own. "We had to defend ourselves. We were under attack."

"Not from my people you weren't. And yet did you distinguish between Pooka and Almadite?"

I threw my hands in the air. "I didn't know there was such a distinction! It was just—"

"Demon or human. No other distinction, eh?"

"I didn't know," I repeated lamely.

"You never bothered to find out. Instead, you relied on the word of an Almadite. Reformed or not, N'yotsu is still an Almadite. Completely different to us."

"I know that now," I said. "I realise that there are many different shades of demon, just like there are human. But we are not all evil and bigoted. Please give us a chance to prove that to you. Help us." They glared at me and I turned to Byron. "You said that some of your kind, the Pooka, have lived alongside humanity for many years?"

"That's right," he said slowly. "In the past there's rarely been any quarrels between Pooka and human. On the whole they've been welcoming to us."

"Until now," grunted a demon in the corner, to an accompaniment of muttered agreements. "The Witchfinders have made it very clear we don't belong any more. Better to go somewhere we won't get hounded out every other day."

Kingdom looked around at his people and then turned back to me. "So you see, whatever goodwill your people may have had has been destroyed by bigotry, personalised by the Witchfinders."

"Which only really cropped up in the past few years," I mused.

"What?"

I felt lightheaded as my mind skipped around thoughts and connections that were in the process of being made even as I spoke. "All was fine until a few years ago, when the Almadites started coming through here in numbers, correct?"

Kingdom shrugged. "Well, maybe not completely rosy, but certainly we were able to live without fear of being lynched."

"And the... negativity has increased over the past few years, at the same time as the Almadite activity increased, yes?"

"Yes. But as we said, your kind will not admit to a distinction between—"

"Maybe," I cut across him, "but isn't there a chance that there's more to this than what we see on the surface?"

A few of the demons were muttering among themselves and Kingdom was clearly growing impatient with me. "I do not follow what you are saying."

"I know from bitter experience that the Almadites are masters at playing very long-term games. You said yourself that Gaap no doubt has at least one other plan in play, possibly more."

"Yes…"

"And you are all warriors?" I asked.

The company gathered around that long table nodded and grunted. "If you are going to berate us for running from a fight then you are either exceptionally brave or more stupid than you appear," growled Kingdom.

"A bit of both," I said. "More the latter than the former, if I'm honest. But that's not the point. What if you were Gaap and wanted to invade a realm? What would you do to minimise the risk of failure?"

Byron rubbed his chin and joined in, warming to my talk of strategies. "I would look to disable or distract the incumbent army. They invaded our home by making us believe that they would attack the Eternal Mines, taking advantage of the main body of our force being deployed to defend those places."

I nodded. "Leading up to the Battle of Greenwich, Andras managed to influence the Generals of our armies, distracting them with promises gleaned from their wildest dreams. It's not a huge leap to expect something like that again. But what if you not only had an incumbent army to deal with but another army that was scattered around the realm, already fleeing your forces because you had previously invaded their homeland?"

"I would want to keep them scattered and preferably on the run. Make sure that there was no chance of them banding up to offer help to the incumbent army." Byron looked at me with wide eyes. "Gods, can it be possible?"

"I had never quite understood why the Queen had created the Witchfinder General posts," I said. "They served no real purpose apart from uniting human against demon, regardless of how benign they might appear, and spreading fear and hatred across the land. I had thought that there was no way that the Almadites would want such a thing. But if they were looking to unite humanity against *all* demons, to make sure there was no chance of us working together with the Pooka, for example…"

"It is a very effective way of doing so," mused Kingdom. He looked at Byron, who had been watching me speak with a broad grin on his face. "What do you think?"

"Makes sense to me," said Byron. "Of course—"

There was a shout from the front of the tavern. "We got company!"

I fought my way to the windows and then cursed. "Speak of the devil."

Outside stood a mob of people holding flaming torches, cudgels and swords, a familiar dark figure at their head. "Come out or we burn you out!" shouted Witchfinder General Morley.

The tavern descended into a confused mass of panic, fear and anger. "Stop!" shouted Kingdom after a few moments. He looked around as everyone subsided, all eyes drawn to him. "We have never willingly killed humans and we will not start now. If what Mr Potts here says is true, then we would just be playing into the Almadites' hands."

"So what, we just wait for them to kill us?" shouted back a huge figure from a corner.

"The plan is unchanged. We will fall back. There are other exits from this place, we will leave before they have a chance to attack."

"And in the meantime they'll set fire to this place and those who manage to get away in time will be cut down in the streets!"

"You need a distraction," I said. "I will go out and speak to them. I am not sure how much time I'll be able to buy you, but hopefully it will be long enough."

Byron shook his head. "Look at you. They will not hesitate to cut you down."

I grinned, trying to appear braver than I felt. "I'm a good talker. And when that fails, I can run bloody fast. You just make sure you all get out in time."

I walked to the door, taking deep breaths and nodding as the Pooka moved aside to clear a path for me. I was not quite sure what I was doing but I knew that I had to do something. As I reached the door, Kingdom put a hand on my shoulder. "Are you sure about this?" he asked.

"Not in the slightest," I replied. "But there's every chance that I am the prize Morley seeks. And I cannot watch while innocent people are killed. I saw women and children in the streets when we came here."

"Yes," said Kingdom. "Hopefully they have gone into hiding. We will make sure they get away safely."

"Do that," I said. "I will buy you as much time as I can. Hopefully this will prove to you that we are not all as bad as you thought."

Kingdom frowned, then nodded. "When you get away from here, make your way back to your friends. I believe they are close to understanding where the Fulcrum will take place. Make sure you stop it before it's too late."

I nodded and then opened the door, stepping out into the night air and staring at the mass of men and flames in front of me.

The mob shouted as they saw me, the ones to the front shirking away in fear while others—many more in number although notably the ones further back—hefted their weapons, faces twisted in animalistic loathing.

"Morley!" I shouted. "I cannot let you do this. These creatures are peaceful, they mean no harm."

He stared at me. "How do you know my name?" he called back.

My lips set into a rictus that stuck to my cheeks like it had been painted on. "Why, everyone knows of you, the famous Witchfinder General. You're a long way from home, aren't you?

"What do you mean?" He frowned, thrown off-guard by my comment.

"I thought you were Nottingham's resident bigot. What brings you this far south?"

"I go where my orders take me," he said, then shook his head and raised his truncheon. "I am not here to converse with the likes of you."

I stiffened. "There is nothing for you here."

"I beg to differ." He sneered at me as he spoke.

"These people are peaceful. They mean no harm to anyone."

"Demons always mean harm to someone. That is your nature. You cannot deny it." He stared at me. "You seem somewhat familiar. Have we met before?"

I shuffled uneasily, trying to think of a way to deflect the conversation. "You said you act on orders. Whose orders, exactly?"

He sneered at me again. "I do not answer to the likes of you. In fact, I don't even know why I am wasting my breath talking with you. We shall storm this place and drive all of you abominations away." He gestured to the crowd behind and they shambled into an advance.

I drew my sword. "I cannot let you do that," I said. "There are innocent people here: women and children."

He laughed, a manic cackle that was echoed by the rest of his mob. "There are no such things as innocent demons, fool," he said. "You are all the same and will be driven from our land." An even bigger roar erupted from the crowd at these words and I raised my sword, stealing myself for the upcoming battle that I surely could not win.

The crowd staggered to an unruly halt and I allowed myself a small rush of pride at how the mere sight of me in arms was enough to stop this murderous mob in their tracks. Then I turned to see Byron and Kingdom standing either side of me, with more demons streaming out of the building behind us. "Gus," said Byron. "We stand with you."

Morley had clearly been close enough to hear these words and gaped at me. "Augustus Potts," he said slowly. "I had been told… but I did not realise that it was this severe." He laughed again. "This is all too perfect. But your little band of deviants cannot stand against us."

I glanced at the demons to either side of me, noting that more and more of them were stepping out to join us, makeshift weapons and pieces of broken furniture in their hands. "What are you doing?" I asked. "I thought this was not your fight?"

"Sometimes even an old, stubborn demon like myself needs to admit when they are wrong," said Kingdom. "Byron here has made me realise that you are correct. This is our home as much as anywhere, and we cannot allow it to fall the way that our home did."

I looked back at the mob tentatively advancing on us. "Well, I'm pleased for the company. I hope you're ready for a fight." I raised my sword above my head and stepped forwards.

Byron grabbed my arm. "No," he said. "Not you. You need to get back to London and your friends to end all of this madness before it goes any further. We will deal with these idiots."

I stared at him. "But I cannot…" I said.

He grinned. "Yes you can. We all have our roles to play and mine—ours—is to fight, something we have not done for far too long."

Kingdom then thrust me aside with a massive paw. "Do not worry," he said. "We will not hurt them. At least, not too much." With a roar he charged towards the oncoming mob, Byron and the others following him. I watched for a moment and then started away into the night.

I had only managed to get a few streets away when there was a shout from behind me. "Mr Potts!"

I stopped and turned to see the dark, hateful figure of Morley advancing on me. He stopped a few paces away, his eyes glinting maliciously in the lamplight.

"Did you really think that you could get away so easily?" he asked.

I held my hands out empty at my sides, my sword safely in its scabbard at my back. "I do not wish to hurt you, Morley," I said.

He laughed. "I, on the other hand, have no such qualms," he said as he charged at me.

I stepped aside, using his momentum to push him down to the ground as he passed. He skidded on the mud and rose with a snarl, raising his truncheon to point at me.

"I heard that you are trying to resist your true nature," he sneered.

I frowned at him. "How did you...?" I began, but he had already rushed at me once more. I darted aside from blow after blow, marvelling at how quick the man was. His hatred had given him a power and ferocity that I found hard to withstand, even in my heightened state. I fell backwards under the onslaught, his eyes boring into me as he swung his weapon again and again.

I knew I should fight back, that I was being hamstrung by not returning his blows. Indeed, if I brought my strength to bear on him then I could have easily ended the fight. But I could not bring myself to hurt him. To raise my fists against a human, regardless of who that was, would surely cement my place in the demon fraternity as an enemy of mankind. And if I killed a human then surely all would be lost; even one as odious and misguided as Witchfinder General Morley.

I batted aside another swing from his truncheon and then felt a sudden wet tightness in my side. I looked down to see a knife protruding from the flesh just above my hip. Morley tensed his arm and the long sharp blade twisted sickeningly slowly inside me. I staggered back, my strength rapidly draining away, and despite my best intentions threw a fist at Morley. He flew across the street and landed against a wall, sliding down to the ground.

I held my hands to my wound, desperately trying to keep the blood and organs inside as I staggered away. I needed to find somewhere safe, somewhere I could rest and sleep... sleep seemed so very, very attractive at that point.

A part of me pleaded with my body to keep going, knowing that to stop would be to die. But a greater part of me no longer cared.

CHAPTER TWENTY-SIX

Flashes of sound, a scramble and clatter, some whispered words.

A face swam into view, a young girl, so sweet and innocent. She should not be allowed to show such pain and sadness on her face, not one as young as her.

Darkness, then a memory. Where had I seen her before? A street corner... my brother's maid... what was her name? Milly?

"My friends needed someone to play with," she said. *"So I killed her."*

Too young for such vicious thoughts.

I heard my own voice from far away: *"Your friends. Who are they?"*

"Why, you've met them already," the child—was it Milly?—said, standing the doll up. *"They talked to us in the sitting room. They're outside right now."* She moved the doll in a slow dance and sang gently under her breath to the tune of 'Ring a Ring o' Roses': *"Will you will you play with me, will you will you stay with me...?"*

The song echoed round my head and I screamed a scream with no sound, my limbs unable to move.

My eyes fluttered open, the sunlight painful as it seared my vision. I groaned and rolled over, wincing at the sharp, stabbing pain in my side. With a shock, I remembered the fight with Morley and the wound that I had sustained, a wound that surely should have been fatal.

I looked down to see my shirt and trousers stained dark with blood that had dried into a hard congealed mess. I stared at it. This alone surely indicated that I had been out for more than just a few hours. Probably more like days I thought, as my stomach started to

251

rumble.

I looked around. I was in a small, dark hut that was probably an outhouse although it looked like it had not been used for quite some time. The wood on the walls and roof was rotting away, with slats leaning on each other for support like drunks at closing time. The floor was covered in a soft grey muck that I did not care to examine too closely, although thankfully I was lain on a large piece of cloth.

The door opened and a tiny figure slipped in, shutting the door quickly behind her. She was a small girl, probably no more than eight or nine years old, and she stared at me through a face that was streaked with dirt.

I held out my hands in as unthreatening a manner as I could manage. "Please don't be alarmed," I said. "I won't hurt you."

"I know that," she said. "You told me. 'I'll never harm you,' you said. Although my name's not Milly or Kate. I'm Sal."

I grunted as I worked myself into a sitting position. "Pleased to meet you, Sal. I'm Gus."

She grinned and shook my hand in a proud mimic of an adult greeting before placing a dirty cloth bundle on the ground in front of me. She opened it to reveal a hock of bread, a lump of hard cheese and a slab of nondescript grey meat. Next to it she placed a chipped mug filled with beer. The sheer weight of my hunger overtook any resistance and I grabbed at the food, stuffing it into my mouth.

She watched as I ate, squatting down on her haunches in front of me. "I wasn't sure what sort of scran you liked," she said, "so I grabbed a bit of everything."

"This is all great, thank you," I said through mouthfuls of gristly meat that at that moment tasted better than the finest cut from the best Westminster chophouse. I met her gaze, noting the innocent curiosity in her bright blue eyes. "Are you not scared of me?"

"No," she said. "You said I shouldn't be."

"But I'm a… I look like this," I said, gesturing at my face with a clawed hand.

"So?"

"But everyone's afraid of demons."

"Are they?" she asked. "Why?"

"Well… demons harm people, kill them."

"But you don't."

"No…"

"I saw you fight that man in the street. You could have killed him but you never."

I remembered hitting Morley hard, sending him flying against a wall in my desperation to get away. I hadn't checked on him, but the force of such a blow could easily have broken a man's neck. "Didn't I?" I asked cautiously.

"I saw him limping away a bit later. Mind you, he didn't look too happy."

I grinned despite myself at the thought, relieved that my conscience could be clear in that respect at least.

"So not all demons are bad," she said. "Or at least you're not."

I frowned. "But many are," I said. "You should be careful; you were lucky with me but you might not be so lucky next time."

"But you said all demons want to kill people. That was a lie."

"I… suppose it was. But sometimes you just need to be careful."

"Yeah, you said that. But not all demons are bad, just like not all people are bad."

I nodded at the truth in the words, grinning as I realised I had been outsmarted by a child, and not for the first time. I marvelled that she could be so much more open-minded than a town full of her elders. But then again, if the way she thought was mirrored in others of her generation then maybe there was hope for us all. Perhaps the bigotry of the Witchfinders would not spread as easily as I had feared.

Not all demons are bad, just like not all people are bad. The words ran round my brain, tantalisingly simple. I had always assumed that to give in to my demon side would be to descend into vicious, mindless depravity, but what if it didn't have to be that way? "I like the way you think," I said.

"Like I say, you didn't do for that other bloke. Why's that then?"

"Because…" I frowned. "Because it wouldn't have been the right thing to do. He is a bad man, but he believes what he is doing is right. You cannot simply kill people because they do not agree with you." My head started to swim with the implications. "Or demons either, for that matter." I thought of all the demons I had killed over the years; how many of them had been truly bad, if such a concept existed? Had I been so wrapped up in our crusade that I had been blinded by the certainties of 'good' and 'evil', not stopping to think that there were shades of grey in the demon world as well as ours? My experiences with the Pooka had laid to rest any thoughts that all demons were simply evil and bloodthirsty. After all, if every demon was evil then what hope did that leave for me?

The memory of Byron and Kingdom swam into my mind. "I had some friends who were trying to stop some bad men from burning down a tavern. Friends like me, good demons. Do you...?"

"There was a big ruckus the night I found you, down by the docks in the Pooka quarter. Lynch mob, folk called it."

"What happened?" I asked. "Did they get away?"

"By the sounds of it, yeah. Both sides gave as good as they got. The demons seem to have got the message though, pretty much all of them have cleared out of town. Apart from you, of course."

"When did... how long have I been asleep?"

"Two days, give or take."

The words were like a splash of icy water. "I have to get moving," I said, grunting as I pulled myself to my feet.

"You had a pretty nasty gash in your side," she said. "Things like that would stop a man dead. But then you're not a man, are you?"

I pulled up my torn, bloody shirt to examine the knife wound. It felt tight, but I knew that caked blood could often cause that sensation. I used some of the beer to soak the crusted scab, peeling it away to reveal perfectly healed skin.

I looked up at Sal and grinned. "No," I said. "I think I'm rather more than that."

I was not so naïve as to believe that Sal's faith in demon-kind was reflective of the rest of humanity and so I was keen to be as inconspicuous as possible as I made my way back to London from Portsmouth. However, I had already lost two days, time that could prove fatal if Gaap's plans had been allowed to advance unchecked, so I could not just travel at night. Nor could I waste time on roundabout routes avoiding thoroughfares and the general population. I therefore had to risk travelling in broad daylight along the London–Portsmouth road or by train.

As one last favour to me, Sal managed to find me a hooded cloak that served to hide my features, as well as a freight train that was heading directly into London. We sneaked up to the side of the tracks, keeping to the undergrowth as we approached a particularly inviting-looking open carriage.

I patted her on the shoulder. "Thank you. For everything. I wish I had some way to repay you."

"You could take me with you," she said, turning those big eyes on me.

"I am sorry, but what I have to do is far too dangerous for a young lady like you." I gave her shoulder a squeeze. "But I will come back and repay you for your kindness. When all of this is over I will take you up to London. I promise."

She frowned at me. "I could help."

I smiled. "I owe you my life, and I am not going to repay that favour by risking yours." The train whistled and started to move. I watched it build up speed and then gave her a hug. "Thank you again. I will be back: promise."

The train had gone past us and was building up enough speed to satisfy me that Sal had no chance of running after it. I burst out of the cover of the bushes and sprinted along the track, catching up with the open carriage and vaulting inside, rolling onto a pile of hard wooden crates. I peered back to see the retreating figure of Sal standing by the track.

I pushed my way as far inside as possible so that I was hidden from view and then lay back. I resolved to make the most of the journey time by getting as much rest as possible, so that I could enter the fray strong and refreshed. That was assuming that there was still some form of battle to be fought. I wondered where Byron, Kingdom and the rest of the Pooka had gone; my memories of the night of the battle outside the tavern were still muddled, and I could not decide whether their standing by me was a sign that they would continue to take the fight all the way to wherever the Fulcrum was or whether they would simply retreat back to the Eternal Mines as they had planned. Of course, if they had been badly beaten by Morley's lynch mob then they may have had little choice but to run away.

I cast the thought aside. There was no point wasting my energies on unknown quantities. More pressing was the question of how I would get myself back in the game. Based on our conversations before I had left, Nonsuch seemed to be the most likely location for the Fulcrum and I wondered whether I should make that my first port of call. It was certainly a more attractive option than braving the crowds in London. But if the battle had yet to be joined there, then I would most likely find myself alone in an empty field.

I settled on my brother's laboratory as the best first step: at the very least, Maxwell could point me in the direction of where the battle was. In the meantime I would keep my ears open for anything that would indicate the commencement of hostilities. I had a feeling that the impact of Gaap's plans would be felt over quite some distance.

There was also the question of how effective I would be in battle. While my body had recovered as rapidly as ever, the memory of my beating at Morley's hands was a raw open wound. I wondered why I had been so reluctant to fight him. I owed him nothing, and indeed I despised everything he stood for. Yet still I was unwilling or unable to inflict even a proper injury on the man. Every time I thought of our confrontation I pictured the scene as though I were watching from afar, seeing a demon with sharp teeth and claws squaring up to a man almost half his size. Even though I knew that the demon in that scene was on the side of right and the man's motives were questionable, seen in this light my instincts were still firmly on the side of the human.

I was certain that I would not be paralysed by the same morals when it came to confronting Gaap and the Almadites, but my encounters with Byron and the other Pooka had muddied my thinking when it came to the question of whether or not demons should be eradicated on sight. I cursed. It had all been so simple once. But then again, if demons were incapable of salvation then where would that leave me?

This circular argument kept me preoccupied for much of the journey to London and I was no closer to an answer when I arrived than when I had left. Even though I knew that it was a nonsense to think of all demons as irretrievably evil, I could not bring myself to permanently align myself with them. I was still a human, surely, regardless of how I looked. Wasn't I?

As the train slowed to come into the station, I jumped down and ran away to safety, half-expecting a hue-and-cry to be raised against me at any moment. I was lucky and managed to slip away unnoticed, vaulting a wall and then joining the throngs of humanity in the street beyond as they made their way through their ordinary lives. I pulled the hooded cloak up over my head and kept my eyes downcast.

For once I was eternally grateful for the natural instincts of the Londoner when it came to other people: that is to act as though no one else existed beyond themselves and anyone they happened to be with. While in other cities a strange figure trying to look inconspicuous would at least attract interest, in London it was almost considered bad form to enter into conversation or even eye contact with a person that one did not have to. Any initial fears of being spotted and harangued as a demon diminished rapidly as I walked through the London streets, my hood covering my features and scarcely a glance being sent in my direction.

By the time I turned onto the busy madness of Trafalgar Square I was marching proudly, my head and hands still obscured by the cloak but cutting a confident figure nonetheless. Just before Whitehall I turned into Spring Gardens and then cut left so that I was in the narrow street running behind number 24. I dashed down the street, keeping myself low and close to the wall that ran along my left-hand side. Without pausing to catch breath or realise that what I was doing was probably foolhardy to say the least, I leapt over the wall, landing in a crouch in the small yard on the other side.

I looked up into a forest of gun barrels pointed at my head. *Yes,* I reflected, *that was indeed a very stupid thing to do.*

CHAPTER TWENTY-SEVEN

I was pushed roughly against the wall, a dozen rifles trained on me as my cloak was torn away and my sword removed. I held out my hands and stammered my innocence but was rewarded by a buttstock to the stomach. I let the soldier think he had hurt me, all the better to hopefully put them at their ease.

"I need to see Maxwell Potts," I said. "I am his brother."

"Yeah," sneered one soldier, "and I'm Florence Nightingale on me tea break, mate."

"Wait," said an officer, frowning at me. "Just keep it here." He ran into the house, leaving me with the group of young soldiers. I looked around at them, seeing naked fear in the way they stared at me and handled their weapons. I recognised a few faces from previous engagements and realised with relief that I had stumbled upon Captain Pearce's Company.

I tried a smile, then realised from their reactions that as far as they were concerned I was baring my teeth at them. I tried a different tack to put them at ease. "Pleasant weather we are having, eh? For the time of year I mean." I turned to a Sergeant. "Jones, is it not? How is the wife?"

He took a step towards me. "If you dare to threaten—"

"Stand down, Sergeant," a voice barked from the doorway. I looked up to see Captain Pearce walking towards us. "Gus, is that really you?" he asked.

"Captain," I grinned. "It certainly is. Sorry about running out on you fellows back at Nonsuch, but I came over a little queer."

He peered at my face and then nodded. "You had us worried back there. But I am glad to see you now; assuming, that is, you can be trusted?"

"Of course I can," I said. "I am still the same person deep down, or at least I think I am. One thing is for sure, though: there is a grave threat posed by the demon Gaap that we need to stop post-haste. I want to get back in the fight. Take me to my brother and N'yotsu and let's put an end to this madness."

Pearce took a deep breath. "Gus," he said softly. "There are some things you need to know first."

We huddled in the shadows of Mark Lane, peering round the corner at the Tower's dark, imposing hulk. "Are you sure this will work?" I asked, looking down at the manacles round my wrists and ankles.

"Unless you have come up with a better idea in the past few minutes," said Pearce, "this is the plan we are going with." After one final examination of the traffic on Great Tower Street he turned to address his men.

"I will say this one final time," he said. "As soon as we step through those gates there is every risk that we could be accused of committing treason. If any of you wish to walk away now, I will not hold it against you."

There was silence among the 50 men all standing in the alley. Sergeant Jones cleared his throat. "All due respect, sir, but we go where you go. And hang the consequences. Sir."

Pearce nodded, a proud smile flashing across his face before being replaced by his familiar stern focus. "Very well. You have your orders. 'A' group: with me."

Pearce and I headed for Great Tower Street, a group of 20 soldiers swiftly forming around us. The remainder melted into the various streets and lanes dotted around the Tower, waiting for the agreed signal.

I looked up at the Tower and then at the pitifully few soldiers escorting us. "Should we not have brought more men?" I asked Pearce.

"Any more would have raised suspicions. Now be quiet and try to look evil and demonic."

I glanced sideways at him. "Is that a joke?"

I had been pleasantly surprised at how quickly Pearce had welcomed me back, although that all made sense as soon as he told me what had happened in my absence. My head had spun as I thought about Maxwell being kidnapped by Gaap, let alone the return of Andras, and for a moment I feared that I would lose all control. Paradoxically, it was the thought of Kate being in the hands of Morley that gave me the focus I needed; we had to get her out of there before he had a chance to do anything irreparable to her.

While Pearce had told me his tale, Lexie and Joshua had appeared and lingered in the doorway, staring at me. "It's all right," I said, "I won't bite."

"Is it really you in there, Mr Potts?" asked Lexie.

"It is," I grinned. "Good to see you both again. At least some of us managed to not get captured or transformed. Without Maxwell, you are probably our only hope of finding the portal."

Lexie puffed out her chest in pride. "And we have managed to do just that."

"Really? You are sure?"

"With circa 80 per cent certainty, we have identified the only logical location," she said.

"Only 80 per cent?" I asked, trying not to sound too worried.

"Don't worry," said Joshua. "For Lexie, 80 per cent is actually really high. It is there, we guarantee it."

"Well—" started Lexie.

"It is there," grinned Joshua. "I would stake our reputations on it."

Lexie pouted and then nodded brusquely, muttering something under her breath.

"So... Nonsuch?" I asked.

"No," said Lexie. "It would appear that that was a red herring. The real location is here." She pointed to a map, at a point just north of St Albans.

"A red herring? But why would Max do that?" They shrugged and so I continued, putting the mystery to the back of my mind for the time being: "Well, the good news is that it is not too far away. Although we will have to make a detour first."

The huge gates swung open as we approached the Tower of London, revealing a couple of redcoats standing guard. They stiffened to attention when they noticed Captain Pearce.

"I am bringing this demon into custody," said Pearce. "We need to place it in a secure cell at once."

The two soldiers looked uncertain and were about to send inside for orders, so I made a show of rattling my restraints and snarling at my captors. Sergeant Jones hit me hard across the back of my head and I subsided.

"We need access straight away, Private," said Pearce. "I am not sure how much longer we can keep this creature contained."

They nodded, glancing warily at me and then darting out of the way as we passed them. We went through the archway and over the bridge, through another archway and then into the passageway between the inner and outer walls. I turned my head slightly towards Sergeant Jones behind me.

"Ouch," I muttered.

"Had to make it look realistic, sir," he said, a hint of amusement in his voice.

"Shush," said Pearce through gritted teeth. "You all know your roles; wait for my signal."

A pair of officers approached us, accompanied by two of Morley's black-coated Witchfinders. I looked around, weighing up the number of troops that I could see. A dozen were dotted around the courtyard while probably the same number looked down from windows and walkways above us.

"Why have you bought that creature here?" asked one of the Witchfinders.

"I thought that Mr Morley would be interested in examining him—it. Where is he?"

"He is currently conducting an interrogation." My heart quickened at these words as the man continued: "I am not sure why he would be interested in this creature. Why not just kill it and be done?"

"The creature's name is Augustus Potts," said Pearce.

The men looked at each other. "Bring it this way." They turned and led us towards the Bloody Tower. Pearce pushed me forwards and half the men followed behind, the remainder staying in the courtyard with Sergeant Jones.

I made a show of stumbling up the rough stone stairs, keeping a wary eye on our surroundings as we made our way down the cold passageway. It was lit by torches flickering in brackets at shoulder-height, giving the impression of us stepping back in time to the Middle Ages.

We came to a thick door and watched as one of the Witchfinders fumbled with a ring of keys. At a nod from Pearce, his soldiers casually milled around so that they surrounded our small group. Pearce checked his pocket watch and grunted as the door swung open. "In there," the Witchfinder said, stepping aside to let me pass. His eyes widened with alarm when he turned to notice ten gun barrels pointing at his head.

"Please," said Pearce, gesturing into the room. "After you."

The Witchfinders and their soldier escorts stumbled into the pitch-black room, followed by the rest of us. A quick-thinking soldier grabbed a torch from outside the room and used it to light the dormant ones inside, providing stuttering illumination to the square windowless space that was scarcely big enough to fit us all in.

"What is this treachery?" demanded the first Witchfinder as I freed myself from the manacles with a satisfyingly sharp snap of my wrists.

"A slight change of plan," said Pearce. "A young woman was brought here a few hours ago. You will tell us where she is. Now."

"We will not assist anyone who consorts with demons," the man spat back. "You will hang for this, Captain."

He and the other Witchfinder displayed the blind hatred of the truly devout; there was little chance of us getting a helpful answer from them in the short time we had available. I looked at the two soldiers who had accompanied the Witchfinders, and they were shuffling uncomfortably as they scanned the room.

"Sergeant," I said to the nearest one. "Do you know who this is?"

"I do, sir. Captain Pearce, sir."

"And do you know who I am?"

"I think you might be Mr Augustus Potts, sir. I'd heard you'd turned demon." He forced himself to look at me. "You might not remember, but I fought alongside you in the clearances of Holborn, sir. Both of you."

Pearce turned and approached the man. "I remember. Clinton,

isn't it?"

The man nodded, his cheeks flushed and his eyes wide. Not for the first time I marvelled at Pearce's powers of recall, given the sheer numbers of men who must have fought and died in his company over the years.

"Sergeant Clinton," continued Pearce, "I accept that what we are doing here is extremely irregular, but these are desperate times. I have strong reasons to believe that Witchfinder General Morley's actions are not in the best interests of the country. Who are you reporting to at the moment?"

"We were put under the command of Mr Morley, sir."

I shook my head as Pearce continued. "Are there any officers here?"

"No, sir. They were all called away, sir."

"Then I am the ranking officer here. Do you accept my authority?"

The Sergeant glanced at the Witchfinders and then nodded, straightening to attention. "Yes sir." The Private next to him followed suit.

"Very good. You and your men are now under my command. You will help us retake the Tower from the Witchfinders. We should hopefully find that my Sergeant outside has managed to persuade your men in the courtyard to also join us. But first, we need to know where the young girl was taken."

"Miss Thatcher, sir? We knows just where she is, sir. Beauchamp Tower, sir."

The Witchfinders in the other parts of the Tower had offered little resistance, especially once the remaining Fusiliers from the Tower's garrison rallied to our cause. We burst into the Beauchamp Tower with weapons raised; Pearce and I both keen to be first through the door. Two Witchfinders immediately inside the room turned and charged at us, one of them firing a pistol at me. I heard Kate scream and dispatched my attacker with a swift blow to his head, sending him slumping unconscious to the floor. I looked down at my body, relieved to note that the man had panicked and poorly aimed his weapon.

"You," snarled Morley, standing in front of a table on which lay a shivering Kate. Her clothes were torn and I could make out a number of wicked-looking instruments placed around her. The sleeves of her dress had been torn away and her left hand was covered in blood, with a nasty-looking burn further up her arm.

"Morley," I said, fighting the urge to murder him where he stood. "Let her go."

"I do not take orders from the likes of you."

I shook my head, trying to control the rising fury at what he had done to my friend. "This ends now."

"I could not agree more," he said, grabbing a long blade from the table at his side. "Abomination!" he yelled as he lunged at me.

I parried, forced backwards by the ferocity of his attack. Again and again he stabbed and slashed at me with an almost animalistic intensity, his teeth bared and eyes flashing as he focused his entire being on killing me. Once again I had a strange feeling of viewing our exchange from outside my body, seeing the righteous man fighting the terrifying demon, knowing that I should instinctively side with humanity but also that things were no longer that black and white, if indeed they ever had been.

My thoughts slowed me and he managed to dodge inside my defences, scraping his wicked blade down my arm. I spun away, putting a hand to the wound that burnt with red-hot pain. The sword throbbed in my hand, runic symbols glowing, and I finally realised the pointlessness of holding back my demon side. Doing so had nearly killed me once before. I glanced at Kate; if Morley bested me once again, what would happen to her and the others?

I could feel the pull of the sword, the swirl of the runic symbols scrolling and circling but held back as always by my own stubborn determination. The effort of keeping that potent force in check was causing me harm and stopping me from focusing on what I needed to do. With a deep breath, I let go.

There was a buzzing like a million angry wasps burrowing through my arms and into my brain, consuming me, changing me, making everything so very clear.

I looked down at the human and saw how weak and insignificant he was. *How dare this insect harm me?*

I charged forwards into the sea of red.

My first blow shattered Morley's blade, the second snatched the remnants of the weapon from his hand. He spun away and I kicked him hard in the legs. As he fell to one knee I followed up with another foot to his face.

He fell onto his back, his face a bloody mess as he laughed at me through broken teeth. "I knew it. Once a demon, always a demon. Your evil must be wiped out." He glared at me defiantly as I raised the sword above my head, ready to strike. "Do it," he spat. "I will be a martyr to show the true nature of your vile kind."

He stood for everything I hated: the sheer, bigoted ignorance that came with a single-minded belief that there was only one true path. That anything different to him was subhuman and did not deserve to live, and that anyone who thought otherwise was likewise damned. To wipe him off the face of the Earth would not be a sin; if anything, it would enhance humanity, the surgical removal of a malign influence.

I glanced round to see that Pearce had managed to free Kate from her bonds and was busy wrapping a length of cloth round her damaged arm and hand. Kate was watching Morley and I, her face blank as she waited to see what I would do next.

"Do it!" Morley shouted.

I looked back at him. It was what he would have done if our situations were reversed, because he believed that it was the only path he could take. To offer mercy would be to acknowledge that it was not as simple as pure good and evil, that there were shades of grey in between.

I lowered my sword. "No." I stepped away. "It is over, Morley. You lose. And we still have a job to do." I turned to Kate. "Are you all right?"

"Yeah," she said, rubbing her wrists. "He gave me a fright and a few scratches, but that's all. You like roughing up girls, do you?" she asked Morley, who had shuffled back into a corner, spitting out globules of blood and eyeing us warily. Then she turned to me and punched me, hard, in the arm.

"Ouch," I protested. "What was that for?"

"For keeping secrets from me, for not telling me about what was happening to you. For not trusting me to understand."

I stared at her. "But... I thought... aren't you a bit horrified by...?" I waved my hand at my face.

"At first I was pretty shocked, yeah," she said. "But you're our Gus. You're one of us. I thought we were a team." She waved away my stuttered apology. "Save it for the ride to St Albans. I expect you to do some serious grovelling."

266

I nodded. "We should get going." I started towards the door and then halted when I saw the looks on their faces. "What is it?"

"Gus," Kate said gently. "You're... back?"

I looked down at my hands. Even in the half-light I could see that the runic symbols had suddenly retreated. I put my hands to my face, feeling nothing but normal skin and bone. Tears sprang to my eyes. Surely this was impossible? I had given in to my demon side and surrendered all of my moral restraints, given up the last vestiges of my humanity. And yet finally I was human once again.

I started to laugh as I remembered Byron's words, urging me to let go of my resistance to the sword's influence and my fearful, pointless stubbornness of losing myself in the process.

Kate and Pearce were watching me with bemusement. "It's finally happened," she said. "He's completely bloody mad—gone to Hanwell with no return ticket."

"No," I said. "I'm fine. I'm not sure I've ever been better in fact." I looked down at Morley. "What shall we do with him?"

"I can think of a few inventive ideas," said Pearce. "But I do not want to stoop to his level. We should leave him here, to be dealt with when all of this is over."

"Why?" Morley spat at me. "Why don't you kill me?"

I took a deep breath. "Someone very wise pointed out to me not too long ago that, just as not all humans are bad, the same applies to demons. Including me. I could have killed you back in Portsmouth and again just now. At first I thought that was because I was holding back my demon nature, but even when I let go of it..." I shrugged.

"I do not believe you," he said. "This is just more trickery. The demons only care for one thing: to destroy peoples' lives. You have been tainted by them and must be stopped."

I was surprised to see tears running down Morley's cheeks. Kate walked over and squatted next to him.

"Whatever they did to you, or your family, you ain't going to make it better by doing all this," she said. "Bad things happen. Yeah, a lot of the bad stuff recently has been the demons' fault, but don't forget that we can do more than our fair share of pointless evil without any help from that lot with the horns on their heads. I'm not saying we're perfect, but we're trying to save the world here, whatever you might think. And we really need to be in St Albans doing that right now. You could fight with us if you really want to do some good."

He shook his head. "I answer to a higher power," he muttered.

"Hmm," I said. "About that. I believe that the Queen is being influenced by Gaap and the other demons; all the better to sow fear across the country, turning everyone against all demons so that there is no chance of us being able to build a force against the invasion from the portal."

"Damn lies," hissed Morley.

"Really?" I asked. "Then how was it that you always seemed to know exactly where to be? The Pooka tavern? When Andras was with Kate?"

He stared at the floor. "I was given orders by an intermediary."

"What did he look like?" asked Kate. "This intermediary? About so tall, glasses, thinning hair, bit dodgy-looking? If so, you might have had a run-in with our old friend the fake Dr Smith. Who's really the demon who nicked Maxwell and brought back Andras."

Morley stared down, mute, while Pearce nodded to me. "It does seem logical," he said. "The more I think about it, the more it makes sense. Divide and conquer."

Morley shook his head. "If the Queen is working for them, then how do you explain her taking the army up to St Albans?"

"The army's gone to St Albans?" asked Kate.

"Maybe all is not lost," I said. "We should go and join the—"

"Wait," said Pearce. "This makes no sense. I met General Gordon only a few hours ago and was given the distinct impression that nothing was happening. If they were mobilising troops to stop a demon invasion, surely everyone would have been summoned?"

"Especially you and your Company, given your experience," I said.

"Precisely." Pearce turned to Morley. "You said the Queen was taking the army."

"Yes," he said hesitantly.

"That precise wording: *taking*. She has gone with them?"

"That is correct. I was ordered to remain here but she is heading up the army and going to St Albans."

"You are certain?"

Kate frowned. "Why would the Queen go?"

"She shouldn't," I said. "If St Albans is going to descend into a war zone, the last place you want the monarch is in the centre of it."

"Unless…" said Kate.

My heart was beating hard. "We have to go. Now. We may already be too late."

"But hang on," said Kate as we ran out the door, "if they wanted to invade then why take the army up there?"

"It is a lot easier and quicker to kill all of your enemies if they are in one place," said Pearce grimly. He shouted for the soldiers to gather everyone in the courtyard and prepare to move out.

Kate stopped beside a door. "Wait. We need to open this. There's someone else we need to rescue. You still got keys?"

Pearce threw them to her. "Be quick," he said. "We will meet you outside. We leave in five minutes."

She fumbled with the bunch until finally one turned and the door swung open. I followed her through and up a narrow spiral staircase that ended at another locked door. Kate pointed at me and then the door and I nodded, holding my sword ready to attack whoever was on guard beyond.

Kate rapped on the door and a man inside opened it, his face paling as he was confronted with the point of my sword. He raised his hands and backed away, revealing the figure cowering hopelessly in a corner, manacled to the wall.

"You have got to be joking," I said.

CHAPTER TWENTY-EIGHT

We met Lexie and Joshua at King's Cross station and managed to commandeer a train from there. Sergeant Jones squatted in the cab to ensure that the driver remained motivated to keep us moving at full speed while the rest of us sat in the passenger compartment and pored over Lexie's map.

"Just past Smallford Station," said Lexie, her finger tracing the train line. She stabbed at a point a couple of inches to the left of the station. "If we can stop the train and get off here then we should be pretty much on top of them."

"And you're sure of this?" asked Kate. "We're not going to be ambushing a dinner party or a field full of sheep?"

"I'm 90 per cent certain," said Lexie.

"It has gone up," I grinned at Joshua.

"I have done some more calculations," she said. "In any case, I suspect it will be very hard to miss it once the Fulcrum is in full swing."

"It is our job to make sure it does not come to that," I said grimly.

The train screeched to a halt by a small copse and we gathered in the shade of the trees, waiting until everyone had disembarked and the train chuffed away before starting to make our way north towards the Hatfield Road, a main thoroughfare that ran parallel to the Hatfield and St Albans railway line. Immediately beyond it lay the site Lexie had identified as the point of the Fulcrum: an estate a few hundred acres in size with the unassuming name of Yewfields.

Pearce sent off three men to scout for the army while the rest of us advanced through the trees with as much stealth as we could manage, all the while keeping a wary eye out for anything that might herald the end of the world.

The copse opened out into a small field beyond which we could see the Hatfield Road, wide enough for only two carts to pass at a time. Beyond the road lay a line of grand oak trees that demarcated the southern boundary of the Yewfields estate.

We hurried across the field, glimpsing in the gaps between the trees the golden-coloured bricks of the estate's mansion house. My heart was in my mouth as we ran, knowing that if anyone were to look our way there could be no doubt as to our intentions.

The soldiers spread out along the Hatfield Road, taking advantage of the tree line for cover as we turned left and headed west towards the main gates.

We knew from the map that the estate was surrounded on three sides by rows of trees with a main gate onto the Hatfield Road at its south-western corner. A modest gatehouse stood to the right of the entrance, which was in turn framed by imposing brick piers to either side. Watching from over the road we could see no sign of life from within the house but decided to approach with caution regardless. The eastern edge to the estate appeared to be open farmland, dotted with the odd outhouse, and so we resolved to approach from the western edge and use the limited tree cover it afforded.

All seemed quiet as we slunk along the rear of the tree line, keeping ourselves as low and inconspicuous as possible. Well, almost all of us.

"You still haven't spoken to me, you know," said Andras, strolling casually along as though we were taking a morning constitutional.

"For God's sake keep quiet," I hissed.

"Well, I suppose that's progress of sorts."

I pulled him down to a crouch beside me. "What are you doing? They will see you!"

"Oh, they know we're here already. No demon worth his salt could miss you lot tramping around the countryside—as I said earlier, many many times. Not that anyone listened to me."

Everyone was now glaring at the demon, willing him to be silent.

"We are trying to reconnoitre with stealth," I said.

"Pointless exercise," Andras muttered, before lowering his voice to a theatrical whisper. "Does this make you feel better?"

I nodded curtly and turned back to the trees, peering to see the buildings beyond.

Andras tutted. "You know, Kate trusts me. No reason why you shouldn't too."

"I wouldn't say I trust you," Kate whispered. "More like, I know the demons don't want you on our side, so I reckon the best place for you is with us. For the moment, anyways."

"Regardless," he waved her words away, "there's no one better placed to advise on strategy and you have ignored me ever since you released me from that cell."

Pearce sighed. "Then what would you have us do?"

"They know we are here, so why give them the pleasure of thinking we're fooled?"

"So you would just march straight in, yes?"

"Why not? What do we have to lose? Giving away the element of surprise is probably the most surprising thing we could do." We stared at him and he sighed in exasperation. "Think about it. They are trying to create a gateway for their army to advance through. If you were trying to do something so important and potentially fragile, wouldn't you post at least a few guards around the place? How many have we encountered so far? Precisely none."

"Meaning we're either in the wrong place or they're so confident that they don't feel the need for guards," said Pearce.

"Either way," nodded Andras, "we're wasting time by sneaking around out here rather than going straight in for a proper look."

"I admit that there is a kind of twisted logic to what he's saying," said Pearce. We spun around at the sound of footsteps to see one of the scouts returning.

"Sir," said the soldier, "the column is about two miles to the south-west and heading this way. From what I could tell, General Gordon is in command."

"You are certain?"

"Definitely him, sir, I'd recognise him anywhere."

Pearce turned to us. "Maybe there is hope for us yet. I shall go and speak to him; with any luck within the hour I will be back with an army to assist us. In the meantime, please stay here and keep out of trouble." He followed the scout back towards his horse.

"Good news," I said as we watched him go.

"So…" said Kate. "Shall we go and take a closer look at the house?"

"Splendid idea," I said.

"Most sensible thing anyone's said all day," said Andras.

Joshua looked from one to the other of us. "But the Captain just told us to stay here."

"Yeah," grinned Kate. "That was never going to happen."

We made our way from the estate's boundary and across a paddock occupied by a handful of apathetic sheep, arriving at a row of lime trees that stood around ten feet tall. The trees lined a carriage drive that meandered from the estate's gates up to the mansion house itself. They were sufficiently spaced apart to not quite offer us complete cover although, given that there were only the five of us, I was reasonably confident that we were at least partly concealed from the casual observer.

We continued along the avenue of trees until we were 100 yards or so from the mansion house, relying on the lengthening trees' shadows to hide our own as the sun dipped down to the horizon behind us. The building was what could be described as a grand gentleman's country house, standing three storeys high and topped off with a steeply pitched roof clearly designed to convey an impression of importance to all and sundry. Turrets, towers and crenellated walls had been added in an attempt to bestow an element of mediaeval grandeur, as was often the fashion with those sorts of buildings. If there was any doubt as to the wealth of the owners, a forest of chimneys sprouted from every available patch of roof space.

A picturesque garden had been laid in front of the main entrance in the style of Lancelot 'Capability' Brown, with well-tended bushes and low trees standing guard in front of the gravelled driveway. To the left of the house stood a squat, rectangular stable block, with windows and doors topped off in half-moon shapes.

I scrutinised every window we could see for any signs of life. Dark forms shuffled behind a first floor window, tall and bulky enough to be demonic. As we watched, a light flickered in a window to the right of the main doorway. I nudged Kate and nodded up at it. She raised an eyebrow in reply. "Take a look?" she asked.

I nodded. "Stay here," I said to Lexie and Joshua.

"What about me?" asked Andras.

"I really don't care," I said as we moved off.

I had struggled to come to terms with the idea of the demon now being a part of our team, my feelings not helped by the fact that his ongoing presence implied that we had lost N'yotsu forever. Kate seemed to believe that the creature really wanted to help us, and had even tried turning my logic against me: that just because he was a demon did not necessarily make him evil. But I knew what Andras was capable of and the depths to which the creature would stoop. I had first-hand evidence of how he could destroy lives, and in killing my parents to advance his schemes he had done more harm to me than any other.

I also knew that deceit came naturally to Andras and there was every chance that this was yet another one of his grand schemes. A scheme that we would no doubt once again fall foul of.

A low ha-ha ran along the front of the house, 100 yards or so from the building. We ducked into the cover provided by the small walled ditch and worked our way along the front of the house, crouching low to keep ourselves out of view from the ground-floor windows. In front of us, a set of three steps led up from the gravelled drive to a boxed and crenellated archway that shaded the main entrance, another nod to the householder's pretensions of mediaeval grandeur. To the left of the entrance a rectangular window was the source of the candlelight that we had seen from the trees.

I peered into the room from our vantage point and the scene jumped out into stark relief thanks to my enhanced eyesight. "Max," I breathed. He was sat in the middle of a long room, angled away from the window with a candelabra on the table in front of him illuminating the side of his face. Thankfully he appeared to be unharmed, engrossed as always in his work.

"Is it?" whispered Kate. "Are you sure?"

"Certain. He's sat at a table tinkering with something. Can't quite tell what. It looks like he's alone, which is interesting. Maybe there are guards outside the door."

She grunted. "You've got better eyes than me. I can only just about see the candlelight."

I grinned. "One of the benefits of being part-demon."

She looked at me and then frowned as she spotted something over my shoulder. "What's that?"

I turned to look where she had indicated, seeing a flat circular device laid out on the lawn a couple of hundred yards ahead and to the right of our hiding place. It stood no more than a foot high and was fed by a multitude of pipes and tubes, all of which led towards the room in which Maxwell was sat.

"I have a horrible feeling that I know exactly what that is," I said. Maxwell's other portal devices had been larger and more erect, but there was still something in the design of this one that was reminiscent of them. "It looks like we have found the point of the Fulcrum."

"Then we need to do something," said Kate. "A few swings of your sword should do the trick, don't you think? Then we can try to bring Max back to his senses."

I nodded. My instincts were to get to my brother first of all, but there was something in the manner in which he was happily working away that made me wonder if he would immediately jump to our aid. I remembered the touch of the Mage on my mind back in Sheffield, the way that that creature could bend anyone's will to do its bidding. It was very likely—nay, a certainty—that Maxwell was acting under the direction of such a creature now. In the circumstances, Kate's instincts to attack first and ask questions later seemed to be the best policy.

There appeared to be no one around and so we scrambled up the side of the low wall and across to the structure. I drew my sword and peered at the device, trying to ascertain the best place to strike. A junction nearest me looked particularly vulnerable and I swung at it with as much force as I could muster.

My sword froze mere inches away from the device. I attempted to pull it back to try again but the blade was stuck fast as though it was held in an invisible vice. I willed every muscle to come to my aid but then realised that my body was no longer responding to my commands. It was at that point I finally noticed the sickly whispers in my mind.

A hand appeared and plucked the sword from my grasp. "Straighten up," a voice said, and my body jerked upright so that I was staring straight into the deep red eyes of the demon we had confronted all those weeks ago in Sheffield: Gaap. Beyond him I could see the cowled figure of the Mage, while out of the corner of my eye I could just about make out Kate, frozen in place just like me. I glared at the demon. Now that we were face-to-face I could see that he was a corruption of the Dr Smith who had deceived us for all that time back in London. I wanted to kick myself: how had we overlooked it for so long? More to the point, how had N'yotsu not spotted the likeness? Surely he of all people should have been adept at noticing his own kind? The thought of my old friend brought another realisation to mind: Andras had disappeared. Had the fiend abandoned us, true to form? Or maybe he was the one responsible for them discovering us?

Gaap hefted my sword, admiring the balance before thrusting it into the ground. He wagged a finger at me. "Very very naughty. Did you really think we would leave something as important as this unprotected?" He looked beyond me, towards the road and I could make out the sounds of horses and marching boots. "Ah, good. The army is here." He grinned at me. "Don't worry, we have this covered."

The crunch of hooves and wheels on the driveway behind us grew in volume and Gaap walked past me, leaving me feeling like a mere ornamental statue. "Your Majesty," I heard him say. "And Prime Minister. So pleased that you have come to welcome my people."

"Not at all," I heard Disraeli say in a dull voice, the words sounding forced out of his mouth. "The pleasure is all ours." There was a pause as he noticed Kate and I. "We understood they were here. We intercepted Captain Pearce. He is under arrest, along with his General. They had plans that were not in accordance with our own."

"Yes," said Gaap. "That is a niggle we should deal with before they have a chance to jeopardise our plans. Please bring your prisoners forwards: we shall dispatch them right now. Mr Potts! How are our plans progressing?"

I saw Maxwell wheel into view, pushed over to the device in front of me by a Berserker demon. I tried pleading with my eyes: surely he of all people would come to our aid?

His head jerked as though he were a marionette being controlled by invisible wires from on high and my heart sank as I realised that he, too, was under the Mage's thrall. "All is ready, and by my calculations the Fulcrum is near. We can trigger the device whenever you wish."

Two figures sprawled on the ground next to me and then jerked upright: I surmised that they were Captain Pearce and General Gordon, not only arrested but now also subjected to the humiliation of the Mage's evil embrace.

From somewhere behind I heard the sound of hooves beating a rapid advance and I felt a faint sliver of hope: could help be at hand?

The horse clattered to a halt not far away and I heard the rider drop to the ground with a squelch. "Your Majesty?" I heard Witchfinder General Morley address the Queen. I held my breath: he had clearly rushed to follow us as soon as we had left the Tower, no doubt to try to warn the Queen of what he saw as our treachery.

"It's no use speaking to her," said Gaap. "I am the puppet-master here. And you have been a fine servant to us, Mr Morley."

"What? I don't—"

"Of course you don't understand," sneered Gaap. "But you may rest assured that you have played your part admirably. Come." He held a hand out and beckoned to Morley. "Come, come," he urged, as though enticing a nervous puppy.

I heard Morley slowly approach until he drew level with me. He looked over at me and the others. "They are working for you?" he asked the demon slowly.

Gaap chuckled. "Oh no, not them. They are an inconvenience that I will soon rid myself of. But don't worry: you did well enough, even though you did let them escape and get here."

I could see Morley's face clearly now as he looked from Gaap to me to the Queen and the soldiers behind us. His usual rock-solid certainty, dented slightly by our encounter in the Tower, was crumbling before me. His mouth opened and closed but no sound came out, while his eyes cast around wildly for something to make sense of the madness before him. I felt a rare sympathy for the man: he had built his entire existence on blind faith in a world that was painted black and white, with his place amongst the angels assured. With one fell swoop, Gaap had destroyed all of that, confirming what we had tried to tell him: that Queen Victoria and all his other masters had been dancing to the demons' tune all the while. And by extension, so had he.

I tried to will him into action with my eyes, desperately hoping that he would turn his confusion into some form of positive, devastating action. His eyes welled up while his face twisted into a confused, sorrowful rage, his hands balled into fists at his sides. "No," he muttered through clenched teeth, "no-no-no-no-no."

"As a reward for your service," continued Gaap, either unaware or uncaring as to the Witchfinder's internal struggle, "I am happy for you to kill any of these yourself." He gestured to me. "I know that you have particularly strong feelings for young Augustus here. Or how about indulging in your soft spot for the girl Kate? You may do with her as you please, then kill her."

Morley blinked and drew his sword from its scabbard, looking at it as though he had forgotten it existed. His eyes flicked from the blade to meet my gaze and for a second I thought I sensed the briefest of nods.

He turned and charged at Gaap with a roar born of all the hatred and despair that had boiled up within his body and mind, swinging his sword over his head as he ran.

Gaap sighed and stepped to the side of the clumsy attack, lashing out with a foot that caught Morley hard in his side. He fell to the ground with a sickeningly loud crunch, flailing around in the mud for his sword. Before he could scramble to his feet, Gaap had crouched down in front of him.

"You don't want to kill me," the demon said. "Think of everything you've done, all that you've become. Is that really what you set out to achieve when you lost your wife and daughter all those years ago? Is all of this what you wanted?" He gestured around them, at the dark, muddy field with us all frozen motionless before the demons and Max's device. "You know what you really want to do," Gaap said, straightening up and turning away.

For a moment, Morley stayed curled in a ball on the ground, his shoulders moving up and down. Then he looked up with eyes streaming tears before plunging his sword into his own chest. With a grunt, he was gone.

"So easy, so predictable." Gaap walked round so that he was addressing us all, a broad grin splitting his hideous features. "Really, it's a wonder that you creatures have managed to become the dominant lifeform in this realm. Until now, of course." He clapped his hands together. "In any case, on to business. I know that you, Mr Potts, have had the pleasure of experiencing the power of my

Mage. Well done for surviving that, by the way. Although sadly your friend N'yotsu will not be able to save you this time."

I steeled myself, trying to summon up any and all reservoirs of resistance I had left. I would not let the creature make me kill my friends.

Gaap let out a slight chuckle, almost as though he could see my intentions writ large in my eyes. "Yes indeed, it would be entertaining to make you all hack each other to pieces, but time is short and I don't want to risk one of you doing something that might hinder our plans, so we'll just settle for you dying now." He nodded to the Mage.

Something hard wedged itself in my throat and I swallowed to try to dislodge it.

"Let them move," I heard Gaap say. "They can't harm us now, and we may as well have a bit of entertainment while we wait for the device to warm up."

I felt the Mage's grip on my body fall away, but what relief I may have experienced was subsumed by the implacable hardness in my throat. I fell to my knees and clawed at my neck, my eyes bulging out of their sockets as I strained to get my lungs to work.

I felt as though I were floating away, my brain pulling itself out of my head as everything started to swim around me. Lights and shapes flashed around the edges of my vision, while everything else condensed to a narrow tunnel.

I could imagine the stares of my brother, of Disraeli and the soldiers, no doubt horrified behind their helpless masks of enforced stillness. We had failed; I had failed all of my friends and now we would die, the world fated to end with us at the hands of these monsters. The grass came up to greet me and I felt my heart slow to a halt. I looked round to see Kate clawing at the ground, her face bright red.

No.

I would not let this happen. I summoned up every ounce of willpower, every part of me, demonic and human, bringing all of it to bear against the Mage's cold hand. For a fleeting moment I felt something slip and a whisper of air made it into my lungs.

I grabbed hold of that small victory and pushed, feeling for a crack in the door of the Mage's implacable will so that I could force my way through it. I looked up to see my sword mere inches away and remembered how it had saved me once before when all seemed lost, when Andras had us helpless and supposedly doomed. I could do it again.

With a hammer blow the Mage redoubled its efforts and I collapsed to the ground, my meagre efforts met by a solid steel wall. I looked up at the creature, willing myself to do something, anything, before it was too late. My world narrowed into a single point of focus, a dull window with the Mage at its centre.

The creature hesitated and looked down to see a blade protruding from its chest. It slumped to the ground to reveal Andras standing behind it.

The Mage's touch immediately lifted and I desperately sucked in air through a throat that felt like it was lined with broken glass. I could hear hacking from the others around me.

"Gaap," said Andras. "Such a pleasure to see you again."

"Andras. What are you doing here?"

The demon stooped to retrieve his sword from the Mage's body, using the corpse's cloak to wipe the blade clean. "That's the one problem with having a pet Mage. It can make you rather complacent. You were so certain you had everyone under your control that you forgot to keep an eye out for any wild cards. And to answer your question: I'm here to stop you."

"You're too late," sneered Gaap. "It's already begun."

I looked up to see a swirling vortex of light hovering above Maxwell's device. Like a thunderclap, a burst of stale wind blasted out over us, forcing those who were standing to take a step backwards. A flash of light blinded the heavens and I buried my face into the ground.

I looked up to see a hole in the world in front of me, a void that had consumed half of the mansion house beside it. Bricks scattered around me as I grabbed Kate and pulled her away with me. She pointed to the side of the portal and I saw Maxwell stranded in his wheelchair, desperately trying to lever himself away.

An army of demons marched towards us from the other side of the portal and our ears filled with the screams of countless beasts coming to slaughter us all.

CHAPTER TWENTY-NINE

Kate and I rushed to Maxwell and pushed him away from the portal. He looked at us, wide-eyed and opened his mouth.

"Just don't say it," shouted Kate. "We'll all have time to say sorry and whatnot if we survive this."

I stooped to grab my sword as we passed it, feeling a relieving flow of power from the weapon as I did so. We ran through the line of soldiers that was being hastily assembled in front of the portal.

Captain Pearce and General Gordon had pulled the Queen back to behind the ha-ha and were hoisting her unceremoniously onto a horse, a group of mounted soldiers waiting to accompany her. Disraeli was shaking his head at Gordon as we approached.

"I should stay here and offer what assistance I can," he said. "I am to blame for this debacle: I should see it through."

Gordon looked him up and down. "Sir, unless you have developed an ability to fire a gun or swing a sword, you are no use to us here. You should go back with Her Majesty and send us whatever reinforcements you can." Without waiting for an answer, the Hero of Taiping marched away. Disraeli watched him go and then mutely accepted the reins of a horse from an approaching soldier.

"She looks smaller than I imagined," muttered Kate as she watched the Queen ride away. She turned to Maxwell. "So that's the Fulcrum then?"

Maxwell looked to where she was indicating, the swirling vortex atop his device. "No. That is a portal to the Aether. The Fulcrum is what is happening to allow the portal to be as large and stable as it is: the confluence of magic and science."

I turned to look at the portal. It was roughly 100 feet in width and ten feet high, large enough for lines of 20 demons at a time to come through shoulder-to-shoulder. Thankfully, this also provided enough of a bottleneck so that we could contain them, although just the mere sight of the small numbers emerging so far was enough to stop a man in his tracks.

They were huge, each approaching seven feet in height and half as wide, casting hideously broad shadows towards us. Each wore chitinous black armour that rippled as they marched, slick scales clacking together, a drum beat from Hell heralding their approach.

Once I would have just seen a mass of identical creatures but now I could tell that they each had their own distinctiveness: different shaped heads or horns, a scar or colouration to the face, even the varied sets to their expressions. What was relatively uniform, though, was the single-minded venom with which they regarded us as they advanced.

Pearce was shouting orders and in no time the soldiers had lined themselves up in double ranks in front of us, stretching from the line of trees on their left flank and in a wide semi-circle around the portal. He ordered them forwards so they were a handful of paces in front of the ha-ha and I nodded at the logic: we did not want to cede any form of higher ground, as even the minimal dip afforded by the ditch could give the attackers the advantage. The front rank went down on one knee while their comrades behind turned so they were ready to aim at the monsters approaching from the portal. At a barked order, they fixed their bayonets to the muzzles of their modified Snider-Enfield rifles.

"Let's give them a warm welcome," shouted Pearce. "Front rank: fire!"

The guns roared as one and the world filled with thick smoke and the acrid tang of gunpowder.

"Front rank: reload! Second rank: fire!"

Reassured that Maxwell was safe behind the lines for the time being, I made my way to the left flank and through the trees so that I could see beyond the smoke. The metronomic firing of the soldiers continued, gunpowder wreathing the land in a pungent fog. My demon-enhanced senses cut through the screen to see that the gunfire was having its desired effect, for the time being at least. Those creatures that had managed to make it through the portal were scattered around the ground, either dying or gravely injured. Nearer to me, Andras and Gaap were engaged in a battle of their own, hacking at each other with their swords.

Joshua and Lexie appeared at my side. "Are you all right?" Lexie asked.

I nodded. "You?"

She blinked at me and Joshua asked: "What can we do?"

"Keep out of trouble," I shouted over the latest report from the guns. "Actually, go to Maxwell over there. See if you can come up with any ideas." They nodded and ran in the direction I had indicated.

"You ready for a scrap?" asked a voice at my side. I jumped and then cursed in relief as I recognised Kate, a sword in one hand, her LeMat pistol in the other.

"What are you doing here?" I asked. "You should be with Max—"

"And nursemaid him while you get to do all the fun stuff?" she asked. "There's an army between him and the demons, and I've got some pent-up frustration to get rid of." She darted forward and fired her pistol at the nearest demon, whooping as it spun away.

I watched Andras and Gaap, tempted to order a few soldiers to direct fire at the two demons. But then if Andras was killed he would take with him any chance of us getting N'yotsu back. And he had saved us from the Mage…

Andras stumbled and I cursed as I ran towards them, swinging my sword at Gaap's back. At the last moment he turned and parried my blow, sending me spinning off to the side. I landed in a crouch a few paces from Andras, who was also recovering his footing.

"Good of you to join me, old chap," Andras said. "In case you were wondering, now would be a really good time to let loose your demon side."

A surge of animalistic joy swept over me as I realised the sense in his words and a switch flicked in my head that released my demonic rage. I felt the runic symbols flow into my arms and move over my body and then grinned at Gaap. A flicker of uncertainty—or was it fear?—passed over the demon's face and then I heard Andras bellow: "That's my boy!" as he threw himself at our foe.

285

Gaap was strong and fast, but he could do little in the face of our combined assault. He stepped back again and again as he struggled to bat away the blows from our blades and I let out a primal yell as I managed to carve a deep wound in his arm. Gaap fell back and yelled as Andras stuck him with yet another blow. He staggered, but before we could close in for the kill a roar erupted from the portal.

It had widened and was now thick with the forms of demons streaming through. While many of them were wilting under the gunfire, still more were making it through and approaching the ranks of defenders. The soldiers shouted as they were given the order to advance with their bayonets, the battle swiftly descending into the chaos of hand-to-hand combat.

"There are not enough of them," said Andras, staring at the ranks of humans advancing on the demon army. There was a sound from the rear and I turned to see yet more demons coming towards us. My heart caught in my throat; how had they managed to outflank us? Andras cursed as he saw them as well.

"Pooka," he spat.

I grinned as I recognised Byron and Kingdom in the front rank streaming towards us. The big demon clapped me on the back as he drew level. "Well, are you going to fight or just stand there?" he shouted as they rushed past us.

I looked to Andras and then down at the ground in front of us. "Gaap," I shouted.

We cast around. The demon had disappeared.

"Worry about that later," shouted Andras, pointing to the battle in front of us. "I'll be damned if I'm going to be out-fought by Pooka and humans!" He launched himself into the fight with a howl.

I looked around, trying to determine the best place for me to enter the fray. Everywhere was chaos and I realised that there was a very real risk that the Almadites could benefit from the inevitable confusion caused by the Pooka. The soldiers would have no idea that the other demons were on their side and as such there was a danger that erstwhile allies could turn on each other unawares in the heat of battle.

I ran after my friends and into battle, ready to tear humans away from attacking Pooka but I need not have worried: there was little doubt who the enemy was. The Almadites that were coming through the portal were bigger and fiercer than the Pooka could ever be. Yet in spite of this, the Pooka were able to match them in aggression and violence, making the most of the increased manoeuvrability that their smaller size afforded them.

A soldier fell in front of me, an Almadite swinging down at him with what was intended to be a killing blow. I threw myself in front of the soldier's prone form, barging my shoulder into the demon's midriff. As we landed hard on the ground I brought my sword up in a clumsy stab that skewered the creature.

Coming up onto one knee, I threw myself at the next Almadite I saw, my blade swinging hard and fast, not pausing as the creature fell but then moving on to the next and then the next. I once again found myself lost in the red mist, and I revelled in it.

The world narrowed into the horrifyingly familiar grind of battle, a place of screams and blood, limbs that ached but dared not rest lest the pause be taken advantage of by a passing foe. My senses were heightened, constantly on the lookout for the next threat and then the one after that. I grunted as I slashed and hacked and parried, cleaving through bodies with ease, focusing all of my energies on just getting past the next foe—on killing before I was myself killed.

There was no time to think, for to do so would be to give my enemy a vital split-second advantage, and so I reacted, simply trusting my instincts and the will of my sword as I worked my way through a never-ending field of demons.

I could not tell how long it had been since I had entered the battle and how many bodies I had left in my wake, but I suddenly found myself looking out into an emptying field. I spun round to see soldiers and Pooka behind and beside me and a dwindling number of Almadites coming through the portal to attack us.

"They're falling back," said Byron. "We're pushing them back!"

"Yep," said Andras. "Now it's time to finish them off once and for all." He started forwards and then jerked to a halt.

Gaap had appeared before us, clearly badly wounded but still more than capable of causing trouble. He was leaning heavily upon Maxwell's wheelchair, with a knife held to my brother's throat.

"Stay back," Gaap shouted. "Stay back or I will kill him."

"No you won't," said Andras, stepping forwards. "He's too valuable to you."

"True. But I could kill him and then reanimate him with a

Djinn. He'd still be of some use to me, and you'd lose him forever."

Andras stopped and Maxwell held out his hands. "It's all right," he said to us. "I can handle this." He turned his head to look at the demon. "You are going to go back through the portal without me. You will also order your forces to desist with this invasion."

Gaap stared at him and laughed. "And why would I do that, little man?"

"When you were in charge of my treatment, under the guise of being my doctor, do you recall treating my brother and N'yotsu for the effects of a rather nasty little compound?"

Gaap looked back uncertainly and so Maxwell continued.

"Before you spirited me away, I took the opportunity to modify my wheelchair. You will find that, rather than being hollow like conventional appliances, the frame of this particular wheelchair is filled with large quantities of that compound. It is rather more potent than the one I used previously, so you will die in quite some agony. Unless, of course, you do as I say."

"But... you wouldn't dare—you would die too."

"I would, but it would be worth it to know that I had taken you with me. As well as any other creatures standing close enough to the portal, of course."

Andras growled next to me. "I do not want that bastard to get away."

I shared his feelings but was also keen to not lose my brother, and watched the exchange in front of us with bated breath.

Gaap stared at Maxwell, his face alternating between sceptical amusement and genuine fear. After a few moments he backed away slowly and then disappeared into the portal, alone.

CHAPTER THIRTY

For a moment we stared at the portal, frozen in place as we reassured ourselves that no more demons were coming through. Then Maxwell started gesturing to us. "Lexie, Joshua: I need you here, now!"

They ran over and Kate and I followed in case we could be of some use in their scientific tinkerings. Predictably, we were not.

Maxwell had them wheel him round to the rear of the portal, where the bulk of the device was still evident. Kate and I followed, ducking warily round the edges of the portal that shimmered with an impossible malevolence. As I passed I noted that it seemed to be the same from whichever angle we viewed it, as though it were a perfect and uniform sphere.

"This is basically iteration number 14 of the device I showed you when you first joined us in London," said Maxwell to Lexie and Joshua. "Do you recall?"

"I do," said Lexie slowly. "We did a bit of work on it but you then said it was an irrelevant mistake and ordered us to do something else. Does this mean it did work after all?"

"Yes. Ah, I am afraid I must confess to not having been totally truthful with you over the past few months."

"What a surprise," muttered Kate.

"But in my defence," Maxwell glared back at her, "I was not acting under my own volition. I now understand that I was acting under the influence of Gaap and his Mage."

"So they forced you to work for them? They made you want to

help them invade our world?"

"Yes. And no. I did not realise that they were demons until they kidnapped me and brought me here. I promise you, I really did think that I was acting *against* the demons, not for them."

He looked at us all for reassurance and I saw in his eyes the same helpless terror I had felt when I was first controlled by the Mage, the disgust that my body and mind could have betrayed me so easily. I nodded and he turned back to the device.

"Lexie, you recall the calculations you were working on before I sent you to Portsmouth with Kate? Well, you were right: they will enable us to create a barrier over the portal."

"I knew it," she smiled triumphantly.

"We need to adjust the flow from this dial here," Maxwell said. "The Fulcrum is not yet strong enough to sustain the portal on its own, so we needed to use artificial means to fuel it."

"You mean it's powered by steam?" asked Kate.

He turned a pale face to us. "Not quite. My God, what have we done? You need to get in there now: follow the pipes. You need to help them."

We didn't wait for an explanation but ran towards the house. I could hear footsteps behind me and glanced back to see Andras, Byron and Kingdom following Kate and I. The pipes led over and through the rubble of the room that we had seen Maxwell in earlier. Thankfully the house was showing no signs of disintegrating further; it was open to question whether that was due to high quality workmanship or because the portal was propping it up. We did not stop to consider this but charged across the room and through a large door into a long hallway. The pipes flowed straight through and then took a right turn up a grand oak staircase. I took the stairs two at a time, following them round as they cut back on themselves and then headed out onto the first floor landing. The pipes ran into the leftmost room and I burst through the door, stopping short as I took in the scene before me.

Until very recently the room had clearly been a grand bedroom with a lavish sitting area. The furniture, or at least as much as had been allowed to remain, had been cast roughly to the sides of the room to make space for the horrors in its centre. The five pipes flowed straight into the space, like a Kraken's tentacles reaching in hungrily for food that lay prone on the tables scattered around the room: Pooka. Or rather, what was left of their bodies, as they were mere husks, drained by the pipes that fed the portal on the lawn outside. Around the outskirts of the room cowered a dozen or more Pooka in chains, clearly awaiting their turn once their friends had been exsanguinated. A rage grew in me; there was no limit to the depths to which the Almadites would not plumb. *Max,* I thought, *what have you done?*

"Of course," said Andras. "The portal is powered by blood. Demonic life-forces originating from beyond the Aether. Forged in one realm and shaped in another, as the texts say: the perfect way to build a bridge between worlds. Ingenious!"

"If I were you," rumbled Kingdom, "I would keep your opinions to yourself." He ran over to the nearest table.

We did what we could to release the victims without harming them any further. One, who resembled more an ancient mummified Egyptian than Pooka, was already dead. The other four still showed signs of life, although we could not be sure for how much longer that would be the case. Kate had managed to gather together a couple of soldiers from outside who had medical training and they busied themselves with doing what they could to save the poor, unfortunate creatures.

"What can we do?" I asked.

"They have lost a lot of blood," a medic said. "We need to replace it as soon as possible but I do not have the equipment here and I cannot risk moving them in this state." He ran a hand across his brow. "I don't even know if their bodies have blood like ours."

"We do," said Byron. "Whatever you need, we can help."

Joshua burst into the room. "They need blood," he shouted.

"We got that memorandum," I said and then noted the pipes in his hands. "What have you got there?"

He squatted in front of us and showed us two rubberised pipes that he had fashioned together with a bulb in between them. He squeezed the bulb and the medic nodded. "That should create enough of a pumping action to transfer blood from one to another. Very inventive." He glanced approvingly up at Joshua. "Can you make more of these?"

Joshua nodded. "Gus, if you can cut me some lengths of these tubes, I can do the rest."

I obliged and then helped him create more of the simple contraptions. "That's really clever," I said. "Is it your idea?"

"No. A friend of our family works at Sheffield Hospital for

Women. Dr Aveling. It's something he showed me last year. He's been dying to try it out, so he'll be really interested to know how we get on."

Byron and Kingdom volunteered to provide blood and we shouted out the window for two more Pooka to do likewise. I looked down at the creatures while we waited. "I am part-demon: could you use my blood?"

"I suspect you would not be compatible," said the medic, frowning over a tube as he struggled to insert it into a vein.

"What about me?" asked Andras. We all looked up at him in surprise and he shrugged. "I would like to do something to help."

Byron glared at him. "Why would we want your help?"

"You weren't so slow to accept my assistance out there when we were fighting—" He stopped himself and held up a hand. "There is no love lost between our people, I grant you. But I am as much an enemy of them as you are. They exiled me from my home, stranded me in the Aether for millennia."

"While we just lost our home and our people thanks to your invasion," snapped Byron.

I was about to wade in and try to broker peace when Kingdom spoke up. "It will take more than one battle for us to trust you, Andras," he said. "But if you are determined to win our confidence then we are willing to let you try. But if you so much as think of double-crossing us, then…" He let the threat hang in the air and Andras quickly looked away.

The medic cleared his throat. "In any case, I suspect you may not be compatible either. After all, there appear to be as many different types of demons as there are creatures on our own world."

"At last you understand it," grinned Byron. "Maybe there is hope for you all yet."

"You and your people fought alongside us and helped us beat back those creatures," said the medic. "That makes you a friend of mine, whatever you look like or wherever you came from. Now sit still, this might hurt a little."

Kate sidled up to Andras. "Of course, there is one thing that would help us trust you: bring back N'yotsu."

He sighed. "I am getting rather tired of explaining this. I am—"

"N'yotsu as well as Andras," she cut in, "yes, I get it. But while you still have the bad bits of you—"

"—I am alive and can function. As you saw rather graphically not too long ago, I cannot survive without those parts of me. But just because I have some rather unsavoury demonic characteristics, that does not make me completely evil. Just ask Gus."

I bristled at the implication. "What makes you evil is the fact that you are Andras," I said.

He shrugged. "I have changed. I will just have to try to prove it to you. But allow me one small victory: surely your adventures into being a demon have shown you one or two things to prove me right?"

I grunted. When Kate stared quizzically at me I nodded reluctantly. "I am part-demon and have accepted that fact. I did think that being a demon would mean I could not help but be evil but, as the doctor so rightly said, there are many different types of demon. I choose to be one of the benign ones."

"As do I," grinned Andras. "For the moment at least. Especially if it means I get to beat Gaap to Hell and back."

"Speaking of which," I said, "it all looks to be in hand up here. We should see how Maxwell is getting on."

As we made our way down the stairs Kate could not resist one last shot at Andras. "So you're planning on staying like that?" she asked.

"I think so," he snapped back. "Why, are you?"

Outside, the chaos that I remembered from the battle and its immediate aftermath had subsided into the restrained, dull horror that I had seen too many times before. All of the soldiers who were still fit were stood in wary watch over the portal, weapons trained and ready for the slightest motion from beyond. Meanwhile, just beyond the ha-ha a makeshift field hospital had been set up where the injured were being tended to. Fires blazed around and about, their flickering illumination merging with the swirling cold lights of the portal to cast the scene in a stark, almost hellish tinge.

I nodded to Pearce as we passed him. "Any change?" I asked.

"None yet. With any luck they will lick their wounds for long enough to allow Maxwell to do whatever it is he is doing."

We approached Maxwell and Lexie. "How are you getting on?"

"We would be getting on a lot quicker if we did not have to

keep answering questions about how we are getting on," he mumbled. I grinned: clearly he was feeling better already.

"As far as I can tell, Max," I said, "it is Lexie and Joshua who are doing all the work. Why don't you try explaining what's going on to us while you're sitting there supervising them?"

He frowned at me and then shook his head in resignation. "The power to the portal has been extinguished and we are in the process of attempting to contain the field that provides the porous qualities to the fabric of space." When we stared at him blankly he sighed: "Think of it like trying to put a barrier in place over the portal. Hopefully it will not take too much longer." He glanced up at the swirling lights of the portal and I followed suit, relieved to see nothing untoward there. Yet.

"If there's no power," said Kate, "then why's it still here?"

"The... ah... elements that were powering the portal—"

"The blood of the Pooka," I said. "Let's be clear about that. The blood of innocent demons was powering the portal."

He looked at me. "Yes. Indeed. Something I regret and will continue to do so for the rest of my life. Are they all right?"

"One is dead. The others... we are doing the best we can."

He nodded. "You must believe me. I had no control..." Tears sprang to his eyes.

Kate walked over and put a hand on his shoulder. "Don't worry Max. We understand, don't we?" She looked pointedly at me.

Empathy cracked the hard shell of my anger. "Yes, we do. The Mage made us all do things that we wouldn't have otherwise done."

"Like try to choke ourselves to death," said Kate.

"By the by," said Andras, "you're welcome. For me stopping the Mage. I did that you know."

We ignored him. "Max, you were saying about the portal?" I said.

"Yes, well," he said, flicking back into his usual matter-of-fact tone of speech. "The elements—the blood—powering the portal served the purpose of punching a hole through the aforementioned fabric of space. Unlocking the door, as it were. A door that was made possible due to the existence of the Fulcrum. Turning off the source of power has simply stopped it from wedging itself open any wider, but does not reverse the fact that it is already open."

"So how do we close it?" asked Pearce.

"I am not sure we can," said Maxwell. "At least, not now;

although the implications of Lexie's formula may point us to a way of being able to do so in time. As I have said on numerous occasions, the Fulcrum is a force of nature, an irreversible event." Lexie cleared her throat and Maxwell held up a hand. "Very well, yes, in time it will reverse, when the balance between science and magic once again tips the other way. But that could be centuries or even millennia from now."

"So you're just stopping it getting bigger?" Kate asked.

"No. We are also in the process of amending the frequencies of the portal so that it will abhor any matter that comes into contact with it." In reply to our blank gazes he added: "So nothing will be able to get through."

"How much longer will it take?" I asked.

"A few minutes," called back Lexie.

Pearce shuffled uncomfortably, he and his fellow soldiers keeping their unwavering vigil on the portal. I looked back at Maxwell and for the first time noticed how tired he looked. "How are you?" I asked, kneeling down beside him.

"I am fine," he lied. "It has been a long day."

I nodded and patted the arm of his wheelchair. "By the way, what you did earlier with Gaap: that was very brave."

He let out a short laugh. "It was, wasn't it? I am not really used to that sort of thing."

"Quite a bluff though," said Kate.

He looked up at her. "Oh, it was no bluff."

I pulled my hand away from the wheelchair and jumped back, imagining myself once more being contaminated by that malignant gas. "What do you mean? You really have filled your wheelchair with that poisonous compound?" He nodded and I threw my hands in the air. "You idiot!"

He chuckled. "Even while I was under the Mage's sway I knew that I could not let something as potent as the compound fall into the wrong hands. This was the safest place I have. In any case, I knew that I needed a back-up plan: that seemed like the most logical way to achieve it."

"But you wouldn't seriously have done it, would you? Released the gas?"

"If I had needed to, yes. Without hesitation."

"But... why? We could have—"

He held up a hand. "I am fed up with you all thinking I am

helpless. Surely you of all people should understand that."

I nodded slowly, my face reddening as I thought about how I had treated him since his accident, like little more than a wounded child. "I am sorry, I meant no offence," I said quietly.

"Before we go all weepy," said Kate, "can we just agree that you're going to take the compound out of the wheelchair as soon as possible and put it somewhere safe?"

He pulled a face. "I am not so sure. It has been quite liberating knowing that I am dangerous once more."

"Max," Kate said firmly, "you are the most accident-prone person I know, after your brother." She waved away our protests. "You bang into one sharp table edge and suddenly wipe out half of Whitehall. Do you want that on your conscience?"

He chuckled. "Fair enough. I promise. Besides, I have other ideas of how I can improve the utility of this device... speaking of which, I had a brainwave earlier and I believe that I know how I can cure you of your... affliction."

"Affliction?" I asked.

"The demonic changes brought on by the runic sword. I believe I can reverse them. Without almost killing you this time."

I looked down at my hands, once again recognisably human. "You know," I said, "I think I'm all right as I am."

Before he could respond, our attention was diverted by Pearce shouting at his men to make ready. I looked over to see dark forms starting to swim into focus from within the portal once more. My heart sank as I drew my sword; I was not sure how many more of these assaults we would be able to withstand.

"Don't get any clever ideas about that stuff in your wheelchair," Kate said to Maxwell. "We need you in the land of the living for the moment."

He was already focused on other matters, though. "Lexie?" he shouted.

"One more minute!" She ran round the front of the portal, ignoring our cries of alarm. Joshua was on her heels, clearly doing all he could to put himself into harm's way first.

I cursed and ran towards them. "The quicker you can do this, the better," I said.

"Thank you for that very helpful insight," muttered Lexie as she adjusted some dials, consulting a crumpled piece of paper as she did so. "There," she said finally. "Just need to activate that lever over there." She pointed to a large switch on the other side of the portal.

"I'll do it," shouted Joshua, starting off at a sprint before any of us could stop him.

The next few seconds stretch out like hours in my mind's eye, like a succession of tragic portraits on a wall that I am forced to crawl past, time after time. No sooner had Joshua set off than he was brought short by a shout of alarm and a volley of gunfire from the soldiers behind us. The demons had started to emerge from the portal once more.

I flinched but then threw myself forwards to try to get in between the young man and the creatures advancing towards him.

"The lever!" I shouted, pointing.

I ran forwards but was overtaken by someone quicker and smaller: Lexie.

A huge form darted out of the swirling lights of the portal, arrowing straight for its closest target: Joshua.

I forced my legs to pump harder, willing every fibre of my being to provide me with just one last surge of energy. Lexie was just ahead of me, running with grim determination.

Out of the corner of my eye I saw another burst of movement: Kate was running towards the lever from the other side.

I threw myself through the air towards Joshua.

A hideous arm and glinting teeth emerged from the portal, a creature unlike any we had seen so far. It put me in mind of a praying mantis in both looks and ruthless intent.

I heard Andras shout: "Furies!" Or maybe it was a memory of something N'yotsu had said a long time ago.

The Fury turned towards us, for I was now in its line of sight too, and I readied myself to defend us.

The creature snapped round and grabbed a smaller form who had thrown herself in front of her brother, ripping Lexie in two.

Joshua and I both shouted.

I grabbed at Joshua as he hysterically screamed his sister's name and attempted to reach her shattered body. Then Kate pulled down on the lever and the world exploded into a madness of white light.

CHAPTER THIRTY-ONE

I struggled to my feet with the taste of blood in my mouth and my ears ringing painfully. The world seemed harsher and sharper to my battered senses. The portal still loomed above us but it was changed, with the beautifully deadly swirls having taken on a slightly fuzzy and indistinct aspect. Dark forms moved inside and I had the distinct impression that they were impotently battering at it.

I looked round and saw Maxwell being helped back into his chair. He nodded at me: it was done, the barrier was in place over the portal. I then registered the look of anguish on his face as he looked over at us.

I staggered forwards and collapsed next to Joshua, who was cradling the battered remains of his sister. She looked at us sightlessly, a faint smile playing on lips flecked with blood and fragments of bone and tissue.

I put a hand on his shoulder, trying to think of something to say.

We became aware of shouting and turned to see a group of soldiers surrounding the Fury which had broken through to kill Lexie. It towered over the men, reaching up to around eight feet in height as it cast around with its triangular head and overlarge eyes. It was topped by a pair of wickedly sharp horns, while rows of vicious teeth snapped and clicked at us. Its skin was a deep black that shone a wet blue as it caught the light, with long, muscular arms flailing round at its would-be captors.

The soldiers were struggling to contain the beast, their bullets and bayonets seeming to do little more than irritate it, and so I threw myself into the fray, barging past the soldiers and squaring up to the beast, my sword raised.

It swung an arm at me, the pointed claw at the end of it aiming for my heart. I threw myself to the side and as I did so I could see blood dripping from its talons. I pushed aside the thought of whose it was and swung with my sword.

The creature screamed in rage as the limb was cleanly severed and I took advantage of its distraction to sweep my blade at its legs, jumping aside as it crashed to the ground.

I approached it with my sword raised, ready for the killing blow, but was stopped short by a cry from behind.

"No!" shouted Joshua. "*It is mine.*"

He pushed me aside and approached the beast, his face pale and drawn so tight that I barely recognised him as the carefree youth we had spent those past weeks with. He muttered some sounds and the creature's limbs burst into flames.

The Fury screamed and thrashed about but could not extinguish the conflagration that showed no signs of advancing up its body; at least, not yet.

I found myself watching the creature with a sick fascination, unable to look away and almost relishing the thing's suffering. It had taken away our friend, and it deserved to suffer.

I looked up and could see my feelings mirrored in those of the others, including Andras who watched with a glint in his eye and a half-smile on his lips.

The sight of the demon's naked enjoyment of the spectacle shocked me back to my senses. Was this what we had become? Watching the torture of a creature, enjoying the spectacle alongside Andras, of all things?

The Fury's screams grew louder, a tortured wail that resonated through my very bones.

This was not right, I realised. Whatever the thing was, whatever it had done, we had no right to do this. I looked across at Andras, remembering all that he had done and was capable of. He and his kind would like nothing more than for us to remake ourselves in their image.

Before I could change my mind I walked forwards and plunged my sword into the Fury's head. It shuddered and then was still.

Joshua charged at me, glaring with hot venom. "You had no right," he screamed. "It was mine! It should suffer!"

I tried to keep my composure as I thought of what he was clearly now capable of, powered by hate and the Fulcrum. "We are not like that," I said. "It is over, Josh. Finished."

He stared at me for a long moment and then turned and charged off, the soldiers scattering in his wake. Kate nodded to me and then ran after him.

"You're wrong, you know," said Andras from behind me. "It's not over yet. Not by a long shot."

I glared at him, then looked around the battlefield, the scene cast in an eerie light by the portal. Soldiers were at last starting to relax, while Maxwell was examining the device under Captain Pearce's watchful eye. Joshua bent over his sister's body while Kate tried to console him. We had won this battle, but only just.

"That's all right," I said to Andras. "I'm not done fighting yet."

TO BE CONTINUED...

AFTERWORD – AUTHOR'S NOTE

First, a gentle plea. Word of mouth is crucial for any author to succeed. If you enjoyed this book, please consider leaving a review on my book's page. Even if it's only a line or two, it would be a *huge* help!

Benjamin Disraeli's first term as Prime Minister lasted from February to December 1868, when he was ousted by Gladstone's Liberal party. Of course, as far as I'm aware he never had to contend with a demon invasion: one of the benefits of being a novelist is that you can stray from the facts in the interests of artistic licence.

As a result, while I've tried to remain as true to the times as possible, I have not been slavish in this: after all, the events of this world and the one we live in diverged in 1865 with the events of The Infernal Aether (and in fact, started to diverge a while before then, but that is a tale for another book…).

Nonsuch Palace was an actual Tudor palace, built and designed by Henry VIII. Work started in 1538 and it was still incomplete by the time of Henry's death in 1547. There is no record of any form of occult connections for the palace, either in its construction or use. I settled on this as a potential location for the Fulcrum mainly because I have been captivated by the name Nonsuch ever since I first stumbled upon it as a child: to my young mind it evoked images of the fantastic and magical, even though the name was really (allegedly) due to a boast that there would be no such other palace to rival its magnificence in all the world.

The method of blood transfusion used by Joshua was indeed the invention of a Sheffield obstetrician named Dr J.H. Aveling. The device used was invented by him in 1866 and was constantly carried in the doctor's pocket until he was first able to use it in 1872, on a young woman suffering from post-partum haemorrhage. The procedure was a success, although Dr Aveling was disappointed to note that "the mental improvement of the patient was not as marked and rapid as I anticipated, but this perhaps was due to the quantity of brandy she had undertaken." I am indebted to Phil Learoyd's paper *The Early History of Blood Transfusion* for these insights.

I have tried to capture the unique spirit and personality of Benjamin Disraeli, although many comments and witticisms unfortunately did not survive the editing process - they are being held in readiness for the next book, *Beyond the Aether*. Among others, Douglas Hurd & Edward Young's highly enjoyable book *Disraeli or The Two Lives* provided much background for my research.

For details of travel and travel routes, as well as many of the locations I used, there was no better source for me than George Bradshaw's contemporary guidebooks, in particular *Bradshaw's Illustrated Hand Book to London and its Environs* (1862), *Bradshaw's Descriptive Railway Hand-Book of Great Britain and Northern Ireland* (1863) and *Bradshaw's Railway Time Tables and Assistant to Railway Travelling* (various). *The Village London Atlas* by the Alderman Press provided me with street layouts to supplement many days spent pounding the streets trying to image what Gus and his friends would have seen back then.

I have taken artistic licence with the location of Captain Gilbert's garrison in Nottingham - I have found no evidence to suggest that Nottingham Castle was used for that purpose at the time, but I needed something large enough, iconic enough and not too far from the train station. So, as with many things in this book, I twisted facts and made things up!

As with the first book, my initial research on demons and demonology was based on *The Lesser Key of Solomon Goetia*, by SL Mathers and Aleister Crowley. I have also relied on *The Encyclopedia of Demons & Demonology* by Rosemary Ellen Guiney, *The Encyclopedia of Witchcraft and Demonology* by Rossell Hope Robbins and the

Malleus Maleficarum (1486) by Heinrich Institoris, translated by P.G. Maxwell-Stuart.

Finally, the location of the Yewfields Estate is based on the grounds and mansion house at Oaklands in St Albans, now a Further Education College and somewhere which I am very familiar, thanks to working there for a number of years. For period detail I relied on pictures in *The Oaklands Story 1921-1971* by E.C. Pelham, as well as invaluable insights from the font of knowledge that is the incomparable Joe Brennan.

A CHRISTMAS AETHER

The Adventure Continues...

A Christmas Aether - a Novella from the universe of The Infernal Aether

Following the events of The Infernal Aether, surely humanity is safe at last?

Get Your Copy Free at **peteroxleyauthor.com/aether**

The story continues in A Christmas Aether, a collection of new short stories continuing the story of Augustus, N'yotsu, Maxwell and Kate.

You can get *A Christmas Aether* for FREE at peteroxleyauthor.com/aether

Find out what happens next, as Augustus finds himself beaten, bloody and helpless in London's demon-infested slums, as well as meet a terrifying new adversary in *The Ballad of William Morley*. Finally, *The Potts Demonology* provides fresh insights into the new world unleashed by the Aether, plus a sneak preview of the terrors to come in *The Demon Inside...*

AN EXCLUSIVE EXTRACT FROM *BEYOND THE AETHER* – THE NEXT GRIPPING INSTALMENT IN *THE INFERNAL AETHER* SERIES

CHAPTER ONE

The sand collected roughly beneath my shirt as I crawled forwards, trying to keep the tall rocks between me and the demons as I squinted against the light from the second, brighter sun high in the sky. If there were any doubts in my mind that we were in another realm, then the three suns circling overhead banished them.

I reached the nearest rock and pressed myself against the hard red stone as I slowly edged my body upwards into a standing position, holding my breath as I peered round to see a group of five demons engrossed in their tasks. I looked back to check that Joshua, Kate and Byron were in position and then counted down with my fingers: three*, two, one.*

We darted round the rocks and ran at the demons, shouting as we closed in. Byron and I threw ourselves at the three Berserkers, which had clearly been brought along as bodyguards-cum-porters. Kate dropped to a knee and started firing her LeMat pistol at the remaining two, who were Warlocks. In doing so she provided Joshua with precious time to work his magic.

I swung my runic sword at a roaring Berserker, exulting as I did so in the animalistic joy that came from being in perfect harmony with the weapon. The beast tried a clumsy swing at me but I parried with ease and brought an end to its challenge with a swift uppercut of my blade, which scythed its head in two. Wrenching the steel free, I twisted out of the path of an axe swung by another demon, arching my back and feeling the rush of wind as it passed me by a mere whisker and buried itself in the ground. Before my attacker could pull it free I kicked hard at the beast's chest and then followed up with a swing of my own. That one hit home, and the demon fell to the ground.

I turned to see Byron still locked in battle with the remaining Berserker and looking like he was gaining the upper hand. Joshua was still struggling with the two Warlocks, and so it was this engagement that I turned to.

I ran over to where Kate was still knelt, firing at the demons with grim determination. I nodded to her as she stopped to reload. "Everything all right?" I asked.

"I'm fine," she said. "Although it'd be nice if they looked a bit bothered by me shooting at them." She snapped the chamber of the pistol closed and started firing again.

I watched as the bullets struck the Warlocks, earning little more than irritated glances from them as they engaged in a battle with Joshua that defied all of my senses.

He faced them from across the sandy plain, his face screwed up in intense concentration. The demon Warlocks' mouths opened and closed rapidly to form words and sounds that, while nowhere near intelligible to my untutored ears, conjured up images and feelings in my mind which were nothing short of breath-taking. Thankfully, though, I was not the target of their utterances, with the demonic invocations being hurled at Joshua and then repelled and returned by him with equal vigour.

As for the forms of the invocations themselves, they were like streams of fire plucked straight from the sun and directed with malevolent intensity; or maybe they were furious dragons arrowing towards their foe. Then again it felt like the cold light of the most distant stars had been wrenched down to Earth and flung outwards like spears of piercing light. To watch was not just to suffer pain in one's eyes and mind, but also one's very soul, for there was something about every hurled projectile that dug down to the very fibre of my being, even though I was a mere bystander.

The Warlocks were clearly powerful, and I had no real idea how long Joshua's resolve could last against their onslaught. Kate's gunshots were stopping the demons from properly focusing all of their ire on him, but surely it was only a matter of time before he would be overcome and battered down.

"He needs help," I muttered.

"What?" asked Kate, straining to hear my words over the

discharge of her pistol.

"I'm going to help him," I said.

She raised her eyebrow at me. "You plannin' something stupid, as usual?"

I grinned. "But of course." My mind made up, I charged straight towards the demons, ignoring Kate's curses and Byron's shout of alarm.

It did not see me until it was too late, and I shouted with joy as my sword cleaved down through its neck and torso with lethal intent. Then I blinked: there was nothing there. Before I had a chance to turn and try to refocus on where the Warlock had gone, my world exploded into a red-hot hell.

I felt as though I had been thrust up into the burning sky, the land countless leagues beneath me. To stay up there was surely to perish, but to fall to the ground would be just as fatal. Everything about me seemed to twist and turn as I realised that I was slowly, agonisingly, being unmade.

It is at this point that it is customary to say that my life flashed before my eyes, but even that cliché was denied me. Admittedly, though, that was a blessing given the numerous trials and terrors that I would have been forced to relive. Instead, I stared into an abyss born of fire and containing at its centre a being I had seen before, months before, a swirling red angry mass that wanted nothing more than my total annihilation. *Who are you?* a distant part of me shouted once more into this hideous, seething hatred.

Your doom came the reply in a cavernous voice that would have snatched away my breath had I any to steal.

Why?

You… are abhorrent, an abomination. You do not belong here; none of you do. I will destroy you all.

Once again, it felt like a million crows attacked me, gnawing into my very soul, like the time when Maxwell had sought to cure me of my demonic tendencies by forcing me to inhale his strange gaseous compound inside his laboratory. But then my attackers exploded in a shower of jagged shadows and I fell to my knees on the ground, my hands buried in the coarse sand as I listened to the Warlock scream his last. I looked up to see Byron and Kate running over to me while Joshua glowered from where he had just torn the demons to pieces.

"You fool," said Joshua. "You could have been killed."

I coughed as I tried a laugh. "I managed to distract him long enough for you to do your stuff though, did I not?"

The young man glared at me and then turned and stomped away.

Byron and I stood on the edge of a cliff, looking down at the end of everything. Or at least that is what it appeared to be, for there could be no other way of describing the madness of the realm in which we stood. Three suns hung in a blood-red sky that was dotted with at least five moons moving across the sky in a perverse dance that was as dizzying to watch as it was surely impossible.

Below and around us, red sand and rocks stretched out to the horizon, with twisting towers of red stone reaching up to the heavens, so high that it seemed they would snag the celestial objects whirling overhead. Nothing lived in that wasteland aside from us and our two friends who were busy examining the demons' work behind us.

"Beautiful, isn't it?" asked Byron.

I grunted. "Not quite the word I would use. A bit too... desolate for my tastes."

He gestured to the skies. "Surely all this astounds you?"

"Makes me sea-sick, more like." I turned to look at him, noting the way the hairs on his elongated ears rippled gently in the breeze. "Is this what your world was like?"

"A little. I have certainly missed having something interesting to look up at. The sky in your world is so... pedestrian. No wonder you haven't explored the heavens: there's bugger-all up there to inspire you."

"You know, it's your world too," I pointed out. Byron and his fellow Pooka demons had played a vital role in helping to repel the Almadite invasion of Earth six months previously. For that service they had earned the gratitude of the government, who had quickly moved to grant them citizenship of the British Empire, if only to ensure that we kept such strong allies to hand in case they were needed again. For their part, the Pooka were happy to have somewhere they could finally call home, having lost their own realm to the Almadites many centuries before. While they had been on Earth for many centuries, giving rise to a multitude of legends and lores, it was not until they had stepped into the light to fight at our side that they found true acceptance.

"Yes, it is my world too. Doesn't make it any more interesting though, does it?"

"We could make Earth more interesting if you would like," I said. "Maybe reopen the portal and let the Almadites come back through. Would fighting them excite you?" I grinned at him.

"That's all right, thank you all the same," he shuddered. He looked at me. "Your kind really do have a bizarre sense of humour, you know that?"

"It is the only way to stay sane in the light of all this insanity," I said. "Speaking of which, how is your prodigy getting on? He seemed to acquit himself well back there."

Byron glanced back at Joshua, who was busy examining the Warlocks' device, Kate stood over him like a watchful angel. "Yes, he did. He is powerful, there is no doubting it, and we are only just beginning to tap into what he is capable of. But…"

I raised an eyebrow. "But what?"

Byron grabbed my elbow and led me away. When we had gone far enough to ensure that we could not be overheard, he continued in a low voice: "He scares me with all that he is capable of. There is so much pain and sorrow there. I fear that his bitterness is what's really driving him."

I felt a cold chill run over me. "Lexie?"

He nodded. "He has not yet recovered from her death. It is as though there is a hole where his humanity should be, if that makes sense."

I shook my head. "He is the most human of us all," I said. "He is grieving; that is only natural."

"It has been six months, Gus, and he has shown precious little emotion aside from anger and a single-minded focus."

"Well, that's good isn't it? Letting his magical studies distract him from his grief and sadness and all that?"

"Ordinarily I can see how it would be beneficial, perhaps. But I know enough about these things from personal experience, and I can tell you that the worst thing you can do is clam up and refuse to talk to anyone about how you are feeling, what you are feeling."

I tensed up with the instinctive reaction of a true Englishman when it came to discussing things like feelings. I had lost my parents when I was a child and, in spite of how I had felt about them, I could not deny that their loss had affected me deeply, sending me into a rebellious funk that shaped my formative years. It sent me spiralling from what could have been a respectable life into a chaotic ramble around the world as I tried to run from my problems. Indeed, my brother Maxwell had often pointed out to me that my tendency towards overreliance on alcohol and laudanum no doubt stemmed from my seeking release from the feelings I had sought to repress over the years. No doubt my addiction to the runic sword had its roots in my troubled past too.

It was somewhat ironic, therefore, that I should have found release and purpose thanks to the one creature that was truly responsible for the loss of my parents: the demon Andras. In driving Maxwell toward creating the portals to the Aether, Andras had also inadvertently pushed me into a position of responsibility, one where I was a key driving force in the battle against the evil Almadites.

Byron, on the other hand, had not only lost his parents but also his entire home. In a hideous foreshadowing of what they intended to do to our world, the Almadites had invaded the Pooka's homeland when their defences were down, constructing an elaborate bluff that led them to believe that the intended targets of their invasion was the valuable Eternal Mines and its endless supply of power and resources. While the Pooka army had readied themselves to defend the Mines, the Almadites, led by Andras, had swept into their realm and enslaved their people, stripping them of everything so that they were nothing more than mindless slaves, unable and unwilling to do anything but serve their new masters.

By the time the Pooka army had realised their mistake it was too late, and their attempts to mount a counterattack fell flat in the face of the vastly superior numbers of Almadite warriors.

I knew from many nights speaking with Byron that he had never stopped thinking about those he had lost and the destruction of his culture, but he and his people had learnt to move on and now had finally established a home once more.

"So he has not talked to you about any of what happened to his sister?" I asked.

"No. Nor has he spoken to Kate or indeed anyone else."

"Maybe he does not wish to think about it just yet?"

Byron shook his head. "His every waking moment is dictated by her memory." I shot him a questioning glance and he tapped his forehead. "I am experienced in such matters, as you know. I wonder whether I should stop teaching him for a time."

"No," I said. "We need all the powerful individuals we can get, especially now. If anything, you should be thinking about how you can accelerate his training."

"Normally I would agree with you, but his aims and yours are not totally in alignment. You see, you believe he is learning how to create portals and fight Warlocks so he can help in the defence of Earth."

"Of course," I said slowly.

"But his real motivation is to find his sister."

I blinked. "But she's dead. We all watched her die. Does he not accept—?"

"Don't worry, he is not delusional. But he is focused on learning all he can so that he can travel to the spirit world."

I could not help but laugh. "I thought Max had proven a long time ago that the Aether is not the spirit world, that the creatures there just prey on those desperate to believe. Even you have told me that there's no such place…"

"No," he said. "I have said that I have never encountered such a place. But I'm just a plain old soldier who sometimes acts as a tutor to desperate humans. What do I know about the mysteries of the universes?"

I paced back and forth for a moment, trying to think through the implications. "As long as our interests are aligned, then surely it is not a bad thing that he explores this other option?"

"Unless he gets distracted at a crucial moment. A weapon is only useful if it fires when you want it to."

I glared at him. "He is not a weapon. He is…"

"What? Do not tell me that you are intimately concerned for his welfare as a person and a friend: you have hardly spoken to him over the past few months."

"Well, maybe I should remedy that.." I folded my arms.

Byron chuckled. "No offence, Gus, but maybe you should ask Kate to make the first move. A woman's touch may be better than you blundering in."

"Have you met Kate?" I asked with a half-smile. "She is probably the harshest out of all of us."

"Regardless. I think she should try speaking to him before it is too late."

"What, before he disappears on some wild goose chase trying to find heaven?"

"Maybe. Or maybe before he gets himself killed. I have noticed a rather reckless arrogance about him in recent weeks. For instance, back then – attacking two Warlocks on his own. He is powerful, but not that powerful. He took quite a risk."

"He still managed to defeat them, though."

"Yes, but only because you nearly sacrificed yourself as a distraction. Do you fancy doing that every time he gets himself in a tight spot?"

I rubbed my head, remembering the horror of that formless voice that had shouted at me: totally alien and yet somehow familiar. "Not really," I said with a wry smile. "I don't like him that much."

A shout from behind made us spin round to see Kate in the grip of a Warlock, holding her in front of him like a shield. Joshua was slowly rising to his feet as we ran over.

"No one thought to check there were any others around, then?" shouted Kate.

"Be quiet!" snarled the Warlock, making her cry out in pain as it squeezed her closer.

"Impossible," muttered Joshua. "I didn't sense it—"

"Time for that later," I said, then louder to the demon: "Release her and we will let you go unharmed."

The Warlock cackled. "Do you really think I am so stupid as to trust the likes of you? Do not make any moves, or I will kill her."

"What do you want?" asked Byron.

"Exactly what you have given us," said the Warlock. A swirling vortex appeared behind the demon and the demon stepped through before any of us could react, taking Kate with him.

We all shouted as one, charging forward, but the portal sealed shut with a pop mere seconds later.

Beyond The Aether will be released in mid-2017 - be the first to find out when it is published by joining my reader's group: **peteroxleyauthor.com/aether**

ABOUT THE AUTHOR

Peter Oxley is a writer, consultant and coach who lives in the English Home Counties. He enjoys reading and writing in a wide range of areas but his main passions are sci-fi, fantasy, historical fiction and steampunk.

His influences include HG Wells, Charles Dickens, Neil Gaiman, KW Jeter, Scott Lynch, Clive Barker, Pat Mills and Joss Whedon. He is the author of *The Infernal Aether* and *A Christmas Aether*. He is also the author of the nonfiction book: *The Wedding Speech Manual: The Complete Guide to Preparing, Writing and Performing Your Wedding Speech*.

He lives with his wife, two young sons and a slowly growing guitar collection. Aside from writing and willingly speaking in front of large crowds of strangers, Pete spends his spare time playing music badly, supporting football teams that play badly, and writing about himself in the third person.

peteroxleyauthor.com

Twitter: @Peterdoxley
Facebook: PeteOxleyAuthor

ALSO BY PETER OXLEY

THE INFERNAL AETHER

The Aether always held the universe together… but in the nineteenth century, it just might tear it apart.

London, 1865.

Betrayed by his closest friend and rapidly drinking through his inheritance, Augustus Merriwether Potts returns to London in the hope of finding his fortune. Instead, he meets a mysterious stranger who thrusts him into a terrifying underworld of demons, ghosts and clockwork men. Fighting back against these new and unusual threats, Augustus and his friends come face-to-face with a creature which has been manipulating them and all humanity: a demon known as Andras, the God of Lies.

Andras has a plan: to recreate the Earth in his own hellish image using the power of the Aether, a terrifying otherworld populated by creatures from beyond humanity's worst nightmares. With the world's governments in thrall to the demons, Augustus and his friends find themselves in the front line of this battle to save the world against all the odds.

Dickens' London has never seemed so scary. *The Infernal Aether* is the first book in a gothic fantasy series which has been described as "an elegant and chilling indulgence". If you like page turners with unpredictable twists and chills then you'll love Peter Oxley's *The Infernal Aether.*

Pick up The Infernal Aether and start exploring this terrifying new realm today.

peteroxleyauthor.com/books/the-infernal-aether/

THE WEDDING SPEECH MANUAL

Worried about making a wedding speech? Nervous? Unsure how to start or what to say?

The Wedding Speech Manual is the complete, practical, step-by-step guide which shows you how to write and perform a personalised wedding speech: something which will be enjoyed and cherished by your loved ones, friends and family.

This book will give you the confidence to approach the wedding day safe in the knowledge that you have an excellent, original wedding speech. Not just that — you will also learn tools to master your nerves and deliver your speech as confidently, coolly and calmly as any professional.

Includes practical exercises to guide you step-by-step through the process of researching, writing and performing your wedding speech, as well as a "Troubleshooting" section covering the most common questions and issues faced by wedding speechmakers.

You will learn:

- What you will be expected to say and do.
- How to master your nerves and stop them getting in the way of your successful speech.
- How to research, draft and edit your speech.
- How to deliver your speech as confidently, professionally and impressively as possible.
- How to handle other typical issues: like props, microphones and difficult audiences.

About the author:

A wedding speech veteran with over 25 years of public speaking experience, Peter Oxley has drawn on extensive experience presenting in a variety of situations, as well as the secrets of the professionals, to write a book which is relevant to all wedding speakers - father of the bride, mother of the bride, groom, bride, best man, maid of honour and bridesmaids.

peteroxleyauthor.com/books/the-wedding-speech-manual/

20832186R00182

Printed in Great Britain
by Amazon